Praise for
JUST ONE NIGHT

"Filled with the salacious, saucy content you'd expect in *Fifty Shades of Grey.* . . . However, beyond the titillating words and visual sexual images, the underlying story is about the choices women make every day."

—*Miss Wordy*

"I enjoyed every second I was with this book. It's intensely sensual, and the sex scenes are incredibly HOT."

—*Sinfully Sexy Book Reviews*

"A quick, fun, and sensual read that left me wanting much more!"

—*Romance Book Junkies*

"Tempting, seductive, and purely romantic."

—*Lovey Dovey Books*

"A refreshing, seductive, and highly enjoyable erotic romance."

—*TotallyBookedBlog*

"So compelling. I could not stop reading."

—*Up All Night Novels*

"I couldn't envision a better ending if I tried!"

—*Jessy's Book Club*

also by kyra davis

Just One Night

Deceptive Innocence

KYRA DAVIS

POCKET BOOKS

New York   London   Toronto   Sydney   New Delhi

Pocket Books
A Division of Simon & Schuster, Inc.
1230 Avenue of the Americas
New York, NY 10020

This book is a work of fiction. Any references to historical events, real people, or real places are used fictitiously. Other names, characters, places, and events are products of the author's imagination, and any resemblance to actual events or places or persons, living or dead, is entirely coincidental.

Deceptive Innocence, Part One copyright © 2014 by Kyra Davis
Deceptive Innocence, Part Two copyright © 2014 by Kyra Davis
Deceptive Innocence, Part Three copyright © 2014 by Kyra Davis
These titles were previously published individually as ebooks.

First Pocket Books paperback edition July 2014

POCKET and colophon are registered trademarks of Simon & Schuster, Inc.

For information about special discounts for bulk purchases, please contact Simon & Schuster Special Sales at 1-866-506-1949 or business@simonandschuster.com.

The Simon & Schuster Speakers Bureau can bring authors to your live event. For more information or to book an event, contact the Simon & Schuster Speakers Bureau at 1-866-248-3049 or visit our website at www.simonspeakers.com.

Interior design by Davina Mock-Maniscalco
Cover design by Anna Dorfman
Cover photographs © Adrian Ricardo/Alamy

Manufactured in the United States of America

10   9   8   7   6   5   4   3   2   1

ISBN 978-1-4767-7313-1
ISBN 978-1-4767-7149-6 (ebook)

part one

prologue

The correctional officer hands me the box without ceremony, here in this dingy room with overhead lights that give everything an unnatural yellow glow. I wait for a moment for the officer, a woman with a soft face and hard eyes, to offer condolences or prayers for the woman I'm mourning, but the words don't come. There is no reverence here, only efficiency.

So I turn my eyes to the box . . . It's so light I can balance it on one hand without hurting my wrist. It's not right. This package is just too small for what it represents.

Under the watchful eyes of the officer, I tentatively open it, mindful of the shiny gold star that proudly announces this other person's authority over this place, over me, and over the woman whose last years of life have been casually tossed into a box.

On top of the contents is a picture of me when I was five, maybe six . . . lifetimes ago. The picture shows me at Disney World dressed like Cinderella, a plastic tiara balanced atop my mass of black wavy hair. My mother is by my side, curtsying to me as if I actually had the power to rule a kingdom.

Back then, I thought any little girl could grow up to be Cinderella. I thought someone—maybe a prince, maybe an employer, maybe just a friend—*someone* would look beyond the trappings of my humble beginnings and realize that I was really a princess. That they would give me the opportunity to live a beautiful life. In a way, that's what my mother was grooming me for. Back then we both believed in dreams. We both thought hope had value. We both believed that mixed up within the dust and discarded crumbs my mother was perpetually laboring to remove, that amid all that dirt . . . there was always a little pixie dust.

Underneath that picture are a few paperback novels: *Cumbres Borrascosas* (Spanish for *Wuthering Heights*), *El Conde de Montecristo* (*The Count of Monte Cristo*). My mother didn't used to be a big reader . . . not back in the days of pixie dust. But back then she had other things to occupy her: me, for one. And then there was her work and her occasional flings with men who lied sweetly and loved viciously. Things that were all taken away. So in this place, she discovered the books of intellectuals, books she wasn't supposed to understand or have an interest in . . . but did.

I flip through the dog-eared pages as the fluorescent lights buzz above my head. So many passages have been circled with faint ink. Words about justice and revenge. All translated into Spanish, the language of my ancestors.

But there is one English book in here: *The Myths and Legends of Ancient Greece and Rome* by E. M. Berens. Serving as a bookmark here among the legends is a picture of a man. A dead man. Murdered in his own home, though in the picture he seems happy, handsome, even worry-free. It's placed between the pages that describe the deity Mars. I've heard stories about Mars before. As far as I can tell he was just another brawling jerk with a god complex.

But then my eyes stop on a name that's unfamiliar to me. Bellona, Mars's companion. The book says that Bellona guides Mars's war chariot. It says that she's armored and is skilled with her weapon. It says Bellona "appears on the battlefield, inspired with mad rage."

"Inspired with mad rage."

It seems an odd choice of words. I've lived with rage for *so* long. At times it's consumed me, I've been lost in it, occasionally immobilized by it. When I did fight, I took on the wrong enemies on the wrong battlefields—

and those had been wars inspired by nothing more elevated than desperation. But now . . . now things are different. I know the faces of my enemies.

I know where they live.

And so maybe, just maybe, this Bellona chick was onto something. Maybe now that my rage has actual direction it also has enough power to inspire. Maybe I don't have to be torn up by my own anger anymore. Maybe that can finally stop.

Maybe now I can use that anger to tear up others.

I think that might be better.

Inspiration and destruction . . . It has a ring to it.

I run my fingers over the name once. And then again. It brings me an odd sense of hope—something I haven't felt since I stopped dressing up as princesses.

The correctional officer loses patience and clears her throat to get my attention, bringing me out of my head and back into the dimly lit room.

"You need to sign for her effects," the officer snaps.

I stare at her for a moment and consider laying into her. But she's simply not worth my time. So I just nod and take her pen to the form placed in front of me. My signature is a scrawl; there's no reading it. It could say anything.

It could say Bellona.

chapter one

My heart's beating a little too fast and my eyes keep darting toward the door. He'll walk through there any moment now. There are only a handful of bar-flies to distract me, and the kinds of drinks they order don't take a lot of thought to make. This is not a Mojito Sparkler type of crowd.

Most of the people who come to drink at Ivan's are men. They come to lose themselves in alcohol and sports. The few women who show up are looking for a special kind of trouble. This isn't the place you come to in hopes of picking up a *nice* guy.

I know these women. Maybe not personally, but essentially I know who they are and what they're about: disheartened or damaged, looking for men who can inflict enough pain to help them forget the pain that's coming from within. Screwing assholes, making themselves vulnerable to emotional predators—it's just another form of cutting, really. Every time they smile at a Hells Angels type I can see the unspoken words hovering over their heads.

Here's the knife. Hurt me so I don't have to hurt myself. Take away the responsibility and just give me the pain.

I get it, I really do. But it's not my game, not anymore.

So I just pour the beer, keep the whiskey flowing, keep my smile evasive, cold enough to scare away the more aggressive ones, warm enough to coax the tips out of the passive . . . and keep my eyes on the door.

And then it happens. At exactly seven fifteen, *he* shows up.

I feel an acute pang in my chest, right where my heart is.

Lander Gable. How many times have I seen this man walk into this bar while I was sitting across the street in a cab or rental car? But now, today, I'm *in* the bar, and he's walking toward me, not away. I've never been so close to him before. I can almost touch him!

And soon I will.

The ringing of the phone momentarily distracts me.

I pick up and ask, "Ivan's, can I help you?" The person on the other end mumbles an embarrassed apology for calling the wrong number and hangs up, but I keep the phone pressed to my ear long after hearing the click, pretending to listen while I study the perfect specimen in front of me: a clean-shaven face, bronze skin, a watch that's worth more than everything I own . . . Only he's replaced the suit he wore to the office today with a pair of Diesel jeans and a sweater. Less conspicuous, but still a little too clean for this place. His physique hints at time spent at a gym, not a dockyard.

You'd think some of the other guys would kick his ass just for entering their bar.

And yet absolutely no one gets in his way.

It's not until he's almost at the bar stool that we make eye contact. He doesn't smile, but there's something there—curiosity maybe, perhaps surprise at finding a woman bartending, definitely appraisal.

I've gotta give myself a major pat on the back for that one. I must have spent two hours putting myself together today for *him*. He's why I'm wearing my wild black hair down, letting it cover my bare shoulders. He's why I matched the loose, low-slung jeans with a fitted tank that subtly reveals the benefits of my new push-up bra. He's why I'm wearing thick mascara and sheer lip gloss. I know this guy's tastes.

He takes his seat, pulls out a ten, and gestures to the bottle of whiskey still in my hand from the last drink I poured. "On the rocks, please."

"You sure?" I ask even as I fill a glass with ice. "I could make a whiskey sour if you like. Maybe throw in a cherry?"

He raises his eyebrow slightly. "Mocking a patron when you're new to the job? Risky, isn't it?"

"How do you know I just started?"

"I'm here a lot."

"Every day?"

"A few times a week." He reaches for his drink, brings it to his lips. Over the glass he offers a bemused smile. "I like your prices."

"Really?" I ask. "Drinks more expensive where you're from?"

"You make it sound like I'm visiting from some far-off land."

"Are you?"

His light-brown hair looks darker in this room, his eyes brighter. "Upper East Side," he says.

"Ahhh." I take a step back and cross my arms over my chest. "That's about a million dollars from here."

He winces. "Not necessarily." On the other side of the bar a few men burst into cheers as a UFC fighter's arm is broken on live TV.

"You living at the 92nd Street Y, then?" I quip.

"No," he answers, his smile returning. "I've managed to avoid that fate." He studies me for a moment, trying to gauge what he's dealing with. "How 'bout you? You live here in Harlem?"

"Occasionally. I'm a bit of a drifter." I fiddle with a glass, playing at cleaning it. "So why do you really come here . . . I'm sorry, I didn't get your name."

He gives me a quizzical look. "Considering how coy you're being about what part of town you live in, I feel like maybe I shouldn't volunteer my name just yet. That way we both have an air of mystery."

"Oh, I'm only coy about inconsequential things." I lean forward, put my elbows on the bar, and cradle my chin in my hands. Ever so slightly I arch my back. "I'm very straightforward about the things I want."

"Really?" He takes another sip. "And what exactly is it that you want?"

"Tonight?" I pause for a moment, pretending to think. "Tonight I want . . . your name."

His smile spreads to a grin. "You think you can coax it out of me?"

"Maybe." Out of the corner of my eye I spot one of the regulars on the other side of the bar waving his empty glass in the air. "When I have the time."

And I walk away to pour the next drink.

The foreman needing the refill is too drunk to notice that I'm trembling while taking his money.

God, is this working? Am I being too forward? Too much

of a tease? My mother would have chewed me out for behaving like this.

But when I look back, Lander's still smiling. I exhale in relief. I have to have confidence. I've studied this man; some would even call it stalking, although I'm not sure I see the distinction. But the point is, I know what kind of man Lander is. He's different. Edgy in that upscale kind of way, and he's rebellious enough to drink in this dive when he could easily afford to knock back cocktails at The Carlyle.

When I return to him I refill his drink without his having to ask. "So I was thinking about this, and before I resort to coaxing I think I'd like to take a stab at guessing."

"I don't have the kind of name that's easy to guess," he says.

"So it's not Rumpelstiltskin?"

He laughs and shakes his head. His laugh is deeper than I anticipated, appealingly unrestrained. "I'll give you a hint," he finally says. "It's English and it means 'lion.'"

"Leo."

"Close. It also means 'landowner.'"

Another well-weathered drinker several feet off has started muttering to himself, adding an odd soundtrack to the scene. He's minutes away from falling off his stool.

"Landlord," I say. "Wait, is that a name? How about Leolord, or Lionlord, or maybe Landlion."

"My name is Lander," he supplies.

"Lander, the landowning lion."

He nods in confirmation. "And what's your name?"

"Bell."

"You were named for your beauty."

I shake my head, a little harder than necessary. "It's a nickname. B. E. L. L. No 'e' at the end. Like Taco Bell."

"Like *Taco Bell*?" he repeats. "Did you just say that?"

"What should I have said? A church bell?"

"No." He takes his drink and downs more than half of it in a gulp. "But maybe like an alarm bell."

I giggle at that and shake my head in protest, though I'm secretly flattered.

"Care to tell me your real name?" he asks.

"Guess," I call over my shoulder as I leave to serve another customer.

I can feel him watching me and I work to make sure my movements are graceful, too graceful for this place. That's what he should think. I want him to be curious about me.

I need him to want me.

"Keep 'em on their toes," my mother used to say. "If they don't know what's coming next, they'll keep coming back in hopes of figuring it out."

I remember that conversation so well, although at the time I pretended not to listen. I had found it distasteful to be advised on men and dating through bulletproof glass.

Looking back on it, I really hope she knew I was listening.

More customers come in: a chick dressed like a prostitute clinging to a guy dressed like a deadbeat, then a dark-skinned man with a scar, and, a few minutes later, a light-skinned guy with a grizzled beard and a bald head. They all glance in Lander's direction but none of them bother him. It's like he's mingling when he shows up here. He doesn't belong. He's no better than those tourists on the double-decker buses, gaping at the sights of the city without ever understanding the first thing about the lives of the people who live in it. Does he know that?

The unspoken question helps me. It sharpens my focus and fortifies me for the next step. When I go back I look him in the eye and silently invite him to restart the conversation.

"Bella," he says, his eyes moving from my hair, to my eyes, to the antique garnet ring I wear on my right hand.

"That would be too easy," I say.

"Belinda."

"Nope."

"Blair."

"Now you're just pulling names out of your ass."

He almost spits out his drink as he holds back an ill-timed laugh. When he composes himself, he opens his mouth again to continue but I gently press my finger against his lips. The move is startlingly intimate and he immediately falls silent.

"That's three strikes," I say as I pull my hand back. "Looks like you're not getting to first base tonight."

He cocks his head. "There's always tomorrow."

"That depends on how you perform next time you're up to bat."

And again I walk away. I serve the other drinkers, and occasionally I throw him a smile or two, but I don't go back to talk. Not yet. I have to tease this out.

It's only when he prepares to leave that I grab his hand. "Do come back another time," I say, my eyes locked on his. Then, slowly, I remove my hand and bite my lower lip teasingly before adding, "For our prices."

He answers me with a smile, puts down a ridiculously large tip, and leaves.

He's back the very next night.

He arrives earlier this time, takes the same seat, and

waits for me to approach. I hold up the whiskey and raise my eyebrows questioningly, waiting for his nod before pouring him a glass.

He throws out a pile of names: Beliva, Bellanca, Benita. The names are foreign to me, unfamiliar, irritating. But I keep my tone teasing and light as I reject them one by one.

The traffic in the bar is also light tonight, but a few distractions manage to pop up. The drunk from the night before is here, the one who almost fell off his stool. This time he's sitting at a table, with a troubled expression that indicates he's watching "his" bartender flirt with "the stranger."

It takes effort, but he manages to get out of his chair and make his way back to the bar. When he puts his empty glass in front of me, he hits the wood of the bar a little too hard so that the placement reads more like a demand than a casual movement. "Empty," he says, staring at the bottom. On the screen behind me "The Most Interesting Man in the World" opens a Dos Equis as this man before me fishes out six crumpled dollar bills and puts them next to the glass.

I shake my head. "I can't serve you; you've had too much."

The man shakes his head in return. "I had too much twenty years ago, but the Lord keeps piling shit on."

"I meant I can't give you more to drink," I clarify. "Go home."

The drunk's head snaps up at the word *home*, as if I've spoken of some kind of coveted prize, as if I've spoken the real name of God. In that moment I know his whole story; the perfunctory telling of it is almost unnecessary. Newly evicted, no family, nothing. The man has no center. I shake my head, whisper useless words of comfort. I recognize his pain, I've lived with it before, but I can't help. I can't give him a home, or a family. I can't even give him the final drink that might make him forget.

"You have to go," I say as gently as I can. "There's a shelter a few miles from here. Perhaps they can—"

But before I can finish my sentence, Lander slams his hand on the bar, and when he lifts it there's two hundred dollars there. "For a Best Western," he says, his voice cool and steady, as if he's ordering a drink, not a bed. "Find one with a free breakfast."

The man gapes at the bills before snatching them up and weaving his way out of the bar.

I stare at Lander, who is now occupying himself with his phone. "He won't get a hotel room," I finally say.

"He might," Lander counters. "Not a Best Western, not a hotel that will buy him a moment of human dignity. But he might find a bed, a room, someplace where he can drink the liquor he's about to buy in private."

I shake my head, still not getting it.

"I feel sorry for him," Lander clarifies.

"Because he doesn't have a family?"

"Because he's chosen despair over anger," he says distractedly as he checks his emails. "It's a bad choice. Despair will kill you. Anger's more useful."

I drop my gaze, toy with my garnet ring. Lander's singing my song . . . my anthem. Again I feel my pulse quicken, just like it did right before our meeting, before I began my game.

I lean into the counter, my hands spread out to either side as if I'm balancing myself. "Are you angry, Lander?"

He looks up from his phone, his expression almost seductive, almost menacing. "Not as angry as you, Bell."

Immediately I step back. "I don't know what you're talking about. I'm—"

"I can hear anger scraping at the underside of every cheery word that comes out of your mouth," he interrupts. "You're absolutely draped in anger. And you know what?" He puts a few bills down, more than enough to cover the drink he consumed. "You wear it well."

My heart pounds in my ears as once again he leaves.

What if he knows?

Dear God, what if he knows I want to destroy him?

chapter two

When Lander arrives on the third night he doesn't bother with the name game.

I pour the whiskey without his having to ask for it. My black minidress is detailed with what the saleswoman euphemistically called "vegan leather paneling" in the front and back and is considerably more brazen than I'm feeling. In fact I'm actually feeling uncertain now; he's not as easy to read as I imagined.

Have I given myself away? How?

The questions and worries kept me up all last night, so I was forced to substitute memories for dreams: memories of my mother, laughing while holding me in her arms, memories of her delighting in my love of fairy tales and storybook princesses.

As the clock pushed past midnight the hue and tone of

the memories changed. Images of my mother gasping as that man, Nick Foley, pulled her into a surprise embrace when he didn't know I was nearby. Memories of the first time I spied Nick kissing the back of my mother's neck while she tried to make the bed he shared with his wife. I was so young, I barely understood what I was witnessing.

And when the clock struck three, that's when the memories were at their darkest. My mother hysterical, blood soaking her shirt—then later, memories of my mother screaming as they led her away.

The memories made me sick. At four in the morning I was on my knees wanting to pray but unable to come up with the name of a God who would listen.

If Lander knows my game, I've failed my mother again, this time in only the space of a week.

So now I stand before him as he drinks his whiskey, waiting for him to show his hand.

Lander's gaze casually sweeps the room. There are more women in the bar than usual tonight. Some of them are actually cute. But he doesn't show any of them special interest. He simply sips his drink and returns his eyes to me, studying me the way I've been studying him.

When he puts the drink down he breaks the silence.

"Why do you work here?" he asks.

"I need a job."

"There are other jobs."

"No doubt," I agree as I take out a rag and wipe some drops of liquor off the bar. "But this is the one I got."

The spill is gone, but I keep moving the rag back and forth with slow, deliberate movements, making it more of a meditative exercise than anything else. Somewhere on the other side of the room a girl breaks out in hysterical laughter.

"I could get you out of here," Lander says quietly, "help you find something better."

The relief hits me with the force of a bullet.

He knows nothing.

And he wants me. I'm sure of that now.

"Are you offering to *save* me, Lander?" I ask as I drop the rag behind the bar.

He chuckles. It's a softer sound than the last time he laughed in my presence, a little more loaded. "I'm not the savior type."

"No, I don't suppose you are."

He continues to study me, the drink in front of him seemingly forgotten. "Would you like to come home with me, Bell?"

Now it's my turn to grin. I look to the left and right, making sure that there's no one close enough to overhear. Then I gently put my hand over his and lean in so my lips are right against his ear and whisper . . .

"No."

* * *

The night moves on at an odd pace. People fade in and out of the bar like phantoms, barely noticeable, never leaving an impression, with the possible exception of the stoned girl with rainbow-colored hair who asks me to turn up the volume on the TV so she can dance to the commercial jingles.

When Benny, the bartender who covers the last shift of the night, wanders in at eight thirty, less than ten people are there.

One of them is Lander.

He's never stayed till the end of my shift before.

I go to greet Benny, tell him which tabs are open and who's paid up. The rainbow girl spins to the sound of Stevie Nicks's "Landslide" as it plays over a Budweiser ad. The drunk from the night before stumbles in, already too wasted to be served. He seems disoriented for a moment as he weaves his way to the bar. He loses his footing and bumps into a biker, jostling him, spilling a bit of the big guy's drink on his lap. As the biker swears, the drunk mumbles his apologies and falls to his knees . . . and tries to use his shirtsleeve to wipe up the alcohol from the biker's pants, which causes his hands to brush up against parts of the other man's anatomy that he should clearly stay away from.

It would be funny . . . except the biker reacts too quickly, yanking the drunk to his feet by his collar, practically holding him in the air as spittle flies from his mouth.

"What the fuck are you trying to do?"

"I'm sorry," the drunk slurs. "I didn't mean—"

But the biker throws him against the wall with enough force to cause a concussion. The drunk is disoriented, unable to stand up straight. He shields his face with his arms as the bigger man advances. Everyone in the bar is frozen, as if the speed of the violence has forced the rest of us into immobility.

All of us but Lander, who gets up and places himself in between the two men. He meets the biker's eyes directly and says in a very quiet but very firm voice, "Don't do that."

The enraged man looks at Lander with his mouth hanging open. It takes him about ten seconds to gather his wits. "What's your problem?" he sneers. "You a faggot too?"

"It's not really relevant if I'm gay or not . . . although your extreme reaction to what just happened is curious. Are you upset that he accidentally touched you or that you sort of liked it?"

There's a startled laughter through the bar as I whirl around to grab the phone. This is going to end badly and

I can't afford to let this man hurt Lander. But I've only dialed 9-1—when I hear the crushing impact of the first punch. Lander's name bursts from my lips as I turn back to the fight . . .

But it's not Lander who's been hit. In fact, I turned just in time to see the biker hit the floor. He tries to get up, still snarling his aggression and holding what looks like a switchblade in his hand, but Lander is having none of it. Another punch and the knife goes flying. Blood is coming from the biker's nose, but he doesn't have time to tend to it because Lander quickly lands another blow to his ribs and then yet another to his jaw. And the entire time, Lander's expression is almost . . . bored. This man is bleeding at his feet as he continues to pummel him, but looking at Lander's face you'd think he was doing nothing more significant than killing a spider.

The biker turns onto his stomach as if trying to protect his face from the blows. But Lander grabs the man's arm, bends it back until it's about to break.

"Are we done?" Lander asks.

The man whimpers and wheezes. "Yes."

And just like that, Lander releases him. The fight's over. The biker, humiliated and teary-eyed, manages to get to his knees and looks up at Lander. And Lander looks down at him, and smiles. With his head low the biker tries to get to his feet, attempts to retrieve his knife from where it lies uselessly under a table, but Lander just looks at him and shakes his head.

The biker nods, leaves the knife where it is, and makes his way to the door. The drunk who started it all with his clumsiness finds a dark corner to huddle up in as he rubs his hand back and forth across the back of his head.

One of the other patrons swears his disappointment as the biker exits.

"That guy's a fucking pussy!" yells out another.

And, of course, they're not talking about Lander.

The dissatisfied audience turns back to their drinks and conversations while Lander turns to me, looks me in the eyes, and then walks out.

In seconds I've gathered my things and I'm following him out the door.

I find him standing just outside the bar, watching as the vanquished man retreats down the block.

I stand only a few feet behind him. He doesn't turn . . . and yet somehow I know he's aware of me.

"Where did you learn to fight like that?" I ask.

"Does it matter?"

I hesitate. The loser has reached the end of the block, where he parked his bike, and the roar of the Harley punctuates what would otherwise be a weak exit.

"Do you think he's steady enough to ride right now?"

Lander finally moves to face me, his expression now impassive. "On that thing he'll end up running into a lamppost before he runs into anything he can hurt."

"He could hurt himself."

"Yes, he could."

We both fall quiet. The streetlights make our shadows long across the sidewalk. "Are you dangerous, Lander?"

"Look who's talking."

I feel a chill run up my spine, I can sense the challenge and the threat he poses . . .

. . . and it makes me smile.

"Would you like to come home with me, Bell?"

I raise my chin and look into his light, stormy eyes.

"Yes."

chapter three

Lander was wise enough not to take his limo into Harlem, so we've caught a cab. We're sitting only a few feet away from each other, not talking, not touching, just . . . thinking.

I'm fiddling with my garnet ring, trying to lay out a plan for the evening. I've never had sex with a man for any reason other than the satisfaction of my own desire, but I'm ready to make the sacrifice for the sake of my cause. I've prepared myself for that.

So sleeping with the enemy isn't a problem . . . but *wanting* to sleep with the enemy is.

That's something I'm not prepared for at all. Over the last few days his self-possession, quiet intelligence, and savagery have been wearing on my defenses. Like the effect of waves against a cliff, the erosion isn't immediately devastating but it's noticeable.

He reaches over and touches my leg, his eyes still on the window. His fingers move up and down, his caress almost casual . . . almost. But there's a soft rhythm to his movement as his fingers rise a little higher, pushing my hem up ever so slightly, then sliding down again to my knee. It's not demanding or insistent. Just confident. Confident in what he's allowed and what boundaries he's able to push.

Being touched by this man, this man who represents so many things that I hate . . . it should be awful.

It isn't.

His hand goes a little higher. He's touching my inner thigh now, just barely, but still, I shudder. The involuntary reaction makes me blush and I quickly look away.

No, this isn't supposed to be happening at all.

When the cab drops us off at his Upper East Side building, he greets the doorman with a word and leads me to the rear of the lobby, his hand on the small of my back.

"Cool digs," I say as he pulls me onto the elevator. When I turn, I more fully take in the lush entry area, its crown molding, its expensive furniture, its little touches of decadence.

"It could be worse," he admits, sticking his key into the slot that will allow us to get to his penthouse. The doors close and he turns to me. "Do you like elevators, Bell?" He steps forward, into my space. Instinctively I step back, but that only serves to bring me up against the wall. His lips touch mine so gently it's practically a caress, nearly innocent.

And yet.

I feel his hands move up to my waist as his mouth quietly, softly moves down to my chin, my neck . . .

"The doors could open at any moment," I say. I try to add a little laugh, but the sound comes out as a staccato breath.

"Yes," he says, "they could."

He leans into me, and his body is different than I thought it would be—harder, stronger.

He doesn't know who I really am; he can't.

His hands are on my hips, and the hem of my dress inches up as his grip becomes firmer, more demanding.

I'm going to destroy him. I'll bring down his entire family.

His lips rise to my ear, his tongue finding my most sensitive spots there.

This is a sacrifice—it's supposed to be a sacrifice . . .

. . . but that's not what it feels like.

I close my eyes just as the elevator slows to a stop. He pulls away, but only a little. "Welcome to my home."

Slowly I open my eyes again and step into his penthouse. The art pieces on the wall are originals, mostly by artists I don't know . . . except for the charcoal nude rendered by Degas.

This man owns a Degas.

I don't comment on it. Instead I just continue down the hall past the kitchen, the home office, into what serves as a living room.

One wall is lined with books, the other with windows. In the corner is a small bar, stocked with expensive bottles that look as decorative as they do sinful.

"You have a view of Central Park." I step up to the wall of glass and stare down at the dimly lit landscape. I can feel his eyes on me . . . It's almost like he's touching me.

This man is my enemy.

"If I lived your life I would go to all the fancy parties," I say lightly. "I bet you get invited to all sorts of red-carpet affairs. I bet you could be in a tux every night of the week if you wanted to be."

"No man wants to be in a tux every night." He pauses, leans back on his heels. "I'd like to guess your name now."

"Oh?" I flash him a bright, playful smile. "You think you can?"

"Yes," he says quietly. "I think I can, Bellona."

My breath catches. I feel a knot in my stomach. Of course, it's not my birth name—he doesn't know that.

But it isn't information I've given him either. "How did you know?"

"I'll tell you tomorrow . . . in the morning." He comes to my side, reaches up, pushes my hair behind my shoulders. "Tonight I want to know if you're like your namesake. Are you a goddess of war?"

"I'm not a goddess," I say quietly.

"And yet I bet you'd hold your own on a battle-field." His fingers slide down my neck. I expect him to lean in for a kiss again, but he doesn't. Instead he just lets his fingers go to the scooped neckline of my dress, tracing it lightly, watching me. When his fingers move lower, over my dress, over the curve of my breast, I look away.

"No, no, warrior," he whispers, taking his other hand and turning my face back to him. "Keep your eyes on me. I want you to see me seeing you. I want you to look into my eyes when I touch you."

Part of me wants to say no. I hadn't planned for this level of intimacy. I don't know how to handle it.

But this is the path I've chosen. It's a path that can lead me to my revenge. And without revenge I have nothing. My whole *life* will be nothing.

His fingers continue to caress, running up and down my breasts. I feel my nipples harden. The fabric of my dress is thick enough to conceal them and yet as he looks down at me I'm sure he knows. It's in his smile, in the mischievous glint in his eyes.

His hands move lower, over my stomach, lower to the hem of my dress, then just below it, forcing his hand between my legs as I lean my back against the window, suddenly needing support. The glass is so clean it looks like I'm leaning against air itself, as if I'm on the verge of falling.

Maybe I am.

Slowly he raises his hand, raising my dress again as he does. The feeling of his palm against the inside of my leg makes me squirm, but as instructed I keep my eyes on his, watching him watching me.

"Do you know what I'm going to do next, Bellona?"

I nod.

"Tell me."

"You're going to move your hand up . . . to my thong."

"And when I touch your thong, will it be wet?"

My heart is beating at an uncomfortable pace. "Yes," I whisper.

His hand goes up, touches my panties, moving back and forth. It's such a thin strip of fabric, no protection at all, really.

"Ah," he says with a smile, "an honest woman."

The irony should make me laugh. But that somehow

isn't right here, and he's made me disinclined anyway.

"What would you like me to do now?"

Step away! The thought leaps to my mind. I need to catch my breath, I need a moment to remind myself of why I'm doing this and why I'm not. I'm getting too swept up in this; I'm losing control.

But I can't say that, not without giving everything away.

"What do you want, Bell?" he asks again, his hand still moving, enticing me, making my body react in ways my mind never intended.

"I want—" I stammer as his free hand moves to my back, then lower, stroking me, exploring me, discovering the spots that make me shiver. "I want you to touch me," I say. "I want you inside me."

He smiles and then slowly, gently, he slips his hand under the satin. His finger finds my clit.

And I shiver.

I close my eyes. I try to focus on the feeling, not the man.

"No, no," he says, weaving one hand into my hair, pulling just slightly as the other hand continues its ministrations. "Look at me."

I open my eyes just as one of his fingers pushes inside me. My hips buck reflexively. I reach out and grab his shirt, but my eyes stay on his.

"Does that feel good, Bellona?"

"Yes."

He smiles, pushes in another finger. I groan, my whole body responding to him. His fingers keep moving, thrusting inside as his thumb finds my clit again. It's overpowering. If I could just pretend someone else was doing this to me, maybe it would be okay.

But I can't do that—not while he holds my gaze.

His fingers move deeper and my pulse jumps again. It's ridiculous that he can make me react like this by simply touching me. It's humiliating. I try to focus my mind, pull myself back from the brink . . .

. . . and I can't do it.

"I do believe you're about to come for me. Is that true?"

I reach out, gather his shirt in my fist, pull on it so hard some of the buttons break away. The gesture is violent, angry, countered only by the softness of my whisper as I say . . .

"*Yes.*"

His fingers increase their rhythm, and my back arches, pushing my breasts into him. There is no control now. There isn't even any thought. Just the sensation of his touching me. My eyes are glued to his and I see him smile as the orgasm overwhelms me.

After interminable minutes, he releases me, steps

back, watches as I stand there, pressed against the glass, my skirt gathered up around my waist, my panties askew. I struggle to catch my breath, but I know better than to look away.

Without breaking eye contact, he starts to undo the remaining buttons of his shirt. And this time my eyes won't behave at all. They travel down to his chest and his stomach. I've been with strong men before, but not one who looks like this man, with every muscle finely chiseled. It's as if he was designed by a Greek sculptor. As he drops his shirt on the floor I step forward, my arm extended, letting my hand touch his chest—his skin is so warm, almost hot . . .

. . . and for the first time I realize that his heart is beating as fast as mine.

He takes hold of my wrist, pulls my hand away. "I'd like you to take your dress off."

The words bring me back, remind me of where I am and who I'm with. There are other beautiful men in the world, but only one is my adversary.

And that's the one I'm going to undress for.

I was shivering before, but now I'm practically shaking as I unzip my dress, pull it down, and step out of it.

"And now the rest," he says. His voice is so polite, and yet it's not a request. Not really. It holds the confidence and authority of a command.

Carefully I unhook my bra.

"Eyes on me," he says softly. "I want you to remember who it is you're showing yourself to."

My heart comes to a sudden stop. Does he know? But as I study his expression I realize he doesn't. He just doesn't want me to slip off into fantasy, the way I had planned. But he needn't worry. I'm finding it impossible to think about anything that isn't happening in this room.

I let my bra fall to the floor.

"You are beautiful," he murmurs.

I don't acknowledge the compliment and instead just hook my fingers into the waistband of my thong and pull it down to my ankles. I force myself to watch his face as he takes me in, force myself to keep my arms by my sides. Resisting the urge to cover myself is difficult.

Resisting the urge to touch *him* is impossible.

Again I step forward, again I put my hand on his chest, and this time he doesn't stop me as I measure his heartbeat with my palm. This man thinks he can control me. He thinks he can dominate me. *This* man. My hand turns into a claw, and my fingernails dig into the tender skin. I watch him flinch as I run my nails down his pecs, his abs, his obliques, never breaking the flesh but nonetheless leaving my mark, reminding him that all his hard-earned strength can't protect him from the seduction of a predator.

I smile almost apologetically and then bring my mouth to his chest, meticulously covering my path of aggression with a trail of kisses. I have to bend to do it and eventually I'm on my knees, my fingers on the small silver buckle of his belt.

My eyes are on his, his on mine . . .

I lower my head just slightly and bite my lip suggestively as I unfasten his belt, the top button of his pants, and move the zipper down until his erection is covered by nothing but the soft cotton of his Calvin Kleins.

"Is that for me?" I ask.

"Only if you retract your claws."

I laugh lightly and begin to pull down his boxers and jeans. I toss the jeans aside, and something in the pocket hits the smooth oak floor with a faint knock, adding an audible exclamation mark to the act.

My eyes are no longer on his. They can't be. What's before me is too . . . impressive.

I lean forward, let my tongue dance over its every ridge. This too was not part of the plan, but something about him . . . I just want to taste him, if only a little.

His hands move into my hair as I continue my exploration, teasing him with my tongue, my hand, even with the warmth of my breath . . .

. . . and this time it's his moan that disturbs the silence.

I take him fully into my mouth, feeling him harden even more. I feel his hands in my hair, hear the way his breathing becomes shallow, taste the salt of his skin, sense the power I have over him.

In an instant he's pulling me to my feet, and for a moment I expect him to throw me down on the sofa and thrust himself inside me with the violence I would expect from a man like Lander Gable.

But he only smiles and then sweeps me up, cradles me in his arms as he carries me down the hall, past the pretty nudes and abstract art, and into his bedroom, where he lowers me onto a low bed covered by a comforter so white and so soft it makes me think of a cloud.

Like a princess.

I can feel my aggression melting away.

It's terrifying.

He leans over me, kisses the contours of my breasts, lets his tongue flick out against the roughness of my hardened nipple before kissing my stomach, my hip . . .

I close my eyes as I feel his tongue against my sex. My head tosses from side to side as he toys with me, drawing out my passion as if it were as easy as pulling on a string.

In battles of passion there are so many tactics that can be used to overpower your opponent: displays of strength, aggression, and dominance, and then there are the equally effective acts of gentleness, attentiveness, romance, devotion.

It seems Lander has mastered them all.

As he continues to make little circles around my clit with his tongue, I grab the comforter beneath me, and I'm writhing under him . . . It's almost too much.

"Look at me, Bell. See who's doing this to you."

My eyes move down, and yes, I can see him, tasting me, watching me.

And when he adds his fingers to the equation, once again thrusting them inside me while his tongue continues to play, it takes only a moment for me to explode again.

He pulls away, raises himself back up so he's hovering over me. He kisses my cheek as he tugs at my hair.

"Bellona," he whispers, "such a beautiful warrior."

I watch, almost in a daze, as he reaches over into his nightstand and pulls out a condom.

I take it from him, feel the aluminum wrapper between my fingers. I know what this means.

It means I'm really going to do this. I'll never be able to say I just got swept up in the moment. This is a purposeful, willful act.

I tear open the package and take him in my hand as I slowly pull the condom over the tip of his cock, rolling it out gradually over every inch, letting my fingers slide along its length as I pull away.

There's nothing stopping us now.

He moves on top of me again, directing my face toward his. I feel his erection pressing against me, but he doesn't move, just hovers there, waiting, a strange glint in his eyes.

I try to reposition myself, force him inside me, but he grabs my arms and holds me against the bed as I wriggle my hips, desperate for satisfaction.

"What is it?" he asks, a teasing melody to his voice. "What do you need?"

My cheeks turn bright pink as I absorb the question, as I come to grips with the answer he requires.

"Please," I whisper, but he just looks at me, silently demanding more. "I want," I begin again in a voice that hovers between pleading and sighing. "I want . . . I want . . . *you*." And then I raise my chin, almost defiantly, as I add, "I need you to fuck me."

And in an instant he's inside me, filling me, making me cry out, my arms still securely held against the bed as my hips rock against his. My body has won the battle it's been waging against my mind, overpowering my thoughts and logic with waves of intense and illicit pleasure.

I can feel that I'm about to come *again*. No, my

mind can't make sense of that at all, but my body tenses, welcomes the building intensity . . .

. . . and then Lander pulls back so that now only the tip of his erection is inside me. Again I try to buck my hips, but he holds me off. He's toying with me, making me ache as he pulls out and then pushes in just a little farther. Again I want to look away—to deny that this desire is real—but I don't. I watch him as my own breathing turns into a pant. Again he pulls out before pushing in just a bit more. The light in his eyes is impish, playful.

"Please," I say again, my body now screaming for release. "Please . . . more."

He pauses for just a heartbeat, and then with intense force he thrusts deep inside me, over and over, setting my whole universe on fire.

Enemy.

He releases my arms and I dig my nails into his shoulders, run them roughly down his back, trying to recapture some of that anger, just a bit of my resolve.

This man is my enemy.

"So you *are* a warrior," he says softly, and in an instant he pulls away. Before I can protest he turns me on my side as he sits up, back on his knees, straddling my left thigh and raising my right leg over his shoulder. With focused power he enters me again, rotating his hips so that every nerve ending inside me feels the impact.

His name bursts from my lips and I quickly cover my mouth with my hand as if I can somehow take it back.

"Look at me," he reminds me. "See me."

The request has a note of vulnerability, and yet as I meet his eyes I know he's the one in control. In control of my body and, in this moment, my mind. In this moment he is everything.

This man. My enemy.

Again I touch his chest, feel the thin layer of sweat, and watch him as he watches me . . . as he brings me back to the brink.

He whispers my name as I cry out again, this time to God, as my whole body spasms against him, responding to him as he grips my leg with one hand, as he touches my face, as he holds my gaze while he climaxes, as he again calls out that name . . .

. . . Bellona.

In a moment he collapses by my side. We both look up at the ceiling, breathless, his scent on my skin, mine on his. Right now everything's mixed up like that, everything's upside down and backward . . . and yet, in this moment, upside down and backward feels disturbingly good.

I reach over, take his hand.

"Please," I whisper, "call me Bell."

chapter four

Seconds turn to minutes as we lie next to each other, embracing the silence. I watched him watching me as I was touched, as I was entered, as I came for him . . .

. . . and now I can't meet his eyes.

He turns on his side, brushes my hair out of my face as I study the ceiling.

"What are you thinking, warrior?"

"I'm . . . I'm thinking this is a really nice place." I can usually deliver my lies with conviction, but not now, not while my body is still trembling, my mind still reliving the way he kissed me, the way he moved inside me.

He smiles, knowing I'm not telling the truth and not caring. His eyes roam the room, as if trying to view his dark wood furniture, the fireplace, the few pieces of designer men's apparel that have been casually left on the floor for the first time. "It fits my needs," he says.

I bite back a laugh. If he *needs* all these things, then he must be the neediest man on earth. "What do you do, Lander?"

I know the answer too well.

"I work for a bank."

"Ah, so you got all this on a teller's salary?"

The way he slid his hand up my inner thigh, the way his fingers caressed me, toyed with me until I cried out.

"I'm a VP," he explains with a smile.

"Wow, you worked your way up in the world at the young age of . . . I'm guessing you're around thirty?"

When he found that spot on my neck, the way he teased it with his tongue, alerting me to sensitivities I didn't even know I had.

"Thirty-two, and no," he says calmly. "My father is the CEO, my brother's a managing director. I was given what I have. I didn't earn a thing."

The admission is unexpected, and it jolts me out of my revelry. I look at his face, searching for either smugness or regret, but neither is there.

"Does it bother you?" I ask. "Having everything come so easily?"

"No," he says, his hand sliding over my stomach, stroking my skin. "I've added my own complications to my life," he continues. "In the end nothing will be easy at all."

"In the end," I repeat, trying to ignore the slow circular movement of his palm. "That sounds so final."

"Endings usually are."

"We should drink to that." I sit up and hold the comforter over my breasts. If there was ever a time for modesty, this is not it. But I'm feeling shy now, unnerved by what he was able to unleash.

"Let's drink to happy endings," I say, keeping my voice casual, flirty.

His eyes sparkle in the dark as he examines me. "I don't believe in happy endings."

"Then what do you believe in?" I pull back a little more, grab one of the dress shirts I spot crumpled by the bedside, and throw it on. "What should we toast to?"

He sighs, but his smile is bemused as I inch out of the bed. "If we have to toast to something, let's toast to justice."

Again I'm hit with a wave of uncertainty. That came out of left field. Does he suspect?

"I don't think I understand," I say slowly. "How did we move from endings to justice?"

"You asked me what I believe in," he says. "I believe that a lot of the things we strive for in this life are either unattainable, illusions, or a matter of luck. Like security, happiness, or even . . . well, *love*. But justice . . . I think we can actually have that. I think that if we work for that, if we make justice a primary ambition, then it's attainable. It's the philosophy I live by."

"But . . . you're a banker."

Lander breaks out in a laugh so rich and warm I can't help but join in. "I guess I wasn't thinking in professional terms," he admits. "I was thinking more along the lines of . . . of social justice, I suppose."

"Ah." I study my ring. "I think I get it. Justice is . . . well, it's a good goal. Very noble. Maybe even attainable, for some—but I'm not sure it is for everybody. It's . . . elusive sometimes, I think."

"Even for the goddess of war?"

"Battles are never easy, not even for the Roman gods." I button the shirt quickly, my eyes now on the floor. "But I'm not craving justice right now anyway," I lie. "All I'm craving is a drink."

He smiles. It's a knowing smile. It's disconcerting. "If it's important to you, I'll get us drinks." He starts to get up, but I put out a hand to stop him. I lean in, touch my lips to his.

"Stay where you are," I whisper as I pull away. "Tonight, at this moment, I want to serve you."

He doesn't respond; he isn't meant to. I smile teasingly and leave the room.

My bare feet pad lightly against the cold hardwood floor, down the hall, to the living room, where the bar is. I reach for the cognac. A strong drink, both rich and flavorful. I select two brandy snifters, pour the liquor, and then, over one glass, gently tap the garnet on my ring. The stone moves aside, revealing a miniature pillbox that forms the base of the ring itself.

A pillbox filled with white powder.

I was surprised by how easy it was to find such a ring and by how affordable they are, as if poison rings are just novelty items, as if their name means nothing.

And no one expects sinister acts from a woman wearing pretty antique jewelry.

I smile as the crushed sedative slips into the drink.

When I reenter the bedroom he's waiting for me, watching me . . . but he sees nothing. Not really.

I step over a discarded pair of jeans. "You shouldn't be so careless about where you leave your clothes, Lander."

"Brazen words from a woman whose clothes are currently strewn all over the living room."

"And whose fault is that?" I sit by his side, kiss him, give him one of the glasses. "To justice," I say, raising the other.

He nods, joins in my toast.

As he takes a long sip, a new sense of calm washes

over me. My eyes wander around the room. There to the right is another expensive nude, and to the left assorted thousand-dollar watches have been carelessly left on his dresser.

"When I was a little girl, the doorman buildings were like castles to me." I toss my hair over my shoulder, fix my gaze on the floor-to-ceiling windows. "They're not, of course, but the people who live in places like this . . . They're a little like royalty, aren't they? Everyone bows before them, craves their attention. They're treated like kings and queens, princes and princesses."

"Yes," Lander says dryly. "My mother was treated like the dowager princess of Wales."

I don't know what that means, other than that he's flaunting his education and it bothers me. I've read all of Lander's favorite Shakespeare plays, learned tennis and chess, studied finance and art—all toward the goal of understanding and manipulating the world of the Gables. I should at least understand this man's references.

Lander takes another sip and yawns. "Where did you grow up?" he asks.

"Brighton Beach," I lie. But it's the perfect answer to give someone like him. It implies that I don't come from wealth, but also not from a place of abject poverty. I need to be an outsider to keep Lander's interest, just not as much of an outsider as I actually am.

With our backs propped up by pillows, we drink and chat for a few more minutes about innocuous things—the gentrification of Brooklyn, the weather, the music we like—and then, as I snuggle up close to him, he yawns again.

"I'm sorry," he says as he puts his empty glass on the nightstand. "I don't know why I'm so tired."

"I wore you out, baby," I say, slipping back to my old speech patterns. It doesn't matter; he won't remember this anyway. I adjust the pillows and then put my hand on his chest. Gently but firmly I push him back so that we're lying down again, his body relaxing into the firm mattress. "You surprised me tonight. You're a lover *and* a fighter."

"Yes," he says, but the *s* is drawn out, making the word sound like the hissing of a snake.

"You learn those moves at Oxford?" I ask, and he smiles, mumbles something unintelligible. "Did you fuck lots of girls in Merry Ol' England?" I ask, my voice laced with venom and sarcasm. I straddle him, my hair spilling forward again as his eyes go to half-mast. "Did the girls line up for you? Did you insist that they look at you when they took off their clothes? Did you make them admit to being wet for you?" I run my fingernails lightly along his throat. "You probably don't think I'm special at all, do you?"

But now Lander's asleep.

I smile, lean over, and whisper in his ear, "But I *am* special, Lander. I'm special because I know who you are. You're the guy who stands by your daddy and brother even when it means destroying someone else's family. Even when it means taking a mother away from her daughter and locking her up for a crime she didn't commit. I'm special because I know that. And I'm special because I'm the girl who's going to teach you and your whole fucking family what karma is. You think I get excited during sex?"

I roll off him and rise to my feet. "Just wait until you see me get off on vengeance."

chapter five

Now that Lander's out for the night I'm free to explore. I sit in his home office, in front of his computer, waiting for it to boot up. The keyboard is cool to the touch . . . just as the glass was cool against my skin when Lander pressed me up against the window.

I shake my head fiercely and turn my attention back to the computer . . .

The computer that is asking for a password before it will open up its desktop.

Fuck.

I try a few numbers, his birthday, the date of his college graduation. But they don't work, and I can't risk trying anything more. I turn the machine off. I hadn't noticed a laptop in the place, and even if there was one, what were the chances that it wouldn't be password protected too?

I stand up, walk over to a file cabinet. But it's mostly filled with things like cable and water bills. I have to assume that all the important stuff is filed electronically. There are a few cell phone bills that might be useful. I use my Android to take photos of each page, vowing to try to decipher them later.

I start opening drawers. In the first I find a spiral notebook. Inside are notes from bank meetings, a few scribbles about new FDIC regulations, nothing that isn't likely already public information. I sigh and look back to the open drawer . . . and that's when I see it: a book that looks suspiciously like a journal.

It seems unlikely to me that Lander is the kind of guy who would tell his secrets to a diary, but you never know. I put the financial notebook down on the desk and pick up the book. But when I open it I don't find words—I find pictures, drawings that look like they were done quickly but are actually pretty good.

They're caricatures. The first one is of a woman with a perversely large bustline and dollar signs in her eyes. She carries a Chanel purse, peeking out of which is a little shih tzu or something with a diamond collar. The words *Dogged Girl* are written boldly underneath the image.

Another is of politicians made to look like marionettes. That one's labeled *Thrusting Spell*, whatever that means.

There's a drawing of a crying woman in a hospital gown, on her knees, clutching at the pant leg of a man wearing a crown as he tries to walk away, titled *A Cad Feels Spewing Sorrow*.

And then there's a drawing of a man in a suit, a nail sticking out where his heart should be. He stands arm in arm with a much older man whose suit pockets are turned inside out as he hands what is apparently the last of his fortune to a smiling boy with shark teeth. The boy looks like he's going to eat the money being handed to him . . . Scratch that, he looks like he's going to bite off the man's entire hand. The title of this piece is actually pretty self-explanatory: *Bite, Torture, Ruin*.

The weird thing is that the boy with the sharp teeth looks a little like Lander.

The last picture I find is of a man who looks a lot like the older man from the last drawing. Except in this image, he's the one with the sharp teeth, and he's snarling down at a man who's lying on his side, apparently sleeping and peacefully unaware of the threat looming overhead. The picture is rendered so we only see the sleeping man's back. The title of that one is *E's Wolflike Indecency*.

Pretty dark stuff for a spoiled rich kid.

But that's not a big surprise. What does surprise me is his talent. I take a moment to photograph each picture. He did these drawings for himself, and they were clearly inspired by things, events, and people, which means this sketchbook is a journal of sorts. I just have to figure out what it's really saying.

I turn the page again. There's a list of names:

> *Ahmadi*
> *Akbari*
> *Najafi*
> *Narndar*
> *Talebi*
> *???*

That's it. Five names and some question marks. Probably just another form of doodling, but I take a snapshot of the list anyway before putting the book and the notebook back and opening another drawer. Perhaps I'll find a flash drive or something—I *have* to find something really good, otherwise what exactly did I get out of the evening?

On my knees, my hands sliding down his hard thighs as I pull off his jeans . . .

Again I try to shake off the image, but it's not so easy this time.

Standing in front of me, naked. I push the jeans aside; something in the pocket hits the floor with a faint knock . . .

Something in his pocket . . .

Maybe?

Possibly?

I immediately turn and go back to the living room, find the jeans . . .

. . . and his smartphone.

I pick it up, activate it . . . and it's not password protected.

Such a small misstep on his part.

And such a major victory for me.

I flip to his text messages. There are a few from women, hopeful texts. You can hear the unwritten words: *Will you save me, Lander? Will you share your life, your love, your checkbook?*

Looking at Lander's responses, when he bothers to respond at all, the answer is always a resounding *No*.

Then there are the texts from his brother. Those are friendly but impersonal. The ones from his father, Edmund Gable, are incredibly curt. He never asks Lander to meet him; instead he tells him to. There isn't one text complimenting an achievement but many cataloging his mistakes. If Edmund loves his son, he doesn't express it here.

Oh, and look at all these texts from Lander's BFF, Sean White.

I study the name on the screen for a moment. It sounds so innocuous. A man with a name like Sean White could be a waiter, a lawyer, an actor, a janitor, *any-*

thing. But of course he's not just anything; he's the head of security for HGVB Bank.

He used to be a cop.

I remember *the first time I saw Sean White, all those years ago. The night had been off-kilter from the get-go. A little before eight p.m., my mother had told me that we were going to meet Nick Foley in Brooklyn Heights.*

Nick had apparently texted my mother on that new, fancy phone he had just gotten her. He had asked us to come over, said he was going to take us out to a movie. It was the first time he had ever offered such a thing, and my mother was so excited. Her lover was acknowledging her. He had chosen her over his wife. At least that's what she had told me this meant. She looked into my eyes and explained that love conquered all. She told me that our lives were about to change. No more run-down apartments with bars on the windows, no more Top Ramen dinners, no more worries about gang-ridden schools.

"Nick is going to take care of us, mija," she said. "He's going to love us."

It was confusing to hear. On the one hand I had desperately wanted my mother to be a real-life Cinderella . . . but then, Cinderella's prince hadn't been married to somebody else.

We got in my mother's run-down Toyota, and by eight thirty we were parked in front of Nick's house. My mother told me to wait in the car.

It felt . . . wrong. Even at ten I understood that my mother had committed a sin, and sins couldn't be rewarded by riches. That wasn't how fairy tales worked.

So I sulked in the car as my mother went to the front door of Nick's five-million-dollar Brooklyn Heights home. I plugged in to my portable CD player and turned up the volume to an eardrum-shattering level as my mother rang the doorbell and then, after a moment, tried the door, which gave way for her.

Watching my mother walk into that house, all I could think about was that she didn't deserve her good fortune. She didn't deserve to ride off into the sunset with this man . . . and yet . . . wouldn't it be nice to live in that house, right here on this pretty street with all these gracefully arching trees? In my bedroom at home I could always hear people outside yelling, drunk, threatening. On the street where I lived with my mother there was always something to fear.

But here? On this street in the nicest part of Brooklyn? Everything felt safe.

That's what I was thinking as I sat alone in the car, admiring the way the leaves glistened under the streetlights, listening to Madonna sing about the equalizing power of music.

I didn't see my mother come running out of the house. I didn't see her until she was flinging herself back into the driver's seat, a cell phone pressed to her ear. The car was dark—our interior lights broken long ago—but when I pulled off my headphones I could hear the panic in my mother's voice. And I saw that there was some kind of stain on her shirt and something dark and wet on her hands.

"*Yes! I just found him! Please come! ¡Dios mío! Please come! There's so much blood! His heart . . . I can't feel his heartbeat! ¡Auxilio!*"

Auxilio: "Help."

In minutes the night was alive with sirens and flashing lights. Soon Nick's neighbors were on the sidewalk, cops were everywhere . . .

. . . and my mother was kneeling by one of those pretty trees and vomiting onto the dirt. A few policemen tried to talk to her, but she was barely coherent.

That's when Detective White showed up. He stood over my mother, seemingly impassive and disinterested.

I knelt by my mom's side and held her hand as Detective White asked his questions.

"*Are you an illegal?*" *he asked her.*

The question was enough to startle my mother into silence, her sobs catching in her throat as she shook her head. She managed to assure him that she was born here, in America, but had been raised in Mexico. She then tried to bring Detective White back to the point. "Did they find the attacker in the house?" she asked. Had he seen Mr. Foley, on the ground, covered in all that blood? Was he really . . . dead? Who could have done that to this man, this man whom she loved? This man who was kind and gentle . . . and important. A senior VP at HGVB Bank. This kind of thing just didn't happen to men like that! It couldn't!

"You were sleeping with him?" Detective White asked.

My mother had simply stared at the detective, open-mouthed. She then glanced at me, shame covering her face.

"Hey, don't worry, I get it," Detective White continued. "You were already on your knees scrubbing his floors, so when he walked up to you, his fly in your face, you figured, 'What the hell, I'll clean his pipes while I'm down here.'"

My mother got up, pulling me up with her. "Mija," she said sharply, "get back in the car."

But it was too late. Another officer came over. A woman this time. "This the kid?" she asked before kneeling down and taking my hand, pulling me gently away from my mother. "It's going to be okay, sweetie," she cooed.

And that's when the world started spinning. Detective White was suddenly slapping handcuffs on my mom while he read off her Miranda rights. He wasn't rough about the way he handled her. There was no hint of the lecherous bully who had been questioning her only seconds earlier . . . not *now that the other cop was within hearing distance. Now he was the picture of professionalism.*

The female officer led me even farther down the street, shielding me from the sight of my mother being hauled away. So I didn't have to see that.

But I heard it.

I heard my mom screaming my name.

Later my mother would tell the police how Nick had texted her, asked her to come over. But Sean White testified that they were never able to find Nick Foley's phone and that when he took my mother's phone the memory had already been wiped clean.

My mother maintained that Nick had planned to leave his wife for her, but Sean White insisted that all evidence pointed to the fact that the opposite was true, that my mother had been stalking Nick even though he had rejected her.

There were people who said that they heard what they now think might have been a gunshot long before my mother arrived at Nick Foley's home, but Sean White "proved" that those witnesses weren't credible. But he was able to find two witnesses who were, two witnesses who swore to hearing a gunshot just minutes before my mother called the police.

There were rumors that Nick Foley had had a recent falling-out with the CEO of HGVB, Edmund Gable, but Sean White was able to squash those rumors well before the *case came to trial. He said that a thorough investigation proved that Nick Foley was actually incredibly fond of Edmund. He admired him! In fact, Nick loved the whole Gable family! Both Lander and his brother made statements supporting this.*

In the end, my mom was sent to prison while I spent the rest of my childhood in a series of foster homes.

Three months after that, Sean White resigned from the force and accepted Edmund Gable's offer to head security for the New York offices and branches of HGVB Bank.

But that detail didn't make the papers.

Sometimes, when I sleep, I can still hear my mom screaming. It sounds like the screams of a dying woman. In the end, that's exactly what they were. The death of her lover, the charges, the trial, the conviction, losing her daughter . . . All these things led to her suicide. It never occurred to me that she would do something like that, but it should have. I failed her in so many ways.

My grip on Lander's phone is now so tight that the tips of my fingers are white. I can literally feel my rage sharpening, stabbing at my heart.

That's good.

That's inspiring.

With a deep breath I bring myself back to the present

and scrutinize the texts. There's nothing incriminating here, not really. But there are a few cryptic messages from Mr. White. A text that reads, I made the problem go away. And another farther down that reads, Made the switch.

What makes these interesting is that there is no preceding text conversation that explains them. They come out of nowhere, as if Mr. White wants to send a signal, letting Lander know what's going on without creating a record that could come back to haunt him.

Which means there are secrets to be learned here. I look around for something to write on and eventually settle on a seemingly forgotten receipt that's peeking out from under the couch and a pen that was left on the coffee table. Quickly I write down the dates of White's messages before moving down to the next contact who's texted Lander. This one is from someone named Paolo. No last name is recorded. The text simply reads, Are you sure they won't check?

That's it. There's no response to the text. Could be nothing, but still, worth looking into.

I switch over to his emails. Budgets and policies, various rules of finance, nothing here of interest . . . but the dates these emails came in . . . there's something weird there. The emails are too few and come too far between.

He's been deleting things. And that would make sense

as a matter of course, except for the things he's *not* deleting. Each email is so exceedingly benign. Some of it con-
tains confidential information but nothing scandalous . . .

. . . which makes me think that what's been deleted
must be pretty damn interesting.

The trash folder has been completely emptied.

"So many secrets, Lander," I murmur as I carefully
put the phone back exactly where I found it.

I climb to my feet and take a moment to admire the
view before going to explore the rest of the penthouse.

I search for hours but I don't find much else and
eventually I call it a night. I pin a note on the pillow next
to Lander. One sentence, two words:

Thank you.

And with that I walk out.

The game is in full swing.

chapter six

It takes exactly thirteen hours for him to call. Since I left at four a.m., that brings it to precisely five in the afternoon. By that time I'm on the other side of the park, on the Upper West Side, preparing for stage two.

I've since programmed his line into my caller ID, but when I pick up I wait for him to identify himself anyway.

"How'd you get my number?"

It's not a real question. I know damn well that the manager of Ivan's gave it to him. He's the one who gave Lander my name too. It took some grilling to get that out of him . . . but I can be surprisingly intimidating when I need to be.

"Your boss gave it to me," Lander confirms, "or I suppose I should say, your *former* boss."

"Yep. Quit this morning." I keep my tone light, even

perky. It doesn't quite match the moody black stretch knit dress I'm wearing: high neckline, hem right above the knee, an extrawide belt wrapped tightly around my waist, and the kind of sleeves that give the appearance of shoulder pads. It's severe and sort of a throwback to the 1980s. I can't say I love the look, but I know my next employer will . . . and judging from some of the leers I'm getting, a lot of other men do too.

"So I was told," Lander says. Even now his voice sounds groggy. There's something comforting about it. I can imagine what it would be like to wake up to that voice, snuggled up in his arms.

It's absolutely not what I'm supposed to be thinking about.

"You also snuck out on me," he continues.

"You were dead to the world. I didn't want to wake you."

"Yeah, that's not like me," he muses. "I'm usually such a light sleeper."

"Well, you did drink a lot." It's not really true; he probably had three drinks over four hours, but that's my explanation and I'm sticking to it.

I stop in front of the building where my interview is to take place. The doorman stares right past me, as stoic as a guard at Buckingham Palace.

"Hate to cut this short, but I gotta go."

"When will I see you again?"

"Soon."

"When's—"

But I hang up before he can finish his question. With a plastered-on smile I give my name to the doorman as well as the names of the people I'm here to see. He nods curtly and calls over to one of the security guys, who proceeds to walk me down the halls and corridors to the correct elevator.

"Are you here for the personal assistant job?" the guard asks. "You look more like a Wall Street power player to me."

"No, not my thing. I manage lives, not money."

"'Lives, not money.' I like that." The guard chuckles, flashes me a grin that is flirtatious and stupidly hopeful.

I return his smile with one that offers no encouragement but doesn't go so far as to completely dissuade. I don't mind his interest. One day I might even encourage it if it suits my purposes. But right now I have more important things to worry about.

When we finally get to the elevator and then I get to the right floor, it doesn't take me long to find penthouse 1400. I press the little doorbell by the side of the door and roll my shoulders back, making sure that my posture is perfect.

In a matter of seconds the door is yanked open by a

man in his late thirties, broad shoulders, short, professionally cut sandy-blond hair. His pale-blue eyes roam over me unapologetically before they reach my face.

"You must be Bellona Dantès."

I smile warmly at Lander's brother. "Everybody calls me Bell."

Once inside the sitting room, Travis Gable motions for me to take a seat on a very sleek but uncomfortable chair. The whole room is done in black and white, the furniture angular and modern to the point of being cartoonish.

"Bellona . . . I haven't heard that name before," he says as he sits across from me, crossing his ankle over his knee. "Is it Italian?"

"Sort of. I was named after the Roman goddess of war."

"Really," he says dryly. "Are you looking for a fight?"

"No, just a job."

His mouth curves up for the first time. "Good answer." He examines me again. His brow furrows ever so slightly. Maybe he thinks I look familiar. But it's been over ten years since we last met. I was almost ten and he was . . . what? Twenty-eight? The cards have been shuffled and reshuffled so many times since then. He'll never make the connection.

"And you go by Bell," he says, tasting the nickname. "I like it."

"Is Mrs. Gable here? I understand that she's the one I'd be working for."

"She's at a med spa." He puts his cell on the glass coffee table that sits between us, next to a display of bleached white coral. "I once assumed personal assistants were just for celebrities. But my wife, Jessica, is disorganized, frenzied, and a little too fond of her dry martinis and prescription pills."

"A risky combination."

He shrugs as if indifferent to his wife's welfare. "She needs help running her own life; that's why you're here. But I'll be damned if I'm going to spend a fortune on an assistant just to keep the world from discovering she's an idiot. If I'm going to hire you, you'll be expected to serve us both."

Serve. It's an interesting choice of word. My feeling is that it's been chosen carefully.

"You speak Spanish?" he asks.

"Fluidamente."

"Good. Every once in a while I'll need you to arrange and keep track of certain off-hour appointments for me or deliver messages. Sometimes I'll use you as a translator when I meet with Spanish-speaking investors. This PA job requires . . . finesse and organization, a strong work ethic, and, if you don't mind my saying, humility. I need someone who's prepared to do it all."

By which he means all the things that an executive assistant should be able to handle on her own, unless some of these meetings need to be kept off the record and away from regulators' eyes. In which case: use your personal assistant.

"Of course, Mr. Gable," I say smoothly. "As I'm sure you've seen on my résumé, I've worked in this kind of position before."

"Right, right, I checked that reference . . . You worked for Stephan George, the real estate mogul." He unbuttons his jacket, drapes his arm across the top of the sofa. "Or at least he was approaching mogul status, from what I understand. Shame about what happened to him."

I nod solemnly, letting my smile slip. "It was completely unfair. He was innocent of all those charges."

It's the right answer. Travis and Jessica have gone through more than ten personal assistants in the last decade; only three of them have lasted more than three days, and *all* of them previously worked for employers who had some dubious legal dealings in a white-collar kind of way—which probably means that Travis likes to hire people who he doesn't think will have ethical qualms about being immersed in his more sordid dealings.

The very thought makes my heart dance.

"Of course, of course," Travis is saying. "Tell me, where is the good Mr. George now?"

"They say he's somewhere in Latin America, but really, it's anyone's guess."

"If you did know, would you tell me?"

"I like Mr. George," I say cautiously, "and I'm very loyal to my employers even after my services are no longer needed for . . . for reasons that are beyond everyone's control."

Travis steeples his fingers. He could pass for a James Bond supervillain in that pose.

"George took off almost a year ago," Travis continues. "Your résumé says you've been bartending since then at some place called Ivan's?"

"It's one of Micah Romenov's bars."

The surprise registers on his face. Romenov is known to have some illegal dealings, although he's never been busted for anything. He's one of those criminals that has a mystique about him, the kind that people like Travis Gable find awe-inspiring rather than repellant. Most importantly, everybody knows that if you're working for Romenov in *any* capacity, even at the lowest level, you have to be good at holding your tongue, turning a blind eye, and, in a weird way, being completely trustworthy. No one steals or betrays Romenov.

Which makes me quite a valuable employee.

"He was a friend of Mr. George and he was doing me a favor. I just needed to earn an income while I looked for work in my field."

I'm momentarily startled by the ringing of the landline, but Travis doesn't show any sign of registering the sound. "I like you," he says.

"Glad to hear it, Mr. Gable." The phone stops ringing and the sudden silence emphasizes the intimacy of this meeting, taking place in a penthouse, not an office . . . and his wife nowhere to be seen.

"Lloyd, Jessica's last personal assistant, was good at his job . . . or at least we thought he was, we *both* thought he was," Travis emphasizes, as if to highlight the shared responsibility for the last assistant's hiring. "Turns out he had a drug problem. I can't have that. People say things they shouldn't to people they shouldn't when they're under the influence. I already have to monitor my wife, so I don't want to have to worry about some assistant too. Are you a big drinker, Bell? Abuse any substance at all?"

"I don't do drugs and I always stop after my second glass."

"That's good. Very good." He presses his fingers to his lips. Studies me a little longer. "And I like your outfit," he finally adds. "It flatters you."

"I try to dress to impress."

There's a sound as the front door opens and closes, then the light click of heels moving down the hardwood floor of the hall.

Travis never takes his eyes off me. "I'm going to give you a chance. You'll mostly be here with Jessica, but remember, if I'm the one who's given you a task, I'm the one you'll be reporting back to on how it went. You will not leave word with my wife or anyone else. Understand?"

"I understand." I lower my head submissively. "I'm truly grateful for this opportunity."

When he only answers with a smile I get up, keeping my eyes on the polished floor. "When shall I start?"

"Monday. Be here at eight."

I nod and turn to leave, and nearly collide with a woman sporting strawberry-blond hair arranged in a low bun. Her dress is a cinch-waisted, full-skirted brocade number. I know she's pushing thirty, but she has that ageless quality that the rich sometimes do when they purchase their sophistication and elegance from Ralph Lauren and Dior. She looks a little like the kind of doll you collect and never take out of the box for fear of decreasing its value . . . except for her bloodshot eyes, which are trained on Travis.

"Hello, darling," she says, looking past me, trying to catch Travis's eye. But he's occupied with his phone. He doesn't even really acknowledge her . . . similar to how she's not directly acknowledging me.

"I just spoke to Lander," she says, now pulling on her fingers nervously. "He'll be here in a few minutes to drop off the piece for the charity auction."

There's a weird dynamic going on between these two, but I can't really dwell on it now. Lander's discovery of my latest career move has to be carefully controlled. Which means I can't be here when he arrives.

"I'll be leaving, then," I say quickly, turning back to Travis. "I'll be here on Monday at eight a.m. sharp. If you need me to work over the weekend, just give me a call."

I move to leave, but Jessica grabs my arm. Her grip is surprisingly strong. "I don't understand," she says, her voice much weaker than her grip. "Have you offered her the PA job?"

"Yes." Travis sighs as he starts scrolling through the emails on his phone. "I did."

"You told me I would be allowed to interview my own assistants."

"You weren't here. I was." His fingers tap out a message on the screen.

"You didn't even tell me you scheduled one!" She glares at me, and her grip tightens. "Sit down. Your interview isn't over."

"Don't be rude, Jessica," he says, but he's distracted and clearly uninterested in the conflict that his wife would like to draw him into.

Exactly how much time constitutes the *few minutes* before Lander will arrive?

"I know you'll be happy with my performance," I say, trying to gently wriggle my arm free without further ticking her off. "If not I'll completely understand if you feel the need to let me go. When I come back Monday we can play it by ear."

"I can't let you go since you don't even have the job yet!" Her voice is escalating, but she sounds more panicked than angry.

Travis sighs, puts the phone back in his pocket. "I just *gave* her the job. And no one is letting her go . . . not unless I decide it's necessary."

"For fuck's sake, she's *my* assistant, T!"

As soon as the words escape Jessica's lips, she presses them together until I can't see her lips at all, as if she's hiding the instrument of her impetuousness.

For the first time I notice the dark clouds that can be seen gathering outside the penthouse's massive windows. It's almost as if Travis summoned them up himself.

"Nothing is yours." Travis's voice is surprisingly calm, almost casual. "Not this home, not the limo, not the clothes or the jewels or even your friends, who only want to hang out with you because you married into my family. It's *my* wealth that pays for everything. It's my name that elevated you. I've *given* you nothing, Jessica. Without me, you *are* nothing. Everything in your life is on lease. The girl is hired. That matter is settled."

Jessica's hand drops from my arm. And for a brief moment I'm too shocked to move. In my neighborhood it's not uncommon to come across men who occasionally throw drunken punches at their wives and girlfriends, but this is the first time I've ever seen a man stab a woman to death with words.

Because Jessica is definitely dying—right here before me, she's bleeding. Travis has used insults to cut open every artery.

I shift my weight awkwardly from foot to foot, my eyes bouncing between Travis and Jessica before settling on the latter. "I really look forward to working with you, Mrs. Gable," I say softly, as if my own feeble words might serve as gauze and Band-Aids. I then turn to Travis and add, "And for you, Mr. Gable."

Before either of them can delay me longer I back out of the room and then rush to the door. Hopefully they'll attribute my haste to a desire to escape an uncomfortable situation.

"Bell!"

I turn to see Travis standing in the hall. "Please remember, this job pays very well. It will be worth it."

Really? Worth watching you demean and humiliate your wife for your amusement? But then, there will be other rewards, I remind myself. *Rewards that have nothing to do with money. Yes, it* will *be worth it.*

"Don't disappoint me, Bell."

"Oh, Mr. Gable," I say solemnly, "I may be many things, but I'm never a disappointment."

And I mean it. To Travis I won't be a disappointment at all.

To him? I'll be a disaster.

chapter seven

Last time I saw Jessica she wasn't more than nineteen and I wasn't even in middle school yet, not nearly on Jessica's radar. Jessica hadn't been quite so . . . strained back then. Her voice, now so thin, was rich and robust as she bemoaned Nick Foley's fate from the witness stand.

And Jessica had been such a perfect witness. A sweet-faced girl from a good family, what could she gain from testifying against my mom?

Nothing. That's what everyone thought.

But isn't it interesting that only six months after my mother's sentencing, Jessica was engaged to a man no one even knew she was dating: Travis Gable, a man who knew Nick Foley quite well.

*　*　*

I tuck the memory away as I walk past the line of co-ops on Travis's block, my eyes quick, looking for any sign of Lander. But he's not here. I got out in time. Pulling my phone out of my handbag, I make a quick call to him, but it goes directly to voice mail.

"Hi, I'm sorry I had to cut you off before. I just finished a job interview not too far from you—right across the park in fact, and I was hoping you had a few minutes to catch up. Call me before I head out of here."

I put the phone back in my purse and keep walking, another block, then two. It would be better if Lander called me before he went to see his brother, though there's a good chance Travis won't actually mention the name of his new assistant. After all, he doesn't know the name means anything to Lander. Hell, he might not even mention that he's hired an assistant at all; surely they have other, more important business to discuss.

Still, there's a possibility that Travis *might* tell Lander that he's hired an assistant named Bellona. The name is notably unique, so he might mention it as a casual comment. It's a possibility I need to eliminate.

I walk another block, picking up my pace a bit. My whole body begs to be in motion, like it's trying to keep up with my mind.

The streets of New York are alive with their usual organized chaos, people with briefcases walking blindly past the tourists, who are taking pictures of the street without even noticing the rock star strolling out of the deli a few doors down. Everyone is blind to what's going on around them.

Just like Lloyd, Jessica and Travis's last assistant, when I tailed him to a dive bar in Queens only last week.

He was standing on the side of the building when I approached him. I smiled weakly, my eyes cast down. "Got a light?"

Lloyd looked up, a Marlboro hanging from his full lips, his eyes narrow as if they were squinting, as if it were the middle of the day instead of late into the night. His posture was tense, his demeanor a little aggressive. Maybe he was hoping for a little action that night.

I was there to make sure he got it.

He reached into his pocket and pulled out a lighter as I held out a menthol cigarette. It's the only kind I can stand. Normally I don't smoke at all. But that night . . . well, I was a different woman.

I was the woman he wanted.

My hands shook as I brought the cigarette to my lips. I struggled not to shrink away as his eyes roamed over my torn tights and my dirty black miniskirt. I felt their cheapness against my skin; I felt the desperation of my sheer, skintight white nylon top over my black bra. I was exposed, easy prey . . .

. . . and Lloyd, with his hair styled for bad-boy appeal and his wifebeater shirt paired with his worn leather jacket, with his pouty lips and perfect skin . . . Lloyd was looking at me like a predator.

That's all I needed.

I shivered as I reached for him, as I took his hand, as I moved into his space. My intentions left no room for sub-tlety. He looked at me questioningly, wondering who I was and what I was up to.

I wasn't quite able to keep my voice steady when I asked, "Wanna party?"

His smile returned. The haze of smoke separated us, keeping the moment from feeling too real or too scary.

"What do you do?" he asked, his eyes hungry. "X?"

It's the question of a novice. Anyone who actually does drugs would have seen my trembling hands, the dark circles under my eyes, my slumped shoulders . . . They'd see all that and they'd know X wasn't my addiction.

"I'm thinking about a different letter," I said. "Like . . . H."

I sounded like a little girl . . . or maybe like Marilyn Monroe or even Jennifer Tilly. It was a new sound for me. I could tell he liked it.

"Heroin?" he asked. "You got some?"

I knew by the way he asked that he wouldn't actually do any . . . but he'd be happy to watch and then he'd take me, making the destruction complete.

I shook my head and gently grabbed hold of his jacket, moving my hand down the jagged open edge of the zipper all the way to the very bottom, which fell below his waist. I let the back of my hand brush against his jeans and felt the evidence of his building desire. His need for me mirrored the need of an addict.

"I know a guy," I whispered. My menthol cigarette was still in my hand. I had only brought it to my lips twice and the neglect had turned it into a cinder, both dangerous and eerie.

"You want me to buy for you?" he asked. "Why would I do that?"

I swallowed and breathed in the smoke. "I got the money," I said. "But the guy who sells . . . I owe him a little more than what's in my wallet, ya know? So . . . if you could help me . . ." Again my hand brushed against his jeans. He was staring at my bra, watching my chest rise and fall, wondering if it was the drugs or desire that made each breath so shallow. "I'll give you the money for the score." I sucked in my cheeks, moved in an inch closer. "I'll give you the money and so much more."

"Oh yeah? What exactly are you going to give me?"

I let go of his jacket and cupped him. I let his smoke sur-

round me, making my eyes water as I pressed my breasts against him. "Whatever you want, baby. I'll get on my knees right here. I'll fuck you in an alley . . . in a cheap motel . . . You can touch me, spank me, tie me up—you can do whatever you want to me." I leaned in farther, grazed my teeth against his earlobe. "You wanna fuck me with a cigar? Or just your cock?" I rubbed my hand up and down. "It's big, isn't it?" I looked up into his eyes, let my cigarette fall to the pavement. "Whatever you want to do to me . . . I'll like it," I whispered. "I want you to use me. I want to be fucked by a stranger . . . by you . . . All you gotta do is get me the hit."

He had pulled back a little, tried to catch my eye . . . but I stared at the ground. I wouldn't meet his gaze.

"This the first time you doing this, babe? Pimping yourself out for drugs?"

I hesitated a moment before nodding.

"But you're doing it now, so you must be jonesing something serious," he said. "And when we're done you'll feel even worse than you do now because then you'll be nothing more than a cheap whore."

Finally I forced myself to look into his eyes. "Have you been with whores before?" I asked.

"Yeah, a few."

"Did you care how they felt afterward?"

"Not so much."

I took a deep breath and voiced the only question that

mattered: "I told you what I'll let you do to me. I've told you what I'll do for you. Do you really care how I'll feel afterward?"

He reached out, stroked my cheek with his thumb. If there was a question in his voice before, the leer in his smile settled the matter. "No. I don't care at all."

It's all I needed to hear. In minutes he was following me down the street, down one alley, then another. He ignored the other pedestrians, drunk stragglers trying to weave their way home. Every few steps he reached out, touched my butt, brushed his fingers against my bra as I smiled, warming my hands in his pockets. "Soon, baby," I promised. "Soon."

In minutes we were in the right place, hidden in a dark alley between two buildings staring at the dealer on the corner. "That's him," I whispered. "He's got the good stuff. It makes every cell in my body come alive—I swear when I'm on it I can fly." I took his hand, pressed the bills into his palm. "When you're inside me we'll fly together. I'll be like a supernova . . . just for you . . . Whatever you want."

His eyes brightened. His hand slid over my hip. "I'm gonna fuck you good."

And with that he turned and approached the dealer. I watched as he pulled out the money. I watched as he made his request.

I watched as the dealer pulled out a pair of handcuffs. I watched as Lloyd was pressed against a wall and read his

*rights. I listened as he cried out in protest, as he tried to ex-
plain . . . but it was too late . . . I was already gone, walking
quickly down the alley, away from the scene, already wiping
away the makeup that created the illusion of dark circles
while whispering to myself, "I bet you care now, asshole."*

*I needed to make my escape quietly . . . but it was hard
not to giggle. Any jerk with half a brain would have been
able to peg that dealer as a narc. But Lloyd didn't have half
a brain. Just a hard-on and a desire to prey on weak women.*

Unfortunately for him, I'm not weak.

*And, of course, it was only a matter of time before the
police found the meth I planted in his pocket, which made
his protests even more futile.*

It was a minor victory, but it was still kinda sweet.

Some might think what I did was cruel. Some might
see it as vigilante justice.

But my motivations were simpler than that and
much more mundane.

The truth is, I just needed him out of my way.

I come to a stop several blocks from Travis's place and
wait to cross a street. Taxis and cars and limos fly past
me . . . except for one limo, which pulls to a stop right in
front of me.

The door opens, but no one comes out. The sun is low in the sky now, and I squint as I try to see into the dark interior of the vehicle . . . but I don't really need to see anything to know who's inside. I know even before I hear his voice:

"Warrior."

Some words carry their own music.

Silently, I slip inside the limo, closing the door behind me, locking out the streets of New York as I take my place by Lander's side.

"When you said 'soon,' I didn't realize you meant this afternoon," he says.

"Actually, it's officially evening now," I counter. He looks good in his slim-cut suit and skinny tie. His hair is neat, but he's unshaven, and his stubble gives his polished look a roughness that's intensely appealing. "Have you been searching all over town for me, Lander?"

"No," he says simply. "If I had been, I wouldn't have thought to look here . . . at least not until I got your message a moment ago."

"Like I said, I had a job interview nearby."

The limo starts to move toward Travis's building. "Another bar?"

"No, something different. Better. Let's get a drink. I'll tell you all about it."

"I'm supposed to stop by my brother's to drop something off for a charity auction my sister-in-law is putting together. If I don't do it now I won't have a chance until Sunday."

"So do it Sunday," I press, adding a slight note of pleading to my voice.

He looks at me expectantly, waiting for me to explain the urgency. When I don't, he chuckles. "You are a study in contradictions, aren't you? Running away from me one moment and then demanding my immediate attention the next." He lowers the partition between us and the driver. "Change of plans, Roger. We're not stopping yet. Take us on a scenic tour, will you?"

"A scenic tour?" the driver asks, keeping his eyes on the street.

"Yeah, you pick the route."

I flash him a grateful smile before turning to look out tinted windows as Lander sends a quick text to his brother, postponing the drop-off. Pedestrians stare at the car, but they can't see who's inside. Limos are so funny that way. They're one of the most conspicuous vehicles on the street and yet when you're inside one you're completely invisible, isolated from the outside world. You're literally living in a bubble, if only for the space of a commute.

"So getting back to last night," he says. "You left without saying good-bye." His tone is teasing but there's a hint of a deeper emotion there. Not anger . . . more like concern.

For some reason that rubs me the wrong way.

"I told you, you were sleeping heavily. It seemed criminal to wake you."

"Now, there's an interesting choice of words," he muses.

I give him a quick sidelong glance, but he doesn't take the bait.

"I don't know why I was so tired last night," he continues. The car rolls past his brother's building. I keep my face arranged in an impassive expression, careful not to give away that I know the place.

"Perhaps," I say, stretching my legs across the spacious limo floor, "I wore you out."

"Not an entirely unreasonable explanation." But he doesn't sound like he means it.

He's beginning to make me nervous. "How long are we going to be driving, Lander?"

"Oh, I don't know, long enough to get some answers."

"You can't interrogate me in a bar like a normal person?"

"I prefer the quiet of the limo," he says with a shrug. "Why aren't you working at the bar anymore?"

"I wasn't happy there."

"I did offer to help you find something else."

"Yes, well, I didn't need your help. That job I just interviewed for? I got it. I landed something better in less than a day."

"Did you? Well, I suppose it wouldn't take much. And why did you disappear on me?"

"I just told you . . ."

"Yes, but I'd like the real reason now."

Again I don't answer, and the limo keeps moving on.

"Were you scared, Bell?"

My eyes shift forward. The driver's back is stiff; his focus remains on the road. "What was there to be scared of?"

"I don't think you were prepared for what happened between us."

"Sex?" I reply. But when the limo driver's eyes flicker to the rearview mirror, I lower my voice. "I knew what we were going to do when I went home with you."

"Yes, but I don't think you expected to like it."

I laugh—a laugh that's meant to show that what he's saying is ridiculous.

It's a laugh that I hope hides the fact that he's right. "Women don't go home with men they don't think can satisfy them."

"*Most* women don't," he concedes. "But you're different from most women, aren't you? Besides, your line of argument is a little weak."

"Oh? And why's that?"

"Because you were a lot more than just satisfied. You seemed almost . . . awed."

Again I laugh, but the sound is harsher now. "You were hardly my first, Lander. I've had other lovers."

"I'm sure you have, but I'm also fairly certain that none of them were very good."

Again the chauffeur's eyes flicker to the rearview. My cheeks heat up as I turn away from his gaze.

"It's not that I'm claiming to be a superior lover," Lander continues. "But I do think . . . I think we have superior chemistry. I think that when I . . . entered you, when I pressed inside you, I . . . broke something. Something that needed to be broken."

"I don't understand you." I want the words to come out derisively, but instead they come out weak, soft.

"Have you been hurt, Bell? Did someone build that armor?"

I chew lightly on my fingernails. I won't answer that.

"Why did you come home with me? Were you really seeking satisfaction or were you craving something . . . darker?"

I stare out the window, holding on to my silence. The limo feels too small now. The air too limited.

He leans forward, tucks a strand of hair behind my ear. "How many battles have you won?" he asks. "How many casualties have there been? Did it feel like you were winning when there was blood on your hands?"

It's a metaphor. He doesn't know the truth . . . but still . . . he's close to the mark without realizing it.

"I don't understand you." I turn toward him, I see the intensity in his expression, I feel his proximity, and again I'm watching him watching me.

No, that's wrong. I'm seeing him *seeing* me. That's different. He may not understand my details, but he sees me with clearer eyes than any other man ever has.

It's terrifying.

It's thrilling.

I have to stop these questions before I do something stupid . . . like answer them.

I let my hand slide over his, lace my fingers through his, feel the warmth of his skin against my palm, a little rougher than mine, a little more weathered, at least on the outside.

I meet the limo driver's eyes in the rearview mirror and raise my eyebrows, questioningly, teasingly, and then I lean forward and gently press my finger against the button that raises the partition, shielding us from his gaze.

I wait for it to close, and then, without a word, I raise myself up and swing a leg over Lander's lap, straddling him. My skirt rides up on my legs as my arms wrap around his neck. "Is this why you stopped for me, Lander? Did you want to give me a ride?"

"A ride is probably all I should want to give you," he mutters, as if talking more to himself than to me. "But for some reason I think I might want to give you more."

I lean down to kiss him as his hands slip to my waist. His mouth is so warm, and the kiss so tender.

From the corner of my eye I can see some tourists gesturing toward the car, looking but not seeing.

The kiss grows more intense. His tongue opens my mouth, pressing inside as he dispenses with my belt, his hands then moving lower, to my hips, to my ass, to the bare skin of my legs.

We've only been together once and yet his touch is already familiar. Gentle but strong. His fingers make their way to the hem of my dress and with one swift motion he pulls it off me. I don't protest. I don't pull away when his hands move over my bra. The limo slows, whether it's for traffic or for us, I don't know.

Placing my hand between his legs, I feel his erection reaching out to me.

I lean in so my mouth is right by his ear. "Careful, Lander," I breathe. "If you give me more, I might take it."

He smiles as I unbutton his pants. He raises his hips as my hands move around them, feeling the perfect, firm curves of his glutes before finding his back pocket. I pull out his wallet and hold it in front of him.

"Are you taking payments now?"

"No," I say sweetly. I search the billfold and quickly find the thing I want. "Today I'm just offering rewards."

The packaging of the condom isn't wrinkled; there's no ring imprinted into the soft leather of the wallet. It might have been in there for a few days rather than a few weeks.

A few days would be good. That would mean he started carrying it around after that night we met at the bar. It would mean that he's been thinking about me, fantasizing about me, hoping for me . . .

I toss my hair over one shoulder before pulling his pants and boxers down, ripping the packaging open, putting the condom in my mouth. Slowly, carefully, I apply it, using my lips to unroll it over his erection, using my tongue to add a little pressure, until he's fully in my mouth . . .

He groans.

It's almost beautiful.

"Will you take me home again, Lander?" I pull myself back up, sliding my body along his as I do. "Will you take me to your pretty parties, introduce me to your friends?"

"I don't have friends." His thumbs link inside the

waistband of my panties, pull them down over my thighs, my calves.

"Then introduce me to your enemies."

He drops my panties on the floor alongside his belt, my dress . . .

His hands grip my waist, controlling my movement as he lowers me onto him, filling me inch by inch. I ache to have more of him, but he holds me firm, keeping his pace deliberate.

I think about the driver. He may not be able to see, but he knows what we're doing only a few feet away from him. What must he think of me? How will he act when he sees me again?

The whole thing is nerve-racking, illicit, intense, agonizing . . .

. . . exquisite.

I close my eyes as I feel my body opening up to him, and when he has finally filled me completely, when I have all of him, I gasp.

My clit is right up against his pelvic bone, and even the slightest movement ignites me.

But Lander pulls me up again, away from the source of my pleasure. Again I fight him, more desperately this time, craving fulfillment, but again he keeps things measured, slow.

I whimper, my body writhing in his grip. And I pull

hard on his lapels as again I feel his body against my clit and moan as he slowly grinds against me, making me quiver.

It's not a big movement. It's small, almost delicate . . . and it's going to make me come in less than a minute . . .

But again he denies me. My eyes fly open and silently plead with him.

"Ah, there you are, looking at me now, like you're supposed to," he says. "Now I can let you come."

And with surprising strength he presses me back down onto him and I cry out as he moves against me, pulling me into him, bringing the sensation to a point where control is impossible for me.

"Will you do something for me, Bell?" he asks.

"Yes!" Although I barely hear the question, barely care what he's asking.

"Will you let yourself truly be seen?"

My heart speeds up to a dizzying pace. I know what he's asking.

And as I groan again I know I'm saying yes.

My eyes are on Lander, so I can't see the partition but I can hear it lowering. I can feel the car slow even more.

My eyes are on Lander as he thrusts inside me, harder each time, rubbing against my clit . . . making me come, all while the driver watches me. My body shakes with the impact and I cry out Lander's name.

The car speeds up again and in an instant I've been flipped over so now I'm on my back. Lander throws off his jacket, adding it to the pile of clothes on the floor. He kneels in front of me on the seat, pushes my knees up to my breasts. Almost self-consciously I squeeze my legs together, crossing them at the ankle.

It only makes him smile.

He pulls my hips into his angled lap, my feet now pressing against his chest, feeling the strength of him, measuring his speeding heartbeat as he pushes inside again. The fit is so tight now, with my legs crossed, the angle so perfect, each thrust brings me closer to another explosion . . .

. . . and I can see he's close too. His fingers dig into my thighs, his eyes holding me as surely as his hands.

This time when I cry out, it's not a word. It's more abstract. It's the sound of triumph. And his voice mingles with mine as he comes as well, completing the victory.

But to whom does the victory belong?

The question flickers through my mind, too weak and insubstantial for me to ponder.

My eyes are still on his, his on mine. He reaches out . . .

. . . and closes the partition.

chapter eight

Only forty minutes have passed since we put our clothes back on, since Lander tried to convince me to go straight to some chic little Upper East Side restaurant. But I had to put him off, if only for a few hours. After what happened, I needed a little time to get my head straight. So after confirming that his brother and his wife were already out for the evening, and that Lander would have to wait until Sunday to see them, I suggested we meet for a late dinner, nine o'clock, in the West Village. I told him I had some errands I needed to do in the area and had him drop me off in front of a Duane Reade. I went in and took my time selecting a few Clif Bars for purchase, reading over the ingredient lists as if I was expecting to find something even faintly interesting there. When I stepped back outside I made sure his limo was nowhere in sight before heading for the subway.

Now as I sit on the train, staring straight ahead but seeing nothing, I wonder . . . *What the hell possessed me?*

I run my hand over my skirt, thanking the gods for synthetic fabrics that don't wrinkle. I don't want to advertise my . . . my activity level during the latter portion of the day.

And yet it's not exactly a secret, is it? The limo driver saw me. He saw me come. And that wasn't some random cabbie I'll never see again. That was Lander's driver. Now every time that man opens the door for me, he'll picture me naked, on Lander's lap, in the throes of the most powerful orgasm of my life . . .

. . . and he'll be opening the door for me quite a lot, because I'm nowhere near done with Lander.

The subway reaches my stop and I hurry off, hoping that no one around will notice the pink of my cheeks or stop to imagine what it could mean.

Of course, the very thought is ridiculous. This is Harlem. And it's not a very nice part of Harlem at that. People here have other things to worry about.

But still, it's hard not to be self-conscious as I walk through the subway station, deep underground. The limo sex was simply *not* part of the plan. Granted, I had initiated things as a means of distracting him from his line of questioning, but it had turned into so much more than that. I lost control—and the plan I've put in place is at least partially dependent on my always being in complete control.

And it's not just events I have to manipulate. What I really need is complete control of how these people—Lander, Travis, Jessica, *all* of them—see me. Gone are the days when I was just a hapless victim in someone else's story. Three years ago I started writing a new story. I wrote myself as a character into a story of revenge and retribution. The other characters will see me the way I want them to because I'm the one holding the pen. This is *my* narrative, damn it! I decide how the story goes, I set the pace, and I decide how and when it all will end.

But every time Lander touches me . . . it's almost like he takes control of the pen. Like he's writing the story *with* me.

And when he touches me, he *sees* me. Not the character, but the author behind the paper. And as exciting as that is, I absolutely can't allow it to ever happen again.

Stupid, I think as I reach the stairs that lead aboveground. My heels click against the concrete steps, adding an accompanying beat to the word as it pounds through my head again and again. Stupid, stupid, *stupid*. I was stupid when I was a child, too stupid to see what was being done to my mom—and now that I know the truth, I'm still just as stupid, letting myself be swayed by something as primitive and inconsequential as physical desire.

When I reach the sidewalk and outside air, I pause a moment, exhale, try to expel the demons of self-doubt. So I made some mistakes. But still, I'm on track. In the end that's all that matters. Whatever feelings I may or may not have for Lander . . . well, those will fade.

But my success? That's something I'll be able to savor for the rest of my life.

I take another deep breath, start walking, find my stride again.

"*To justice*," I said as I handed him the drugged cognac.

And justice is exactly what I'm going to get.

The sunset's pretty today; the pink hues make the streets of my neighborhood look deceptively safe. But there are little indications of a lurking danger: the occasional collection of glittering glass where a car was once parked, the subtle shabbiness of the local market, the shifty eyes of the boys who hang out on the corner, their pockets stuffed with danger and vice.

I'm a bit out of place right now in my expensive career dress and sex-kitten heels, but no one bothers me. They know me around here, and even those who don't still recognize my walk—confident, forceful. Anyone who's ever watched a nature show knows that predators look for weak victims, ones who will be easy to take down. They'll target the wounded animal that reeks of fear first.

That's not me.

Were you scared, Bell?

I shake my head, pushing away the memory as I walk on.

"Don't let that man get under your skin, honey!" a gravelly voice yells.

I stop in my tracks and turn to see a homeless woman sitting on the pavement, a purple pen in one hand and a coloring book in the other. Lined up beside her are several broken crayons and stubs of colored pencils.

"What are you talking about?" I ask warily.

"I know your story," she says. The streaks of gray in her mass of curly brown hair make her look more wild than unkempt. "You fell in love with the wrong man."

I laugh, suddenly relieved that this woman doesn't know anything about me and embarrassed that for a moment I worried she might. "I'm not in love with anyone," I say gently.

"Girl, you just keep telling yourself that!" The woman chuckles, turning her attention back to her coloring book. "I fell in love with the wrong man once. No, make that twice—or three times . . . You know what?

They're all bad. Those men are all just a bunch of horned-up motherfuckers if you ask me."

Again I burst out laughing. But the woman keeps her eyes on her coloring book, her pen moving swiftly over the page.

Glancing at her work I'm surprised to see how meticulous she is about staying inside the lines. The picture is of a mother and daughter walking hand in hand through a park. She's colored the landscape in shades of green, yellow, and lavender, making the already pacific scene seem joyful and alive.

I once saw the world that way, back when I was young enough to hold my mother's hand.

"But not all of God's creatures are bad," the woman continues. "Last night a raccoon came through here. Walked right up to me, gave me a nod hello, and then just kept on walking. Like a real gentleman."

"You gotta be careful of those things," I warn. "Some of them have rabies."

"Yeah, well, at least a rabid raccoon has an excuse for bein' mean. What's the men's excuse? They all got rabies too?"

"No, they're just men." I study her for a moment. "What's your name?"

"Mary," she says as she selects another color from her collection.

"Are you hungry, Mary?"

She looks up again, her wide brown eyes answering for her. I reach into my bag and hand over the Clif Bars. "Hope you like Blueberry Crisp."

She puts her colors down as she tears open a wrapper. "Chocolate Chip's better." She takes a bite, her eyes still on me. "Don't let him hurt you, okay, honey?"

"Oh, don't you worry. No one's going to hurt me, not ever again," I say before turning to walk the last block home.

I try to convince myself of my own words as I walk up to my building, but as I glance at the bars on the first-floor window my confidence wavers. I can handle living in a poor area, but damn do I hate these bars. They scare me so much more than the drug dealers on the corner. I can escape men like those, but you have to be Houdini to escape a cage.

I grit my teeth and put my key into the lock of the front entrance, quickly stepping into the lobby. I stick another key into one of the tiny metal mailboxes to the left. The box is so small the postman has no choice but to crumple the mail before stuffing it in, as if people in my building aren't even entitled to birthday cards that don't have the appearance of discarded garbage. But today it's all junk, except for one envelope addressed to a woman whose name I don't use anymore. I tuck it into my purse and head up the narrow staircase to my apartment.

When I get inside I double lock the door before applying a thick chain.

My studio is sparse. There's a little nightstand by my futon, where the picture of me and my mother at Disney World resides regally in its cheap plastic frame. My desk is completely buried, strewn with copies of newspaper and magazine articles about HGVB Bank and about Edmund Gable and the "Gable Boys" (as *Esquire* refers to Lander and Travis). THE KING OF FINANCIAL INVESTORS, reads another title boldly printed below a picture of Travis.

And then there are the old articles, articles about Nick Foley. A VP at HGVB Bank murdered in cold blood by his maid. A sordid tale of infidelity, jilted lovers, perversion—everything the media loves . . . except maybe the truth.

But the articles sound so confident in their reporting. According to one, this woman, this murderess, this *maid*, had been rejected by her lover, the wealthy, respectable Nick Foley. You see, in a moment of weakness, Mr. Foley had fallen into the centuries-old tradition of fucking the help. But when his wife found out, the remorseful Mr. Foley tried to break it off. Clearly that was to be expected. But in this telling, the maid didn't take it well. This maid had hoped that Mr. Foley would leave his wife for her. She didn't understand.

She didn't understand her place.

None of the papers actually say that, not in those words. But the sentiment is there, glaring between the lines. The silly maid thought that being fucked by her employer made her special. She actually presumed that an important VP would leave his blond debutante wife for a little Mexican housekeeper, a woman who cleaned his toilet to earn money for groceries, food to feed herself and her bastard daughter. She was delusional . . . but more than that—she was dangerous. Only a few months earlier, a Haitian nanny who may or may not have been suffering from post-traumatic stress disorder had been caught trying to kidnap the children in her charge. And months before *that*, a Chinese limo driver had been exposed as being part of a crime ring—he was signaling his burglar associates every time he picked up an important client, letting them know which specific houses would be unoccupied for a while and would make good targets.

So this story about the maid? It fit that narrative. The enemy lives among us, disguised as loyal servants. They have to be stopped, and quickly.

It's the kind of narrative that can influence a jury, the

kind of boogeyman story that scares people into ignoring things like lack of evidence and due process.

Of course, most of the information I have now was never discussed during the trial. Never even brought up. And I know from experience—painful, frustrating experience—that the authorities have absolutely no interest in looking at any new information now. They got their conviction, their headlines, their promotions; any new twist would just be inconvenient at this point.

Just as well, perhaps. I touch the papers on my desk. All this information in the hands of a bureaucrat would be useless.

But in the hands of a vigilante? It's invaluable.

In the dim light of my place, I smile to myself and reach into my purse, pull out my Android, and flip through the pictures I took at Lander's place. The drawings catch my eye first. I study the one with the guy who is about to bite the hand of the man handing him money. *Bite, Torture, Ruin. Is* that supposed to be Lander? It's really hard to tell. But it would be interesting if it was; it would be *really* interesting if this is how he sees himself.

Lander left the country right after my mother's trial, off to Oxford to add to his elitist portfolio of accomplishments, while at home his father destroyed lives and his mother died.

Yes, that's right. Lander's mother died of cancer while his father was in the middle of divorcing her. Lander didn't even bother to come back to see her until it was time for the funeral. And as soon as he graduated, he tucked himself neatly into his father's organization and took a position at HGVB. They were side by side on the golf course in no time. As far as I can tell, Lander has never even bothered to visit his mother's grave. He just sucked up to the rich parent, the one with the prestigious name and ability to dispense trust funds. *That's* the kind of man Lander is—no matter what my body is trying to tell me now.

My mind falls back to the night before, the way Lander kissed my neck, pulled me against him, the way he entered me slowly, gently, only increasing in intensity once he was sure that my eyes were on his, after he felt secure in our connection. No one had ever looked at me like that. No one had ever managed that balance between gentleness, power, and passion before.

But it was an illusion. Nothing gentle lasts long in this world.

Perhaps Nick was gentle when he kissed my mother, for all the good it did them.

Again my mind travels back . . . back to that bed, back to the trail of kisses that had moved from my breast, to my stomach, down, lower, between my legs, the warmth of his tongue as he toyed with me, the sound of his voice when he raised himself back up, tugged gently on my hair, and whispered my name:

"Bellona, such a beautiful warrior."

"I'm sorry, Lander," I say as I open the top drawer of my desk and lightly caress the gun that I've hidden there. "But even beautiful warriors are killers."

chapter nine

The dress I picked for the interview was based on Travis's 1980s "Addicted to Love" aesthetic tastes. There's nothing more pathetic than people who think "retro" and "modern" are interchangeable fashion concepts.

But that look isn't for Lander. For him, I put on a pair of skinny jeans, a white tee that's just fitted enough with a cropped secondhand brown leather jacket and a few long silver chains I picked up at the Hell's Kitchen Flea Market.

Funny, but the clothes I know will impress Lander are the clothes I actually like to wear.

A tiny voice in my head tells me to be wary of that, that any commonality with the enemy is a warning sign, not a convenience.

He had wanted to pick me up—or maybe he just

wanted to find out where I lived. I came up with an excuse for why he couldn't arrive at my doorstep, but I didn't bother coming up with a *good* excuse. It didn't matter if he believed me or not. It only mattered that he wanted me enough to ignore the fact that he didn't believe me. Men are incredibly easy that way.

When I arrive at the restaurant—a popular Italian place, his pick—he's already there, waiting at a table in an outfit that looks almost designed to complement mine: dark-blue jeans and a creamy cotton pullover, long sleeves pushed up on his forearms, five buttons at the neck, the top one undone. Very casual and, oddly, very sexy. He's drawing something on a piece of scratch paper, but when he spots me across the room he folds it up and puts it in the pocket of his jacket, which hangs over the back of his chair. The pen he leaves idle on the table.

"You've gotten all your errands done?" he asks as I sit down, his tone somewhat bemused.

"Virtually." I take my seat across from him, giving away nothing.

A waiter arrives with two cocktails. "I hope you don't mind," Lander says. "I thought you'd like their specialty."

I examine the two cocktails. His drink, which appears to be bourbon on the rocks, looks considerably simpler than mine, which is . . . something mixed with several other things and garnished with a twist.

"You like to add interesting flourishes to your alcoholic beverages, don't you?" he asks, his voice casual, though immediately I think of my garnet ring.

"Why do you say that?" I ask, matching his tone.

"You're a bartender. All bartenders like intricate mixed drinks."

Is he playing with me? I can't quite tell. I hold up my drink and smile. "Well, let's see if this ends up being a little too interesting for me."

We clink glasses. My drink tastes of bourbon and grapefruit and bitters. A little comfort, a little tart, a little bitter . . . not a bad balance to try to strike in life. But then, I gave up striving for balance a long time ago.

"You realize that this is our first date?"

I smile, nod. "It's very . . . traditional of us, isn't it?"

"What would have been traditional is if we had started with dating and worked our way up."

"I meant that having dinner together is normal, and up until now nothing about us has been . . . normal. *You're* not normal."

"You don't think so?" He picks up his menu, studies the choices. A few tables over a group of slightly drunk voices launch into a rendition of "Happy Birthday."

"I've been to your penthouse," I say, taking another sip of my drink. "I've been . . . in your limo."

That causes his eyes to flicker up to mine, his smile growing a bit more mischievous.

"I know how you live," I continue. "I know that the clothes you wear are expensive as hell . . . and I know you don't have to go to a dive bar in Harlem to get cheap drinks. It's totally out of your way and it takes you way out of your element. Yet you're a regular there. *That's* not normal."

Lander hesitates a moment before lowering the menu. "I like . . . I like the clarity of the people that frequent Ivan's."

"Seriously? Most of the people in that bar are too wasted to have clarity about anything."

"That's not what I mean . . ." He takes a moment, gathers his thoughts, and starts again. "That girl with the rainbow hair, it took me about fifteen seconds to realize that she has a drug problem."

"Wow," I say as I scan the appetizers on the menu. "You're a real Sherlock Holmes."

"That's my whole point." He picks up the pen and starts drawing on the back of a paper napkin. "I didn't have to figure it out. If she were advertising her addiction with a neon sign it couldn't have been any clearer." From my position I can make out that he's drawing someone in a biker's jacket. "That man I got in a fight with, he doesn't like himself very much, so he uses violence and intimidation to give himself a sense of self-worth. The guy I gave the two hundred dollars to, he's an alcoholic with no family and no home and a lot of money problems."

"Lander, he literally told you all that. He stood by your side and he said—"

"I know what he said, I was listening." His pen is still moving. It's almost as if he's unaware he's the one moving it. It's like a tic, except in this case his "tic" is creating something rather interesting. "That's why I like Ivan's so much. All I have to do is watch and listen to know what the people there are all about. I *know* what their issues are." The biker he draws has his fist raised as he shouts at an invisible foe. "The people I work with, the people who live in my sliver of Manhattan, they have a lot of the same issues. But it can take months before you realize that your secretary has a Valium addiction. Alcoholics disguise themselves as wine connoisseurs because they have enough money to float their addiction 'responsibly,' and others who aren't making enough to support their way of life are buttressed by credit cards. You never know what *anyone's* issues are."

"And the bullies?" I ask. The waiter approaches our table, but Lander waves him away.

"There are plenty of those, and they all look and dress like me. We all shop at the same stores, work in similar jobs . . . It can be incredibly hard to distinguish them from everyone else, and many of them are so subtle in their aggression that you don't know you're a target until you're already down for the count." He studies his picture for a moment, his forehead creasing as if he's in the middle of solving a puzzle.

"I spend all day, every day," he says, somewhat distractedly, "trying to peel back the layers, trying to peek behind the curtain, trying to figure out who the people I'm dealing with really are, trying to figure out what they really want and what they really need. It's a game . . . and I'm not bad at it." Carefully he writes the word *Cries* under the picture. "But I get tired," he continues. "So I go to bars where the people aren't hiding behind curtains pretending to be Oz. I go to places where the patrons dance around with rainbow-colored hair or snarl behind grizzled beards." He writes the word *in*. "I go to places where I know exactly who and what I'm dealing with at all times." He smiles to himself as he finishes the title of his art with the word *Rebuke*. *Cries in Rebuke*. "At Ivan's, that's the way it is." He suddenly looks up from his picture and meets my eyes before adding, "I've always known who I'm dealing with at Ivan's . . . except when it comes to you."

My mouth rises into a one-sided smile. "I'm the only one at Ivan's you couldn't figure out, so I'm also the only one you took home. You say you don't like complications, but"—I lift my drink, take another sip—"I think the lady doth protest too much."

Lander laughs and now catches the waiter's eye, letting him know it's all right to approach. "Are you a fan of Shakespeare?"

"I know a few of his plays."

The waiter takes our orders. For himself, Lander gets the escolar appetizer and fettuccine as an entrée, then he orders for me, a spring pea salad and branzino, before topping it off with a rather expensive bottle of wine to share.

"So you're an artist?" I ask and take another long sip of my cocktail.

"I doodle," he says quickly. He briefly holds up the picture, giving me just a few seconds to examine it before folding it up and tucking it into his pocket. It's as if he's suddenly embarrassed to have it in the open, as if he hadn't thought I'd notice what he was doing.

It is *a kind of tic*, I think to myself. When he ponders things he draws . . . it's a little odd, but then, at least it's helpful to me. It means that those drawings I saw at his place are a peek into something . . . deeper.

"You're right, you know," he says as if trying to draw my attention away from the picture. "I did choose to take home the most complicated girl at the bar. For instance, after talking to you for five minutes I sensed that you were well-educated . . . most well-educated women don't work at bars like that."

"Most well-educated men don't frequent them," I counter.

Our conversation is momentarily put on hold as the waiter comes back and pours a small amount of red wine into Lander's glass. Lander swirls it almost impatiently before tasting it and giving his nod of approval. When my glass is filled, I take a moment to admire the color, which is so dark it's luscious. I would wear this color if I found it in a dress. Lander's right: The rich disguise their sins so well. Their vices are actually made pretty . . . before they turn ugly.

"When you quit, you didn't do the expected thing," Lander continues as the waiter retreats again. "You didn't seek employment at a different, better bar. No, I run into you on the streets of the Upper West Side looking like you just stepped off the pages of some cutting-edge style guide. That's a pretty dramatic switch."

"Guess I'm a Renaissance woman."

"And then when I asked you to come home with me, you said yes, but you were conflicted. There were moments when I thought . . . the way you looked at me sometimes . . ."

"It made your heart melt," I say teasingly.

"It made me think you wanted to hate me."

I hesitate a moment, take another drink. "I don't want to hate you," I lie.

"Who are you, Bellona?"

A warrior. That's what I want to say. But instead I

shrug bashfully. "If I'm mysterious, Lander, I'm certainly no more so than you. I've . . . *been* with you twice, I'm about to share a meal with you now, and I still don't even know your last name."

He's taken aback for a moment and then laughs, genuinely. He truly didn't realize he'd kept this fact from me. "I guess I haven't been so forthcoming either, have I?" He smiles and casually says, "My last name is Gable."

"Gable," I repeat, then I widen my eyes with practiced surprise. "*Gable?* You're not any relation to Travis Gable, are you?"

"Yes," he says warily. "He's my brother."

The waiter returns with a breadbasket as I prepare to launch into a performance. "Lander—that's who I just interviewed with. Travis and Jessica Gable. I'm going to be Jessica's personal assistant!"

Lander looks at me for a moment, his face washed of emotion. I can't read him at all.

"Seriously," I press. "I mean, what are the odds? I can't believe—"

"No."

He says the word so quietly I'm not sure I heard him correctly. The restaurant is bustling with laughter and chatter. "Did you say—"

"NO."

Our appetizers come but neither of us reaches for our utensils as the food is placed in front of us. "No . . . what?"

"You can't work for my brother."

"Actually, I can." I pause before deciding to throw on a carefree grin as if he hadn't overstepped. "Although technically I'm working for Jessica." I pick up my fork and stab my salad. "I'll only be doing things for your brother when . . . well, when he needs me. I still can't believe the guy's your brother. Are you sure we're talking about the same—"

"Don't do this."

"Lander, I was a personal assistant before I started working at Ivan's. The bartending gig was really more of a holdover than anything else. This PA job is just perfect. And the pay—"

"Listen to me!" he snaps, stopping me short. The people at the next table send him a quick, curious glance before turning their attention back to their meals.

"Bell, you have to understand," Lander continues. "My brother—" He pauses as he searches for the right word before finishing with "My brother is an *asshole*."

I break into a fit of giggles, making a display of levity as I mentally parse out his reaction and comments. The sibling rivalry between Lander and his brother isn't exactly a secret, but from all appearances it's a *friendly* rivalry. In fact, my studies and observations had led me to believe that the two brothers had actually become closer over the last few years. I'm pretty sure that's what *everybody* believes. But that's apparently not the case. So perhaps the brotherly love is all just for show?

I let my laughter die down and take another forkful of salad.

"This isn't a joke," Lander presses.

"I can deal with your brother. I've always been skilled at managing men."

"I didn't say he's a man. I said he's an asshole."

"There's a difference?" I snap before I can stop myself, then grin teasingly to take away the impact.

"Bell, please don't do this."

I sit back and really study his face. He's completely serious, but he doesn't look angry . . .

. . . he looks worried.

Could he actually be *worried* about me?

"I need you to trust me," I say. And in a way it's true: I need him to trust me so I can betray him.

I stare down at my hands clutching the fork and knife.

This is the first time you've thought about what you're doing in terms of betrayal.

It's the silent whispered voice in my head, moving me

toward something that bears a dangerous resemblance to guilt.

"I can handle myself," I continue. "But if there's something I should know about your brother, you should tell me now. Don't ask me to step away from a very lucrative job just because you have sibling rivalry issues. Tell me *why* your brother is an asshole. What *exactly* has he done?"

Lander chews on the inside of his cheek for a moment. It's the first time I've ever seen him look uncomfortable. "He's a womanizer."

"Mm-hmm, so was Bill Clinton. That didn't stop Janet Reno—"

"See, like that. How is *that* a reference you can just pull up at the drop of a hat? Who the hell are you?"

"Well, I *was* a bartender—who followed politics somewhat—but I'm about to be your brother's personal assistant, at least I will be if you can't pull up an objection that doesn't reek of complete bullshit. Give me *specifics*, Lander."

"He sleeps with his assistants, Bell."

"Really? Your sister-in-law told me that his last assistant was a guy, so if that's the way Travis rolls, I think I'm covered."

"Fine, he probably didn't sleep with the last one—"

"Probably?"

"*Definitely* not with the last one, but . . . Bell . . ." Again he chews his cheek, and his eyes move aimlessly around the room. "I wish you could just take my word for this."

"I can't," I say dryly. He winces at my refusal, making me soften slightly. "Look, I'm taking the job . . . but I will promise you that if your brother steps out of line or does anything blatantly . . . *unethical*, or immoral, I will let you know about it."

His eyes snap back to me.

I just offered to spy on his brother for him. He knows it; I know it. Now all that's left is for him to take me up on it. Or not.

And his decision will tell me so very much about Lander's relationship to the Gable family dynamics.

The restaurant noise that seemed held at bay in the background throughout our conversation now envelops our table, ringing in my ears, making me wonder how we were even able to hear each other speak only moments before.

Seconds pass, then a minute, and as the waiter takes away our plates, behind us someone's cell phone rings the notes of Vivaldi . . .

. . . and then Lander nods and just like that, the noise of the restaurant just sort of falls away again, and my ears, my eyes, and my . . . well, my everything . . . are tuned in only to him.

"I still wish you would just walk away from this. But if you insist, then yes, you should tell me about anything . . . anything my brother does that makes you uncomfortable or makes you . . . wary." He's choosing his words so carefully now. It makes me smile. "I want you to be okay, and if you let me know what's going on I can make sure of that."

I shift in my seat as new dishes are brought back to our table. "Okay, I promise to tell you if things get weird, or even if I think they're about to. But you have to do something for me too."

He raises his eyebrows, digs into his fettuccine.

"I want this job to work, Lander." I bring my voice down an octave, emphasizing my earnestness. "Assuming everything's basically on the up-and-up, of course. But I worry . . . if your brother knows that we're . . . well, that we *know* each other like we do, then it could make things difficult for me."

Lander takes another sip of wine in lieu of answering.

"I just . . . I don't want him or his wife to think of me as the woman his brother is fucking."

"Bell." Lander says the name softly. "It's not like that."

Actually, it's exactly *like that*, but I keep the thought to myself and wave his concern away with a flick of my hand. "I don't want them to think of me as the woman

Travis's brother is *dating* either. I don't want any kind of special treatment any more than I want them to look at me like I'm some little gold-digging whore."

"Bell!"

"Just let me establish a relationship with my new employers on my own merits. If the job goes well and this"—I gesture to myself and Lander with a quick swing of my fork—"if this goes well too, then we can act like we met and started dating well after I took the job. But if the job ends or *this*"—again I gesture with my fork—"ends, then . . . I mean, why screw things up by revealing everything too soon? Why not just let it all run its natural course before we start merging things together, like work and family, too soon?"

"I've been merging work and family all my life," he points out.

"Well, I haven't, and I don't want to start quite yet. Are you okay with that?"

Are you okay with lying to your brother and his wife? That's the real question. I look at him calmly as my heart pounds against my chest. *What's the answer, Lander?*

"Yes, I think we can hold off on letting them know."

I have to stuff my mouth with fish to keep myself from grinning ear to ear.

Travis doesn't trust his wife. Lander doesn't trust Travis. And now Lander has just given me what I need to make sure that Travis doesn't trust Lander either, if he ever did.

It's the trifecta of family dysfunction.

It's going to make it so much easier to do what I need to do.

chapter ten

By the time we leave the restaurant we've each had a cocktail and shared the bottle of red. The streets of New York seem to have a warm, hazy glow and the honking of horns and growl of engines almost sound musical. I have to resist the urge to clap my hands in time, adding my own harmony to the city's symphony. Lander gestures to his limo. "I'll take you home."

I shake my head. "Not necessary."

"It's no trouble."

I look up at him, into his perfect smile, at the little crinkles that are just now beginning to form at the corners of his eyes. They make him look . . . kind.

Again there's that stab of guilt. Of course, it's just an illusion. The kindness, the decency . . . It's a trick of the light, like so many other good things in this world.

I swallow the moment of weakness as I slip my arms around his neck. "It's not necessary, because *I'm* coming home with *you*."

The crinkles deepen as his smile expands, his hands wrapping around me, pulling me into him so I can feel my breasts push into his rib cage, his breath in my hair.

"I like you, Bell. Why is that?"

"Because we're two of a kind, Lander." It might be true. He hides his ruthlessness as well as I do. His is tucked inside the corners of the friendship he offers and concealed inside his sleeve like a magician's trick. Now you see it, now you don't.

First I'm the upright rich kid who's a little out of his element in a dive bar, and now I'm the guy beating the shit out of a Hells Angels prick.

Now you see it, now you don't.

I shudder in his arms. I've studied, practiced, and prepared for this fight. Lloyd, the PA I'm about to replace, the one who now spends his day in an orange jumpsuit picking up trash on the side of the highway, he's part of my history now. And there are others, other men I have quietly torn apart in my journey here . . .

. . . here to this battlefield . . .

. . . here, wrapped up in Lander's embrace.

Lander is the first worthy opponent I've ever engaged

with. He's the first one who has surprised me. He's the first one who's inspired even an ounce of guilt.

And weirdly enough, he's also the first one who has ever made the game fun. Really, *really* fun.

"Take me home," I say again, and he leads me to the limo.

The driver comes out to open the door for us. He meets my eyes, making me blush. Before Lander I never blushed . . . not since I was a little kid, not since I learned to breathe anger and live with pain. I raise my hand to my own cheek and feel the warmth. There's something . . . appealing about it, thrilling.

We get in the limo, the door is closed behind us, and the noises of the city are instantly gone.

As we drive through the streets, we're quiet, like the first time we rode in a cab together . . . Was that only yesterday? It's hard to keep track of these things when you've just started a relationship with a man you've been studying for years. Time gets all mixed up and confused. You have to remember what you've been told versus what you've secretly learned on your own. That's what always trips people up in the movies and on TV.

I reach over, squeeze Lander's knee, gaze at him with wide, innocent eyes. The trick is to not overthink. To always stay in the moment. To pretend that you don't know *anything*, that you can't even remember what he told you an hour ago. Pretend that all you can remember and feel is the sensations he provokes, the pulsing need you have for him when he smiles with those crinkly eyes.

With Lander I don't have to pretend too hard.

In minutes we're at his Upper East Side home, walking past the doorman, moving into the elevator, not touching but feeling each other's presence. His hunger for me is tangible. It tickles my skin and pulls at my heart.

When we walk into his penthouse, I lead the way. I don't bother with the living room but instead crook my finger, beckoning him to follow me into his office.

I stand in the middle of the room, turn to him, reach out my hand. "I don't know how much time we have," I say softly. "Maybe we'll last a month, if we're really lucky a year. Maybe you'll tire of me tomorrow."

"Bell, I won't—"

"But I want to treat every moment like it has value," I interrupt. "I want to make love to you in every room of your home. I know what it's like to be pressed up against your window, the entire city at my back. It wasn't like flying—it was more unstable than that. It was like . . . like the only thing that kept me from breaking through that glass and falling was our lust. Like passion actually kept my feet on the floor."

"Bell," he breathes, but this time the word is not the

beginning of a promise, or an exclamation. It's the sound of admiration, maybe even respect.

It's the way a goddess's name *should* be spoken.

"On your bed it was all about the luxury," I continue. "The softness of your blankets, the grandness of the bed frame, pricey comforts. Decadence."

He doesn't reply. He's worshipping me with his eyes.

He worships me. Right here, in this moment, he worships me. *Me*, the embodiment of war. What does that say about his heart?

"And now . . . now I want to make love here, where you work, where you *think*." I step forward and slide my fingers down his arm. "I want you to enter me here," I say, taking his hand and pressing it between my legs. He immediately begins to move his hand, making me shiver. "And I," I continue as I run my index finger along his forehead, "I want entry into *here*."

He doesn't answer. Instead he continues to move his hand, adding pressure, watching as I respond. Then slowly he bows his head, lowers his lips to my neck, makes a trail of warm, sensuous kisses up to my ear before whispering, "Bell, you've been in my head since the moment we met."

It's not what I meant, but it's not a bad start. Desire and longing make men careless.

And yet right now he doesn't seem careless at all. Not

as he deliberately pulls his hand away, removes his jacket, then mine, and throws them both on the desk already covered in papers . . . papers I'll look through later. But not now. Now all I can do is look at him.

He quietly removes my shirt and then steps back, just a little, as he runs his fingers down my bra straps.

"That's nice." He runs his thumb over my nipple as it hardens, his touch making me jump ever so slightly. "I like that."

I grab the bottom of his shirt, yank it off him with considerably less grace and much more urgency. In a moment I feel my bra loosening, then falling to the floor, right as I move into him, pressing my bare flesh against his, feeling the competing drumbeats of our hearts. His lips press against mine again, making my whole body warm and vibrant. My jeans loosen around my waist, and as his lips move back to my neck and then to my shoulder, my jeans are pushed down inch by inch until I finally bend over to pull them off. Again he sweeps me off my feet and into his arms, but instead of bringing me to the bedroom, he lowers me onto the black leather sofa. And there he is, by my side, on one knee, his fingers looped into the waistband of my panties. With the perfect precision that I've come to associate with him, he pulls them off slowly, their motion both scratching and caressing my skin.

And when they're off, he just stares at me.

"If you don't run away from me, if this is more than a moment, then one day I want you to pose like this, for a painter. I want a master to paint you, as you lie here, naked, on my furniture. I want him to paint you when you're exactly as you are now, all sex and longing, aching for release."

"And what would be done with this painting?" I breathe.

"It would hang in the best gallery in New York . . . or perhaps it would be presented at Christie's . . . and men would bid for the right to hang you on their wall. They'd bid and compete for you, because they would never have seen anything so beautiful in their lives."

"You want my image to hang on some rich man's wall for everyone to leer at?"

"Oh, they wouldn't leer, warrior. They'd admire you, like I do. You're a work of art. You're everything that's beautiful about eroticism."

His words border on insanity. He doesn't know me . . .

. . . does he?

Does he know who I am? Am I being made a fool of?

But then, I'm not the only one whose desire is exposed here. I can see that even now. I reach my hand out, touch his pants where the fabric is now pulled taut.

Slowly I raise my arms above my head, naked but no longer trembling, no longer hesitant.

His hand caresses me, from my breast, down my leg again, and then he bends down, kisses my stomach and navel, then my hip. I feel his tongue flick against my inner thigh and then he blows gently on that one spot, making my skin feel cool and alive. He continues to nip and tease until finally I feel his tongue against my very core, circling my clit. I begin to writhe against the sofa, the leather gently pulling at my skin as he increases the pressure, his tongue just a little more demanding, pressing flat against my clit now, making me moan. And it's then that I feel his finger press inside me. I suck in a sharp breath as his index finger makes a circle inside my walls and his tongue circles in reverse around my clit . . .

And when the second finger enters me, the world explodes. My nails scratch at the leather as I search for something to hold on to, something external to stabilize me as I lose all sense of control.

But there is no stability, not right now, not anymore. All I have is this fiery, unpredictable passion for Lander. When he raises himself up, pulls off his jeans, it's all I can do to keep from tearing into him, throwing him on the floor and mounting him.

He steps away, but I grab his hand, easily reading his

unspoken intentions. "I'm on the pill; you don't need a condom."

He looks at me questioningly. But I smile, squeeze his hand. "It's okay," I say again. "I want to feel you, the real you." He takes a step closer, strokes my cheek, lowers himself over me slowly, hesitantly. "Now, Lander," I whisper. "I want you inside me now."

It's as if my whisper has sparked a wildfire. Immediately he enters me forcefully, pressing deep inside me as I arch my back and clutch his shoulders, feeling his skin against mine. Nothing's keeping us apart. Nothing's dividing us. I kiss his neck, my hands sliding down his back as he puts my leg over his shoulder and thrusts even deeper.

"You feel . . . perfect, this is perfect," he breathes, lowering his mouth to mine. I respond by gently biting his lower lip, letting him know that given the chance I would devour him.

He pulls my other leg up so they are now both hovering over my head and again he thrusts inside me, even deeper now than before, the friction driving me wild, making me cry out.

In this moment there is no plan. There is no revenge.

There's just Lander.

And as he thrusts again, his eyes penetrating me with an equivalent force, I realize that in this moment that's all I want.

I don't even blush as I call out his name; I react with unadulterated pleasure when he calls out mine. I feel him pulsing inside me as he comes.

As he eases away, bringing my legs down to the leather, his breathing uneven and labored, I whisper his name again. "Lander." My eyes slide away, almost too tired to focus, my body spent. His jacket is on the floor now, having fallen at some point during our revelry. Peeking out of one pocket is the drawing of the biker . . . along with another drawing.

It's a drawing of me.

chapter eleven

I didn't wear my ring tonight, which was careless. It makes sneaking into his office all the more precarious. Of course, my focus needs to be on gathering information I can use against the Gables . . .

. . . but what I really want to look at is that drawing.

As before, Lander left his clothes on the floor, and I silently thank God for his bad habits. I pull out the drawing of the biker, *Cries in Rebuke* . . . such an odd title, and he seemed to be so deliberate in the way he chose it, taking a minute between writing each word; *Cries*, and a minute later, *in*, and a minute after that, *Rebuke*. Yes, my Lander is an odd one. But I don't really care about the drawing of the biker, so I carefully put it back in the coat pocket and take out the one he drew of me. In it, I'm lying on my side on the floor, one leg draped over the other to hide my nakedness from the waist down. He's covered my chest with a kind of ornate, jeweled bra or bikini top. It looks a little retro, like what might have been worn by an exotic dancer in the first decades of the twentieth century. On my head is a headdress perched way back on my skull, the way you would wear a tiara. Except this hat looks almost Asian in its curved details . . . almost like something that would be worn by a princess from the Far East . . . or maybe something that would be worn by a goddess.

It's all oddly familiar to me, the pose, the costume . . . Perhaps he's modeled me after a famous painting, one that I've seen but can't fully remember. Maybe . . . maybe something that relates to his interest in history? That would make sense since it's period dress. But it's more than that—this drawing is ringing a bell. If he modeled it after a painting with some kind of historical significance, then it's probably in relation to World War I or World War II. Those are the periods of history that Lander is most fascinated by, and therefore the periods I've spent the most time studying over the last few years. Although how this picture could have anything to do with war is beyond me. Particularly when I consider the words written underneath the drawing:

Kind, Witty Heroine.

That's what he wrote. That's how he titled his drawing of me.

I touch the image lightly, tap it as if expecting that it will disappear. I've never seen a drawing of myself before.

In it I'm beautiful.

I stand there for a full minute, studying the lines he built me up with. And the line he wrote: *Kind, Witty Heroine.*

No one has ever seen me that way. I have never been the heroine . . . and it's been a very long time since I've had the luxury of being truly kind.

But I can't let myself get caught up in this. I have other things to do.

Slipping the picture back where I found it, I start looking through the other documents. There's something here about mortgage rates and risk analysis.

What was the inspiration for that drawing? Was it what happened in the limo? Or perhaps what happened the night before?

I flip to another paper. Something about interest rates.

Does he really think I'm that pretty? Does the period dress mean something? Does he see me through some kind of classical lens?

There's a currency conversion chart, comparing pesos to dollars.

That drawing might be the most romantic thing I've ever seen.

As soon as the thought runs through my head, I freeze, the conversion chart still in my hand.

What the hell am I thinking? I'm not supposed to care about whether or not Lander feels romantic about me. I'm only supposed to care about whether or not he gives me access to his home and office—so I can get my hands on the information I can use to make sure the Gables suffer the exact same loss, pain, and humiliation my mother experienced. By the time I'm done, they'll all be behind bars, protesting their innocence to guards who don't care and won't listen. They'll lose their family, friends, reputations . . . If all goes as planned, at least one will lose their life.

It's actually less about justice and more about karma. When they say karma's a bitch, they're talking about *me.*

. . . But what if Lander isn't as guilty as I think he is?

I have pretty compelling, albeit circumstantial, evidence that Travis was involved in Nick's death in some manner, and I'm positive that it was Travis and Lander's father who set my mother up to take the fall, thereby tearing apart my family . . .

But, really, other than Lander's being friendly with Sean White and testifying about an argument my mother had with Nick Foley's wife—an argument that might have actually happened—what do I have that ties Lander to the whole thing?

I squeeze my eyes closed, trying to block out the doubts. The evidence against Lander might not be as strong as that against the other players, but it *is* there. And I've seen Lander's dark side—it's not just pretty pictures and romantic dinners. He was savage when he fought that biker. And he enjoys that dive bar because he thinks the people there are simpler, easier—not really human at all in some sense. And those other pictures he drew, the ones in his sketchbook, they're a little frightening . . .

It would be easier if I didn't find his dark side as compelling as his romanticism.

We're two of a kind.

I'm in trouble.

With trembling hands I put down the rest of the papers and take a deep, stabilizing breath. Lander could wake up at any second. I have to get back in bed with him. But more importantly, I have to refocus and remember *why* I'm getting back in bed with him. I'm not slipping in there to cuddle with a lover. Getting in bed with him is nothing more than a tactic. I'm Bellona, not Venus. In the mythology, Venus just fucked Mars. Bellona's the one who got to lead his chariot and kick some ass.

I chose the name Bellona for a *reason*.

When I get back to the bedroom I can't help but notice how innocent he looks while sleeping.

An illusion, just an illusion.

I sneak into bed, my back to him. And then I feel the mattress shift beneath me as he wakes just enough to throw an arm around my waist, pulling me to him as if I'm a teddy bear . . .

. . . or as if I'm his love.

While he sleeps, holding me tight, it feels a little like love.

chapter twelve

It's not quite seven on Monday morning and I've just powered down my laptop. I spent some time googling the names I found in Lander's notepad, but I've come up with nothing so far. I can see that they're all Middle Eastern, but so what? It's not like the Gables, the kings of capitalism, are going to join forces with some radical Jihadist cause. It's much more likely that these are the names of sheikhs, oil tycoons, and international businessmen who hold their investments with HGVB. That doesn't interest me.

What interests me is that the Gables are the sort of people who set an innocent woman up for murder . . . It's just not the kind of thing you get yourself involved in if you aren't already involved in other illegal activity. I just have to figure out exactly what *kind* of illegal activity they're engaged in and exploit that. And Lander . . . well, he just has to be involved. He *has* to be. I've decided.

Standing in front of my bed, staring down at several wardrobe choices I've laid out for myself, I want to pick wisely to set the tone for what's next. Today will be my first day at work as Travis and Jessica Gable's personal assistant, and dressing is a bit of a challenge. If I really want to get in with Jessica, I should wear something sweet, traditional, almost sarcastically feminine. Jessica herself always looks like she's trying to channel Audrey Hepburn in *Funny Face* . . . except Audrey never looked so incredibly despondent.

I sigh and push down the bubble of sympathy that keeps threatening to emerge. From the corner of my eye I watch a small cockroach scuttle across the floor, making sure it doesn't come near me.

We all live in our own individual hell. Some of us are just better at dealing with it.

I turn back to the clothes. Travis's tastes are . . . well, they're different from his wife's, but if I look like I'm dressing for *him*, she will become suspicious. Plus she'll be reminded that in every way that counts I really work for her husband, not her.

I don't want to remind Jessica of that. Later, maybe, but not today. So I opt for a suit I scored at a consignment store on the "right" side of town. The color is what fashionistas would call burnt umber, and what I call reddish brown. The jacket drapes in front (just like the matching sleeveless shirt meant to be worn beneath it) and it nips at the waist and flares at the hips. The skirt is fitted just enough, and the hem hits the knee. Both Audrey and Jessica would approve. I'm sure Travis will appreciate it enough too.

I dress, apply my makeup, and then stare into the full-length mirror. I cleaned the glass less than a week ago, but there is already a thin layer of dust on it and a few smudges that give my reflection a slightly hazy and warped quality. Still, I can see the rewards of my efforts. I've pulled back my hair into a tight, low bun, not all that dissimilar from how Jessica wears hers. The heels are sort of Mary Jane style.

Cocking my head slightly, I study myself some more. "Is this me?" I ask aloud. For a second I feel the stab of anxiety. I've played so many parts . . . at what point does my real self disappear? I look down at my newly manicured fingernails. Not a single chip there.

"It doesn't matter," I whisper.

And it's true. Who the hell cares who I was or who I am underneath all the polish and costumes? Who cares who I'm going to be when this is all over? My own life hasn't meant much for some time. It didn't mean much to the various foster families I boarded with, it didn't matter to the people who locked up my mom, it never meant anything to my father, whoever the hell he is, and at a certain point it stopped meaning much to me. The thing that motivates me to get out of bed every day is revenge. I educated myself for the sake of revenge. I studied fashion, Shakespeare, tennis, finance, politics, commerce, art, and law—all for the sake of revenge. If it wasn't for revenge, I wouldn't have even bothered to do my nails. I wouldn't bother to eat. I might have killed myself, but even that seemed like a wasted effort. Without revenge, my death would be as meaningless as my life. Which raises the question . . .

What happens when it's over?

The question is always there, coiled up like a snake in the back of my mind, waiting to inject its venom into my thoughts. What happens after I win? Without revenge and vengeance—without *war*—what's left of me?

"Did it feel like you were winning when there was blood on your hands?"

I close my eyes and take another deep breath.

"It doesn't matter," I say again. Because it doesn't. It's why I didn't need Lander to wear a condom. I doubt Lander has anything, but at this point my future health isn't all that important. If I stop . . . existing . . . after my victory . . . well, that'll be all right. I'll have fulfilled my purpose. I'm a soldier—my objective isn't to preserve my own life. My objective is simply to win. That's it.

I open my eyes in time to see another cockroach. I raise my foot and stomp on it, crushing it under my heel.

It doesn't matter who I am underneath it all, not really.

All that matters is that I'm ruthless.

chapter thirteen

When Jessica opens the door, she's wearing a pale aqua-green sheath dress that hangs stiffly from her shoulders. It's not tight . . . in fact on someone else it might be frumpy. But Twiggy-thin Jessica wears it well. My mother used to call women like her "human hangers." Their figures are designed to make clothes look good, but it's all silk and mirrors. Take their clothes off and there's nothing there for a man to sink his teeth into. Nothing soft or feminine for him to hold on to. According to my mother, naked stick-skinny women have all the sex appeal of a paper doll.

My mother never mentioned that Nick Foley's wife was very skinny. She didn't have to, I knew who she was thinking about.

Jessica isn't smiling as she stands in the doorway,

blocking my entrance. But she doesn't look angry either. She just looks kinda . . . spacey. "Are you early?"

"Only ten minutes." I check my watch to confirm. "Is that all right?"

Jessica waves her hand in the air. I can't tell if she's making a dismissive gesture or practicing her princess wave.

Then from the back of the penthouse I hear the laughter of children. It's startling. It's not that I forgot that Travis and Jessica have kids; it's just that they're both such terrible people it's the kind of thing I didn't want to remember.

As the echoes of laughter come rolling down the hall, I find myself turning away from the sound.

"Oh, my children weren't here during your interview, were they?" Jessica's voice sounds so hollow it has the quality of an echo. "Let's meet the children." She turns on her heel and leads me into the penthouse.

In the living room, sitting in the armchair, there's a woman in her early forties with olive skin and a mass of thick curly reddish-brown hair. She's possibly Puerto Rican. Standing near her are a seven-year-old boy and a girl who's not quite three. The boy is tossing a Nerf football into his sister's waiting arms from about four feet away. Each time, she closes her arms a moment too late, letting the ball drop soundlessly to the floor, but each time, the girl is delighted by her own failure, squealing with laughter as her brother fetches the ball and tries again.

She looks up at me with clear blue eyes. They're the eyes of her father, except on this child the eyes don't look cold at all. They sparkle.

She's the picture of innocence.

When I destroy this girl's parents, I'll destroy this girl's world.

The thought hurts my heart. I look down at my hands and for a moment I imagine myself as Lady Macbeth, trying to scrub imaginary blood off my hands . . . and failing.

"Did it feel like you were winning when there was blood on your hands?"

Is that how Lander sees me too? As Lady Macbeth? Or does he see me as a muse? A work of art?

Jessica distracts me from my thoughts by bending down and throwing her arms open. "Give Mommy a hug, darlings!"

The girl doesn't hesitate, throwing herself into her mother's arms, almost knocking her backward, but the boy hangs back, the corners of his mouth turning down, his face darkening at the sight of his mother's plastered-on smile.

So it would seem a few layers of the boy's innocence have

already been stripped away. Soon he'll be as raw and bitter as the rest of us.

It isn't a pleasant thought, but then, in the end, innocence is nothing more than a vulnerability. The innocent are the ones who are most frequently betrayed.

"Kamila," Jessica says as she turns to the Puerto Rican woman, "don't forget Mercedes has her gymnastic lessons today, and Braden has soccer after school."

"*Swim* lessons," the woman who was addressed as Kamila mumbles as she takes little Mercedes's hand.

"Excuse me?" Jessica looks up at her, bewildered.

"She said Mercedes has swim lessons today," Braden explains. I'm not sure I've ever heard a seven-year-old sound so condescending. "And today I have karate, not soccer."

"Oh." Jessica walks over to the sofa and sits down on the very edge of the cushion. She stares out the window as if searching the morning light for answers. "What day is it, Kamila?"

"It's Monday, Mrs. Gable," the nanny says patiently.

"Oh."

Not another word is spoken as Kamila leads the children out of the penthouse, taking Braden to school and Mercedes to whatever activities she has planned for her. If Jessica ever intended to actually introduce me to her kids, she's clearly forgotten about that.

"It must be hard," I say, making my voice heavy with sympathy.

"What?" Jessica asks. She's still staring out the window, maybe at the sky, maybe at nothing.

"Raising two kids when your husband works so much."

"Oh, not at all." She raises her hand up, rotates her wrist a few times. "What's hard is not being allowed to raise them at all."

"Not being *allowed* to?"

Jessica stills her hand so that now her wrist is flexed back, her diamond ring unable to reflect the natural sunlight. "There are things I'll need you to do," she says, ignoring the question. "Errands you'll need to attend to for me . . . I'll need you to show me respect in public and in front of the children, and please . . ." She turns to me, her eyes unfocused and misty. "If you fuck my husband, keep it to yourself."

I don't answer right away, allowing the room to fall into silence as we both take inventory of the moment: How much hostility is in the room? How much understanding?

"I'm not going to sleep with your husband," I say quietly.

Jessica smiles again, staring past me as if I'm not there. "Of course. See, that was good practice for the future."

I don't answer. Instead, I watch the way Jessica is sort of swaying as she sits on the couch. I don't know what she's on, but I know that she's stoned out of her head. She's floating, vulnerable . . . She's made both her mind and her will weak, which means she can be easily manipulated.

It's perfect.

I sigh loudly enough for her to hear and take a seat by her side. "Why are you married to him?" I ask. "Why don't you leave?"

It's a ballsy thing to ask, but what I've seen of her marriage has been so mind-bendingly horrific that *not* asking would be almost insensitive . . . and I don't want Jessica to see me as insensitive. I want her to see me as someone who feels for her. More importantly, I want her to see me as someone who is on her side.

"It's a long story," she answers.

"You're literally paying me to listen."

Jessica laughs softly, shakes her head. She's still swaying slightly and I can't help but wonder what I'm supposed to do if she passes out.

"Seriously, though, I *want* to listen," I press. "I don't care what your husband says, I applied for a job to be *your* assistant, and as far as I'm concerned that's what I am. I like *you*."

"Why?" Again she tries to look at me, but her pupils

are so dilated it's difficult to imagine that she can see much of anything.

Why *would* anyone like this woman? Pity her, maybe . . . the kind of pity you would feel for a woman in a horror movie, the one who is too stupid to hightail it out of the haunted house.

"I admire you" is what I settle on. "Wife, mother of two, philanthropist, fashion icon . . ."

"Fashion icon?" Jessica's voice shows the first sign of real animation I've heard from her that morning.

"Yes," I say with a smile. "Before I arrived for my interview I did my research. I've seen your features in the society pages. You always look perfect." I drop my head as if deflated. "I've never been able to look as polished and put together as you. And I don't have half as much on my plate as you do."

Jessica gazes at me, her brow trying to crease through the Botox. "You're not like the other assistants Travis hires," she says. And then she gets up and teeters down the hall.

I'm not sure if I'm supposed to follow her, but I do. She leads me into what looks like a home office. On a desk there is a laptop and a large pile of mail, unsorted, unopened.

"I need you to deal with this," she says, pointing down at the envelopes. "I can't."

She walks out of the room, leaving me to figure out what it means to "deal with this."

I sit down at the desk, but it's the computer I attend to before the mail, in hopes that there might be something interesting on it. When I look through Jessica's email and browsing history, it becomes immediately evident that she likes forums. She's commented in forums about weight loss and skin care, about plastic surgery and med spas—always under one alias or another, but her email account has a record of when people have replied to her.

I tiptoe to the doorway and look down the hall. "Mrs. Gable?" I say softly. There's no answer. Quietly I walk down the hallway, peeking inside each room until I find her back on the sofa in the living room, sitting up but with her head lolling to the side, snoring softly. It's actually more of a squeak than a snore, kinda like a mouse, which is appropriate considering how timid she is with her husband.

"Mrs. Gable?" I whisper. But she's completely dead to the world.

So I return to the office . . .

. . . and open up a new email account for Jessica.

It's incredibly easy to do. I have all her information right in front of me. I can even reply to and then erase the email that is sent to her existing account to verify that it really is Jessica setting up the new account. Once that's taken care of, I use her new email address to register her on a few new forums dealing with abusive relationships and another dealing with self-defense. I even write a quick comment on an overwhelmed parents forum, just to round things out. As I continue to work for Jessica I'll be able to forward certain emails sent to her real account to this new one. I'll reply to senders and ask them to update their address book. Of course, that won't work for her friends, assuming she has any, but there are plenty of emails in her real account that were sent by nonprofits soliciting contributions. Jessica won't notice if a few of those organizations stop filling her email inbox. This way, everything will look legit.

And when it's time for her to send and receive *incriminating* emails . . . well, those will go through this new address too.

I take a moment to erase the browsing history from the last hour . . . but of course, once you do something on the internet, you can't entirely erase it. That's good, because for now I only want to hide my activity from Jessica and Travis. When the police eventually look at her computer . . . well, they'll find what I want them to find.

Satisfied with the work I've done so far, I pick up the envelopes and start going through the mail.

An hour later, I find Jessica in the living room, awake

again but now she's just staring out the window, a glass of white wine before her. It's not quite ten a.m.

"I went through the mail," I say, sitting next to her again. "I entered the invitations into your calendar. If you like, we can go through them now and decide which should stay there and which should be removed. And, of course, I'll RSVP for you."

She says nothing.

I look directly at her, using my best girl Friday tone. "You've also been sent several donation requests; we could go through those too. And the ballet would like to know if you can organize another silent auction for them. They emailed a few days ago. You did want me to go through the emails too, right?"

She shrugs, still not looking at me.

I pause for a moment, put my hands in my lap, and angle myself toward her. "Interview me."

At that she turns, her expression questioning.

"Go ahead. If I'm going to be your assistant, you should be the one to interview me. If you don't like me I'll leave. You can tell your husband that I just up and quit of my own accord."

"If I don't like you . . . you'll . . . you'll just quit?"

"If you want me to, yes. I don't like being anywhere I'm not *really* wanted, and I don't like making people feel uncomfortable."

She shakes her head, unsure of how to respond.

I straighten my posture, meet her eyes. "Interview me."

The corners of her mouth turn up, slowly at first, and then they move into a broad grin.

"Where did you go to school, Bell?"

That's how it starts, and it goes on like that for about twenty minutes. Jessica asks all the questions that one is supposed to ask during an interview, and I give her all the answers that I know will please her. She isn't creative, and her vices are still pumping through her veins, so she's unable to come up with any questions that are clever or unpredictable. I have a well-practiced lie to give her in exchange for each one.

But I can tell Jessica thinks she's putting me through the wringer. When she asks questions like, "In what areas do you think you need to improve?" her face glows with self-congratulatory enthusiasm. She loves it when I pretend to think seriously about the question, when I nervously bite my lip.

Jessica loves feeling like she's in control of something . . . even if it's just the employment status of an assistant.

And people don't usually let go of the one thing they have control over. They tend to hold that close.

No one is going to be asking me to quit. My inferior position gives her purpose, justifies her.

When we're done Jessica gives me a nod of satisfaction and brings her glass of wine to her lips. "Do you have any questions for me?"

I take a deep breath and look down at my hands. "What were the other assistants like?"

"They were . . . well . . ." She hesitates and then takes another long sip before continuing. "I probably shouldn't say this . . . but they were all a bit . . . shady. I couldn't figure out why my husband hired them." Her face darkens, her improved appearance slipping quickly as she downs the last of her wine. Whatever medication she's taking, it's not doing a great job at handling her mood swings.

"Of course, we've only had three in ten years," she continues, her voice a little higher, a little more shrill. "Three that lasted more than a couple of days. We've had *lots* that lasted less than that."

"Why's that?"

"Damned if I know!" Jessica gets to her feet and walks to the window, glaring out at the skyline. "We go through this whole long interview process to find a personal assistant *for me* that *he* likes and then invariably during their first few days on the job he calls them to his office to do some kind of errand—and then they never come back!"

I laugh nervously and cross then uncross my legs. "What happens to them?"

"Perhaps they just can't stand him. Perhaps they get scared off. Maybe he chops off their heads and throws their bodies in the Hudson. I. Don't. Know. All I know is that my time has been *wasted* and then we have to interview scores of people again so he can . . . can—"

"Chop off someone else's head?"

Jessica's mouth twitches at the corners.

"Wow, your husband's a regular Henry the Eighth."

And now the laughter comes—still nervous, a little rueful, but I got her laughing.

"Our last assistant lasted less than a month," she says once she collects herself. "That's not usual. It's always either a few days or it's years. But Lloyd lasted a few weeks. Of course, in that case I do know what happened. There was an . . . incident. The other two who were with us for a while, they didn't get in any trouble, and it's not as if they stole from us or anything—"

"That's good."

"—and they certainly performed their duties to satisfaction, but . . ." Her voice fades off as she tries to explain and then settles on waving her hand in the air dismissively. "I don't know. They just came across as a couple of miscreants. I hated having them in my home. But you . . . you're different. You don't seem like . . . like . . ."

"Like a miscreant?"

Again Jessica chuckles, but this time the laugh

quickly fades and she puts one hand to her head and the other on the wall to steady herself. "Oh dear, I'm a bit woozy."

I quickly stand and lead her back to the sofa. Jessica thanks me softly and then stares out the window again. "I'm taking a new . . . medication. I may have gotten the dosage wrong."

"Happens to the best of us."

Jessica flashes me a small, grateful smile. "You're very . . . sweet."

I suppress a smile. Clearly Jessica is a horrible judge of character. "Like I said, I like you. I'm sorry you've had so much trouble with your other assistants." I place a careful hand on Jessica's shoulder. "I hope you'll feel differently about me. I mean . . . okay, I'm never going to be anything close to your equal in *anything*." I pause, giving room for Jessica to interject with the expected *Now, now, don't be silly*, but that doesn't come. As far as Jessica's concerned the inequality between the two of us is a given.

"I still hope we can be friends, of a sort," I continue. "Anytime you want to talk . . . well, I'm a great listener. It just feels like you need somebody in your corner. Somebody to *hear* you."

Jessica's eyes water a little. She doesn't say anything, but it's clear she's absorbing what I'm saying. She's welcoming it.

"So tell me, how did you meet Mr. Gable?" I ask. "Was he romantic then—did he sweep you off your feet?"

Jessica folds her hands in her lap and stares at her ring. "It was more like the other way around. Years ago, back when I thought there could be nothing better than being Mrs. Travis Gable, I truly . . . went out of my way for him. I did anything and everything he asked. I . . . proved myself to him. I proved myself worthy of being a Gable." Jessica giggles softly and shakes her head. "I really did. I'm worthy of all of this. I got everything I deserve."

I'm silent as my eyes wander around the room. On the wall is a Warhol. On the coffee table is a Waterford crystal vase. The rug is something obscenely expensive, I'm sure. I turn back to Jessica's profile. Her skin is perfect, the product of regular facials, chemical peels, and monthly microdermabrasions. Is this really the price Jessica thinks she deserves to pay for sending my mother to her death?

I reach out, take Jessica's hand in mine. "You're wrong, Mrs. Gable. You deserve so much more than this."

Jessica's lip begins to tremble as her fingers link through mine. "Do you think so?"

"I do," I respond, smiling.

The sad woman looks into my eyes wonderingly.

"I'm not going to sleep with your husband," I continue. "But it does appear that I'm going to be working with him a lot, and I'm going to try to help him see things differently. I promise you, Mrs. Gable, I'm going to do everything I can to change your life."

"You're so nice," Jessica breathes. "No one is ever nice to me anymore . . . except for Mercedes, and she'll outgrow that in time, just like Braden did. Oh!" She pulls her hand away and covers her mouth as if shocked by her own behavior. "I'm being so inappropriate. I'm sorry, I'm not . . . not myself this morning."

Really? It's out of character for you to be fucked-up by ten a.m.?

"You're just talking, Mrs. Gable. You're talking to someone who wants to listen."

Jessica exhales, the kind of exhale that suggests a person has been holding their breath for a very, *very* long time. "Thank you, thank you so much, Bell."

"Oh, trust me, it's my pleasure, Mrs. Gable."

I spend the morning doing little tasks for Jessica. I send responses to invitations to various events, I send out Evites for a fund-raiser Jessica is throwing for a politician her husband is fond of, and then I address engraved invitations for Mercedes's third birthday party.

Jessica's in and out. She has a manicure scheduled and then she stops by her dermatologist's office for a Ju-véderm touch-up. It's tempting to post on the forums I've signed her up for while she's out, but of course I can't risk it. It's important that she be near her computer when I'm using her identity to post things. Can't have a time-stamp online contradict an alibi from someone else in real time. But now, when she's home, she sits in the same room as me, tells me about the other women who are on the board for the symphony—all absolutely awful, ac-cording to her—and the woman who lives on the floor beneath them, who is always nice to Jessica when Travis is around, but rude to her when he's not. I don't mind. The forums and emails can wait. Right now I'm just grateful for her confidence.

She talks about how Travis is the one who picks up her pills at the pharmacy. She talks about how that's the one kindness he still extends to her. Well, that and the fact that he gives her a big enough clothing allowance to buy out Bergdorf Goodman.

She talks about how she knows Travis isn't faithful but that she's learned to turn the other cheek . . . for the sake of the children.

Translation: She knows that if it comes down to a custody battle, she'll lose. And, in addition to that, her access to the prescription meds she's now addicted to might be cut off. So she sucks it up and tries to ignore the constant humiliations her marriage subjects her to.

I cluck my tongue, offer soothing words of comfort, and stock up the bits and pieces of information like so much ammunition.

It's well into the afternoon when Travis calls and asks for me.

Jessica hands me the phone, her hand shaking, her eyes downcast, studying the ground. I press the receiver to my ear while trying to give Jessica an encouraging smile, if only she would look at me.

"Mr. Gable," I say lightly, careful to keep any notes of flirtation out of my voice. "How can I help you?"

"Is my wife driving you crazy? Has she done anything stupid yet?"

"No, Mr. Gable."

"Don't lie to me. It's almost four; she must have humiliated herself at least five times today." He laughs as if he's just told a particularly good joke. "Tomorrow I want you to come to my office at HGVB."

"All right. Tomorrow morning Mrs. Gable requested I deliver—"

"I don't care what she wants you to deliver. She has feet and a limo at her disposal. She can deliver it herself. Tomorrow I want you here. Who is it that pays your salary, Bell?"

"You do, Mr. Gable."

"So then it's rather important that you please me, isn't it?

"It is."

"Good girl. Be here at nine thirty a.m."

The phone goes dead and after a moment I gently place it back in Jessica's hand. Jessica, who still won't meet my eyes.

"He wants me to do something for him at HGVB."

"He wants you to 'do something *for him*,'" Jessica repeats, spitting out the words.

"Just business," I assure her. "He won't touch me, I promise you that."

Jessica looks up, meets my eyes, and then smiles . . . and then laughs. She laughs so hard that for a moment I worry she's going to choke.

"It's ridiculous," Jessica finally manages. "Ridiculous that you should have to promise me that. Ridiculous that I should have to ask!"

She walks away from me, sits down on the settee. "The Gable men are highly intelligent individuals. My husband was first in his class at Princeton. His father says he could have been a chess master if he had put his mind to it. His brother too . . . although Lander was always more into Scrabble, anagrams, crossword puzzles, things like that. Used to create crossword puzzles too. Three of them were published in the *New York Times* . . . although none of them made the Sunday paper. These men, their minds absorb information and knowledge like sponges . . . but their hearts . . . nothing gets inside there. Nothing at all."

I don't say anything; there's nothing really to say.

Jessica's lower lip starts to quiver. "And will you come back, Bell?" she asks. Her voice is soft, almost pleading. "When Travis starts using my assistants—"

"I'm coming back," I assure her. "I'm not going to be one of those assistants who lasts only a day."

"You promise?"

"Oh yes," I say sweetly. "I'm the kind of girl who sees things through."

chapter fourteen

I surprise Lander by showing up at his doorstep with grocery bags full of food. It's not that he wasn't expecting me; it's that he thought we were going out.

"Why would we do that?" I ask with a laugh as I breeze past him, into the kitchen. "We have everything we need right here." I start unloading the bags. "I make the most amazing lasagna you'll ever taste."

"Lasagna?"

I turn to him with a wide smile and wrap my arms around his neck, pulling myself close to him. "Mexican lasagna. It's kinda spicy. You think you can handle it?"

He smiles, kisses my forehead. "I can handle anything you can dish out."

"Lucky me." My intention was to just give him one little flirtatious hug before turning to dinner, but now, in his arms, I don't really want to pull away. I think about the coldness that emanates from Travis. His voice could give you frostbite. His touch, hypothermia. But Lander always runs somewhere between warm and hot. Being with him is like lying out in the sun. It feels so good you forget that it can burn you.

I try to remember what he looked like when he was beating that man in the bar. I try to remember the hidden viciousness. But sometimes it's hard, like right now, while I'm in his arms.

"You said you wanted to make love to me in every room in my home."

"I did say that." I kiss his neck lightly. "Maybe that'll be our dessert."

"There are a lot of rooms. Maybe it can be our appetizer too." He lifts me up, places me on the counter, next to the extra virgin olive oil and red chili powder.

"Aren't you hungry?" I ask teasingly.

"Starving." He bites down lightly on my shoulder.

I thread my fingers through his hair, then grab on to it and pull him back so he's looking at me. With slow, languid movements I stretch out my legs, then wrap them around him. I move my hands from his hair to his cheeks, cupping his face. "Would you like to fuck me, Lander?"

"I would," he says with a brightly lit smile. "I would like to fuck you, Bell."

I laugh. Only Lander can make the word *fuck* sound like romance. I think about that drawing he made of me. *Kind, Witty Heroine.*

It's not who I am. But right now I want to pretend. Pretending is part of my plan.

It's also part of my pleasure.

I lower my mouth to his, my hair enveloping us both.

I think of Jessica, married to a man who can't even pretend to like her.

But here I am, pretending to fall in love with a man who is pretending to be good.

I pull off his tie and drop it in the sink.

"Hey!"

I shrug as I pull off his jacket. "It's ugly and you're rich. Buy a new one."

"Well, aren't you sassy today?"

"I'm sassy every day." I throw his jacket across the room. "If you're just noticing now, you haven't been paying attention."

"Trust me, I've been paying attention." He pulls off my jacket. "For instance, I know that you like it when I kiss you here." He kisses the base of my neck, sucking slightly, making little circles with his tongue.

"Oh please," I breathe. "Everybody likes to be kissed there."

"And here." His tongue flicks across that little hollow spot atop my collarbone.

"Less obvious, I admit," I concede as I pull his belt from him and wrap it around my hand.

"Hmm, here." He leans into me, gently biting down on my nipple through the fabric of my shirt.

"A lot of women have sensitive breasts. That's to be expected," I whisper as I wriggle against him.

"True." He pulls my shirt from me and his lips find the delicate skin inside my elbow, sucking it gently.

I breathe in, close my eyes. Who knew that was a "spot"?

Lander . . . Lander knew. He's learning my body like a geographer learns the landscape, testing it, feeling it, mapping it out to ease his future travels.

"And you like it when I pull your clothes off you slowly," he adds. "Like this." He pulls my skirt down my legs, so that the fabric rubs against my skin.

"Take off the rest of your clothes," I instruct.

I sit and watch as he removes his shirt, his pants, as he stands before me naked and beautiful . . . so strong . . . and so surprisingly vulnerable. That dominant man I slept with on that first night isn't here right now. This man is playful, sweet . . .

. . . and sexy as hell.

Lander is such a versatile actor.

I stay on the counter as I remove my bra, slowly at first, and then I rip it off, swing it over my head, and throw it toward his jacket.

"Very pretty," he says, his eyes lingering on my curves, the smile on his mouth a little wistful, a little mischievous. "You do know you're not done."

I pucker my lips teasingly and then slip my thumbs into the waistband of my panties and wriggle out of them as he watches closely.

He's getting harder.

"My beautiful warrior." He gently lifts my chin. "You're mesmerizing."

"Yeah? Well, you're going to have to come out of your trance." I uncurl the belt, swing it over the wide part of his back, and use it to pull him to me. "I want you *now*."

His mouth spreads into a grin as his hands grab my thighs. With hard-won flexibility and grace I uncurl my legs and put one over each of his shoulders so now I'm in a perfect V.

"Did you not understand me when I said 'now'?" And with that I pull again on the belt, drawing him even closer. In an instant I feel him pressing against me and then inside my walls.

He groans as I lean back, using the belt to support myself. "Do you know how good you feel?" he asks.

I answer by pulling harder on the belt, bringing him

closer, deeper, feeling his bare skin against mine, nothing separating us. He's so deep now, he's filling the emptiness I've lived with for so very long.

He doesn't have to ask me to look into his eyes tonight. Tonight I don't want to look anywhere else.

I'm pretending, of course . . . I'm an actress swept up in a role. It doesn't have to be real, it can't be. But tonight I'm losing myself in the fantasy. That's my decision, my choice.

He pulls the belt away from me and I wrap my legs around his waist again as he lifts me off the counter. Still buried deep inside, he pushes me up against a wall, holding on to my thighs, keeping my hips against his as he starts to thrust again. His face is right against mine; we're so close that he's a bit of a blur as I cling to him, feel him, every inch of him. I lower my legs so they're now wrapped around his and squeeze with my thighs, making myself tighter, feeling the friction of his movement.

That's all it takes. The orgasm rolls through me and I cling to him as he pulls me down onto him with increasing force.

Again he lifts me up, this time breaking our connection as I protest. He sits down on a kitchen chair, pulling me onto his lap. I immediately straddle him, pressing him inside again. My breasts are pressed against his chest, my mouth on his. Using my legs I push myself up and down, savoring our connection and the tension. I feel his every breath, smell the hints of his cologne as I increase my pace. I can see what I'm doing to him, feel what he's doing for me. I'm holding on to him so tightly you would think I was drowning.

Maybe I am in a way.

I increase my speed again, and that's when Lander reaches between us and toys with my clit.

Which sends me over the edge. I cry out, my face pressed against his as he comes inside me at the same time.

For a moment we just stay there, pressed against each other, our foreheads touching as we both try to catch our breath.

"Lander," I whisper.

"Yes?"

"Is this the way you're greeting all your dates these days?"

"No, Bell, just you."

Just me.

I wish that didn't sound so wonderful.

Twenty minutes later we're both dressed and the skillet's on the stove. Lander's putting on his coat because I forgot to bring the onions. I've also convinced him that some Coronas and limes would be a nice addition. I talk him out of calling his driver for this even though it's about a ten-minute walk to the grocer. Everybody deserves a night off.

He kisses me on the cheek before he leaves. "I like this," he says quietly.

"What? Kissing?"

"You're cooking, I'm getting groceries. It feels . . . nice."

I laugh. It's so domestic. So sappy sweet.

It makes me smile.

I watch him leave, almost wishing I hadn't purposely left the onions at home.

When I'm sure he's gone, I go into his office and head straight for his desk. There in the top drawer is his sketch of the biker. I start to push it aside to look to see what else is in there when something about the picture stops me.

It's the biker's face. His expression seems worried . . . even scared. It isn't the look of a man who is angry or of someone who *Cries in Rebuke*, per the title.

I look at the title again. I remember how carefully Lander selected it. He didn't exactly come up with a phrase. He seemed to come up with each word individually, as if he were solving a puzzle rather than naming an image.

"*Lander was always more into Scrabble, anagrams, crossword puzzles, things like that.*"

Word games . . . Lander plays word games. I study the title again before grabbing a blank piece of printer paper and a pen and getting to work.

It takes me several minutes, but eventually I get it.

C.R.I.E.S. I.N. R.E.B.U.K.E. . . . it's an anagram. It's an anagram for INSECURE BIKER.

And if *that's* an anagram . . .

I put the picture back and open the drawer where he keeps his sketchbook. I find it on top of some insurance papers for various artworks, a fountain pen that's probably worth upward of five hundred dollars, his passport, and his social security card—a number I memorized over a year ago.

I flip open the book and start with the picture of the woman with the dollar signs in her eyes and the diamond-collared dog, *Dogged Girl.*

I almost laugh. I can't believe I didn't see it before.

D.O.G.G.E.D. G.I.R.L.

Switch those letters around and you get GOLD DIGGER.

Anagrams.

I flip to the picture of the politicians drawn to look like marionettes. It's titled T.H.R.U.S.T.I.N.G. S.P.E.L.L.

At least that's what he wrote. It takes a while, but eventually I get PULL THE STRINGS.

Giddily I flip to the page with the drawing of the crying woman, clinging to the pant leg of the crowned man. A. C.A.D. F.E.E.L.S. S.P.E.W.I.N.G. S.O.R.R.O.W.

This one isn't so easy. I sit hunched over the desk, writing out different possibilities. Maybe one of the words is *eel*? *Pew*? *Rad*? Three minutes pass, then five. I have PRINCESS but I'm not sure that's right. Still, with the guy wearing the crown and all, maybe he's king and the crying woman is a princess? But I can't come up with the word *king* from this anagram.

Princess of . . . Could she be a princess of *something? Of what?*

I'm getting a little frustrated now. Lander draws these pictures and creates these anagrams when he's working out something in his head, when he's thinking things through . . . and I sense that of all the pictures this one will offer me the insight into his mind that I really need. I could do this later but now that I'm in the middle of it I want to finish working out this puzzle *now*. I feel like I'm on the brink of something here.

My mind runs through all the things I know about Lander. Which is a lot. Perhaps too much for it to be useful. I look at the woman again, at the man. I can't see the face of either person, but the woman has her hair in a

French braid down her back. Not very many women wear their hair like that anymore . . .

. . . but Lander's mother did. I've seen pictures.

"But the people who live in places like this . . . They're a little like royalty, aren't they? They're treated like kings and queens, princes and princesses," I had said.

And he responded . . .

"Yes, my mother was treated like the dowager princess of Wales."

I work with the letters and there it is: DOWAGER PRINCESS OF WALES. His mother the dowager princess. And the man . . . That must be his father.

It gives me pause. I'm going to have to think about what that means . . . research it. But now something else has caught my eye. Peeking out from under those insurance papers is the drawing of me.

I pull it out and study the picture with new eyes.

Why *did* he put me in period dress? And the dress is so . . . so *specific*.

Kind, Witty Heroine is the title.

I start to work with the words, writing out every possibility. NOWHERE—no, that doesn't make sense. KID, but there's no child in the picture.

One minute passes, then two, then three . . . I'm not making progress.

Until I look at the costume again. I look at my position . . . I look at my *hair*, swept up in a low bun, loose enough to reveal my waves. Again it just looks so familiar, and I *know* it has something to do with history. The problem with having studied so many of Lander's interests over the last few years is that all that new information is crammed into my head and getting mixed up. If I remember the name of a battle, I forget the date or vice versa. And to be honest, the battles themselves are of less interest to me than the people who waged them. During my studies I found that the women of World War I and World War II were much more interesting than the men. The sly strategies they employed in order to survive while still advancing their cause . . . well, it's just something I can relate to. Like Virginia Hall, a civilian woman who trained battalions of the French Resistance and gathered intelligence on their enemies. She successfully became a master of disguise in order to fool the Germans, even going so far as to train herself not to walk with a limp despite her prosthetic leg. And conversely, in World War I there was Mata Hari . . .

Oh.

I look down at the drawing again. The picture it's modeled after is so famous I'm embarrassed I hadn't figured it out before. And yet I can't help but double-check. I pull out my phone and do a Google search, hoping that by some miracle I'm wrong. That I'm misremembering.

But I'm not misremembering anything, because there she is: Mata Hari, wearing the exact costume I'm wearing in the drawing.

Mata Hari the seductress.

Mata Hari the whore.

Mata Hari . . . the Frenchwoman who worked as a double agent for the Germans in World War I.

Mata Hari the traitor.

My hand is shaking now as I move the letters around. I KNOW HER . . .

. . . and there it is. The solution to the anagram.

The memory of Lander's warm touch against my skin now turns very, very cold. His prints chill me as I recoil from the drawing. I want to throw up. I want to run from the room. But instead I just read the unscrambled note again and again. Four little words:

I KNOW HER IDENTITY.

part two

part two

chapter fifteen

I'm sitting on the floor of Lander's office. My hair hangs heavily over my shoulders as I hold his drawing of me in one hand and the solution to his anagram in the other. He had titled the drawing *Kind, Witty Heroine*. But the anagram for K.I.N.D. W.I.T.T.Y. H.E.R.O.I.N.E. relayed something entirely different:

I KNOW HER IDENTITY.

Twenty minutes ago he had kissed my cheek, breathed in my scent.

I know her identity.

Twenty minutes before that he had been inside me, pressed against me, my sweat mingled with his.

I know her identity.

I had told myself that I was pretending. I had told myself I didn't care about Lander at all. I just needed to get *him* to care about *me* for the sake of my plan, a plan designed to make his family pay for setting my mother up for a crime she didn't commit. That's it.

But that's not entirely true.

I thought that Lander was taken with me. I thought he saw me as someone who was true and kind.

But that's not right. He sees me as Mata Hari, the enemy. And that's what I am.

I'm Mata Hari.

A seductress.

A whore.

A traitor.

And what we're doing . . . it's nothing more than a game of poker. We place our bets. We bluff, we hide our cards . . . We're *opponents*. One of us will win and the other will lose *everything*. Just a high-stakes game of poker, nothing more tender or sentimental than that.

But when he holds me in his arms, it feels like something else. I wanted, just for a moment, for it to be something else.

I keep trying to pretend that the only thing on my mind is revenge and how I can overcome Lander's suspicions in order to achieve that goal . . .

But that's simply not the case.

And now, as scary as it is, I might have to stop lying to myself.

And if I do I'll have to admit that I want at least one person to see me as good, even though it's not true. My mother saw me as someone good when I was a child, but that changed. By the time she killed herself she had seen me for what I am: rotten, ruined, hateful . . . stupid. I don't like to think about it, but when my mother was alive I had been stupid. After she passed, I had hoped that in honor of her memory I could at least overcome that one shortcoming. I had tried to be smart . . . even clever.

But I failed. I'm just as stupid as ever.

I've bet everything I have. He saw through my bluff and now he's about to lay down his winning hand.

I'm about to lose everything.

That can't happen.

In an instant I'm on my feet, the drawing clutched in one hand, the solution to the anagram crumpled in the other. With a jerk of my arm I throw the latter into the wastebasket.

I do have a contingency plan. I know what needs to be done if one of the Gables learns who I am.

But it involves violence.

And I don't want to hurt him.

I just want to keep pretending.

I walk into the living room and gaze out his floor-to-ceiling windows to the city below. It's a beautiful view. Manhattan looks like a carpet of lights, the windows of the skyscrapers glowing gold. They look like low-hanging stars.

I'm about to lose everything.

I put my hand to my head. Press the drawing to my heart. I feel sick.

And I wonder . . . how strong is the glass? I had leaned against it as Lander touched me. It had felt as if his touch was the one thing that kept me from falling.

But he's not touching me now.

What would it take to break this glass? What would it feel like to really fall? What kind of relief can really be found in death?

"Bell?"

I don't move. The drawing is still pressed against my chest. I won't be able to hide it.

And suddenly I realize I don't want to hide it. If the hellhounds are going to be unleashed I'd rather fight them now than cower in the corner waiting for their attack.

I whirl around and there he is, looking almost guileless in his untucked pin-striped shirt and faded jeans. The natural highlights in his brown hair almost match the glow of the city lights.

But this is not a guileless man.

I swallow hard and slam the picture onto the coffee table.

He pauses a moment, staring down at the drawing. "How did you—"

"I saw it last night while we were having sex," I snap, cutting him off.

I can see his mind working quickly. He's still thinking about how I got my hands on the picture, but now it hardly matters. If he knows I'm a spy, clearly he knows I'm capable of rifling through a desk or two.

"What does it mean, Lander?" I ask, my voice icy.

"*Kind, Witty Heroine*," he says slowly. "Isn't it self-explanatory?"

"Right." I cross behind the armchair, putting one more piece of furniture between him and me.

"I would think you would be flattered," Lander adds.

"I was . . . until Jessica started telling me all about your love of anagrams. And then I started thinking about how you came up with the title of the picture you drew of the biker."

"The biker?" he repeats. He's studying me now with a cold curiosity. He doesn't look confused and he certainly doesn't look worried. He may not have been expecting this confrontation, but now that it's here he's ready for it. I can just tell.

"Yes, you know," I say sarcastically, "the guy who *Cries in Rebuke.* The way you came up with the title . . . It was like you were working out a puzzle. And you were."

"Was I?"

His voice is so steady, so utterly emotionless, I find myself a little unnerved. This is not the passionate man I made love to less than an hour ago. This is not the man I've been studying over the years.

This is a stranger.

"Insecure biker," I say, trying to keep my tone confident. "It's an anagram. And so it makes sense that the other drawing you made that night would be titled with an anagram too. I mean . . . it makes sense for *you*. Normal people don't turn random thoughts into anagrams. But there's nothing normal about you, is there, Lander?"

"No, I suppose that's something we have in common. You and I are two of a kind."

I inhale sharply. It's not his words that scare me. It's his calm.

Right now I'm afraid of Lander.

I walk around the chair and slowly lower myself into it, keeping my eyes on his . . . just like I do when we make love. But the chemistry, while still intense, is totally different now.

"Kind, witty, heroine." I say the words slowly. I gesture to the picture. "I was so flattered. I didn't even recognize that you had me dressed up to look like Mata Hari."

"Ah, you know your history."

I don't answer. My jaw is so tight it aches.

He sits opposite me, reaches for a pen, then pulls the drawing toward him. Below *Kind, Witty Heroine* he writes the words *I Know Her Identity*.

Seeing him write it out like that makes me think about his window. It makes me think about how easy it would be to fall.

He turns the paper around so the words are facing me. I read them over and over again, using them as an excuse to avoid his eyes.

"You're not who you say you are, Bell."

I hold my silence, reading and rereading those words and thinking about what they mean.

They mean it's over.

I've failed, Mom. I didn't get you your justice. I am as stupid as I've ever been.

"You act like you're this carefree party girl, but that's just a façade. You're calculating, ambitious, determined . . . and you're very manipulative, aren't you?"

"Just more things we have in common," I snap. But only my words are brave. Inside I'm trembling.

"That's true. I've manipulated enough people to know what it looks like." He leans back into the sofa. "You knew who I was when I walked into that bar, didn't you?"

I swallow hard before whispering, "How could I have known that?"

"Come now, your Miss Innocent role's played out. You have to be a more versatile actor."

I lift my chin defiantly, hold in my fear.

"You thought I was going to change your life, didn't you?" he presses.

No, I thought I was going to destroy yours. But I don't say it out loud. Instead I wait for his accusations to become a little more specific.

"You knew how much money I had. You knew who my family was. And you sure as hell knew who my brother was. That whole thing about your not wanting my help, that's bullshit, isn't it? You were hoping that if you slept with me I would get you an *in*. Maybe, with my help, you could get a job at HGVB or a job working for the Gable family that paid—probably one that pays a little bit more than the one my brother just gave you. Fucking me for career opportunities . . . it's just another form of prostitution. At least Mata Hari was honest about being a courtesan."

For a second I don't move. I'm holding my breath, waiting for him to start laughing. Waiting for him to admit that this bizarrely mundane accusation is just his way of giving me a false sense of security before he pulls the rug out from under me. Any moment now he's going to tell me that he really and truly *does* know my identity.

"Tell me, Bell, what's the real reason you don't want me talking to Travis?"

It takes a moment for me to find my voice. "Why don't you tell me?" I finally say. "You seem to have this whole thing figured out."

"I think you've come to realize that Travis isn't faithful to his wife. I think you're beginning to wonder if *he's* the brother you should be sleeping with. As you once pointed out to me, I'm neither as rich nor as influential as he is."

"Wait, are . . . are you serious? Who in their right mind would—"

"I'm convinced you're a lot of things," he interrupts, "but I'm not sure that being in your right mind is one of them."

I feel dizzy. Sitting across from Lander, being accused of something so ridiculously idiotic . . . I'm almost indignant. The man rides around the city in a limo, his last name is Gable, and he has a multimillion-dollar penthouse with a Degas hanging in his hallway. There are literally tens of thousands of women who would love to use Lander for his money, and I'm sure hundreds have tried. And all of those gold diggers would happily ditch Lander for his richer brother if Travis showed them even an iota of kindness.

But can Lander really not see the difference between

those women and me? Do I really seem that *common*? That pathetic? *Really?*

Still, as incensed as I am, I'm also incredibly relieved. Part of me wants to fall to my knees and praise God for making Lander such a moron.

But as he sits there *glaring* at me, a completely different emotion takes hold: confusion. He's so *angry*. Have I hurt him? In the short period of time we've been dating has he come to care so much about me that I have the power to do that? Have I disappointed him?

I've spent a lot of time figuring out new and creative ways to screw up this man's life . . . and yet right now the very thought that I might have inadvertently caused him pain cuts into my lungs and makes each breath a little painful.

"I didn't know who you were when we first met," I say carefully, but as Lander rolls his eyes I quickly add, "but of course I knew you had money. You reek of it, Lander. And there aren't a lot of Bill Gates types who walk into that particular bar, so maybe . . . maybe I saw an opportunity there."

"Maybe?"

"I looked you up online just a few hours after we first met," I continue. "I figured out who your family is and . . . Okay, it took some digging, but I eventually discovered that your sister-in-law was looking for a personal assistant. I got my last PA job through a personal connection. It was sort of my first real job and it was a good one. But then the guy I worked for dropped off the face of the earth. You can't even talk to him to check a reference. You have to talk to someone else who worked for him—and half of those people are currently under indictment. I was screwed, Lander."

"A heartbreaking story."

"You're right to be angry." I lower my head, as if abashed. As if. "I was going to use you. I *wanted* to use you . . . and that was wrong. But, Lander, I didn't do it. I got the PA job all on my own. In the space of twenty-four hours I had started dating a truly amazing man and I landed a killer job without any help from anyone. And for a brief moment I thought maybe I wouldn't have to play games anymore. Maybe the manipulations could stop."

Lander shifts his position. He's staring past me, but his expression isn't as hard as it was minutes ago.

"I initially didn't want you to tell your brother about us because I have something to prove . . . to myself. I got this job on my own merits. And I was afraid that if he knew that we were dating—"

"You said initially," Lander interrupts. "What's your reason for not wanting me to tell him now?"

I get up from my seat and then perch myself on the edge of the coffee table, right in front of him. I reach forward and put my hand gently over his. He looks past me, staring out the window, completely unmoved by the intimacy I'm trying to infuse into our exchange.

"You think your brother's up to something, don't you?" I ask.

He doesn't answer, but I can see I have his attention.

"I don't know if you're right, or what you think is going on," I say softly, "but if you are, I'll find out for you."

For a moment he doesn't move. And then, slowly, he turns his gaze back to me. "What are you suggesting?"

I take a deep breath—what I'm about to say is a gamble. If I've misread Lander's feelings about his brother, I'll be making a huge mistake.

But poker is a game of skill. It's all about reading your opponent and spotting his tells.

I'm a good poker player.

"I already said I'd keep my ears open," I say, pressing forward, "but now . . . If you tell me where to look, I'll look. Lander, please let me do this for you. Let me make up for making you not trust me. Please."

"Do you know what Travis would do to you if he thought you were spying on him for me?"

"Fire me?" I ask. "Give me a bad reference? What?"

It's not an idle question. I want to see Lander's reaction. I need to gauge how dangerous he thinks Travis is.

He answers me with a look that tells me he thinks

I've grossly underestimated his brother. Without saying the words, he's telling me that I might be putting myself in harm's way.

"Will he hurt me, Lander?" I ask softly.

Lander hesitates a moment and then shakes his head, releasing an uneasy laugh. "He's not a gangster," he says. "He's not going to throw you off the Brooklyn Bridge. But his reach is long. If he doesn't want you to work again . . . well, it'll be difficult for you, Bell."

He's underselling it. Blackballing me would only be the beginning. But I simply smile and shrug my shoulders, pretending I can't see the truth behind the words. "So we won't let him find out," I say. "Later, when I've had time to do a little digging, we'll act like we just met. We'll start dating in the open. We'll let Travis think that he saw you ask me out for the first time. If it turns out he's not hiding anything . . . well, no harm, no foul. And if there *is* something . . ." My voice fades, letting him mentally fill in the blanks.

Lander smiles. "You *are* a good manipulator, Bell." He impatiently brushes a piece of lint from his jeans. "And I feel like you know me a little better than I'm comfortable with."

"I know your dark side," I say gently. "I've seen it . . . and it doesn't bother me." I scoot in a little closer. "I like it, Lander."

It's a risky angle. I'm not so much explaining my be-havior as I am trying to distract him by offering him something he truly wants. But he's buying into it. I can feel it as he spreads his fingers wide under mine.

"I should kick you out of here," he says quietly.

"I know," I whisper and lace my fingers into his.

"You had to go through my stuff to get that drawing."

"Yes," I admit. "I was just thinking about what Jessica had said about you and anagrams and then thought about the doodle you were making. I just had to see it."

"You shouldn't go through my stuff."

I nod. "It won't happen again."

Again he scoffs, and this time it's for good reason.

"I need to ask you something," I add.

He meets my eyes, and I see something there, a dare, a spark of confidence . . . and maybe . . . maybe a bit of mischief?

But it all disappears in an instant as his face hardens and his voice turns gruff. "Let me guess. You want to know why I acted like everything was fine before if I didn't think it was. You're wondering why I've been both-ering with you at all."

I bite my lower lip and nod.

"I acted like everything was fine because you *are* a good actress, Bell. I kept thinking we would have this confrontation. I'd imagine slamming the door in your face. I thought I could turn the tables and that I could be the one to use *you*."

"But you didn't."

"No, I didn't. I'm not entirely sure why. Maybe because you're so good at acting that what we have actually *feels* real. And sometimes . . . sometimes I'm a person who likes to pretend."

I have to fight to keep my eyes from widening. I don't want him to know that I understand exactly what he means. That I understand in a way that I can never share with him.

"The woman you think I'm pretending to be . . . maybe it's the woman I am. Or at least maybe it's the woman I can be if I just keep trying."

His sigh is more dismissive than exacerbated. He simply doesn't believe it. He raises his hand to my cheek, caresses it with his thumb. "Why are all the sinners so beautiful? Why can't I fall for the angels instead of the warriors?"

"Because angels ask you to sacrifice too much."

"Ah," he says, and an impish smile plays on his lips. "And warriors know how to have fun."

"We do." Slowly I rise from the coffee table and straddle his lap. I slide my fingers into his hair. "We do know how to have fun." I lower my lips to his. I feel him respond. His hand moves to my lower back, his mouth opens for me, and he caresses my tongue with his. As I shift in his lap, pressing myself against him, I feel his desire build.

And like that, I can see everything's going my way. I'm back on track, and without resorting to violence. His suspicions, while merited, were misdirected, and now I've been able to spin the story to my liking.

But I'm not pleased with myself.

His hands move down to my hips, pulling me even closer as his kisses move to my chin, then my neck, and I feel his hands move between my legs, adding a tantalizing pressure to this seduction.

I didn't want him to see me as a gold digger. The truth is worse than that, but his accusations scrape against my skin, making me raw.

He holds me firmly as he raises me up, then flips me over onto the couch. I'm lying on my back, my legs still wrapped around him. I feel the flicker of his tongue against the hollow of my throat, as if attempting to coax out the words I wish I could swallow.

If he had worked out the truth, our poker game would have turned into a knife fight and Lander's blade surely would have sunk deeper than mine. There would have been so much pain. The wounds he would have inflicted would have been debilitating.

But then again, at least when I bleed I know I'm *real*.

As it stands now, I'm a ghost. A fantasy composed of nothing more tangible than my imagination and his misdirected suspicions.

I grab his hair, this time pulling him back. "I don't want your money," I say quietly as my grip tightens.

He doesn't answer, but his eyes are warm and almost patient. I let go of him and pull off my shirt. Lifting my arms above my head, I drop it over the edge of the couch.

"What *do* you want, Bell?"

I press my lips together as the truth struggles to escape:

I want justice.

I want revenge.

I almost tell him my real name.

"I want . . ." I whisper. "I want . . ."

What? What can I say? What hateful little lie will I choose to ruin us now?

"I *want*," I breathe and then pause as I again catch that flash of mischief in his eyes, the impish curve of his mouth. It's a challenge. An invitation for wickedness.

I love it.

I slide my hand down his chest, his stomach, his waist, his hips, until I can caress his erection through the rich denim fabric. I raise my eyebrows suggestively.

He may not know what I want for my life . . .

. . . but he knows what I want right *now*.

For a moment neither one of us moves as we taste this moment, testing its potential.

And then the gates of our passion are blown wide open with an exhilarating smash.

I tear at his shirt, yanking it off him, and for the second time today I see buttons fly. But the last time it was purely playful. This time it's more complicated, and more delicious.

His teeth graze my nipples through the fabric of my bra. His hands are rough against my skin as he presses me to him.

He knows my body so well . . . but he doesn't know me at all.

I bite down on his shoulder, almost breaking the skin. He rolls us over and together we tumble onto the soft area rug, into that narrow space between the coffee table and the sofa. I'm on top now, my skirt bunched around my waist as I pull off his belt, and, tugging off his pants and boxers, I tear away my panties and straddle his waist. My sex is pressed against his stomach and he reaches for me, but I slap away his hands as I take off my bra, exposing myself to him. With one hand I grab his jaw, making sure he doesn't turn away from me.

"Look at *me* now, Lander," I say, my voice hoarse with emotion. "See who I am. *Know* who I am."

Again he reaches for me, but this time I don't stop

him. His hand caresses my breast; his fingers pinch my nipple just enough to make me jump. "I know you, Bell."

Bell. For the first time the sound of that name stings. What the hell had I been worried about before? Lander doesn't know my identity. He can't.

I no longer *have* an identity.

I raise myself up on my knees and then lower myself onto him, feeling the friction of his cock as he fills me. I ride him slowly at first, my hand on his chest, keeping him in his place as I take control.

"This is who I am, Lander," I say as I increase my pace. "This time it's you who needs to see *me*."

I feel myself getting wetter, feel him growing even harder inside me as I continue to move, rotating my hips to a rhythm that I desperately want him to hear.

In a flash he sits up, grabbing me by my waist to keep me from falling back and losing our connection. I stare into his eyes and slowly start to lean back. His hand supports the curvature of my back as I continue into a full backbend, my head resting between his legs, my hips pressed against him, my knees pushing into the soft rug, my arms stretched out, hands clinging to his ankles.

And that's when Lander leans forward, bringing him in so deep I can't help but cry out. He kisses my breast as I cling to his legs, bracing myself against each thrust. The ecstasy is overwhelming. *This* is real, this feeling, this passion, this crazed intensity.

This man . . . he knows my body.

He knows how to make me *feel*.

I'm trembling against him. Being with him like this shouldn't feel this powerful. I've forgotten who I am. Maybe that was inevitable.

But I shouldn't forget who he is.

And yet right now, he *is* this feeling. He's rage and rapture; he's tenderness and grace.

He's the closest I'll ever get to love.

My orgasm rocks through me as he pulls me back up so I sit on his lap and give way to his motion.

And when he comes . . . I feel that too. I feel him throbbing inside me. I feel him shake as he explodes. I feel his warm breath against my skin and how desperate his hands are by the way they grasp me.

And I wish he knew me.

I wish we were the man and woman we pretend to be.

I wish I didn't have to destroy him.

chapter sixteen

I don't spend the night. I need Lander to feel the luxury and loneliness of an empty bed. The minute he gets used to me is the minute he'll start losing interest.

But I also leave because I need to prepare. After all, the next day will be my first working with Travis.

When I wake up that morning I take care selecting my outfit. I end up with a charcoal suit made of a stretch wool-poly blend with a leather collar and leather patches on the elbows. It's cold commerce with splashes of rebellion.

Travis will appreciate it.

I smile at my reflection and snatch up my bag, ready for battle.

But on the way out I pause to grab a Clif Bar, not for me, but for Mary. It's a knee-jerk reaction that I don't seem to have the strength or desire to squelch.

On the way to the subway, I spot her sitting on the pavement, her back to a wall as she uses a stub of a colored pencil to work on her coloring book, two felt-tipped pens in her hair held in place by the thick, tight curls.

"Hey," I say as I reach into my purse. "Hungry?"

Mary flashes me a yellow-toothed smile and holds out her hand. "So nice of you. My name's Mary."

"So you've told me," I say as I hand over the Clif Bar. "It's your favorite, Chocolate Chip."

She rips open the package enthusiastically. "Chocolate Chip's okay," she says as she bites deep. "But Crunchy Peanut Butter's my favorite."

I laugh and start to excuse myself, but then she jerks her head up and meets my eyes, staring at me with a new kind of clarity. "You look just like my daughter," she says. "You know her?"

"No," I say uncertainly. Mary's so nuts it's hard to tell if she really does have a daughter or if she's referring to the raccoon she befriended the other night.

She reaches down into her shirt and pulls out a small, weather-beaten photo, holding it up for my inspection. It's of a girl several years younger than me standing in front of a fountain in Central Park. She's fairer than Mary but she has Mary's reddish-brown hair and broad nose. Feature for feature, this girl and I have nothing in common, but in her expression—in the anger in her eyes—I can definitely see the resemblance between the two of us.

"She don't talk to me no more," Mary says. "She says she ain't got no mama, but I'm her mama, all right. She may not like it, but I'm her mama."

She looks down at the coloring book in her hands, and for the first time I look at it too. The hues that she always keeps so contained are now spilling recklessly outside the lines. Scribbles of purple, red, and gray scratch over the printed drawings of the happy family, decimating their white-picket-fence world.

"You know what I think?" Mary asks. "I think she forgot who I am."

Did my mother ever think I forgot about her? Did she think I had erased her from my life?

There are memories that I simply do not want to relive. And there are things I don't want to acknowledge.

For instance, the similarities between me and Mary's daughter.

"She remembers," I finally say as I try to quiet my thoughts. "Every time she looks in the mirror she remembers."

Mary smiles up at me brightly. "That's nice! I like that!" She bobs her head up and down as she seems to replay my words in her head. "'Every time she looks in the mirror' . . . Yeah, that's real good. I'm Mary, by the way."

I take a deep breath and excuse myself from the scene, wondering where I can buy her a new coloring book. For reasons I refuse to examine, I feel I owe her that.

It only took me twenty minutes to get to HGVB via subway; twenty minutes to push the unsettling encounter with Mary out of my mind. Twenty minutes to refocus on the Gables and my objective. Twenty minutes . . .

But now I've been cooling my heels on the marble floors of an HGVB waiting room for a little over half an hour, growing impatient again. Men like Travis Gable always make people wait, even when they don't have to. I know that, and I'm prepared for it, except . . .

My eyes slide over to where the elevators are as I shift uncomfortably in my sleek black leather chair. Lander could walk through at any moment. I neglected to tell him that I'd be working with Travis, not Jessica, today. I had my reasons. But if Lander walks in, it won't look good. He's infatuated with me perhaps, but I now know that he's not falling in love with me.

I smile inwardly. It's ridiculous that something like that would bother me. It's only important because it means my value to him is tenuous. That being the case, I need to ensure that at the very least he sees me as a reliable informant.

The only reason his feelings for me matter is because of how they affect my plans. That's it. That has to be it.

My mind travels back to last night—the drawing, the confrontation, the sex, the words of appeasement afterward. My own feelings for Lander are as mercurial as a tropical climate. One moment it's sunny, the next stormy . . . and you never know exactly when the hurricane is going to hit.

Of course, that's my own fault. Years ago I used to imagine what it would be like to be with Lander in his penthouse. I imagined standing next to him at the bar. (I always knew he'd have a well-stocked, elegant little bar.) I imagined him slipping his arms around me as I reached for a traditional corkscrew, something simple with a polished wood handle that would feel smooth and right against my palm. I imagined kissing his cheek as he leered at me. I imagined that his face would be flush with drink. I imagined the crude insults he would frame as compliments while his hands roamed over me, squeezing and pinching.

I imagined taking the corkscrew and sinking the long helix into his throat.

I imagined the blood. The way he would clutch at his neck uselessly.

His pain.

Him dying.

I haven't played that particular game of pretend for quite some time. Those were the clumsy imaginings of a simple and resentful girl, one who indulged in gruesome fantasies rather than pursue any real course of action. Justice had seemed like too grand a concept, completely out of my reach. Back then I didn't bother to think about what I was or wasn't capable of.

And I didn't actually know what Lander was like. We had never spoken. I had stalked him online and in person. But that doesn't tell you what it's like to be around someone in the flesh, interacting with him. I had imagined that he would be condescending and crude, not challenging and passionate.

Back then I had never felt the warmth of his smile.

Back then it was all fantasy.

Now I have a plan. And now I have the maturity to know that I can cause more pain with a kiss than I can with a blade.

But still . . . The fantasies of killing him weren't that long ago.

I glance again at the elevators as people wander in and out. It's a thin crowd; this isn't a high-traffic floor. It's a place for the elite. The people who step out of the elevators are dressed in a way that subtly advertises their

power and success. Five-hundred-dollar ties peek out
from beneath wool crepe suits. Delicate heels skinned in
various reptile patterns click carefully across the marble.
These are the people who get to gamble with the econo-
mies of nations. Fortunately Lander's not among them at
the moment.

The receptionist at the front desk looks up from her
computer and gives me an apologetic smile. She's an incredibly pretty woman and very well dressed, probably
around my age. She could be a model . . . or a mistress.

I pick up a *Forbes* magazine from the low table,
vaguely thinking about office romances and human re-
sources departments. If HGVB does have restrictions in
that area, would the rules apply to people who have the
Gable last name? Probably not.

An elevator opens again, making me jump, but he's
not there.

Has Lander ever slept with one of the girls in this
office?

"Mr. Travis Gable will see you now," the receptionist
says, interrupting my thoughts.

I get to my feet so fast it leaves me a little dizzy, but I
don't let it slow me down as I follow close on the heels of
the receptionist, who is leading me down a hall, away
from the elevators. She reaches for a door, but I beat her
to the punch and swing it open myself, quickly stepping

out of the hall and into the privacy of Travis's office.

Lander's brother is sitting at his desk, talking on the phone, sounding important, possibly for effect. He waves me in without looking up from the papers spread out before him. The suit he's wearing today is a little nicer than the one he wore on Friday, and his hair is combed a little more carefully. There's a faint hint of cologne. Whoever he's trying to impress is no mere client.

The receptionist hesitates only a moment before stepping out. I let out a quiet sigh of relief as I hear the door close, effectively hiding me from anyone in the hall.

Travis also reacts to the sound, looking up from his desk for the first time. His eyes immediately focus on me, and he lets them wander over my figure.

He's wearing the expression I used to fantasize Lander would have right before I stabbed him with a corkscrew.

"Dave, I gotta go. But I expect you to handle this thing quickly. Understood?" He hangs up the phone before the person on the other end could possibly have had a chance to answer. "You're looking good, Bell," he says. "You'll represent me well."

"Thank you, Mr. Gable."

I wait for him to offer me a seat.

He doesn't.

"I have something that needs to be hand delivered to Brooklyn."

He reaches under his desk and pulls out a rather distinctive crocodile skin briefcase. From it he takes out a small but fat manila envelope that drops onto the desk. I hesitate for just a moment before picking it up.

"Open it," he instructs.

I do, carefully peeking inside . . .

It's filled with money. All in twenties and hundreds.

"Count it."

I flip through the bills: $40, $60, $80, $100, $200, $300 . . .

"There's twenty-five hundred dollars in here," I say when I'm done.

Travis smiles, puts the briefcase away, and crosses his arms over his chest. "Discretion will be necessary."

The comment makes me look up sharply from the envelope. I study his face, but it's completely unreadable.

Twenty-five hundred dollars. It's not a lot of money for Travis—basically enough to buy his wife, Jessica, half a handbag. But it's still a lot to carry around in cash.

"Where exactly shall I deliver this?" I ask, trying to keep my voice matter-of-fact.

He pulls out a piece of notepaper and writes down an address before sliding it over to me. "It's an apartment building. There will be a man who answers to the nickname L.J. You'll give him the money and he'll give you a package to bring back here. Do not under any circumstances open the package."

My heart is pounding against my chest so hard I'm sure Travis can hear it. It can't be this easy, can it? Can he really be on the verge of revealing some felonious secret that I can use against him?

I *so* want to believe that . . . but . . . why would he give a veritable stranger that kind of power? It doesn't make any sense. So if he isn't giving me the tools to take him down, then it's possible I'm being tested.

Or maybe it's worse than that.

I know her identity.

The things Lander had accused me of—they had been stupid, banal things, all easy for me to spin and explain. But what if he really *does* know my identity and he's the one misleading me . . . again?

If so, did he share that information with his brother?

And if he did *that* . . . is this the beginning of some kind of setup?

My hands are shaking, but I hide it by busying myself with making space for the envelope in my purse.

Of course I could just hand the envelope back to Travis . . . and lose my job. And then my whole plan falls apart.

I steel myself and zip up my purse. "Shall I go now?"

"You don't have any other questions?"

I meet his eyes, hold his gaze. He looks so much like his brother . . . but he's so very different.

"No," I finally answer. "You've told me all you want to tell me. My job is to do what's asked of me."

When he doesn't respond, the room dives into silence. I can feel the chill of the air conditioner. With Lander I'm constantly having to remind myself that he's the bad guy, but with Travis no reminder is necessary . . . and I can't even put my finger on why that is. Is it simply because Travis is mean to his wife? I *hate* his wife. So what do I care how he treats her?

Although how he treats her highlights the fundamental truth about his nature. Travis is very successful and he's reportedly very smart.

But underneath the money and the intellect, he's just a bully . . .

. . . a bully who might be setting me up just like he and his family set up my mom. If he's figured out who I am and what I'm trying to do . . . well, that would be motive enough.

The money is probably only adding a few ounces to my purse, but its significance is heavy enough to make my shoulder ache.

I think back to the blood on my mother's clothes the night she was taken away from me. I'd give anything to go back in time and stop her from walking into Nick Foley's house.

I wish I had never seen that blood. Or, at the very least, it would have been better if the blood that stained my mom's pink shirt was the blood of a man who actually deserved to die.

The envelope is so damn heavy.

"When you've completed this errand you'll come right back here."

I nod, step backward. "I'll see you a little later then, Mr. Gable."

"Till then," he says and turns his attention back to the papers on his desk. He's done with me. I'm dismissed.

I feel unsteady as I walk down the hall, past the receptionist, and toward the elevators.

My mind is still awash with memories of my mother crying, memories of the blood. I've spent years turning my mind and body into a weapon in order to seek justice through cleaner means.

Despite my earlier willingness to act, thinking about my mother's ordeal also makes me never want to see that kind of violence up close again.

But if Travis is setting me up . . . if violence is the only option left for me . . . isn't it worth it? That's always been my plan B, and isn't that fair? Wouldn't that at least *resemble* justice?

I get on the elevator thinking about Lander, and then Mercedes, Travis's daughter. Mercedes, who is still innocent and who still seems to love her parents.

The elevator door opens after descending two floors, letting in strangers, just random employees of this dreaded bank. They don't acknowledge me as they press the button for the lobby.

I nervously rub my left thumb over my right palm. After a moment I realize that I once saw my mother make this same jittery motion after she found Nick. She was trying to scrub his blood off her hands.

And Lady Macbeth had scrubbed her guilt-ridden hands and asked: "Yet who would have thought the old man to have had so much blood in him?"

It's a quote from one of Lander's favorite plays, one that resonates with me. I switch my purse to my other shoulder, hoping to balance the weight. I've daydreamed about hurting the Gables for so long . . . but if I literally end up with their blood on my hands, how will that affect me? When it comes down to it, how far am I willing to go? Could I actually shoot Travis? Could I watch him die?

More people come into the elevator. I press myself against the wall to make room. The elevator slides down to another floor and then another. One of the men leans over and whispers something into the ear of a female colleague, who barks with laughter. The soft and loud sounds only serve to make the space feel tighter. Feeling claustrophobic, I think about the last time I laughed. It was with Lander, the brother of the man I'm thinking about killing.

The elevator reaches the lobby and everyone swarms out, moving in one direction like so many salmon.

I wipe my guilt-ridden hands on my skirt and follow them out, my purse adding weight to every step I take.

chapter seventeen

I catch a cab to Brooklyn rather than take the subway. No need to make this process longer or more dangerous than it needs to be. Still, I have the cabbie drop me off a block from my destination . . . just in case.

The address is on the outskirts of Brooklyn Heights, and as I close the cab door and listen to it drive away, I assess the street. It's nice. Nothing to fear here but conformity and Chihuahuas.

And yet it's not far from where Nick Foley was killed, in his three-story town house with a pretty view and expensive furnishings. The security systems, the prestige, the money—none of it had kept out the bloodshed.

I glance around the area again. There are a handful of pedestrians, lots of yellow cabs and town cars flying by. Two are double-parked, probably waiting for their fares to pay them.

Walking toward the address, I wish I had worn different shoes. These high heels limit my speed and agility. Studying the addresses as I proceed down the block, I spot the one Travis wrote down. It's a small apartment complex with a bank of individual buzzers by the front door. I reach out to press the one that corresponds to the apartment I'm meant to visit. But then, before I can actually press the button, I stop. Something's amiss, I can sense it . . .

Someone is watching me.

I step back, look both ways. A woman with a designer bag and a screaming child in tow marches past me without a glance. Across the street there's a couple strolling easily, holding hands. Farther down a man almost runs into a lamppost as he tries to walk and text at the same time. No one seems to notice me . . .

. . . but I could have *sworn.*

My hand goes into my bag and I feel the outlines of the envelope. I could leave right now. Call it a day.

And then I would have to walk away from the whole game. And after all I've done to get here, if I do that, I deserve to be set up. If I do *that,* I'm the one who deserves to die.

I press the button next to the number: 555.

"Yeah." It's a male voice, heavy with a Brooklyn accent, not exactly the norm here, in Brooklyn Heights.

"Hello, is this L.J.?"

"Yeah, what of it?"

"Travis Gable sent me."

There's a grumbling and then the sound of a buzzer as I'm let in.

Yeah, what of it? I consider the phrase as I take the tiny elevator to the fifth floor. It's cliché tough-guy talk. So cliché I've never actually heard anyone who isn't in a movie say it. When the doors open, I see a man dressed in ripped jeans and a T-shirt featuring a rapper who was popular about a decade ago. The man's eyes are moving left and right as if he's checking for unwanted company.

It's suspicious . . . in a cartoonish kind of way. All he's missing is a puffy jacket and a gold tooth.

"You have something for me?" he asks, his eyes again darting up and down the empty hall.

"Yes." I start to reach into my bag but he stops me and steps backward, opening the door to the apartment behind him.

"In here," he instructs.

I don't move. Looking through the doorway, I can tell the space beyond is in mild disarray. Boxes are stacked up against the wall. The only furniture is a beat-up couch and a crate serving as a coffee table. On a built-in kitchen counter is an old pizza box, a few used paper plates, plastic cups, and a scale.

As far as I can tell there's no one else in there, which means I'll be alone with this man.

"Are you coming in or what?" L.J. snaps.

I take a deep breath. "Can't you just give me the package here?"

His eyes light with condescension and disgust. "You scared, little girl? You think I might bite?"

"I just think—"

"You do look like you're worth a nibble," L.J. interrupts, laughing at his own joke. "But I don't got time for that shit. Just get your hot ass in here so we can get it done."

I still don't move. It's as if my feet are tethered to the floor.

"Fine." L.J. shakes his head. "You go tell Travis that you were too scared to do what you been told."

He turns to walk in himself, but my hand automatically shoots out and grabs his arm to stop him. "No, of course I'll come in."

Stepping past him into the stifling room, I think about my gun sitting uselessly in my desk, neglected and aching to justify its existence. I clench and unclench my fist, thinking about the comfort that weapon could provide.

L.J. comes up behind me, presses himself into me. His hand moves up to massage my breast. "Is there anything you wouldn't do if Travis asked?" he grumbles, his breath hot against my neck.

In a flash of movement, I jab my elbow into his solar plexus and demurely step away as he falls to his knees.

"So, do you have a package for me, L.J.?" I ask calmly as he gasps for air. "Or am I going to have to tell Mr. Gable that you failed him?"

He raises his hand, silently requesting that I wait while he struggles to regain the ability to speak.

I step around him so I can peruse the room. Pieces of foam peanuts can be found tucked in random corners and under the sparse furnishings. The boxes that aren't sealed are already halfway full. I wonder if L.J. is moving up or down in the world. I turn back to look at him, and he's on one knee now as he struggles to get to his feet. This is not a man who has ever called the shots.

"All right," he says, and coughs as he drags himself up. "You got the money?"

I take the envelope out of my purse and hold it up.

He nods and moves behind the counter, where he pulls out a brown paper bag. "I'm gonna need you to see this measured out."

"No, I don't want to see what's in the bag."

L.J. looks up sharply. "Listen, bitch," he says, his voice still raspy. "If you think I'm going to let you leave without you and me agreeing on what it is you're buying, you're out of your fucking mind."

I look away but it's too late. From the paper bag, L.J. takes out a large plastic bag of white powder and puts it on the scale.

I also see that L.J. is regaining his strength too rapidly.

He walks across the room and grabs my arm, yanking me toward what I can now see is cocaine. "Look, can we both agree that we got a clean ounce here?" He gestures to the scale.

"Yes," I hiss, and he throws me aside so I have to balance myself on the counter to keep from falling. I watch as he puts the merchandise in question back into the paper bag.

"The money?"

I put the stack down on the counter and he snaps it up. He counts out the bills silently, his face red with discomfort and embarrassment.

"Grab it and go," he says once he's done.

I hesitate only a moment before gingerly taking the paper bag.

"Tell Travis that if he's going to send you here again you better be ready to make up for that little elbow move. I mean I'm gonna expect you bare-assed and ready to bend over my knee for a little *corporal* punishment. You tell Travis that, got it, baby?"

"Got it," I say distractedly as I put the bag into my

purse. "You want Travis to force me to let you touch me because you're not enough of a man to get laid without his help. I'll be sure to tell him." Not waiting for his response, I stride out of the room and head straight to the elevator. When it finally arrives, I enter and lean against its wall as the door closes.

I know getting caught with narcotics is never a good thing. After all, I got this job by setting up Travis's last personal assistant for drug possession. Perhaps Travis knows that. Maybe he believes in poetic justice.

But when I set up the assistant it was only with a very small amount of meth—a misdemeanor. But this is *not* a small amount of cocaine. In fact, there's so much cocaine in this bag it wouldn't be unreasonable to accuse me of dealing, not buying.

The elevator opens and I glance around, checking to make sure that there are no police waiting to haul me in. But the lobby's empty, so I quickly exit to the street.

There aren't quite as many pedestrians around now. I make some quick calculations as I walk. In New York, carrying this much cocaine is considered possession in the third degree. I could serve up to nine years in prison, and even if I didn't, *any* felony drug conviction means I will no longer be eligible for welfare or public housing or any of the other things I'll need when employers start rejecting my job applications due to my felony record.

I walk a block, then two, wanting to get as far away

from that building as possible before hailing a cab. I try not to appear conspicuous, refusing to look over my shoulder even though I'm still haunted by the feeling of being watched.

Maybe this is a legitimate errand . . . Well, not *legitimate*, socially speaking, but maybe it's what it seems to be on the face of things. Maybe Travis actually uses cocaine. Or . . . well, okay, maybe he and fifty friends use this much. Or it's possible that he's trading the coke for some kind of favor. If either of those scenarios is true, he's just handed me the fuel I need to put my plan into overdrive. With a few added creative flourishes I'll be able to take him and the rest of his family down within a week . . . two weeks tops.

But Travis just doesn't strike me as the user type . . . *at all*. And while I can see him loading his wife up on Zoloft and Ambien, I can't imagine him giving her cocaine. The last thing that man wants is a hyped-up wife with chemically induced narcissism.

I hail a cab, and as I slide into the backseat I finally allow myself to look back for the first time. Everything seems normal. A few scattered pedestrians, a few cabs . . . not a cop in sight.

I tell the cabbie to take me to HGVB Bank and then shut down his attempts to strike up a conversation as he starts our journey out of Brooklyn.

Clenching my teeth, I open my purse and peek inside. I run my fingers over the brown bag without taking it out and think about something Lander told me over a recent dinner, something about the bullies in his world:

"There are plenty of those, and they all look and dress like me . . . Many of them are so subtle in their aggression that you don't know you're a target until you're already down for the count."

So if that's true, what's Travis playing at? Am I a target or does he take me for an ally? Or perhaps something in between?

God, there are so many possibilities, I can't keep them straight.

I stare out the window, watching as New York rushes past me, from the Brooklyn Bridge to the more industrial areas to the coldly sophisticated architecture of the Upper East Side.

The taxi pulls up in front of the HGVB Bank building. The meter flashes the fare.

I'm about to walk into a major American bank with a bag full of cocaine.

I pull out my phone and find the voice recording app I've recently downloaded. I'm not sure if recording the impending conversation with Travis will help or hurt, but I want to be ready, just in case.

As I get out of the cab, walk into the lobby, and pass

the security guards, I find myself wondering exactly how this fucked-up day will end.

Travis has a cup of coffee in one hand while the other lazily pecks away at his computer. By his bemused, somewhat bored expression, you'd think he was flipping through the blog pages of *OMG!* rather than uncovering new ways to manipulate the world's economy.

"You have something for me?" he asks in lieu of a greeting.

Without a word I pull the brown sack out of my purse and put it on his desk. I'd like to turn around and see if there's a cop there, an undercover officer ready to kick my plan into a violent new direction.

But I keep my eyes on Travis. Again I remind myself of my poker metaphor: I can't see Travis's hand, but I know how to bluff.

Travis picks up the bag. "Did you look inside?"

"Your guy took it out of the paper bag before I could stop him."

"Hmm, I'll have to give him a call and talk to him about that," he says distractedly as he pulls out the plastic bag filled with white powder. With slow, lazy fingers he feels the edge of the Ziploc, but then his fingers stop . . .

I watch as his fingers now follow the path of a strand

of hair caught—or more likely, placed—in the bag, which I failed to notice earlier. It's longer than L.J.'s, but even from where I'm standing I can see it's a different color from mine.

Again he looks up at me, and the hard line of his mouth softens a little. It even turns up at the edges into something that might, in dim lighting, be mistaken for a smile.

"You didn't open the bag."

I shake my head. "Will there be anything else, Mr. Gable?"

He responds by raising his eyebrows . . . again, looking a little too much like his brother. For some reason their resemblance disturbs me.

He opens the bag and holds it out to me, as if in offering.

"Taste it. See if it's any good."

Goose bumps are rising all over my skin but I keep my expression calm. "I told you, Mr. Gable, I don't do drugs. I wouldn't be able to tell good from bad."

"Have a little faith in yourself, Bell." He stands up, walks around the desk, holds his offering no more than a foot away from me. "Just one taste. I want to know what you think."

This is feeling more and more like a setup. I bought the cocaine and now he wants to get it in my system. Of course a little taste won't be enough to do anything to me. I should know; I've tasted it before. I'd like not to ever taste it again.

"I'd rather not," I say quietly, hoping that he might be moved by meekness.

"I'd rather you did, Bell."

I smile and zip up my purse, being careful to leave it open just enough as I press the record button on my phone.

"I don't do cocaine," I say again. "But if you're telling me that trying this is a requirement of my job . . ." I let my voice trail off, waiting to see if he'll actually walk straight into such an obvious trap.

"That's not a bad way to look at it." He licks the tip of his index finger like a stamp and then dips it into the bag. Once it's coated in white powder he holds it up to my lips.

This is becoming less and less appealing by the second. "Since you insist, Mr. Gable." I step forward and with seductive finesse wrap my lips around his finger, letting my tongue absorb the powder . . .

. . . and then I gag and jump back, sticking my tongue out as if that will take the bitter taste away.

"What the hell is that?"

Travis cocks his head and stares at me with mock concern. "What, you've never tasted crushed-up Tylenol before?"

I lick the back of my hand like a cat, trying to wipe

the taste away. "Tylenol? You had me buy twenty-five hundred dollars' worth of Tylenol?"

Again he laughs, and he drops the plastic bag into the wastebasket.

"You didn't think I would send one of my employees out to buy *illegal drugs*, did you?"

I shrug and cast a longing look at the bottle of water on his desk.

"I would never do something like that. You really thought you were buying cocaine? You were willing to do that without offering a single moment of protest? Do you really think so little of the law?"

"Your instructions are not for me to question, Mr. Gable," I say quietly.

Travis smiles, leans back against the edge of his desk. "You didn't run off with that envelope full of money," he notes. "You gave it to L.J. You didn't call the police. You didn't run off and try to snort that stuff yourself, and you didn't throw it in a Dumpster like some scared little rabbit. No, you did exactly what you were told, without question, without hesitation, without fanfare. Do you know what that means, Bell?"

That I'm an idiot? A submissive? But I keep the thoughts to myself and simply shake my head.

"It means," Travis says, drawing out the words, "that I can trust you."

My lips curve up into a Mona Lisa smile. "And *that*,"

I say softly, "truly means the world to me, Mr. Gable."

Travis grins and looks up at the ceiling as if he'll find his next move there. "Your résumé says you speak Spanish fluently. Is that true?"

"*Sí.*"

Travis chuckles as if I've made a joke. "*Sí*, that's good. Tomorrow at eight I would like you to come to a meeting with me, off the premises, with one of our prospective clients. Since he is a *prospective* client I would like to keep the meeting confidential. No need to broadcast news before it's been made."

"Shall I meet you here?"

"No, be at my home. I'll get you when I'm done here. Just be sure Jessica doesn't send you out on any useless errands during that time." He pauses a moment before adding, "How *is* my wife, by the way?"

"She's . . . sad, Mr. Gable."

"Sad. Now, that's interesting." Again he chuckles. "I've given her everything any woman could ask for and yet she's sad."

"If I remember correctly, you told her those gifts were simply on loan . . . or leased . . . I believe the words you used were 'on lease.'"

"It's still a good deal. She gets my name, one of the best penthouses in Manhattan, all the Botox and Juvéderm money can buy, a wardrobe that would make any supermodel jealous. I already got two kids out of her, so I won't ask her for more. I paid for the mommy-job plastic-surgery session. She has access to drivers, maids, chefs . . . She's never even had to dust a picture frame."

"It's a privileged life," I agree.

"Yes, and all she has to do is lie on her back for me every once in a while, and not very often at that. Fucking her these days is a little too much like necrophilia for my tastes."

Yes, because in so many ways your wife is already dead. You've been killing her for years.

"*You* would be grateful, wouldn't you, Bell?"

The question is loaded.

There's a line to walk here. I can't fight Travis with the easy insults and brutality that I used on L.J., and, considering my goals, a little flirtation and seduction are fine . . . But I don't want to sleep with this man. It shouldn't be necessary. In fact, if he is in pursuit rather than satisfied, he'll be easier to manipulate.

Sleeping with Lander was a prerequisite to getting into his home. And now I've managed to convince Lander to hide his relationship with me from his brother, a detail that will be very useful in the days and weeks to come.

Plus, with Lander the act is not . . . unenjoyable.

But being with Travis?

I shift my eyes to the window, hoping to push out the image of him laboring on top of me. The brothers look so much alike, but while Lander makes me want to throw him on the bed, Travis makes me want to throw him down a flight of stairs.

"If I were Jessica, I would be very grateful," I say carefully. "She's an incredibly lucky woman."

"Luck has nothing to do with it. She earned her place . . . just as you'll earn yours."

He steps forward, lets his hand brush against my hip. "I'm a very generous man . . . or at least I can be when people do what I want them to do."

I slide my eyes back to him. "And when they don't?"

His hand moves to my ass. "Things go badly for them. But we don't have to worry about that, do we, Bell? You've proven yourself to be very . . . obedient."

I open my mouth to respond before I know exactly what I'm going to say—

The intercom buzzes then. "Mr. Gable?" It's the voice of the receptionist. "Your father wants you to bring— wait, I have it here—the Ramirez report to his office right now. He wants the hard copy, he doesn't want you to email it."

"Your father works here?" I blurt out. "In the New York office?"

Travis glares at the intercom. "He usually works in

London, but he's back for a few weeks." He jams his finger against the intercom. "Tell him I will be there in a few minutes."

"He wants to see you now, sir." The receptionist sounds almost chastising.

Travis snatches up the phone but then seems to think better of it and slams it down again.

"Wait here," he growls before striding past me and leaving me alone in his office.

For a second I don't move. Edmund Gable is the only Gable I've actually spoken to before all this. I was ten, but still there's always the chance he'll recognize me.

He was supposed to be in London!

I close my eyes and count to ten. I need to stay calm. Travis went to his father's office. That means that I should be safe in here. I need to stave off the panic and think.

I open my eyes again.

"Think!" I whisper to myself. "What's the smart thing to do right now?"

I look around the room, smile to myself . . . and then I walk around to his computer and get to work.

chapter eighteen

It was just yesterday that I set up a dummy email account for Jessica. As soon as I can break Lander's password, I'll give him one too, but so far the code that will earn me entry into his virtual world has eluded me. Favorite sports teams and birthdates have yielded nothing but glaring error messages. But given time I'll work it out.

And with Travis, all I have to do is use his email account that I can access with this computer to email Jessica's new account. I'm starting a paper trail. She'll never read it. She barely reads the emails sent to the accounts she knows about. My fingers fly across the keyboard as my eyes keep darting toward the door. Once done I sit back and read my work:

Jessica,
Please be a little more careful with the

information you share about my dealings,
particularly with Lander. You know what I've
gotten away with in the past. Think what I could
get away with doing to you.

—Travis

It's a good note. Vague enough for me to fill in the
blanks once I get a few insights about whatever rules and
laws Travis is actually breaking. A little truth, a little fiction. It's a magical combination that allows opinions and
verdicts to be shaped and manipulated. Creating fiction
is easy. Finding incriminating truths, well, that just takes
time.

I press send and then quickly go to his sent mail
folder and erase the message.

I'm removing my visit to Travis's email account from
his computer history when I hear his voice in the hall.
Quickly, I bring everything on his computer screen back
to how I found it and rush to the other side of the
desk—knocking over his Fiji water bottle in the process.

I start to bend to reach for it but then I hear Travis
right outside the door. The doorknob turns and I immediately take a seat in front of his desk, only to immediately pop back up and greet him as the door swings
open.

As Travis enters, I can see that his leering smile has
been replaced with a nervous one.

And right behind him is Edmund Gable. Tall, slim, wearing a gray pin-striped Kiton suit and an effervescent smile, he manages to look ten to fifteen years younger than his age despite his shock of white hair. The lines across his forehead are faint from lack of worry. He gives his son a jovial pat on the back as he walks past him.

With what I hope is a subtle movement I reach for the back of my chair. I need the support to help stabilize me as my stomach drops and acidic bile burns my throat.

Edmund smiles brightly at me. You'd think he was the nicest man in the world.

"Ah, you must be Jessica and Travis's new personal assistant!" He offers me his hand. "You'll have to forgive me, but Travis didn't give me your name."

I place my hand against his. It's unlikely he'll remember me. He hasn't seen me in more than ten years. I was a child. Actually I had been less than that. I had been nothing more than a pawn, almost impossible to distinguish from any of the other dispensable pieces on his chessboard. On the face of it, the circumstances that led to our meeting back then couldn't have been more benign . . .

He had called my mother personally, asking if he could hire her to clean his two-story penthouse. He said Nick

Foley had referred him. That Nick had given him her number.

But it was a lie.

"Bell Dantès." I say the words carefully. I can't afford for any of my venom to carelessly spill out now.

"What a lovely name . . . appropriate for such a lovely woman." His grip is firm . . . a little too firm. My fingers tingle as he releases me. "I'm Edmund Gable, Travis's father."

I see Travis shift uncomfortably as he stands toward the back of the room as if waiting for his father to give him permission to make himself comfortable in his own office.

"So tell me, Bell," Edmund says, "are my son and daughter-in-law treating you well?"

"They've been wonderful, sir."

My mother had brought me to Edmund's house. She had nowhere else to leave me, but Edmund had been very understanding. He had video games left over from when Lander and Travis used to play. He let me occupy myself with that while he asked my mother to chat with him in the kitchen about the job.

* * *

"My father has taught me the importance of being a generous and respectful employer," Travis says as he holds his place by the door. He's wearing a smile, but it's strained, and his posture has grown rigid, as if he's a soldier awaiting inspection.

I remember playing Resident Evil for about fifteen minutes while my mother spoke with Edmund downstairs. But the game wasn't my thing. I was into Disney fantasies back then, not Japanese-style horror. Plus, it occurred to me that Edmund and my mother had been talking for a very long time. How long did it take to ask a woman to vacuum? I had taken my shoes off, so they didn't hear me approaching the kitchen, but I heard them . . . They were talking about Nick.

"Let me get that file for you, Dad," Travis says as he finally moves from his spot and quickly goes to his desk.

"No rush, Travis." Edmund takes a small step forward, his voice getting a little louder. I glance down at the water bottle lying on the floor next to the desk, but Travis doesn't seem to notice it. He pulls a key from an inside pocket of his suit and unlocks the bottom drawer of his desk. As he pulls out another fat manila envelope, I glance back at Edmund, my palms sweating, my mind drowning in memory.

"He loves you, *I'm sure of it," Edmund had said to my mother. "You need to fight for him. Do it publicly and do it aggressively. Confront his wife, let her know you won't allow her or anyone else to take him away from you. Let it be known that Nick is yours and that crossing you in this matter would not be wise. Trust me, it's the only thing she'll understand and it's the only way Nick will be able to grasp how strongly you feel about him. True love is always worth a battle."*

Beside me, Edmund crosses his arms over his chest, his smile fading slightly as he watches Travis close the drawer but neglect to lock it.

For a while *the things Edmund said to my mother hadn't meant much to me . . . It took years before I was able to look back at that moment and realize that Edmund had been planting the seeds of my mother's self-destruction. He wanted her to make scenes. He wanted her to appear to be obsessive, unwilling to take no for an answer. He wanted everyone to see my mom as a poor man's Glenn Close, ready to boil her lover's rabbit. It made it that much easier to set her up.*

It worked.

And now my mom's dead.

Travis holds out the envelope for his father, who is now barely smiling at all. Travis notes this and swallows hard before walking around the desk and putting the envelope in Edmund's hand.

"Thank you, Travis." His tone is just slightly cooler. But then, in an instant, the smile is back, not quite as bright but certainly containing a practiced warmth. "Well, I'll be going then." He turns back to me. "Have we met before, Bell? You look . . . familiar."

My heart slams to a stop and my eyes sting as I struggle to keep them focused. "I don't believe so, sir."

"Are you sure? I'm usually right about these things."

I shake my head and smile apologetically. "I'm quite sure we haven't. I would remember."

He laughs. "Oh, don't be so sure. Without the suit I look like your run-of-the-mill senior citizen. You know what they say: clothes make the man. In any case, it was good meeting you."

He turns and walks to the door, leaving Travis behind without another word.

I glance at Travis, who seems lost in thought as he studies the door his father just exited through. His silence gives me the time I need to collect myself. So far his father hasn't placed me. He may never place me . . . or if he does, hopefully it will be too late for him to do anything about it. I clasp my hands behind my back to keep them from shaking. Focus and calm, that's all that's called for. I take a quiet breath and will my heart to resume a regular pace.

"Your father's quite a . . . presence."

"He is that." Travis leans back on his heels and stares at the door. "HGVB is . . . I suppose it's as close to a family business as an international bank can get. All the Gable men work here. Me, my father, and, of course, my brother."

And there's the opening I've been waiting for.

"Oh yes!" I say enthusiastically. "I know! I assume Lander has talked to you about us by now. It's a small world, isn't it?"

Travis's eyes snap back to me. "Excuse me?"

"Lander . . . He's . . . he has talked to you, right?" I ask, now feigning uncertainty.

"How do you know Lander?" Travis's eyes are narrowing, his jaw growing more rigid.

"Oh no," I whisper, putting my fingers gently to my lips. "I just assumed . . . But I promised . . . Oh, I really screwed up!"

"What are you talking about?"

"He specifically asked me not to say anything, I thought he just wanted to be the one to tell you! Like he was going to make some kind of joke out of it and he didn't want me to spoil the punch line . . . But I was so sure he would tell you by now . . ."

"What the fuck are you talking about?"

His words cutting the air, Travis seems startled by his own outburst. I, on the other hand, can take it in stride. But perhaps that's because this is the reaction I was actually trying to provoke.

"I'm . . ." I hesitate, bite down on my fingernails like a scared little girl. "I'm dating your brother, Mr. Gable. I thought he was going to tell you. He *asked* me to let him be the one to tell you. He said he was going to do it right away or I would have told you myself. I swear, when I met him I didn't even know he was your brother. It was all a total coincidence."

"A coincidence," Travis repeats. He turns away from me and walks to the window.

"Yes, I mean . . . it sort of was. I met him on the elevator of your building right after our interview. He asked me if I lived there and I told him I had just been hired to be a personal assistant to the couple in 1400. He didn't tell me his last name right away. I think he was afraid that if I knew he was the brother of my boss I'd be scared off . . . and I suppose I would have been. He took me out for dinner and drinks and . . . well, by the time he did tell me who he was—"

"What?" Travis snaps. "You had already slept with him by then?"

I don't answer right away. Travis still has his back to me as he glares down at the lesser skyscrapers beneath us.

"He—he—" I stutter. "He told me you would be okay with it. He promised me that this wasn't the kind of thing that would upset you at all. He said I should just let him handle it and it would all be fine. He . . . he promised me, Mr. Gable." Travis turns just as I dramatically slump into a chair. "Please, Mr. Gable, I honestly didn't mean to keep anything from you. I . . . Oh, God, I can't believe how badly I screwed this whole thing up. I mean, on the one hand I promised him I would let him tell you—and I'm so good at keeping confidences, I swear I am—but if I had known that he was going to keep it from you for this long . . . I mean we've seen each other three times in four days . . . I thought for sure . . . And if I had suspected for a moment that he *wasn't* going to tell you, then I would have not only let you know but I would have also broken it off with him! I mean, I've only been seeing him for about a week now and you're my *employer*! Obviously my loyalty lies with you!"

I'm rambling . . . by design. Let him think I'm flustered.

Let him think he can manipulate me.

Let him think that his brother already has.

"I. Don't. Understand." Travis pronounces each word separately, as if they aren't connected in a sentence. Almost as if he's creating one of Lander's anagrams. "Why would he keep this from me?"

I shake my head, dab my eyes with my sleeve.

"What do you two talk about?" he asks.

"Excuse me?"

Travis just looks at me, refusing to repeat the question. I shrink back into the chair and shake my head.

"We talk about all sorts of things," I say. "Politics, food, history, and pop culture . . . And work, of course. He's had a lot of questions about my work for you and Jessica, but I suppose that's to be expected."

"You've only worked a day and a half for us."

"True . . . He wanted to know all about the interview. He had lots of questions about my first day with Jessica. He was really interested to find out what my first day would be like working with you, asking if I would be helping you with bank-related business, or if you would be meeting with any clients or investors during the day, and if you would meet with them on-site or not. He was just intensely curious. Of course I certainly won't tell him any of that and I absolutely won't tell him about today's errand. I doubt he'd believe it anyway," I say with a nervous laugh.

"No," Travis says, his voice completely cold. "You won't tell him about that." He then shakes his head, absorbing. "I knew something was up with him. He's been too nice of late. Too accommodating."

"Well . . . he *is* your brother. Is it really so strange that he would want to accommodate you?"

"You don't know Lander," he snaps. "You may know who he is in the bedroom, but there's not a soul on earth who knows what's going on inside his head. Although I'm beginning to suspect . . ."

His voice trails off, and his eyes glaze over as his thoughts move outside the room to wherever Lander is.

"Suspect what?" I ask softly, wanting to share in his mental journey.

"I want you to keep seeing him."

I don't say a word.

"Yes," Travis continues, "don't let him know there's a problem at all—"

"You ask too much."

Travis stops short and stares at me with dawning surprise.

"I bought what I thought were drugs for you. I even tasted them, although I didn't want to. It's not for me to judge what your recreational activities are. And if you want me to stop seeing your brother I'd understand. I can see why that might interfere with our professional relationship. But you can't tell me who I should sleep with, or *continue* to sleep with. I choose my lovers; no one chooses them for me." I take a deep breath before adding, rather dramatically, "I'm a lot of things, Mr. Gable, but I'm not a whore."

"I didn't say—"

"It was implied."

Travis studies me, trying to find a way to cajole me to do the very thing I already have every intention of doing. But he doesn't know that. It's essential that this always feels like the setup is completely his idea.

"Lander told me that he was going to talk to you," I continue. "He misled me at best and lied to me at worst. Why would I want to continue to see someone like that? I've only gone out with him a few times. He's a passing fancy . . . it's not like it's love."

"There is no such thing as love," Travis mutters, almost more to himself than to me.

"I think . . . I think you might be right about that," I say, and they're the first honest words I've ever uttered to Travis. We sit quietly for a minute or two, both of us thinking about all the things that have brought us to that conclusion. It's disconcerting to realize that perhaps Travis has been hardened and molded by circumstance rather than by nature. If so . . . what if *this* is the brother I have the most in common with? Was Travis ever kind?

Hopeful? Is there a part of him underneath all that darkness that's good?

Ah well, it doesn't matter now. I don't have time to analyze the thoughts and feelings of the enemy soldier.

"If you and I—" I break off, immediately regretting the initial framing of my argument. With an embarrassed smile I start again. "If it's true that there is no such thing as true love, then that's just all the more reason not to keep around a man who would be dishonest with me. There are other men who are just as pretty as he is. Men who won't complicate my professional life."

It almost makes me laugh to listen to myself. I'm talking about my "professional life" as if I'm a surgeon or a partner in a law firm, not a personal assistant to a drug addict and her Tylenol-snorting husband. But I do like the way Travis listens to me when I talk about my job this way.

Travis grabs a chair that's against the wall and drags it next to mine, taking a seat beside me. "There's a reason you've spent so much time with Lander over the last few days," he says. "I grew up with the man, I know how fun he can be. I know he can be clever, and his dry sense of humor always keeps everyone laughing at dinner parties. He's a tennis player, but I always thought he should give golf a go. Not because he'd be good at it but because so many people would be eager to hang out with him on the course."

"He is a charmer," I say with a little smile.

"He used that against you." Travis's eyes slide past me as he stares off into space. "He does that sometimes."

"Most men do."

Travis smiles—it's the smile of a fox. "You're a smart woman, Bell. I can see that. You see Lander for what he is. A charmer, a deceiver . . . a *typical* man. So if you're going to be with a man, why *not* be with him for a while? And why not give back a little of what he's given?"

"You're talking about revenge," I say calmly. "But he hasn't hurt me . . . not unless you fire me for this."

"It's not revenge, it's survival," Travis reasons. "Survival is finding ways to use the people who would use you."

"Ah." I smile to myself. I'm fairly sure that Travis thinks everyone on this earth is trying to use him, in which case we're all fair game.

"Enjoy him, Bell. Use him. It's what he planned to do to you, so there's nothing to feel guilty about. You don't have to give anything up and you can gain so much."

"What can I gain?"

Travis smiles, shrugs. "That depends on what secrets you can pry from him." He reaches over and puts his hand on my knee. His touch makes my skin crawl.

"It's just a little game of espionage," he continues. "We could have fun with it."

"A game of espionage," I repeat. "Or, if we employ

your philosophy, this would be a bit like the game of survival."

"Sometimes they're the same thing."

I nod calmly as I feel the spark of excitement. Thanks to Travis's bizarre and rather extreme litmus test, I have already proved my loyalty to him. Now I can prove my usefulness.

It's funny, though, his thinking that I would seek revenge for something so petty as a simple deception. I would never do that. I have a much higher bar.

My phone beeps and I pull it out of my bag to find a text from Lander.

"He knows I'm here," I say out loud to Travis, the surprise in my voice genuine. "He wants me to meet him on the fifth floor, room 552."

"It's a conference room. It should be empty about now." Travis stands up, offers me his hand to help pull me to my feet. "Meet him. See what he wants and call me afterward." Again he smiles . . . Such a wide grin doesn't fit well on his face. It's false, and a little grotesque. "Like I said, we're going to have fun with this, Bell."

"Yes," I say, grinning back, matching him tooth for tooth. "I actually think we will have a lot of fun."

chapter nineteen

Lander is exactly where he said he'd be, room 552. He's leaning against a long table, his arms crossed, his foot tapping impatiently. Yet even in his impatience there's something . . . kind. Yes, there's something kind about him.

Minutes ago I betrayed this man's trust . . .

. . . but then can you betray the trust of a man who doesn't trust you?

"You didn't tell me you were coming here today," he says as I enter the room, quickly closing the door and locking it behind me.

"Travis called me in at the last minute," I explain.

How would Lander react if he knew that I had just made sure that his own brother didn't trust him at all? Would he lash out at me? Would he reach out to Travis in solidarity?

Would he hate me?

"And what did you do for him?" he asks, his voice dripping with the assumption that whatever I did, it wasn't platonic.

"I told you, it's not like that. I work for him, that's all."

"That's not an answer."

"That's because you didn't really ask me a question. It was more of an accusation."

He looks away, muttering something under his breath.

I study his profile. Was there ever a woman who looked at this man who didn't also want to touch him? How unfortunate for him that he gave that permission to me.

If I needed to justify my recent actions beyond the parameters of revenge, I could point to the fact that Travis really *shouldn't* trust Lander any more than Lander should trust him. All I'm doing is pulling on a string that has already begun to unravel.

When Justice calls the brothers' names and their lies are laid bare for all to see, they'll have no one to blame but themselves.

So why do I feel guilty?

"How did you know I was here?" I ask quietly.

"I was told that Travis was meeting with his personal assistant," he says, before adding with a bit more acidity, "a meeting that 'couldn't be interrupted.'"

Funny, I think, *your father obviously wasn't given that same message,* but I keep that observation to myself.

"I get why you're upset," I continue. "You still don't know me very well, but you *do* know your brother and . . . well, I can see why you're suspicious of his intentions."

"What do you mean?" Lander asks sharply.

I pause for a moment, suddenly a bit off-balance. I had planned this exchange. I had been prepared to lie to him by telling him that his brother was lecherous and generally up to no good. But the thing is, Travis has made lying unnecessary. Not only is he awful, manipulative, and sexually aggressive, but he's also crazy. Any man who would send me out to buy Tylenol disguised as cocaine has to be seriously whacked in the head.

So Travis has turned my lies into facts . . . now I just have to decide which facts are the most useful.

"Your brother is . . . a bit aggressive," I say slowly. "He's made it pretty clear that he wants me. Lots of innuendo and all that. But I told him . . . I told him that while I wanted to work for him, I wouldn't be his whore."

Lander's jaw tightens, making him look all the more like his brother. "What did he do?"

"Like I said, it was just some innuendo, a few *accidental* brushes of his hand." I use my fingers to make quotation marks around the word *accidental.* "But he heard me, Lander. It's been dealt with."

"It's sexual harassment and it's illegal."

"What—shall I report him?" I ask with a bemused smile. "Do you think the district attorney of New York City will drop everything if a personal assistant reports that her boss leered at her? Or maybe you'd like me to go to the media? Do you think this is a story for the *New York Times*?"

"It's not funny."

"Last night you practically called me a whore, and now you're offended that some guy thought he had the right to leer at me. I'm sorry, Lander, but yeah, I do think that's kinda funny."

"I didn't call you a whore, I called you—"

"A courtesan," I interrupt with a smile "You're right, I've misquoted you."

"Did you?"

I shake my head and slip my hands around his waist. "Your brother doesn't respect women. Having that so clearly out in the open actually makes things easier. With him I know where I stand and what I have to deal with."

Lander pulls away. "You don't have a problem with being disrespected?"

"If he treated me with respect, I might resent you for asking me to spy on him. As it is, I don't really mind."

Lander doesn't answer. Instead he moves away from me, his eyes on a promotional poster explaining how HGVB's customers should always be treated like family. I can't imagine handing over my money to someone who would cause me as much pain and grief as my family has—with my disappearing father and a mother who consistently partnered up with men who hurt her and all that—but perhaps whoever conceived of the poster had a different life experience.

"As flawed as he is, I want . . ." His voice trails off for a moment as he studies the poster. "I want my brother to be successful and happy. If he's doing anything that might stand in the way of that, I want to be in the position to help him . . . redirect."

I smile, impressed with the skill with which he delivered that fabricated sentiment.

I move up behind him; lifting myself up on my tiptoes I manage to rest my chin on his shoulder. "I'm sorry," I say lightly, "but what you're asking of me? It's not a request inspired by brotherly love."

Lander chuckles. It's the soft sound of acknowledgment. "Why are you doing this? I told you I could get you another job . . ."

"But you don't really want me to take you up on that now." I gently turn him around and lay my hand on his cheek. "Do you?"

Again he doesn't answer.

I move in a little closer. "He's hiding something from you."

"Oh?"

"I got a glimpse of an email he was sending to his father—"

"*Our* father."

"Of course," I say with a placating smile. "Like I said, I only got a glimpse, but it was something about some HGVB client. And your father had written that he agreed it was 'unwise to bring Lander into the loop.'"

Lander gives me a skeptical look.

I shrug and pretend to think about what I read. "Does the name Talebi mean anything to you?"

It's a name I found in the sketchbook Lander uses as a diary. It could be nothing . . . but it's worth testing.

"Talebi," Lander repeats slowly.

Again I shrug. "I could have gotten that wrong . . . but the client's name . . . it was something like that. I really didn't get anything else."

"That's useful," Lander says, his eyes moving past me as new thoughts and ideas flicker through his mind.

"Just promise me you won't let Travis know I gave you that information," I say, taking his hand. "Protect me, Lander."

Lander laughs lightly. "It's like being asked to protect a great white shark."

I give him a wry smile. "Well, we *are* listed as a vulnerable species."

"Yes, vulnerable." Lander glances toward the door as we hear the passing voices of people walking through the hall. "Vulnerable and so misunderstood." His eyes move back to me. "I compared you to Mata Hari."

"Yes, you did."

"But that's not who you are, is it?"

I shake my head, bite my lip. "What finally clued you in?"

"Mata Hari was working for the Germans. But that's not you. You're much more like me."

"Mmm, how so?"

"You're like me in that you're only working for yourself. I don't know why you're spying on Travis for me, but I have a feeling it has more to do with your anger than it does with some desire to please me."

I feel my heart sink into my stomach as I release him and take two steps back.

But his expression is gentle as he reaches out and gently holds my chin, guiding my face toward his. "Does your anger spring from fear? You're scared . . . of what? Are you scared that if you let people get too close they'll hurt you? Or is it that you think you'll hurt them? Tell me, Bell. Have you ever hurt someone you care for? Maybe even someone you love?"

"Stop." The word shoots out of my mouth before I can suppress it. This isn't a turn I want the conversation to take.

His fingers lace through my hair, running through the waves of black. "I suspect you believe that all men are enemies in one way or another." His gaze moves from my eyes to my lips. "That's all right," he says softly. "I'll change your thinking. That's already starting."

"Your ego is unreal."

"It's not about ego. It's about observation. I'm learning you. I'm learning your mind." He kisses my forehead. "And I'm learning your body." He leans in and kisses my neck.

He finds that spot, right at the base near the shoulder, his tongue darting out, sending little shivers down my spine. "You don't have to act tough for me, Bell," he says, whispering the words against my skin.

"I don't have to do anything," I say, my hands going to his shoulders, my fingers digging into the fabric of his jacket. "I don't even have to listen to you."

He picks me up and puts me down on the table. My legs are open as he steps between them, his hand now on the back of my neck as I look up at him.

He nuzzles his face in my hair before moving down to my ear, grazing my earlobe with his teeth.

Gently, I pull his jacket from him, tossing it onto the floor.

"Careful, warrior," he says as his hands move up and down my back. "I have to wear these clothes all day."

I grab his tie and pull him to me, smiling. "Not my problem." I reach down with one hand and let it run over his erection before pulling his belt free and dropping it on top of his jacket.

He raises his eyebrows, pulls my top off, and throws it down. "Now we'll both look guilty. Tell me, when Travis sees your wrinkled clothes, your mussed hair, your smeared lipstick . . . How *will* you explain that to your employer? Will he question you? Will you lie?"

"I won't have to lie," I say as I undo his pants and then yank them down, pausing long enough to allow him to step out of them. "I don't have to explain myself to anyone."

"Oh, but you do." He unfastens my bra. Changing the pace he slowly pulls it down my arms. His fingers dance over my nipples and I feel myself flush as he looks at me. "We all have to explain ourselves, no matter how strong or independent we think we are."

"Do we?" As his fingers continue to toy with me and his tongue tastes my ear, I find myself wriggling in my seat, my words coming out as a staccato whisper.

"Yes." His free hand runs up and down my thigh. "In the end we're all just pieces of a puzzle. Your piece may be more decorative in its imagery than others, but you still have to find a way to fit into the world, just like the rest of us. We all have to make our connections, link our lives to the people and places that fit us best. Otherwise we're nothing more than fragments."

I smile, my guard temporarily slipping. "You're always such a philosopher. Always seeing the world in metaphors." His fingers continue to circle my nipples, making them hard as my breath catches in my throat. I hear more voices in the hall. A lost visitor tries the doorknob before being redirected by a companion to the correct room. "Perhaps we shouldn't do this here," I whisper.

"The door's locked," he reminds me. He takes my skirt and pulls it off me, carefully putting it on an empty folding chair near him.

"But someone might hear us . . . And if they see us walk out together . . ."

"Then they'll be envious." His hand moves between my legs, and his fingers slide under the fabric of my panties. "They'll know I've been inside the most sensual woman in the world."

"I'm not the most . . . " I lose my words as his finger slips inside.

"I'm learning you, Bell," Lander repeats. "I'm learning your rhythms, your moods and tempers."

As his finger continues to explore I feel myself rock against him.

"I know you like risk," he says. "I know that you use the air of mystery you've cultivated as a shield. And I know how to break through that shield now. I know how to make you lose control."

His thumb rises to toy with my clit and he continues to move his finger inside me as I get wetter and wetter. I can hear voices in the hall. I have to press my lips together to keep from adding my groans to the sounds around me. Once again my hands rise to his shoulders, but this time I'm not digging in my nails, I'm simply holding on for support. The day, the odd errand Travis sent me on, seeing Edmund for the first time in years . . . Even with all my planning, it was enough to make me dizzy and unsteady on my feet. But Lander, he's here, he's solid.

And as impossible as it is, it feels like we fit, like . . . like he's the piece of the puzzle I need to reconnect with the world.

While the rest of the time I feel like nothing more than a shard of broken glass. A fragment.

I let myself give in to the sensation of him. The sounds in the hall now are nothing more than background music, adding the beat of excitement to our dance. My head falls onto his shoulder as his fingers continue to move. I feel myself shaking as my body contracts around him, holding him in place, making us whole.

He gently steps away, but only enough to pull down my panties. He lets them drop to the floor.

"Lie down," he instructs. "On your side."

At a seductive, unhurried pace, I pull my knees to my chest before shifting my position and lying down on the conference table, on my side, facing away from him. I feel him climb on top of the table with me, kneeling beside me. I hear laughter in the hall. I feel him stroke my back, then lower. I feel his knee press between my legs and then I feel him pressing against me. I don't say please this time. I don't ask. I just turn my head slightly and smile into his eyes.

When he enters me, as I feel every ridge slide inside me, rubbing against each nerve ending, in that one fleeting moment the puzzle is complete.

"Bell," he whispers, and I extend one of my legs forward, straight in front of me like a dancer preparing to rest her slippered foot on a ballet bar.

But his movement is not so gentle. The table creaks slightly as he thrusts with increasing force, his hands slipping to my hips as he pulls me against him.

Outside I hear a woman call out to a colleague. On

the wall I see more promotional posters for this hated bank. But all I *feel* is Lander.

And he feels perfect.

I throw my head back as the passion continues to build. I feel the orgasm coming and I'm not sure whether I still care if we're caught or not. Everything outside that door is so complicated and messy. This is so simple.

We just fit.

Again he thrusts inside me and I manage to compress my cries into whimpers as he pulls my leg back to him, turning me to face him as he lies down with me so that now my legs are scissored through his. My face is against his as he penetrates even deeper. I cling to him and he continues to move. The whole table shakes with us, and for a moment I wonder about its stability. But then, what would I know about stability?

His lips are on my chin, my cheek, and then my mouth as we continue to rock. I grind against him, circling my hips, raising the intensity for both of us. I feel him tensing as my orgasm overwhelms me. It's the intimacy that does it. It makes me forget about the compounding lies and the schemes.

Here, naked on this table, in an office building with people walking up and down the halls outside, here with my enemy deep inside me . . . here I feel safe.

It's been a very long time since I've felt safe.

The feeling goes to my head, sharpens my passion and lust as I move against him, as he holds me firmly in his hands. I press my mouth against his neck to muffle my cry as he comes in me, filling me, bringing our dance to a graceful close.

For a moment we just continue to lie there, holding each other. For a moment I forget my plans, forget where I am. I forget all the lies.

Until he whispers that one word, "Bellona."

And that's when I open my eyes, release my grip, and pull sheepishly away.

Because that's who he's making love to: an imaginary woman. A goddess made up of nothing but myths and legends. That's who he can't resist. He doesn't know the first thing about me.

In the end it was just a false sense of safety . . .

. . . just like it always is.

chapter twenty

On my walk from the subway station to home, I stop to see Mary and hand her a plastic bag from Duane Reade. "Three Crunchy Peanut Butter Clif Bars, one Smartwater, one Strawberry Shortcake coloring book, colored pencils, and a new sharpener," I say proudly.

"Aren't you nice!" she says. She reaches for the food first. "Crunchy Peanut Butter's good . . . but Apricot's my favorite."

I start to say something, but she nods over toward my apartment building. "There's one of 'em fancy cars parked down there. You think the president's come for a visit?"

I follow her gaze and see that there is in fact a limo in front of my apartment building.

That's not normal. It's a little smaller than Lander's

limo, so it's not him, thank God. I don't want him to know where I live. Still, its presence here is odd.

"Mary, I gotta go," I say distractedly as I walk toward the car.

"Hey, how'd you know my name?" she calls out behind me, but I keep walking. As I get a little closer I can see that there's a small dent near the back of the driver's side, giving this luxury ride a little roughness.

I slow my pace as I watch the back door open, and a large, bald man wearing a suit that almost succeeds in hiding all his tattoos steps out.

I know this man.

"Hello there, Sweet!" he booms in his unusual accent.

I flash him a nervous smile. "It's been a while, Micah."

"Too long," he agrees. "I was just in your neighborhood and figured I'd see if you'd like to grab a bite. What do you say?"

He knows the answer is yes. No one ever says no to Micah Romenov.

And yet I almost like this guy. He's been a kind of friend to me, partly because he's always been able to compartmentalize his brutality and has never used it against me.

And if he ever decides to withdraw his friendship . . . if his opinion of me ever becomes less favorable . . . well,

I might not be around long enough to change my opinion of him.

"Do I have time to go upstairs and change?" I ask.

"Of course, of course." Micah laughs. "I'll be down here making some calls. I just thought we'd take some time to catch up is all."

"Catch up about what?" I ask as nonchalantly as possible.

"Lots of things, Sweet. Life, family . . . and your new job. Oh, are you still okay with me calling you Sweet? Or do you prefer people call you Bellona these days?"

"Sweet is fine," I say, pulling nervously on my fingers. "I'll only be a minute."

For the second time today I think of the little gun in my desk. Of course, if Micah ever turned on me, such a small piece of metal wouldn't be enough to protect me.

Less than forty minutes later we're walking into a chic Tribeca restaurant. It's hard not to feel a little overwhelmed by the place. The ceiling is comprised of a series of arcs. Everything in the room is sumptuous: even the upholstered chairs with their padded armrests and curved backs have a regal quality to them.

But then, perhaps all of that is appropriate, since the man I'm with is kinda like a king . . . or at least a dictator.

The hostess recognizes him right away and we're seated within a minute. Our table's right up against the wall, just the way he likes it. We're both served vodka martinis before I even have a chance to unfold my napkin. The waitress stands by as Micah raises his glass, holding it with all the subtle grace and practice of an old-moneyed country-club boy. You can barely see the tips of his tattoos peeking out from underneath his long sleeves. He takes a sip and then nods his approval to the waitress, who swiftly leaves us.

"Forgive me," he says. "I should have started with a toast. But it's my habit to taste the martini first. If it's not crafted well, I send the shit back."

Again I smile. Micah was born in Russia but lived in England for much of his young adult life. He hobnobbed with the lesser-known royalty before moving his operations to the States. So now he's a bizarre combination of the two cultures. He prefers vodka, but he sips rather than gulps. He's a key figure in the Russian Mafia, but he's so polite when you're talking to him that you almost forget about all the men he's buried. Some would say that the men he killed were also bad guys, but still, to use Micah's words, "It's a fucking messy bit of business."

"Now we'll toast." Micah raises his glass and I follow suit. "What are we drinking to?" I ask.

"To your new job, Sweet, what else?"

My smile wavers as I bring the drink to my lips.

"You did get the job, didn't you? I made sure my people gave you very good references."

"Yes," I say uncertainly. "I got the job. Thank you for your help with that."

"Bellona," he says, sounding out the word with a touch of distaste. "What kind of name is that? It sounds like a piece of lunch meat."

I shrink a little in my seat. "It's the name of a Roman goddess. I just like it is all."

"Bellona," Micah says again, shaking his head. "When you told me that you needed false references—some cooked-up proof that you worked for that lousy Realtor—you neglected to tell me you were applying to be Travis Gable's personal assistant."

"Would that have made a difference?" I ask lightly, picking up the menu. "Do you know him?"

"Simple question, complicated answer." Micah leans back in his chair, his eyes skipping toward the door and then back again. "You've gone to a lot of trouble for a PA job. I assumed you'd be going for something better. Hell, I could have set you up with something *a lot* better."

"I don't think I have the skills needed for your particular line of work."

Micah's brow creases for a second and then he breaks out laughing. It's such a warm laugh, I find myself tempted to relax . . . but I know better.

"You must try the ravioli," he says, waving his hand toward my menu. "It's fucking fantastic."

I put the menu down, happy to let him pick my entrée. He raises his hand in the air and the waitress jumps into action, almost knocking over another guest as she hurries over to take our order.

"I wasn't suggesting you work for me," he says once we're alone again. "I owe your mother a debt. I'm not gonna repay it by getting her daughter mixed up in a bunch of nefarious bullshit."

Part of me wonders if he plans his sentences out ahead of time, figuring out which words to mix in order to amuse and captivate. When you're as dangerous and powerful as Micah you can afford to be silly.

The other part of me wishes he hadn't mentioned my mother. But then, he always does. If it wasn't for her I wouldn't even know Micah.

Again he sips his martini. "Why the personal assistant job?"

I shrug. "It's not a bad gig. It pays well, really well. And once it's on my résumé that I worked for the Gables, I'll be able to work for anyone."

"As a personal assistant."

"There are worse jobs."

"Yes," he agrees. "More than a few." He looks around the restaurant and shakes his head. "I miss the days when you could smoke in restaurants. Don't you? Do you

smoke? I've never seen you light up, but maybe that's because the fascists who run this city have made sure there's
no place where you can."

I roll the stem of my glass between my fingers. "I
don't smoke."

"Why not? You're afraid it's gonna kill you?"

"No, I don't spend a lot of time worrying about what
is or isn't going to kill me. I just don't like the taste."

He studies me a moment before slowly shaking his
head. "It's why you wouldn't do very well in my profes-
sion. I've never gotten the impression that you care much
for your own life, Sweet. And in my business, if you don't
fear death you die."

"But they die anyway . . . the people in your business."

"Yes, but if they didn't have that fear they'd die faster.
The fear of death always extends a person's life a little,
even if it's only by a few days . . . sometimes a few hours."

"A few hours?" I laugh and shake my head. "Gee,
what a privilege."

"It is," Micah says, his face completely serious. "Every
minute of life is a gift. Do you know what happens to
you after you die?"

I shake my head as a waiter pops a bottle of champagne for a couple celebrating a few tables over.

"Neither do I," he says. "I don't know if we go to
heaven, or hell, or purgatory. Maybe we all just rot in the

earth with the worms sliding through our skulls. All these preachers and scientists who try to tell us what's going to happen to us after we die, none of them *know*. But I do know what happens when you live. I know what the air feels like when it fills my lungs. I know what it's like to have the sun on my face and beer in my belly. I know what it's like to lie awake in a dark room. I know I gotta die one of these days. Not too many people in my line of work reach a ripe old age. But even so, if a little fear can buy me two extra hours, I'll take it."

I run my fingers along the edge of my bread plate, take another sip of my martini.

"I know what you're thinking," he says.

"Yes." I tap my foot against the hard floor. "I'm sure you do."

"Go ahead and say it, I won't be offended."

I look up, meet his eyes as a busser brings over a basket of rolls before making a quick retreat. "I'm thinking," I say, "that you rob people of those last few hours, weeks, and years all the time."

"Yeah, well, I only give people what they deserve. And even then I don't always take pleasure in it. What can I say?" He selects a roll from the basket before adding, "Every job has its drawbacks."

I burst out in startled laughter. It's not that what he's saying is funny. He's a horrible person. I know that.

But he's also the only person I'm in contact with who actually knows my real name, even though he never uses it. I should probably want to avoid him just for that reason alone, but oddly enough it draws me to him.

I take a roll and tear into it, trying to figure out if I should ask why I'm here or if I should wait for it to be revealed.

But Micah makes that decision for me.

"What are your plans for Travis?" he asks after a moment of silence.

"He's just my employer."

"Hmm, does he know you know me?"

"He knows I worked in one of your bars."

"Yes, but only for about a week."

"He doesn't know that detail."

A plate of ravioli is placed in front of me and my wineglass is filled with white wine. Micah nods his approval to the waitress. "I always ask for my wine to be poured just as the food arrives. Wine's supposed to be a complement. If you want to get fucked-up before dinner you should stick with tequila."

Again I giggle and shake my head as I eagerly dig into my ravioli.

"I spoke to Andreea today," Micah says as he sips his wine. "She says hello."

It's not a passing comment. I shift uncomfortably in

my chair. I've never actually been introduced to Andreea, but I've heard about her.

I've dreamed about her too.

"She's doing well," Micah adds. "She's getting married."

"Anyone you know?" I ask as I sink my fork back into the pasta.

"Of course, I introduced them. He's my lawyer. It's perfect, really. He walks the straight and narrow, but he's familiar with my world. He's not shocked by it, and he's never going to say a word about anything to anyone. And I can protect him, and her, if it ever comes to it. I can keep them both close."

"You know, she may not want you to keep her *that* close. She's an adult, not a child."

"She was legally an adult when she got herself locked up too. Adults are just as idiotic as children, and frequently just as dependent. Sometimes I think the only difference between the two groups is that kids have legitimate excuses for their ignorance while adults just invent them."

I smile and nod my agreement. The white wine in my glass is reflecting the light perfectly, making the color as warm as the room. I've always preferred the shadows of dimly lit restaurants. The hints of mystery found in a flickering candle put me at ease. I don't live in the light. I don't know what to do with it.

"Your mother had such an influence on her," Micah continues as he twirls his own linguine around his fork. "Andreea may be blood, but she's just not cut out for my line of work, and my brother certainly didn't raise her for it. But when I tried to set her straight she wouldn't listen. But your mother? She was able to get through to her. All those college courses she convinced Andreea to take while she was in the pen . . . Andreea's got her degree now and everything. I'll always be grateful for that."

I take a sip of my wine and glance toward the windows.

"I think your mum needed Andreea too, since you had stopped visiting her by then . . ."

"We've already talked about this," I say irritably. I finish my wine and reach for the bottle, but Micah takes hold of it first and with a patient smile refills my glass.

"I've brought it up before," he says, "but we've never actually talked about it. You've never wanted to."

"Yes," I say coolly. "Some things never change."

"Now Andreea, she's been talking about it a lot lately," Micah adds, ignoring my comment as he carefully puts the bottle back into the bucket. "Must be because we're coming up on the anniversary of your mum's death."

I don't say a word as I scrape my nails back and forth against my leg.

"Andreea says you thought your mother was guilty. Do you still think that?"

"She was innocent," I snap.

"That's what Andreea says. But that's not what you always believed."

It's not a question, so I don't bother to create an answer.

"It shouldn't matter, you know," he says. "Guilty or innocent, she was still your blood. If she did kill that guy, well, maybe she had her reasons, or maybe she just made a mistake. But even if she was guilty of taking a life she was still responsible for *giving* life to you."

"All right." I put my utensils down on my plate and lean back in my chair. "But just so we're clear, she didn't kill Nick. She wasn't a murderer."

Micah nods, accepting this. "So you think your mum took the blame for someone else's crime?"

I grit my teeth and reach for my wineglass.

"If that's true . . . that would mean that you believed the cops over your own mum."

Again I don't answer.

"Is that why you don't fear death, Sweet? Because you think you don't deserve life, not really?"

I smile as I swallow more wine. "I wasn't aware that you moonlighted as a shrink. Am I being charged for this bullshit?"

Micah breaks out laughing. It's a full-throated laugh and it almost makes me smile . . . But the subject of our conversation is too sour for me to enjoy the sweetness of this little moment. I finish my second glass of wine and allow Micah to pour me another.

"It doesn't really matter if any of us deserve to live or die, Sweet. I don't know if any of us *deserve* all this." He gestures around him at the world at large. "But we all owe our lives to our parents. When we don't at least fight for those few extra days, months, years, hours . . . When we give up on life, we're reneging on our greatest debt. If there's one rule I live by, one that I've spent my life enforcing, it's that you never, *ever* renege on a debt. If you do . . . well, sometimes you have to pay with your life. But in your case?" He lifts his barely touched wineglass and holds it up to the light. "In your case you pay by living."

I shake my head, let my eyes wander the room, looking for celebrities among the überchic Tribeca crowd. "You're a study in contradictions, Micah."

"And you're a liar, Sweet."

My eyes snap back to him, my heart suddenly beating hard against my chest.

"Why are you working for Travis Gable?"

The question confuses me. Why the interest in my new job with Travis? I've never discussed the Gables with Micah. I've thought about it, many times. Micah became a regular visitor of my mother's after he realized that she was guiding his niece in a direction that he approved of. He had made promises to her about being there for me if I needed him. On my birthday and at Christmas he always gave me a few grand to help keep me afloat. I know who Micah is. I know what he does to people, and there have been many nights when I lay in bed fantasizing about what he could do to the Gables. But then *I* want to be the one to throw the knockout punch. I want that satisfaction more than I want anything else in this world.

Besides, Micah's unpredictable and he can't be controlled. I know he's sincere about the importance he puts on debts. But the debt he seems to think he owes my mother is flimsy and unsubstantial. If he were to help me with the Gables, not only would that debt be paid, but I would owe *him*.

I like Micah, I really do. But I don't want to be in debt to a mob boss. And while I don't worry about getting myself killed, I do worry about pain.

Micah acknowledges my silence with a nod. "Just tell me this, then," he says, cocking his head to the side. "Should I be investing my money with HGVB right now or not?"

I smile wanly. "I think you could find safer investments."

Again Micah laughs, softer this time. "You're a tricky

one. All right, but just remember, you abandoned your mum when she needed you. You can only make up for that by living the life she wanted you to lead."

"Really," I say flatly. "Are you living the life your mother wanted you to lead?"

"My mother wanted me to be KGB. What I do now is a step up."

"How is everything?" a chipper voice says, and both Micah and I look up at the same time at the waitress who is smiling down at us, her blond hair cut pixie style to frame her face.

Micah gestures to our plates, indicating that we're done. "I believe we're ready for cognac." His eyes twinkle as he adds, "Nothing better than getting fucked-up on digestifs."

I smile and try to look relaxed, but memories are coursing through my veins, making my skin itch and my soul ache.

It's memories that push me to finish off the last of the wine and rush through my cognac, hoping and praying that I can find amnesia at the bottom of a glass.

chapter twenty-one

I leave the restaurant alone, insisting that I can catch a cab home.

I'm a little drunk, just not drunk enough. I think about that man . . . that depressed drunk who asked me to serve him at Ivan's only a week ago. All he had wanted was a kind of nonprescription morphine and I had denied him. Lander hadn't, though. Lander gave him the means to further his self-destruction.

I would pay for that form of kindness right now.

I wander around lower Manhattan, glaring at the Manhattanites in their deceptively casual clothes. As if a cotton T-shirt could distract from a two-thousand-dollar purse or a four-thousand-dollar hair weave. As if their excesses were details rather than the main attraction. It didn't used to be like this. All these chic restaurants and expensive boutiques that offer to sell you a bohemian look for the cost of a car—it's all relatively new. Once there were warehouses here, and *real* bohemians, unpublished writers and struggling dancers. There were drug addicts trying to ride their high to an artistic breakthrough. There was a coarseness that reminded people of what New York was really about.

Evolve or die—that's always what they tell you. Adjustment and assimilation are the mechanisms of survival.

But I wonder as I walk unsteadily through the pedestrians, do we ever really change? Or do we just cover up the parts of ourselves that don't fit in anymore? Look at these buildings—warehouses converted to lofts. If you look closely you can see what they are underneath the new packaging. The bones of the city are what they've always been. New York has dyed her hair and put on a new coat. But she's still the same city.

I turn down Cortlandt Alley and there it is, the real New York, hiding in the shadows behind the polished storefronts. This alley is different from so many of the others. It spans three blocks and has but one streetlamp for its entire length. Scaffolding that's older than me lines some of the buildings, but for the most part it's just bricks and concrete. I run my fingers along the buildings as I walk into the alley's depths, squinting at the iron shutters bolted to the windows. They're not there for effect. They were constructed to stop the spread of fires that terrorized the textile factories once housed here. And as I continue to walk, I can also make out artfully rendered graffiti and drunkenly scrawled gang tags. Traces of a forgotten past and a repudiated present can be found scattered throughout this place. I understand it. In so many ways it's a reflection of me.

I keep walking, moving a little farther from the honking horns and boisterous laughter of the street. I discovered this place when I was thirteen, two years after I had abandoned my mother.

I keep walking into the darkness, hoping it will blind me to my own mistakes. But . . .

I had been so young. My mother had been sleeping with a married man. She sought to destroy a family, and then they told me that when she didn't get her way she killed the man she loved. To my unworldly mind, every sin was a gateway to another. So my mother had cheated . . . and that sin led to the sin of murder. It was a simple, well-packaged idea. One that was so easy for a ten-year-old to understand and accept.

My mother was the only family I had. She had been my world, my teacher, my comforter, and my role model. When the boys teased me at school about my bookwormish tendencies or the frilly dresses I insisted on wearing, I would run home and she would kiss the tears away. When I was with her she made me feel safe. She had been the only person on this earth who loved me. And when the hardships of poverty had crushed down on us, her love had been enough to keep me smiling. It was enough to keep me believing in the richness of our possibilities.

Yet I believed them *when they told me that with one violent act she had taken all that away. My feelings about it at the time were ridiculously simple:*

She abandoned me.

And that was a betrayal.

The alley stretches out in front of me. The name of a now-defunct business is painted in white on a dirty glass window. You can barely make out the lettering in the dim lighting, but it's there—these ghosts of the past are always there when you take the time to look.

By twelve I was skipping school. I lashed out at any foster family stupid enough to take me in. When they gave up on me, I took satisfaction in it, allowing their rejection to reinforce my rapidly forming worldview. I threw away the moral teachings that my mother had handed down to me, feeling that every good word she had uttered was now corrupted. I didn't stop reading, but when I opened a book I did it in

secret, under the covers with a flashlight, hiding my intellec-
tual curiosity the way other kids hide alcohol and drugs.

When I turned thirteen . . . well, that's when I started
dating. I made it my mission to only choose boys my mother
would hate, letting them touch me in forbidden places just
to make a point.

I did occasionally visit her—usually because one of my
series of foster parents insisted. I would sit across from her,
picking at my nail polish as she tried to give me parental ad-
vice under the eyes of her keepers, guards who were amused
and appreciative of the disrespect I paid to their prisoner.

I called my mother a whore once, and the guard later
gave me a lollipop.

I feel my phone vibrate in my purse and I take it out to
see Lander's name across the screen. He wants to know
where I am.

I'm lost.

I type the words carefully and examine the way they
glow, adding another faint light to the dark. And then I
erase the letters, one by one until the screen is blank.

My mother seemed to age five years between every visit.
Her shoulders slumped, her head drooped. Eventually she
stopped offering me advice on boys and school and life. We

would sit in silence, both of us thinking about how it used to be, our nostalgia breeding bitterness rather than sentimentality.

I look at my cell phone again. Cortlandt Alley, I write. If you can find it you can have me.

So coy, so insincere. As if any man could have me, as if there was a "me" to have.

I get to the end of the first block and am once again confronted with the hustle and bustle of the street lined with whitewashed chain stores that have eaten away at New York like an invasive species. Quickly I make my way through the pretenders and cross the street, slipping back into the alley, into the darkness.

As a teen I moved from party to party, dabbling in vice. I took hits of Molly at raves and then further dulled my addled mind with the monotonous beat of the electronic music. I had sex with pretty boys who had bad tempers. Sometimes they were my age, sometimes older. It didn't matter. The sex itself wasn't all that enjoyable, but the destruction was. My teachers and various foster families told me I was falling apart, but I didn't think so. To say I was falling apart would be to imply that what was happening to me was somehow accidental. As if I had dropped a glass I was trying to polish. My world wasn't falling apart; I was tearing it apart. I had control. I had found outlets for my anger and my pain.

I knew my mother loved me, and I knew that anything loved by a woman as duplicitous and evil as her couldn't be worth much.

I knew what I was doing.

The memories surround me as my heels continue to click against the pavement. I pause briefly in front of a rusted loading dock, corrupted by neglect.

School had been easy for me. I aced all my tests from English to math to social studies. Part of me didn't want to, but I couldn't resist answering questions I knew the answers to. I read my textbooks and I understood my lessons, but I rarely did my homework, which was enough to keep my grades down and prevent me from being loved by any of my teachers. And I continued to hide my love of books. Books filled with history, fantasy, and politics—I adored them all . . . I loved escaping into other people's worlds, other people's dramas, other people's minds. But the only ones who knew about my passion were the local librarians, who delighted in giving me their recommendations but never bothered to learn my name. They liked books better than people too.

I kick aside a discarded beer can as I consider the littered path that's led me to this point in my life.

Shortly after my sixteenth birthday, my foster family took me to see their son perform a one-man show. I remember sitting in that tiny theater listening to their son launch into one pointless tirade after another. To this day, one-man shows annoy me.

But that night, as I sat in the audience, it occurred to me that there was a parallel between this fledgling actor and me. This college kid was verbally beating himself up in his one-man show. But me? I was fighting a one-woman war.

I was all alone on my little battlefield and I was killing . . .

. . . and I was dying.

Ahead of me is a single lightbulb mounted on the wall under a folded-up fire escape. I stand in front of it, noting how it casts a welcoming light on the gang insignias scrawled beneath it.

I look down to the end of the alley and see a man walking toward me. I recognize the gait. It's Lander.

I step out of the light.

The first time *I saw Lander, he was on TV; testifying at my mother's trial. I was ten; he was almost twenty-one.*

The second time was by accident and I wasn't quite seventeen. I saw him outside HGVB Bank. I had been living in a shelter for homeless teens for almost three months and, coincidentally, I had been working at a used bookstore near the bank's offices. I was saving up my pennies, even performing a little better in school. I was looking for new ways to survive.

When I saw him that time he was standing with his father and Sean White. They were all jovial and appeared to be very close.

At that moment my mind started to spin.

I knew Lander from the trial.

I knew White from the arrest.

I knew Edmund Gable from the time he had urged my mother to publicly fight for Nick Foley . . . a few weeks before she found Nick's body.

Three separate events that all led to my mother's downfall.

And now there they were, all together, their hands in

their pockets, in their gorgeous suits, free in the streets—laughing.

And for the first time since the trial I began to wonder about my mother's supposed guilt.

Lander is moving slowly, each careful step bringing him a little bit closer. I back up a little more so that I'm now standing under the edge of a scaffold, making my position all the more discreet.

I can feel suspicion and concern emanating from him in equal measure. They vibrate through the narrow alley, bouncing off the graffitied walls like the echoes of a scream.

After I saw Lander and his crew outside HGVB, I started doing research. I spent hours in front of the library computer, poring over articles and court documents. Memories I had long since discarded found their way back to the forefront of my mind, but now they were weighted with new meaning and significance. Details that I hadn't been able to make sense of when I was ten set off new alarm bells.

And slowly a new, horrible idea took hold:

What if my mother was innocent? What if I had wrongly turned on the one person in this world who loved me?

Yes, I had been fighting a one-woman war . . . but per-

haps my mother had been an innocent civilian who'd been caught in the cross fire.

I could blame the Gables for giving me the ammunition to fight, but I'm the one who pulled the trigger.

If she was innocent, I was guilty.

I *was the monster.*

Lander is only a few feet away now. He reaches out to me in the shadows, stroking my cheek. So gentle, so sweet.

I close my eyes, my mind still in the past.

I *became determined to set things right. I would get my mother an appeal. I vowed that when I visited her again it would be with news that I had found her a path to freedom. And maybe . . . maybe then she would forgive me. Or if not, then maybe at least she could recapture some of that love she once felt for me. Maybe I could scrape off this feeling of self-loathing with the edge of justice.*

Maybe . . . maybe there was still hope.

Lander's hands are in my hair. "What is it, Bell?" he asks softly, his voice barely carrying over the noise of the street only half a block away. "Where are you?" he asks.

I keep my eyes closed as I remember what it was like . . .

I took mountains of circumstantial evidence to the police. Evidence that pointed toward the Gables and away from my mother. I remember what it was like to be scorned by those officers. I remember the very moment they swept aside all my research and told me that my claims and accusations were nothing more than the wishful thinking of a child. I remember what it was like when lawyer after lawyer dismissed me, often refusing to see me at all. I remember how the ones who did see me smiled as they told me how much they charged, knowing damn well I couldn't pay. I remember all the unanswered messages I left for my mother's public defender.

I remember the feeling of failure and shame. I couldn't face my mom—and just when I thought I could, just when I thought I had built up the nerve . . .

. . . she died.

She hung herself in her cell.

When I look down at my hands, it's her blood I see, staining my nails, darkening my frustratingly long life line.

I trusted the word of strangers over my own mother's pleas. I was just as guilty as Lander and Travis and Edmund. In a very real way we were all killers.

And now we all have to go.

*   *   *

My eyes fly open as Lander continues to stroke my hair. His brow is creased as he studies me, his eyes imploring me to explain the pain he sees in my expression.

With all my strength I push against his chest, taking him off guard. He falls back against the wall and I'm immediately on him, tearing at his shirt, biting at his neck. Around us are the ghosts of the past, the bones of the city, the reality behind the façades. And as Lander grabs me and whirls us around so that now I'm the one against the wall, I'm the one immobilized as he presses my arms above my head.

This is the violence of us.

His mouth is crushed against mine, hungry and needing. His hands reach under my skirt, pulling my panties down, letting them drop to my ankles where I impatiently kick them away. A cacophony of sound rolls down the alley from the street, encircling us and filling us with an energy much more primitive than the sophisticated restaurants and cocktail lounges only steps away.

But those things are the façades—the city's pretenders. Lander and I can play the game, but we aren't pretending tonight. We're here, in the stripped-down, raw ruthlessness of the city—embracing the brutality that scores of mayors and gentrifiers have tried to erase.

But they can't. They can hide the truth, dress up the history, cover up the savagery . . . but they can't erase the past. You can't erase what's real.

I bite down gently on his lower lip. His hands slide down my arms, releasing some of the pressure. I take the opportunity to weave my fingers into his hair and then I pull, forcing him to look me in the eyes, just as he has so often asked me to do.

But there will be no asking tonight.

"We're two of a kind," I whisper, softening my grip, running my hands under his shirt, digging in my nails as he lifts me up. My hips are pressing into his hips, my feet supported on the shaky bars of the scaffolding as he holds me to him.

"Yes," he breathes. "And that's the danger of it."

I smile, raising one hand to his neck as the other works on his belt. I can feel his erection underneath the fabric, and then I pull the fabric away and feel his length pressing against the inside of my thigh.

Ah, Lander, always ready to lend a hand to poor souls in need of delicious self-destruction.

I grab him by the shoulders as he enters me right here, in this alley, pressed up against the bones of the city as the sounds of the night vibrate through me.

My feet still on the scaffolding, I use my leverage to lift myself up and then press myself down onto him, arching my back, feeling him rubbing against me. He swiftly turns us around and I find myself having to wrap my legs around him in order to keep my balance. In seconds my back is once more pressed against the wall. I'm shaking as I continue to claw and bite. I hear him moaning as he thrusts inside me deeper and deeper.

How can people not see the brutal romance that beats through this city? How can they not see the raw strength and the bitter carnage? How can they not see the cruel history and the passionate victories? The lust, the desire, the anger?

How can they not see *us*?

But it doesn't matter. In this moment, in the illuminating darkness, I see him. And he sees me.

He pushes even deeper inside and I call out, knowing that the city will absorb my cries, adding them to its own rhythmic melody. And I feel Lander fill me, feel him explode. I feel . . .

. . . everything.

In a moment I will have to lie to Lander. I will answer to my made-up name. I'll hide my intentions and my ambitions.

But right now? Right now he's holding *me*. Not some pseudonym. *Me*.

And I'm holding him.

In the city of the blind, we see.

chapter twenty-two

Lander wanted me to go home with him, but I refused.

For just a moment everything had felt so raw, so real. If I were to lie next to him in his bed, we'd start to talk, and with the words would come all the old manipulations and deceptions. Just for one night I want to put all those words aside and savor this feeling. It's funny because Micah knows my story but he doesn't know anything about who I am. Lander doesn't know a damn thing about my history . . . and yet he sees me with clearer eyes than anyone ever has. Sometimes I think that if all my interactions with Lander were in silence, he would know *everything*. But with words I can throw him off and distract him from the truth he so clearly senses but can't yet pinpoint.

So I sit in the back of a cab, replaying the events of the night as the driver rushes through the busy streets, breaking traffic laws like they're nothing more than false promises.

I spent so much time studying Lander from afar, but none of that prepared me for the man he is. I don't know if I hate him or love him . . . but then, I feel the same way about myself.

My cell rings in my handbag, and reluctantly I fish it out. Travis's number flashes across the screen. I know I have to answer but I really don't want to.

I let it ring again. When I started this game I had lumped all the Gables together. They were a singular enemy. But now I can see that my categorization of these men was much too simplistic. They're all charged with the same crime, but if I were Lander I'd want to be tried separately.

My phone rings again. I squeeze my eyes closed and pick up, pressing it against my ear without saying a word.

"Bell? Is that you?"

No! I want to scream. *I am not Bell!* But instead I put a smile in my voice as I answer, "Yes, Mr. Gable, it's me."

"What did he say?"

I look out the window of the cab. On the sidewalk a woman laughs as a man waves his hands about, desperately trying to make some point. And over there is another man who looks homeless. He's trying to sell a knockoff purse to a pampered child.

"Bell?"

The cab keeps moving and the faces keep changing. I spot a woman crying as she taps out a message on her phone. There's a man in a suit walking past her, not seeing her at all.

Winners and losers. It's the formula for the world.

"Bell, can you hear me?"

"Yes," I say, my voice soft and appeasing. "But I think our connection is weak because you don't seem to be able to hear me. I just said that Lander asked if you mentioned any names in my presence. He specifically asked if I've heard you mention the name Talebi."

"Talebi?" His tone sounds more worried than confused . . . I'm definitely onto something.

"He thinks you're involved with some people you shouldn't be. But of course I didn't tell him anything. Besides, you *didn't* mention any names . . . except for L.J., of course, and I didn't tell him anything about that."

There's a long silence on the phone.

"Oh," I add as I look down at my nails. "He also asked me to check into your HGVB files . . . see if I can find any business correspondence in your private email account. I really think I should leave him."

"No, no, he trusts you," Travis says quietly. "The appointment I need you to accompany me to . . . the one at eight . . . I'm going to pick you up early so we can get a drink first and talk a few things over."

"No need, Mr. Gable. I promise I won't ever tell Lander a thing."

"It's more complicated than that, Bell."

Now it's my turn to fall silent as I wait for him to explain. But instead he just clears his throat. "I'll pick you up at six forty-five from my place. Be sure Jessica doesn't send you out on any errands at that time."

"Very well, Mr. Gable."

I hang up and turn my eyes back to the window. By the time I'm done, there will be so much distrust between the two brothers they won't even consider turning to each other in their hour of need. They certainly won't compare notes.

I lean back into the fake leather seat and close my eyes.

I like Lander. I really do. But we're two of a kind. And so I believe, with all my heart, that he should know what it means to truly be like me.

And that means learning how to lose.

The next day, I spend the afternoon sorting through Jessica's appointments, brainstorming ideas for a charity auction, and responding to the various invitations sent to her from assorted organizations. In the beginning of the day she reminds me a little bit of Pigpen, except instead of a haze of dirt around her she has this miasma of intoxication. Whether it's only the prescription drugs that are allowing her to float through her sorrows or she's adding a little something else to the mix is an open question. But as the afternoon wears on, she comes a bit closer to earth. And when she's a little more lucid I begin to realize that Jessica is capable of being rational. She's even got a sharp wit, with a sadness and bitterness that are even more mind-bending than the high she clearly prefers. At five, we're in her home office and she's listening to me read off her calendar for the next week.

"I can't possibly go to David's party," she explains with a sigh as I list off yet another event she's been invited to. "He's in recovery and doesn't serve alcohol at his events—and *none* of his friends are bearable when they're sober. They're not great when they're drunk either, but at least then you can insult them without worrying about anyone remembering it in the morning."

I laugh as I make a note to send her regrets.

Jessica cocks her head to the side as I turn back to the calendar. "Travis tells me that he's taking you to dinner tonight?"

I look up from my work, surprised . . . although I shouldn't be. Travis isn't the kind of guy who would feel the need to offer any kind of reassurances to his wife, even when there's nothing of note to hide.

"Mr. Gable is interested in investing in some Spanish start-up, but the CEO isn't fluent in English so he's bringing me along to translate," I explain. "That's all he told me, but it's certainly not a social thing."

Who knows, I think, *it might be true.* Although the litmus test he used to make the decision to bring me to this meeting—putting me through all that to see if I would buy cocaine for him without question or hesitation—suggests that the agenda will be a little darker than what one would normally expect to find in an investment meeting. At least I hope so.

Jessica smiles weakly and turns her eyes to the floor. "He made it seem like a date. Funny, isn't it? That a husband would purposefully make a business meeting sound like a date when talking to his wife?" She laughs and smooths her white skirt with her perfectly manicured hands. "I suppose it's also funny that I trust what you're telling me more than I trust what he says. But then, you don't seem to make a sport of hurting me. That makes you a more reliable source."

I let her statement hang in the air between us for a moment before scooting my chair a little closer to hers. "Has he ever raised a hand to you, Jessica?"

Jessica looks up quickly. "No one's ever asked me that."

"Has he?"

She sucks in a sharp breath and looks away. "Once. He was . . . frustrated with me. Perhaps I was genuinely *being* frustrating . . . So hard to remember how these things start. But then he slapped me. Open hand, not a bruise to speak of. He just slapped me to get me in hand."

"To get you 'in hand,'" I repeat.

Again Jessica laughs. "The way you say it . . . it all sounds so ominous. But that slap has never bothered me much. If another man had slapped me like that I could still love him. It's the poison in his words . . . That's what I can't recover from."

"Does he trust you?" I ask.

This time her laughter fills the room.

"But he used to trust you," I press, "back in the beginning?"

The memory seems to quiet her. "Yes," she finally says. "Once upon a time in a land far, far away."

He trusted you when you lived in Brooklyn Heights, I think. *Back when he asked you to testify against my mother and rewarded you with marriage into the family. Or is Brooklyn now a land far, far away?*

But to her face I smile. "What would he do if you gave up his secrets now?"

She furrows her brow as if confused by the question.

"He's awful to you," I continue. "Surely you've thought about hitting back at least once. You don't have a lot of ammunition and you're not built for a brawl. But every woman knows how to spill a secret. Just some embarrassing little detail whispered into the ear of the wife of some business associate? Just enough to make him squirm a little. God knows he's earned it."

The perpetually foggy expression Jessica wears clears; her eyes seem to sharpen as her mouth sets in a thin line.

"He'd kill me," she says simply.

"I didn't mean that you would have to spill a big secret . . . or even that he would ever have to find out that you were the leak . . ."

"He'd find out it was me. And it wouldn't matter how big or small the secret was." She leans forward, her eyes still on mine. "Do you think I'm telling you secrets, Bell? All my complaints about my husband, all the sad stories about my marriage, do you think I'm telling you anything the whole world can't already see? Even the gossip columnists know it, but Travis has his connections. My little tragedies will never be printed, so I might as well sing them to whoever will listen. I can do that because my husband doesn't care about those stories. Travis may not trust me, but that doesn't mean I'm not trustworthy. I keep the secrets I'm entrusted with."

"Because if you didn't . . . he'd kill you?"

Again she looks away.

"Are you scared of him, Mrs. Gable?"

"Silly," she says, her tone returning to the light notes of a few minutes ago. "Everybody should be scared of my husband."

I nod and, given the change in her mood, turn back to the calendar. As I do so, I discreetly reach into my purse for my phone and turn off the record button.

Less than an hour later Travis arrives, and with barely a word to his wife he whisks me away to his "appointment." We don't speak on the limo ride up and out of the Upper West Side, through the nicer parts of Harlem, and then into neighborhoods that I know too well, but that Travis shouldn't know at all. He's on one side of the bench seat and I'm on the other, more than arm's length from each other. He may like to leer but he has no interest in touching me here, in view of his driver.

So different from his brother. But I suspect that Travis finds his adventures through more troubling means.

Besides, he seems preoccupied tonight. He's looking out the window, but I don't think he's seeing anything. I can almost hear him thinking.

"May I ask where we're going?" I eventually say as we turn onto FDR Drive.

"To my meeting."

I give him a sidelong glance, wondering if he's being obtuse or purposely vague. I settle on the latter.

"Where is this potential client from?"

Travis shoots me a disapproving look.

"I only ask because people speak Spanish differently depending on where they're from. People from Spain pronounce some of their consonants completely differently from people from Latin America, while Caribbean Spanish is a whole nother beast entirely."

"You'll understand his Spanish and he'll understand yours. That's all that's important."

I smile sweetly and stretch my legs out in front of me. Destroying Travis's life is going to be such a pleasure.

Eventually our limo arrives in the South Bronx, which is not even close to being the worst area of the Bronx, though it's not exactly trendy either. We park in front of a little bar not far from Yankee Stadium under the watchful eyes of the locals. Travis walks two steps ahead, opening the door for himself without bothering to hold it for me.

Inside we find a seat at the bar and Travis orders us two scotch and sodas.

"Mr. Gable, is everything all right?" I ask tentatively.

"We have cameras," he says as our drinks arrive.

"I . . . I don't think I understand," I say as I sip delicately at my cocktail.

"At HGVB, in the conference rooms, we have cameras. I just checked the tape this afternoon."

I feel my cheeks heat up as I stare into my drink. "Oh."

"I know my brother is—"

"Please, let's not do this."

"I just need to make sure you don't fall for him . . . I mean *really* fall for him."

I look up, surprised. "But you know that will never happen. The only reason I'm still with him is because you talked me into it."

"Yes, but . . . I saw how you were with him." For the first time tonight he lets his eyes roam over me and I instinctively shrink back, crossing my arms over my chest. "That didn't look like just sex."

"No?"

"No. It looked like lovemaking. You made love to my brother."

I take a deep breath, knowing what tack I'm going to need to take but really wishing there was another option. "I have certain tastes," I say quietly. "I like it to feel tender . . . even when there's no real connection there at all."

Travis studies me as I continue to stare into my drink. I try not to flinch as he brushes my hair back over my shoulder and then smirks with amusement.

"Please, Mr. Gable. I'm so embarrassed. It didn't

mean anything. He just . . . He kept questioning me about you and it seemed like the best way to get him to shut up."

At that Travis barks in laughter. The patrons at the tables look up from their menus and conversations to see what's going on before turning away from us again.

"I need to trust you. There is nothing more important in an employee than trustworthiness."

"I bought cocaine for you," I spit out. "I think you can trust me."

"But it wasn't cocaine."

"I didn't know that. Really, what more do you want?"

"Well," Travis says with a cruel smile, "I wouldn't mind seeing a live performance someday. The tape was grainy. I don't think it'll fetch much on the open market."

My cheeks go from pink to red. "You wouldn't."

Again he laughs. "Trust, Bell. As long as I can trust you, you can trust me."

I don't answer. *It's like a football game*, I tell myself. The other team tries to provoke you into a penalty. They taunt you and so you reply with a little shove, a slap to the helmet. Just one stupid mistake, one little penalty, is all it takes to lose the entire game.

So I press my lips together, keep my eyes down, and keep playing.

"I don't know what Lander's up to," Travis says

thoughtfully. "But I'd like his phone records. I'll need you to get those for me."

"I don't know where he keeps his phone records."

"You're a resourceful girl. Find out."

I straighten my posture as I consider this. My mind runs back to our last conversation about what I would and wouldn't do for Travis.

"You told me that you would not be my whore," he says, as if reading my mind. He leans forward and puts his hand over mine before continuing. "But you see, I saw the tape. I *have* the tape. You had sex in what amounts to a public place. There isn't a privacy law in this entire country that will protect you, and the internet has a strong appetite for this kind of thing. If you don't want the world to see you as a whore, you'll do as you're told."

I meet his eyes. I see the way he's looking at me. He's looking at me like the guards looked at my mother. He's looking at me as if he has complete control.

What an idiot.

Does this guy actually think that I would allow myself to be blackmailed with a sex tape? Yes, it would be humiliating, but we don't live in Saudi Arabia. We don't stone women who appear in sex tapes in America. We give them reality TV shows.

And it's not like I have any parents to shame.

But I play my part and give him the shaky smile he

expects. "I'll try to get the phone records," I say softly. "Please, just don't show anyone that video."

"Trust, Bell," he says again, his smile broadening. "I trust that you'll do what you need to do and you can trust that I'll reward you with my discretion."

I take another sip of my scotch. "Shouldn't the man we're meeting be here by—"

"Travis Gable." The name is spoken with a heavy Mexican accent and I turn around to see a tall man with a military-style haircut, thick dark eyebrows, and a closely clipped goatee. His eyes only brush over me as they return to Travis.

"Javier, this is my translator," Travis explains as he shakes the man's hand. "She goes by Bell."

Javier looks at me again and this time he chuckles. "A translator," he says in Spanish. "I can guess why he picked you. It's not so different from those female body-guards that Gadhafi used to surround himself with."

"Gadhafi was a dictator and a tyrant," I answer, also in Spanish. "Mr. Gable is just my employer."

Travis's eyes jump back and forth between us. "What are you saying?" he asks irritably.

"He says I'm far prettier than Gadhafi's female body-guards," I tell him. "And I replied that those women had no choice but to serve Gadhafi, whereas I *decided* to work for you."

It's a test of sorts. I want to see if Travis will recognize that I've bastardized the translation or if Javier understands enough English to correct me. But Travis accepts what I say and Javier remains silent.

"Shall we get a table?" Travis says amiably, which I translate. Javier is dressed head-to-toe in Gucci. His watch is a Rolex. He's waving his wealth around like a flag. In so many ways he could fit into Travis's world . . .

. . . except there's something about the way he walks . . . and the way he keeps glancing toward the door and windows, and the way he insists on taking the seat where his back is to the wall.

It all reminds me too much of Micah.

We're seated and I give a weak smile to Javier, who smiles back with a little more enthusiasm. He smells of expensive cigars mixed with dabs of cologne. In minutes we've given our order and are drinking our margaritas on the rocks. Travis immediately launches into an explanation of what kind of account he'd like to open for Javier and the virtues of HGVB, and for his part Javier asks about the security of the bank and exchange rates. It's an odd conversation, not just because it would be more at home conducted in a bank's office than in a bar, but also because of what's not being said. Travis's words are being carefully chosen. He tells Javier about the bank's privacy policies and security more than he goes over growth rates or investment opportunities. Interest rate information is glossed over. Loan options aren't even mentioned. Instead he talks about recommended currency exchange houses and remote deposit capture.

Javier listens attentively, if unenthusiastically. The men continue to talk in numbers and policies as I work as a go-between, conveying information without gaining much insight myself.

But there's something here. For one thing, between Travis's over-the-top loyalty test and his eagerness to blackmail me, I just know he's bringing me close to secrets, secrets he wouldn't let me anywhere near unless he had strong assurance that I could be a trusted witness to his duplicity.

But it's not until I drop my fork and have to bend under the table to get it that I realize that Javier is armed. A gun is tucked neatly against his waist, only exposed now because of the way his jacket has been allowed to hang open as he sits.

The only people authorized to carry concealed weapons in New York are law enforcement. And this guy isn't law enforcement.

I get back up slowly and Javier smiles at me again, this time the glint of menace strong in his eyes. He *is* like Micah . . . except this gangster has no loyalty toward me. There is no one here I can rely on to be concerned with my safety or even my life . . .

I'm not even sure I can count on myself for that.

I swallow hard and continue to translate. Accounts, figures, policies, privacy—the words interweave from English to Spanish and back again. The message ranges from boring to incomprehensible, but the energy at the table feels different to me now. It's . . . viperous.

As Micah would say, this is some nefarious shit.

Eventually, about an hour into the night, well after our dinners are consumed and our glasses drained, Javier hands Travis a folded piece of paper.

"Do you want me to translate?" I ask Travis, trying to sound more helpful than eager.

"No, Bell. I think this note will be easy enough to understand."

My eyes shift quickly between the two men who have been completely unable to directly communicate for the entire night. Now all of a sudden Javier can write a note to Travis that Travis can understand?

I don't think so.

I fold up my napkin on the table. "Will you excuse me for a moment, gentlemen?" I ask in English and then don't wait for a response as I go to the ladies' room. There are a few women in front of the mirror when I get there so I stand in a stall until I'm sure I'm alone. Glancing through my purse I can see that I left my phone at the table, but after doing some quick calculations I realize that pen and paper will serve me better anyway.

When I step out of the stall, I pull out a pen and a frozen-yogurt punch card. I write my name and phone number on the back of the card, then fold it up as small as I can and hold it in my fist, which I press against my purse.

I open the door to the ladies' room a crack. I can see that Javier is sitting back down at the table as if he's just returning to it. Perhaps he stepped out a moment for a smoke. Or perhaps he stepped out to call in a hit on an adversary. With this guy, neither possibility would shock me.

I close the bathroom door and take a deep breath. Yes, Javier is a dangerous guy. But as Micah pointed out, I'm not afraid of death. I'm just afraid of losing.

Within fifteen minutes we're all walking out together and I am again translating a few words here and there. But once outside it's time for good-byes.

"Tell him I look forward to doing business with him and that he may contact me anytime, day or night."

"Mr. Gable says he looks forward to working with you," I say to Javier in Spanish. "And I hope that perhaps I might see you again sometime soon. If you have free time, call me." I extend my hand for him to shake, secretly pressing my number into his hand.

Javier pauses a moment, my hand still in his. "You

don't want him to know?" he asks, also in Spanish, his eyes briefly shooting toward Travis.

I give Javier's hand a little squeeze of confirmation before releasing him and turning back to Travis. "He wants to be sure that you don't mind his calling late at night," I say, pretending to translate.

"I wouldn't have offered if it was a problem," Travis replies impatiently.

I turn back to Javier. *"No vamos a decir nada,"* I confirm. We will not say anything.

Javier grins, discreetly tucks my number into his pocket, and leaves.

Travis zips up his jacket as I rub the backs of my arms for warmth. "You were very friendly with our client, just now," he notes.

"He clearly tried to make my job easier," I say casually. "Using short sentences that were simple to translate, avoiding slang and colloquialisms. I just wanted to let him know I was grateful for that."

"*And* you thought he was attractive," Travis says irritably.

"For better or worse, I'm dating your brother," I retort. "I can only handle one man at a time."

"That sounds like a theory worth testing," he says with a smile. "If I take you home will you treat your employer to a nightcap?"

It's a struggle not to roll my eyes. Travis, the master of

cold lechery, is incapable of pulling off even an inappropriate flirtation.

"I'm going to get those phone records for you, Mr. Gable," I say gently. "But I hope you understand . . . I'd like to be alone tonight. I just want to go home and go to sleep."

"Of course, Bell." Travis's cool smile is back as his limo pulls up. "I assume you'll find a cab."

He doesn't wait for me to answer as he gets into his limo and rides away.

Standing alone in the Bronx, I decide that loitering probably isn't a good plan. Walking toward the subway, I think about the train transfers and various stations I'll have to go through to get home from here. It's offensive, but not surprising, that Travis would leave me in this situation. Then again, I'd rather put up with the inconvenience of transferring trains and even the risk of wandering around the Bronx at night than spend more one-on-one time with Travis. Plus I wouldn't have been able to let him drop me off anywhere near my real home anyway.

Being a mystery can be an enormous amount of work.

I wonder if Travis thinks the same. I run over the conversation in the restaurant. So the guy wants to open an account. So what? Travis had gone over all the tedious details involved in that. What information they were required to share, what deposit amounts have to be reported to the IRS—so much talk about Mexican currency exchange houses. As far as I could tell there's a currency exchange house that Javier works with and he wants HGVB to work with them too . . . I think.

I frown as I follow the steps down into the subway station. I've spent a lot of time studying the things I thought might be helpful when taking on the Gables, but clearly not enough. Spanish and English are my two languages, but it's like reading about Chaos theory from a textbook. I can read the words but that still doesn't mean I get it.

The financial world will always be foreign to me.

But Javier? There's something about him that seems more dangerous than the average gangbanger. And danger is something I *am* familiar with.

I wait on the platform for my train, ignoring the woman who is retching by one of the pillars.

If Javier does call me . . . well, then perhaps I'll give Micah a call. I'll want him or someone who works for him nearby. I'm not going to let anyone end my life before I make sure the Gables are wishing someone would end theirs.

chapter twenty-three

t's almost one a.m. when Lander's text comes through.
I need to see you.

I'm lying awake in my bed, staring at the cracks in
my ceiling, trying to play through the night's events in
my head in hopes of making some sense of them.

But the truth is I can't focus. As soon as I slipped out
of the armor I wear for Travis and into the soft cotton of
my nightshirt, it's Lander who occupied my mind. I
smile as I read his message. He doesn't really think I'm
going to rush over to him in the middle of the night,
does he?

I haven't seen him since that incident in the alley, just
over twenty-four hours ago now. Part of me wants to
hold on to that memory a little bit longer before we meet
again. I want to imagine what it would be like if Lander

wasn't Lander and I wasn't me. I want to imagine what it would feel like to be touched like that by a nameless man with a nebulous past. I want to imagine what it would be like to be with Lander if we both had the opportunity to send our demons to hell where they belong.

But that's not how life works.

I pick up the phone. I'm sleeping, I write.

I press send and wait. A minute passes, then two . . . and then the text comes: Obviously you're not.

I giggle to myself as I consider my response.

Fantasize about me tonight, I write, and then tomorrow I can make your fantasies come true.

I send the message. I turn on my bedside light in time to see a spider gracefully drop from my ceiling fan as he spins a web almost as complicated as the one I've woven for my own prey, though perhaps not as delicate.

Another text comes in.

The man you met with . . . his name isn't Javier.

I stare at the message a long time. The spider rises again, flying on his invisible string.

Again my phone vibrates in my hand.

Please come to me now, Bell. You're in danger.

I sit up in bed, my heart beating in time with the thoughts that are racing through my brain.

How do you know who I was with tonight?

I wait one minute, two . . . but there is no answer.

Lander?

Enough of this, I have to call him—but then I get the next text.

He may have followed you, Bell. He may know where you are and where you live. Come to me now. Before things get bad.

I jump to my feet, take the gun out of my desk. With shaky hands I load it, nestling each bullet in a separate cold metal cocoon.

How much does Lander know? Was he following me? But if so he'd have to have done something like go into the bar after we left and start asking questions of the other patrons until he found one who overheard me or Travis refer to our companion as Javier.

And I don't think any of the patrons in that restaurant were close enough to hear us.

So does Lander know Javier? Or has he talked to Travis?

And if it's the latter . . .

I shake my head. Once again I find myself questioning what Lander does and doesn't know. I throw on a pair of jeans and an oversized sweater as I tuck my gun into my waistband . . . just like Javier.

The metal feels uncomfortable against my stomach, serving as a reminder of the precariousness of my situation. If I could just hold it in my hand it would bring me a sense of comfort and strength—which, I realize, is not unlike the feelings I've had while holding Lander's hand.

How odd that holding Lander is like holding a lethal weapon.

I almost laugh at myself. How can I be having romantic thoughts about Lander when my life could be in danger?

More importantly: my plan could be in danger.

I transfer the gun to my purse. It will be easier to reach and more difficult to drop. I pull on my tennis shoes. I'm not sure what I'm doing or where I'm going. To Lander? Is that wise?

I exit my apartment and take the stairs two at a time until I'm outside in the still night air. On the corner I spot a dealer, which is, strangely, almost reassuring. The world is as it was yesterday and the day before.

What would scare me more now is if the man on the corner was a banker.

I need to get out of here quickly. I start heading toward the subway, keeping my breathing even. I won't go to Lander's, not right away. But I will get far away from my apartment, maybe go to one of the all-night cafés near his penthouse and call him from there. I need to figure out what he really knows and what he doesn't. The worst thing I can do in a crisis is tip my hand.

I'm walking swiftly down the street, praying for a cab, when I hear a voice.

"Psst! Clif Bar lady!"

I look up and see Mary just a little way up, her head peeking out from an alley. Even in the dim street lighting, I can spot the colored pencils sticking out of her hair.

"Clif Bar lady!" she says again, gesturing for me to come forward.

I pick up my pace as I move over to her.

"Mary, I don't have—" But before I can finish my sentence, she grabs my arm and with surprising strength pulls me into the wide alley . . . where a limo is parked.

And outside the limo are Micah and Javier, standing side by side.

"These guys say they're family," Mary says almost scornfully. "Don't you know better than to ignore your family?"

Javier smiles a slow, treacherous smile as he holds up my phone number in one hand and his phone in another.

I look down at my own phone, which is clasped in my hand. With a shaking finger, I tap on contacts and then look at Lander's number . . . and realize that someone has changed it, likely while I was in the bathroom at the bar. The texts that came with Lander's name on them weren't from Lander at all.

"I really need to talk to you again, Sweet," Micah says.

"Is there a problem, Micah?" I ask, doing my best to keep my voice steady.

He opens the limo door. "How 'bout you take a ride with us and we'll discuss some things."

"And what if I don't want to?" I ask. The gun is still hiding in my purse, but it's no use to me now. No matter where I aim or fire, there will be another man, with another gun, and the driver is undoubtedly armed as well.

"What if you don't want to?" Micah laughs and translates for Javier in Russian-accented Spanish. Javier's smile broadens a little more.

"Sweet," Micah says as he stuffs his hands into his pockets. "What did I tell you the other night? You have an obligation to live. Don't make choices that will undermine that objective."

"*Móntate en el coche,*" Javier says, as if I am now the one who needs a translator.

Slowly I walk to the car. In the background I hear Mary muttering to herself. My phone vibrates as I approach the door but Micah takes it out of my hand before I can even look at it.

"Well, look at this! Now Lander really *is* texting! He

says he just had a dream about you. Aw, that sounds nice."

I don't say anything. Instead I just stand there looking at the car's interior, wondering about what lies ahead.

"Maybe we should call him up, make it a foursome." Micah laughs. His laugh sounds warm, even friendly.

I've been so stupid.

Micah tucks my phone into his coat pocket as I get into the car.

It's funny, but it's Lander I'm thinking about as the car carries us away. It's his face that I'd like to see again more than all the others.

But now . . . it seems doubtful that I'll have the chance.

part three

chapter twenty-four

Everything outside this limo is familiar to me: the run-down apartment buildings, the little grocers, the scattered homeless, the dealers, the neighbors who despite their struggles always manage to maintain a sense of community that is completely foreign to the truly wealthy. This is a world that I can easily manipulate and survive in. It's an oddly comforting place. It's my home. Harlem.

If I could just open the door to this limo I would be home.

But no one is going to let me do that. Not Micah, who is on my right, flipping through my phone and looking at my texts and call records. Not Javier, on my left, scratching at his stubble while his free hand casually rests on the butt of his gun.

"What's this?" Micah holds up my phone and flashes

me the picture I took of one of Lander's illustrations, the one that depicts the man with sharp teeth snarling down at a sleeping man. Underneath it is an anagram I've yet to work out. But I don't need to know the anagram's solution to understand the darkly aggressive energy of that drawing. I understand it because I understand the artist. Lander's work reflects his passion, his meticulous attention to detail, his darkness, even his humor.

It's possible that I've seen Lander for the last time. I may never again feel the warmth of his skin as I rest my head on his shoulder. I may never again hear his whispered compliments as he slides off my clothes.

And with that I may be robbed of the opportunity, in my quest for revenge, to rip my new lover's life to shreds.

I may have lost everything. Failing would mean losing my mom all over again.

Micah's still holding up the picture and I turn my eyes away. "It's just a doodle," I say, allowing him to think I'm the one who created it.

Micah raises his eyebrows and looks at the picture again. "Not bad. You didn't tell me you were an artist, Sweet."

"And you didn't tell me you were a kidnapper."

"Yes, well, I also failed to mention that I piss standing up, but you can assume as much," he says with a chuckle. "Some things just come with the territory."

"I don't understand—" I begin, but Micah cuts me off.

"You know, I've been saying those three words a lot lately. I told you a long time ago that I would help you get any job you wanted. You're a good-looking woman and smart as hell. I could have set you up at a nice art gallery where you would have waited on respectable wealthy gentlemen until one of them made you his wife. I could have gotten you modeling gigs, or if you wanted to use what God gave you, I could have made sure you were the highest-paid call girl in New York. I would have made sure that every client treated you right."

"So you think being a personal assistant is beneath me, but serving or fucking wealthy men is not?"

Javier's eyes slide in my direction. Javier speaks very limited English, but everybody knows the word *fuck*.

"It's my experience that fucking wealthy men is something most women enjoy," Micah notes mildly.

I straighten my posture and meet Micah's eyes. "You told me that I could fabricate any work history I wanted."

"I did. I did," Micah confirms. Outside I can hear the calls of young men as they stumble out of a bar.

"You also said I could use you and your people to back up any professional references I chose to invent," I continue. "I made up a career history, one that qualified me for a personal assistant position. I didn't try to convince an employer that I passed the bar or went to med school. I didn't tell a property development firm that I knew how to build a building that could withstand a storm. I chose not to apply for a job where my lack of real qualifications could lead to someone dying or spending their life in prison. So what exactly is your problem?"

I can see the beginning of a smile pulling on the edges of Micah's lips. "Here you are, in a confined space, surrounded by men with guns, and you're giving me attitude. Like I said, you lack a healthy fear of death."

I flinch slightly at that. I don't want to die. Not yet. In a month or two . . . maybe. Maybe someday soon I'll see death as a relief. But that's later. After I do the things I need to do. After I get my mother justice.

Still, if I must die now, I refuse to spend my last minutes on earth kissing the asses of the men who are going to kill me. I simply will not do it. And so I can't help but be emboldened by the futility of my situation.

Micah powers down my phone and slips it into his jacket pocket. "I would have understood . . . if you had wanted to pretend to be a lawyer or a doctor. I would have counseled against it," he says with a light laugh. "But still, I would have understood. You've always struck me as a go-big-or-go-home girl. I respect that. But a personal assistant? Not your style, Sweet. So I got a little worried."

Javier shifts slightly in his seat so that now his leg is

lightly touching mine. The noxious quality of my own vulnerability is overwhelming. These two men could do anything to me. And all I can do is curse them until they cut out my tongue.

"I was so worried," Micah continues, "that I thought maybe you were under duress of some kind . . . or maybe you had lost your senses. So, out of concern, I assigned you a . . . a secret chaperone."

"A chaperone," I repeat.

"Yes, just someone to follow you at a discreet distance to make sure that you were all right. Don't worry, they weren't following you every day. You're not that high on my priority list . . . But you can imagine my surprise when I discovered that you're not only working for Travis Gable but also 'dating' his brother, Lander."

"I can date who I please."

"Of course you can, Sweet." Micah pats my knee reassuringly. "Of course you can . . . Still, I found it all a bit odd. There are a lot of rich men in New York. Men who are known for being more generous and more gullible than the Gables. So why them?"

It's not a question, not really, and I don't answer, just keep my eyes on my fists, which are now clenched in my lap. Outside I hear the distant wail of a siren, a sound that everyone in this neighborhood associates with an approaching danger rather than an impending rescue.

"Anyway, I started doing some research," Micah continues, "and, well, here's a funny coincidence, but it would seem that the Gables knew the man your mother killed."

"My mother didn't kill anyone," I hiss through clenched teeth.

Micah throws up his hands as if to ward off my anger. "I meant no offense. Nonetheless," he says casually, "when I looked over the news reports about the case I found myself hoping that she did."

My eyes shoot up and meet his. "Why?"

"He deserved it. Your mum was a good woman. If that Nick Foley wanted her, he should have treated her better. He should have put the two of you up in a nice place; he had the money for it. He shouldn't have had her cleaning up after his wife. Scrubbing the missus's toilets, removing her hair from the floor of the shower he shared with her, washing her perfume from his sheets. That's just bad taste, Sweet."

"He didn't deserve to die," I whisper.

"Didn't he? He was extraordinarily disrespectful. He humiliated her, *degraded* her. He treated her more like an indentured servant than an employee. Like she was his property to fuck and discard as he pleased without ever thinking about the needs of her and her daughter. Are you honestly suggesting that shit doesn't piss you off? Let me tell you something: if your mum didn't kill that bastard, then whoever did pull the trigger did her a favor."

"A favor? Whoever pulled that trigger let my mother take the fall for his crime!"

"Or *her* crime," Micah says slowly. "Even if it wasn't your mother, the killer could have been a woman. The missus maybe? Or another scorned lover? No reason to assume your mother was his one and only mistress. I seriously doubt she was."

I shake my head. I don't want to hear this. But Javier's hand is still on his gun and the limo keeps moving.

"But you don't think it's a woman," Micah says calmly. "You think the Gable family was involved."

For a moment the world gets very, very quiet. I can't even hear my companions breathing as the car bounces over the potholed streets.

"A lot of other people thought that too, Sweet," Micah continues, his voice dripping with sympathy and tinged with condescension. "The papers didn't buy it, but the rumors were there. There were a few coincidences that guided suspicion in that direction. The cops checked into it . . . and discovered *nothing*."

"*You* trust the cops?"

Micah smiles. "About as much as I trust the stock market. There are a few good stocks and a lot of bad ones, and there's a whole bunch of corrupt bullshit going on behind the scenes that nobody gets to see. Still, I gotta admit, while they harass innocent people all the time, they're not in the habit of sending innocent people to prison. Occasionally it happens, but it's rare. And if the cops had *any* evidence, boy they would have loved to have sent even one of the Gables to prison. It would have been quite an impressive bust, a career maker for some blue-collar detective eager to bust a banker. But there was nothing, Sweet. I checked. As for Travis, well, I do a little business with him."

"Wait, you—"

Micah holds up his hand to stop me. "All aboveboard of course. But if I thought Travis was capable of doing what you seem to think he's done, I would have brought him into my operation."

"Micah!"

"Sorry, Sweet, but it's true. See, there are a lot of people who are capable of giving themselves over to violence. For those people, violence is a drug that they get a euphoric high from. And like all addicts, they end up using their drug recklessly and in excess so that in the end they make a big mess out of everything. I'd wager you've met a lot of people like that in your life, am I right?"

I give a curt and impatient nod, silently urging him to get to his point.

Micah continues, "But to set someone up as effectively as you seem to think your mother was set up? A man who uses violence as a drug couldn't do that. He would have slipped up, made some careless mistake in the heat of the kill. He would have shot Nick at an angle that would have been impossible for someone of your mother's height or shot him when your mother had a clear alibi. It's the rare individual who is capable of mastering violence and applying it with discretion and care so that it can grant specific results. A man who can turn every gunshot and punch into a business decision? *That's* a man I can use. But Travis is not that man. Neither is Lander nor their father, Edmund. The sad truth is, they're simply not that ruthless."

I press my lips together and stare at the closed partition blocking off our driver. I think about Lander raining down blows on a man who was already on the ground. I think of Travis cutting his wife to pieces with his words. These are violent men. I don't know if Lander has the ability to wield his anger in the way Micah appreciates, but I'd bet everything I have that Travis does.

And I know that if Micah is doing business with the Gables, what they are or are not capable of is completely irrelevant. Micah will do everything he can to make sure that I don't tamper with his interests. If that means he has to kill me, that will happen.

When they ushered me into this car, Javier had taken

my purse from me and placed it on the seat across from us, right next to a small black duffel bag containing God knows what. But no one has bothered opening my purse. They don't know about the gun that hides inside it. Then again, they might not care. It's too far away for me to reach without getting up, and they're certainly not going to let me do that.

"I don't know who killed Nick Foley," Micah says. "If you want, I'll look into it a bit more. See what I can dig up. In the meantime feel free to serve Travis, fuck Lander, kiss up to Edmund, whatever. All that's fine."

"What are you going to tell them?" I ask, although I'm not sure I want to hear the answer.

"Nothing," he replies jovially. "The Gables may not be ruthlessly violent, but they don't make life easy on their enemies, and I told your mum I would look after you. So, for now, I'm keeping my mouth shut. "

"Really?" I ask, genuinely surprised and relieved, but also more than a little confused.

"Sure! Maybe you want to see if you can take them for some cash or use them to gain a little power. Or perhaps you want to mess with Travis's marriage or Lander's heart. If so I won't interfere. Make 'em cry, see if I care. But, Sweet?" And with this he takes my chin in his hand, forcing me to hold his gaze. "Don't do anything that interferes with their ability to perform their professional duties at the bank. Do not mess with my investment. That won't work out well for you."

Without taking his hand off the gun, Javier places his other hand on my thigh.

"He likes you," Micah says nonchalantly. "He told me as much. He said he'd pay good money for a turn with you. A lot of men would. If you like, I can still set you up to take care of some of my more respectful business associates. Like I said, I'll make sure none of them hurt you. I can even advise them to . . . to put some effort into it, give you a little fun. Normally my cut is seventy percent, but your mum was good to my niece, so for you I'd bring that all the way down to ten. So you see, there would be very good money in it for you and it's a lot less complicated than playing cat-and-mouse games with the Gables."

Carefully, I pull Micah's hand away from my face and turn to look at Javier as he begins to caress me. *"¡Quita tus manos de mi!"* I hiss.

Javier looks up at Micah, who gives a slight nod. With some reluctance Javier removes his hand.

"Have it your way, Sweet," Micah says with a sigh. "It was just a suggestion. But I really do want to help you." He reaches forward and takes the duffel bag off the seat and puts it in his lap. When he opens it he reveals bundles of money.

"There's fifteen thousand dollars in here," Micah says, holding up a handful of hundreds. "It's all for you. I should think it's enough to cover the rent for the shithole you live in for quite some time."

"Why are you paying me, Micah?" I say coolly.

"Because," Micah says with a light laugh, "I'm very good to my friends. Of course, when someone makes the mistake of becoming my enemy, well, then I'm not so nice. But you don't have to worry about that because you're never going to make that mistake, are you, Sweet?"

I swallow hard and stare down at the floor.

"I believe I asked you a question."

"I won't make that mistake," I say quietly.

He smiles and again relaxes back in his seat. "It's like I said, you're beautiful and smart. Such a wonderful combination."

He gets my purse and puts it on top of the duffel bag, then pulls my phone from his jacket again. "I'm just going to put your cell in your handbag . . ." he begins, but when he opens my purse he sees my gun. He pulls it out carefully and studies it. Beside me Javier grins.

"What an adorable little pistol," Micah muses. He checks the chamber and then takes out all but one bullet before putting the gun and the loose bullets back into my purse. "Every woman should have protection," he says. "Of course, both Javier and I have our own guns.

Tell me, do you think that if we were enemies you would be able to shoot one of us and then reload before the other shot you?"

"Of course not, but it's a silly question, Micah," I whisper. "I would never attempt to do something like that. We're friends."

"Yes, Sweet," he says, patting my knee. "We truly are."

chapter twenty-five

It's almost two in the morning. I should be home. I should be restrategizing. I've put years into this plan, and I can*not* just sit back and allow Micah to screw it all up. I need to think! And when Micah dropped me off back at my apartment that's what I tried to do. I tried to think. I tried to focus . . .

. . . but I couldn't stop shaking.

If Micah doesn't think the Gables are methodically violent, then he doesn't know them. Of course, it's possible that they hired a hit man to kill Foley, but they were definitely the ones behind the murder. But then, Micah isn't interested in the truth. He's interested in his business. And he knows that I'm not in the position to question him.

At least not to his face.

And if . . . no, not if, *when* I proceed with my plan, will Micah find out? What will he do to me? Will there be pain?

He's right about one thing: I'm not afraid of death. But I am not so ambivalent about the process of dying.

There have been lots of moments over these last few weeks when I've felt anxious, maybe even a little scared. But tonight, when I sat between Micah and Javier, I was *frightened*. And I haven't been frightened since the night they took my mom away.

When that policewoman first delivered me to the social workers, I had been desperate for the comfort of my mother's arms. But I was told that was impossible. So I remained frightened until I began to believe the lies of strangers. All those liars, the ones who told me that my mother was a villain? The ones who convinced me that I should blame my mother for everything? They cleansed me of my fear and baptized me in anger.

And I was reborn.

But now the fear is back, and in that fear I feel traces of my former self. I want comfort.

And this time I'm not that little girl, and I can have it.

Which is why I'm now on the Upper East Side, standing across from Lander's building, trying to talk myself out of going to him. Even now, after I've traveled across the city to see him, I'm still trying to convince myself that I don't need to do this. I want to believe that I can go home, curl up in my anger and Micah's blood money, and draw strength from that.

But the problem is, I'm still shaking. So I left Micah's money on my bed, unprotected and unwanted, and now here I am.

The traffic is light this time of night. There aren't many pedestrians around, and the ones who do pass me give me quizzical glances. I must look odd, standing here in the middle of the sidewalk, shivering as I stare at a mostly dark building.

But this is New York, so no one stops to ask if I'm all right or if I need help. And to be honest, I'm not sure it would be any different in Kansas or California. That's the thing about fear—people can smell it on you. It repels the lambs and attracts the wolves.

E's Wolflike Indecency. I still don't know what that drawing's title is an anagram for, but the image says enough. I look around me, wondering when the wolves will come. I imagine Micah with a mouthful of razor-sharp teeth advancing on me, redefining our relationship, calling me enemy.

I can't be thinking like that. Fear is simply not an emotion I can work with.

Anger. I need anger. I squeeze my eyes closed and imagine Travis leering at me. I think about Jessica lying her ass off on the witness stand—*anything* that will bring me that warm feeling.

But then those images give way and I'm in that limo again. I can feel Javier's hand on my thigh. I can smell the cigarettes on Micah's breath as he calls me friend and unloads my gun.

I'm shaking.

"Bell."

My eyes fly open and I take a step back. Lander is standing before me, wearing a long coat partly covering up cotton jersey pajama pants and a white cotton undershirt.

"The doorman just called and told me you've been standing out here for the last half hour."

I stare at him for what feels like minutes but is probably seconds. I don't say a word. I can't even find my voice.

He reaches out to me and I fall into his arms. Clinging to him, I press my head hard against his chest as he pets my hair.

"Warrior," he whispers, "what's happened to your armor?"

I still keep my mouth shut. I can't risk saying anything. And if I could, what would I say? As it stands, I can't even explain my presence here to myself. I'm seeking comfort from the man I want to destroy, and the reason I need comfort is because someone is trying to keep me from destroying him.

It's enough to make me giggle. Lander pulls away so he can see my face. But when he looks at me he can tell that my short burst of laughter wasn't attached to any actual delight, more like an encroaching madness.

He wraps his arm around my shoulders and leads me to his front door, through the brightly lit lobby, and then up to his dimly lit apartment. I sit down on the couch, still not speaking. He walks to the bar, resting his hand on a bottle of brandy before shaking his head.

"I think tonight might call for something gentler," he mutters.

He leaves the room, and for a few minutes I can hear cabinets being opened and closed in the kitchen and then finally the alarmist whistle of a kettle. When he comes back it's with a cup of chamomile tea. I take it in both hands, warming them and allowing the steam to roll across my face as he stands over me.

"Want to talk about it?" he asks.

"I shouldn't be here."

He doesn't respond right away and for a minute I think he's not going to. But then Lander cuts the silence with three softly spoken words: "You belong here."

I inhale a sharp breath and gaze out those floor-to-ceiling windows. "No," I say as the lights of the city sparkle beneath us. "I belong down there, with both feet on the ground. I don't think I was designed to be above it all."

"Essentially we're all primates, Bell. Our instinct will always be to climb."

I laugh and bring my cup to my lips, taking some pleasure from how the hot tea stings my tongue and throat on the way down. "Are you a goal-oriented person, Lander?"

One corner of his mouth curls up. "You have no idea."

"I am too. I can be . . . single-minded."

He gestures to himself with his thumb. "Same," he says, and takes a seat beside me.

"I've made so many mistakes," I whisper. "I just keep screwing up over and over. Every time I think I'm on the right track, I'm confronted with a new challenge or twist that I just don't know how to deal with and then I screw up again."

"I believe that's called life, Bell."

"Well," I say with a small smile, "it's certainly called *my* life." But then my smile fades. "How long have you hated your brother?"

"'Hate' is a strong word."

"It is," I acknowledge without bothering to amend it.

Lander sighs. "I have . . . disliked my brother all my

life. Every once in a while I'll feel a spark of sympathy for him, but he's pretty good at stomping that out. Why?"

I shake my head. "I want to know you. And I don't. I've made assumptions about you, maybe even drawn a few premature conclusions . . . but I don't actually know you." And then finally I turn to him and meet his gaze before adding, "And you don't know me."

"I know that you're scared. And I can see that you're shaking."

Again I close my eyes, willing my body to still.

"Did my brother do something?"

"Oh, I'm sure your brother has done a lot of things. But he's not my problem right now. *I'm* the problem. I'm scared because . . . because for the first time in years I feel a need for human comfort. I'm scared because I don't know you and yet I'm beginning to feel like part of me needs you. I don't know how to handle this. I'm not equipped to handle this."

Again the room grows quiet. I can't believe how brazen I'm being. I don't even know what it means. Am I playing him? Am I digging for information that I can use against him? Or am I searching for information that will allow me to drop my vendetta against him? Is it possible that I really want to be closer to this man, that I need him?

How terrifying it is that I can no longer read my own

intentions. I've played so many roles: the easy temptress, the vengeful angel, the affectionate and loyal girlfriend, the opportunist, the eager student . . . So many different identities and now they're all trying to merge. But that's not really possible. My body can't be a melting pot for the various facets of my personality, and so instead they battle it out inside my heart and my head, driving me fast toward something that feels like insanity.

Lander runs his hand over my hair. "Ask me anything."

I look up at him wonderingly. "Tell me," I say quietly, "about your mother."

"Ah," he removes his hand and crosses his ankle over his knee. "My mother was a martyr. She was always sacrificing herself for lost causes. Before I was born she was a small-town schoolteacher in Florida who publicly campaigned against the use of 'under God' in the Pledge of Allegiance. She thought the pledge should be read in its original form. She did a whole lesson plan on how the pledge was written by a patriotic American socialist. Sure, it was true, but it predictably cost her her job."

I give him a quick, quizzical look. "The Pledge of Allegiance was written by a socialist?"

"A Christian socialist. But that's not my point. My point is that incident was indicative of how my mother lived her life. She was always seeking out lost causes. She met my father when he was traveling for business. He was already married but had told her that his wife had announced her intention to abandon him and their son. So of course my mother gave up her dreams of being a college professor so she could devote herself full-time to raising someone else's child and taking care of my dad."

"Oh." I look down at the light amber liquid in my cup. I think about Travis's hardened demeanor and penchant for cruelty. "I didn't know Travis's mother abandoned him," I say softly.

"Well, as it turns out, she *agreed* to abandon Travis," Lander says, "in exchange for a hefty divorce settlement, and that was only after my unwitting mother had accepted the burden of my father's proposal. I realize that a lot of women don't think marrying a ridiculously wealthy and powerful man could possibly be a hardship, but those women don't know my father. And then when you throw Travis into the mix?" Lander shakes his head. "Trust me, my mother had a better chance of getting God out of the Pledge of Allegiance than she did of making either one of those men happy."

"How long did your father wait between divorcing Travis's mom and marrying yours?"

"He married my mother one week after his divorce was finalized. I was born seven months after that. My father tells people I was premature, but I wasn't."

"A week," I repeat. I've done a lot of research on the Gables, but I failed to dig up that detail. Of course, until recently I wouldn't have thought any of this was relevant to my goals, but now, sitting next to Lander, I wonder. I've spent so much time studying what kind of people Travis and Lander are, but I hadn't thought about what *made* them that way, which is odd. If anyone knows the importance of cause and effect, it's me. My whole life has been little more than a series of reactions. Perhaps it's the same way for Lander. Perhaps it's the same way for everybody. "How did Travis handle the . . . the mom switch?"

Lander scoffs. "He resented the hell out of it, which I suppose is understandable. He took out his anger on my mom. My entire life I sat back and watched him shower her with abuse and scorn, and I watched her take it and repay him with nothing but affection and kindness."

"Did your father try to smooth things over at all?"

"My father is not a peacekeeper. He has no interest in the sport."

"The sport of peacekeeping," I say with a smile. "I can't say I'm very good at that one either. So your mom and dad . . ."

"They're not together anymore," Lander says, answering a question that I hadn't actually intended to ask. "And when he left her she found new ways of martyring herself. This time she martyred herself for me.

But that's just the way she was, always looking for a cross to die on."

"You're talking about her in the past tense." I stare at the floor as the statement leaves my lips. I know his mother is dead and I hate that I'm forced to feign ignorance. This moment feels something close to pure, and I hate poisoning it with this deceit.

"She died," Lander says, his voice completely cold. "Cancer."

"I'm sorry."

Lander stares out the window, not answering.

"Did you love her?" I ask quietly.

"I did love her. I respected her too. But I didn't always admire her."

"And your father?" I ask. "How do you feel about him?"

"My father," Lander says with a dry laugh. "Now there's a man only a stranger could love. But respecting him? I suppose that depends on your definition of the word. In a way *everyone* respects my father, particularly his enemies."

"Are you his enemy?"

"I'm his family," Lander says vaguely. "Words like 'enemy' and 'friend' don't apply so well when you're talking about family. A family's conflicts, resentments, and affections are rooted in such a deep history. *That's* the distinction. When we argue with a friend or lover it's because we disagree with something they've said or done. Their offenses are exterior events. When we argue with family it's because of disagreements that are so old they've become part of our fundamental nature."

I think about that for a moment. My mother was the only family I ever had the pleasure of knowing, and I hadn't been given nearly enough opportunities to disagree with her. Resent her? Ignore her? Yes, I'm certainly guilty of that. But if things had been different, if I had been allowed to grow up with her, what arguments would we have had? Would they have been over my curfew? Over what I could or couldn't wear to school? Or would they have been more fundamental? Did my mother and I have similar political views? Did we have different views on the importance of science or higher education?

I never asked her. My knowledge of my mother is that of a ten-year-old.

"You're shaking again," he says.

The feeling of Lander's hand, now on my back, is disturbingly soothing.

"When you were younger," I say slowly, "were you ever afraid of your father?"

"Terrified," he says in a hoarse whisper. "I was a scared little boy, always hiding behind my mother's skirts. He never raised his voice, but he could be cruel. Back then I was never really clear about what he was and wasn't capable of. And that scared me to death. It definitely kept me in line."

"And now?" I ask softly.

"Now I know exactly what he's capable of. When you remove the unknown it's easier to be brave. I know where I stand with him. I know how to talk to him. I know how to draw my own line in the sand."

I think back to the time Lander testified against my mother. I had seen it on TV. Not only did he praise Nick Foley, but he testified that he had witnessed an explosive exchange between her and Mrs. Foley. He said that my mother had made threats and that she wasn't in her right mind. Many of the details of the testimony now seem dubious at best. But now, when I think back on it, what stands out to me is Lander's appearance. He had been just under twenty-one. I remember he had looked harried, exhausted, and anxious all at the same time. If it hadn't been for Jessica's and Sean White's testimony, Lander's testimony might have been useless. He had been too unnerved to be given too much credibility, despite the influence of his family name.

Had his father strong-armed him into taking the stand? Looking at him now, it's hard for me to imagine anyone intimidating him, but he just acknowledged that he wasn't always this confident. And the relative boy I saw on that witness stand was so very different from the man sitting by my side.

I'm reaching. I know that. Lander's motivations for perjury shouldn't matter to the law, and they sure as hell shouldn't matter to me.

But he had been young—admittedly not much younger than I am now, but the rich age slower than the rest of us. A pampered lifestyle encourages immaturity. So maybe he was scared. When you're scared you do stupid things.

I'm making excuses for him.

I think about seeing him with Sean White back when I was still a teenager. I think about his current relationship with his father. Hate him or love him, Lander still works for his dad. That is Lander's choice.

But perhaps there's a reason for that too.

"Has there ever been a time when things were better between you and Travis?"

"Oh, there was a short period when he seemed to soften up a bit. When I was an undergrad and he was nearing thirty. He had met some woman, I didn't like her much, but she seemed to be able to reach him in a way that the rest of us never could."

"What happened to her?"

Lander shrugs. "I'm not entirely clear on that. All of a

sudden it was just over. And then in a year or so he announced his engagement to Jessica, and shortly thereafter the other woman's wedding announcement popped up in the *New York Times*. She ended up marrying some millionaire philanthropist. His family isn't as rich as ours, but they have fewer enemies."

I smile. My guess is that most political dictators have fewer enemies than the Gables. But then, dictators are probably more aware of their vulnerability to those enemies too. Gables seem to think that the only people capable of hurting them are other Gables.

"I've told you a lot about my history," Lander continues. "May I ask about yours?"

"No, not tonight," I say quietly.

My audacity startles us both and together we laugh.

"I know I'm being unfair," I continue, "but I just don't have the energy to comb through my history."

"Is there something I can do for you? Is there something you need?"

I nod, and then I do something that surprises even me. I reach over and take his free hand in mine. I've been underneath Lander, had him inside me. I know what it's like to have him caress my skin. I know what he tastes like. But other than a fleeting, thoughtless moment in the bedroom, this is the first time I've ever held his hand.

His eyes spark with something warm and he pulls me to him so I'm tucked into the crook of his arm.

And that's when the shaking stops.

We sit there, just like that, silently looking out at the city, until eventually I feel sleep pulling at me and I close my eyes, slipping into unconsciousness while I hold his hand.

chapter twenty-six

Hours later I wake up. We're still both on the couch, his right arm still wrapped around me as his body leans to the left, his head lolled to the side. The sky has an orange glow and its color penetrates the room, making everything look a little bit magical. The rhythm of Lander's breathing is slow and sweet.

Everything about this moment feels blessed.

Gently I put my hand on his chest, feel the methodical and determined beat of his heart. His eyes open and he takes in the room and our place in it before turning to me. When he presses his lips against mine the sensation is gentle and filled with more adoration than lust.

I let my arms wrap around his neck and press myself into him. As he leans me back my legs wrap around him. I sigh when his mouth finds my neck and smile when his breathing transforms from deep to shallow. I arch as I feel his hands on the small of my back, feel my shirt bunch as he pushes it up. I love the way the sunrise reflects in his eyes. So many complex colors and shades. Some soft, some violent, all of them perfectly beautiful.

I pull his pajama bottoms from his hips, down his thighs, to his knees in an unhurried fashion before grasping the fabric with my toes and using my feet to remove the cotton from his legs. Then I lie back as he frees me from my jeans. I can feel his erection pressing against me and there's something beautiful about that too, something both primitive and graceful about his desire as I open myself up to him and he pushes inside.

I buck my hips and let my hands run up and down his back as I lick his ear, kiss his cheek, whisper the word *yes*.

We're in sync now, dancing to a melody that's so much more tender than any we've ever danced to before. He kisses me again and we continue to move. Each thrust moves him a little deeper inside and I feel myself expand for him, I feel myself getting wetter. The room is growing brighter by the second as the sun rises in the sky.

I will not have this man as my enemy.

His hand slides between us as his fingers find my clit, bringing this loving ecstasy to a new height.

I will not destroy him.

"Warrior." The word is there, mixed up in his moan as he rotates his hips against me, as he continues to toy with me, bringing goose bumps to my skin. *Warrior.* He says it with such affection and passion.

But for me, the word has the edge of a curse.

I raise my arms, hold his face in my hands, and as he looks into my eyes he momentarily stops, studies me as I respond with the only healing word I can think of . . .

"Lover."

Once more Lander moans and he again goes into motion, rocking my body with his, kissing that spot on the base of my neck, the spot that makes me descend into blissful madness.

I feel myself moving to the brink. The sweet tension inside my body is being pulled so taut I know it's about to break, and when it does, when I finally call out his name, I feel the throb of him as he fills me.

Everything has changed.

chapter twenty-seven

We walk back out into the world only an hour later, me in the worn jeans and sweater I arrived in, he in a wool gabardine suit and silk tie. If Lander's tired, he shows no sign of it. He strides confidently into the sun like he's Icarus with a tougher set of wings. But me? For the first time in years I feel timid. How long have I allowed anger to extinguish any uncertainty that dared to spark?

But although the lion's share of my heart still belongs to anger, a small sliver of it belongs to something—or *someone*—else. That sliver is weakening me and now uncertainty has a fighting chance.

Lander kisses me gently before jumping into a cab, pressing into my palm enough money so I can take one too. I have to get back to my apartment and change before rushing to take my place at Jessica's side. Well . . . perhaps not rush. She expects me at ten a.m., but it's unlikely she'll even look at a clock before ten·thirty. It usually takes her at least that long to recover from whatever ordeal her husband and children have put her through on their way out the door.

I actually relish the cab ride home. It gives me time to think, which I desperately need. As my car bumps along I consider the facts.

Fact: My mother didn't shoot Nick Foley.

Her fingerprints weren't even on the damn gun! Of course, the prosecutor explained that away by positing that there were no fingerprints because someone wiped it down. But if my mother had had the presence of mind to do *that*, then why didn't she also refrain from prostrating herself over Nick's dead body? When she called the police, she had his blood all over her shirt. And really, if she was trying to cover her tracks, why would she bother calling the police at all? No one was on the street that night. I was the only one who saw her enter that house. She was the housekeeper, so even if they found a few of her hairs around the room, it wouldn't have been damning. Why didn't she just leave?

Of course, the answer is that she didn't leave because it didn't occur to her that she might be considered a suspect. It's not the kind of thing that occurs to innocent people in a moment of grief. It's a shame I didn't think all that through when I was ten, but it's a *travesty* that her public defender didn't think it through either.

Fact: Jessica Gable is a liar.

On the stand she claimed that she had heard a gunshot less than five minutes before my mother called the police. The police told me that I probably hadn't heard the shot because I was listening to my music, but at the time I hadn't realized that Jessica lived five houses down. I was right across the street. If Jessica could hear the gunshot from that distance I should have heard *something*. My music hadn't been *that* loud. Jessica also claimed she had heard my mother and Nick arguing on the street several days before the murder. She said my mother was threatening him. None of the other neighbors had witnessed that particular argument, which was odd, but not as odd as the idea that Nick would have an argument with his mistress in front of his house for all to see. It was ridiculous, and if my mother's attorney hadn't dialed it in, the jury would have realized exactly how ridiculous Jessica's claims were.

Fact: Travis is an asshole.

Even his brother knows it. And he helped set up my mother. There's no ambiguity there, at least not for me. Just because I didn't see what was going on then doesn't mean I can't see it now.

* * *

I was a month away from my tenth birthday and my mother was cleaning Nick Foley's home while I found little corners of the house where I could stay out of the way. When my mother said that Mr. Foley needed to show her what cleaning needed to be done in the second-floor bedrooms, I took the paper and pencils he gave me and went down to the first-floor dining room. When I heard the doorbell ring ten minutes later, I didn't think much of it, nor did I contemplate the sound of Nick stomping down the stairs, cursing to himself as he did. I remember hearing the door open, but I don't think I really started paying attention until I heard the contempt in Nick's voice when he said the name of the man who stood in his entryway . . .

"Travis."

That was so many years ago. I suppose it makes some sense that the police wouldn't believe me when I recounted the conversation seven years later. "Memories are unreliable," the police officer had told me. "It's the hearsay of a ten-year-old," said the defense lawyer who had refused to take up the case.

All true, but I would bet my own life on the accuracy of this particular memory.

If she were still alive, I would bet my mother's life too.

"This is how business is done," Travis had said, his voice carrying from the living room where he and Nick were talking. "Every industry, every company has its own religion. And this is HGVB's religion. It's our code."

"Religion?" Nick had asked incredulously. "Nothing that's going on here is going to earn any of us a seat in heaven."

There had been a slight pause in the conversation before I heard Travis's low voice float through the house again. "Heaven is a corner office and a seven-figure salary," he had said. "And you don't get there through good works. You chose this church and now you have to live by its rules. You need to obey. I'm telling you now, Nick, any other path will lead you quickly to hell. And that's not a metaphor."

"What do you mean?"

"I mean that you're going to hell and if you don't play ball, someone will send you there before you can even say the words 'whistle blower.'"

The words had sounded so silly and foreign to me. Companies didn't have religions . . . did they? And how could heaven be an office? And what the hell was a whistle blower? I had imagined a high school PE coach with devil horns *blowing his whistle at all the young sinners he hoped to send to hell while on the other side of the gymnasium a heavenly angel sat at a desk studying some business papers. The whole thing made me giggle . . . which is what brought Travis into the dining room: he had heard me. I remember the look of alarm when he entered the dining room and the calm that had washed over his face when he saw that the person in the room was only a child. "A little young for you, isn't she, Nick?" he had asked as he turned his back to me.*

Nick, who was now in the doorway, had flushed. "I'm—"

"Fucking her mother?" Travis had finished for him.

I remember how white Nick became upon hearing those words. It was a silent but damning confirmation of Travis's accusations. And I remember my heart dropping to the floor.

I hadn't known. Until that moment I hadn't grasped what was going on—right under my nose—between Nick and my mother. Travis had barely looked at me, wouldn't even recognize me later, and yet with those three words he had stripped me of a protective layer of innocence.

If Travis hadn't said that last part, I might not have been able to recall the rest of the conversation at all. It would have been just a jumble of silly words I didn't fully understand and I would have tossed out the memory before I even reached seventh grade.

But he did say it, and so I do remember that conversa-

tion vividly. And now that I'm older I see that conversation differently, because now I know what a whistle blower is.

More importantly, I know what a death threat is.

Sometimes I wonder if Travis already had a plan before he made that visit, or if finding me in the dining room had gotten him thinking, opening his mind to newer and darker possibilities. Perhaps he had run right home to Daddy and told him how he had found a perfect scapegoat. How he had found a way for the Gables to get away with murder.

I do sort of wish I had told my mother about the encounter. Maybe then she would have been more suspicious when Edmund Gable called her out of the blue and asked her to clean his house. But even that's unlikely. She would have had to know that Travis was Edmund's son for the alarm bells to ring. How would she know that? I certainly didn't.

So Travis needs to pay and so does Jessica and so does Edmund . . . and I have to find a way to make that happen before Micah can stop me.

But what about Lander? Am I really so ready to give him a get-out-of-jail-free card? Based on what? Am I giving him brownie points because he doesn't like his father very much? Because he had a sad childhood? So did Travis. So did 80 percent of the people I've ever met in my entire life. But most of those people don't go around setting up innocent people for murder.

But it's *Lander*.

I wince at the dreamy tone of my own internal voice. Outside the wind is picking up as we drive into Harlem, blowing through the hair of the gentrifiers and old-timers alike. It's oddly unifying. White, black, or brown, today we're all going to have a bad-hair day.

It's odd, but I actually have a lot in common with the Gable boys. Deceased or absentee mothers, a difficult childhood, a chip on the shoulder. But while I can kind of relate to Lander, Travis seems like he's from a different species.

The cab moves out of the nicer areas of Harlem and closer to my neck of the woods. Now the cars on the side of the road have all seen better days. Scattered glass can be seen on the pavement where one of those cars was once parked. The chain stores that have moved into South Harlem are a lot harder to find here, up near 155th Street. There are fewer leaves blowing around and more litter. The change of scenery reminds me of how separate I am from the world I'm invading.

With a little restructuring of my plan I can protect Lander from the worst of it. But still, when all's said and done Lander will have lost his brother and his sister-in-law. Not necessarily to death, but definitely to a kind of obliteration. And since I'm going to ruin his father, he may be unemployed in addition to being called upon to raise his niece and nephew.

To be fair, that's probably enough. My heart rate increases as I evaluate new formations for my revenge, and I smile as I realize that, perhaps, if I do things right, Lander will never even know that I'm behind the chaos.

chapter twenty-eight

As predicted, Jessica doesn't even notice that I'm a half hour late.

"Bell," she says in a hollow voice that matches her cloudy eyes, "how are you this morning? I'm sure my email account is bursting at the seams with new Evites. I haven't had a chance to even look at it in over a day. Could you see to that? Oh, and did you happen to run into Mrs. Jennings on the way up? A very fair-skinned Nordic-looking woman almost six feet tall? She just left here. She's donating a diamond necklace to a silent auction to benefit the ballet. It was very kind of her, of course, but what I really want to know is what you thought of her new haircut! It's perfectly awful; it makes her look even more manly than usual."

She yabbers on and on but never mentions or even

alludes to my dinner with her husband, which she clearly objected to. And she certainly doesn't bring up the last time we spoke, when she shut me down after I tried to push her to strike back at Travis. Maybe she's forgotten all about that. It's a real possibility when you consider the number of brain cells that have fallen casualty to her little internal drug war.

I'm beginning to learn Jessica's patterns. She spends her days floating around the penthouse, complaining about Travis to anyone who crosses her path—house-cleaners, deliverymen—occasionally lapsing into intense moments of depression and sadness, only to be partially revived by another pill or spa treatment. But at least she's predictable. And when you consider the craziness of what's been going on lately, Jessica's predictability is kind of soothing. When she takes a nap at noon I'm able to check the email account that I've set up for her, the one she doesn't know about. Sure enough, the email I wrote from Travis to her is still there. I see no sign that anyone has been on this account other than me. There's no trace of it in the browsing history, which hasn't been wiped clean since the last time I erased it.

And there are lots of responses to "Jessica's" last post on a forum that deals with abusive partners.

The responses are annoying to say the least. Using the alias I had assigned her, I had posted that my husband occasionally raised his fist as if he was about to hit me and then blamed me for making him come so close to losing control. I had written that he called me a cunt in front of our youngest child and once even told me that the world would be a better place if I wasn't in it.

Several of the women on the board had recommended couples counseling.

People are pathetic.

So after adding Jessica's voice to a few conversations started by others in the online community, I write another post, this time saying that things have escalated. I tell them that I got a little drunk and provoked him unnecessarily, verbally taunting him and even snatching away his phone when I suspected he was about to text a mistress. This enraged my husband, who then grabbed me by the hair before pushing me up against the wall, wrapping his hands around my neck and choking me.

In the end it doesn't really matter what the other posters think. What matters is what the police find.

Still, I'd like to make an impact. I'm creating a drama here; is it too much to ask for an appreciative audience?

By the time Jessica wakes I've done everything I need to do and even ordered her lunch from a local spot that delivers. She sips unsweetened iced tea and pops amphetamines while we go over her social calendar.

"Next week is the political fund-raiser," she reminds me. "Travis has great hopes for this particular candidate, this Sam Highkin. He must have what it takes. I've never known Travis to bet on a horse that didn't win."

"Is Highkin a good guy?" I ask.

Jessica looks at me blankly.

"I mean, do you like him? Is he decent?"

"He's a politician," Jessica responds, as if that alone explains the state of his character. And she might have a point. Still . . .

"Do you agree with his politics, then?" I press.

Jessica shakes her head impatiently. "I don't really follow that sort of thing. I know that if he wins his next race it'll be helpful to Travis. And," she adds thoughtfully, "I know that despite his being a virtual unknown I've managed to almost sell out the event at a thousand dollars a ticket. It's the black tie, of course."

"The black tie?

Jessica shrugs. "I suppose I don't have many friends, but I do have the Gable last name. So when I send out an invitation it gets read. And when I announce that the fund-raiser is a black-tie affair, the wives start nagging their husbands to take them. Even within our circle there are really only so many opportunities to pull out your best full-length evening gown." She sighs and shakes her head. "People simply don't dress up anymore. We've become a culture of jeans and T-shirts. It's really rather objectionable, don't you agree?"

"Absolutely," I lie.

"I mean, there's no reason we have to dress like factory workers or schoolteachers, is there?" she continues. "Personally, I'll be wearing Gucci. And my girl at Stuart Weitzman called to tell me about a new pair of metallic silver heeled sandals they got in. They're accented with Swarovski crystal. Of course I had her bring them right over and when I tried them on I felt . . . transformed. They're works of art, really."

"I'd love to see them." You'd think she was describing a new level of spiritual enlightenment.

Jessica jumps to her feet. "They're divine," she says. I detect a note of giddiness in her voice as she starts to lead me out of the room. I've never heard Jessica sound happy before, let alone giddy. These new pills must be good.

But we don't quite make it out of the room before my cell phone rings. I'd ignore it, but it's the special ringtone I assigned to Travis.

He's not calling his home phone, or Jessica's phone . . . he's calling me.

Maybe he's doing that to hurt Jessica.

Or maybe he's doing that because he's talked to Micah.

Renewed anxiety begins to trickle through my heart. I don't know exactly what Travis's connection is to Micah. I don't have any guarantee that Micah will remain quiet about his suspicions, no matter what he promised me.

This call could be nothing.

Or it could be the end of everything.

I do my best to give Jessica a calm and apologetic smile as I answer the phone and press it to my ear without a word.

"How are you, Bell?"

His voice scratches at every nerve in my body.

"I'm fine, Mr. Gable," I say, my voice surprisingly steady. Jessica gives me a sharp look and I make a show of rolling my eyes, letting her know that the last thing I want is to be talking to her husband. She smiles weakly, and after a second of uncertainty, goes back to her chair and picks up a magazine. Even the careful way she turns the pages broadcasts her discomfort.

"I was just watching that tape again," he says.

"I'm sorry?" I ask, momentarily disoriented. I sink into a chair across from Jessica. Did Micah make a tape of our exchange?

For Jessica I keep my face calm.

This must be what it feels like to have a heart attack.

"The tape of you and my brother," he clarifies.

Even after I hear the words it takes a few more seconds to register. I'm so scared about what Micah may have told Travis I completely forgot about the sex tape.

"I have to say," he continues, "my brother is a lucky man. Your breasts are exquisite."

"Is there a task you need me to attend to?" I ask, lowering my head so my hair falls forward. If I left the room, it would be inexcusably suspicious, but I also can't afford for Jessica to see my face right now. I've practiced hiding my anger, but humiliation is a more difficult state to conceal.

"Is my wife there?"

"Yes, she's right here, Mr. Gable. Would you like to talk to her?"

"No, I would like you to touch yourself, Bell. I would like for you to touch yourself in front of my wife while talking to me on the phone. I'd like for her to know that her husband is making you come right in front of her. Would you do that for me?"

I don't answer right away. So far he's made no reference at all to Micah or Javier . . . but he *is* taking his harassment to a new level. Something must have triggered that . . . What would that be?

I take a deep breath and try to steady myself. "No, Mr. Gable," I finally answer. "Of course not."

"That's not very cooperative of you. I am the one

paying your salary, aren't I? And I do have this tape to do with as I please."

I squeeze my eyes closed. Using that tape as a threat, that's rather desperate . . .

. . . and it gives me hope. If he had something more solid to threaten me with, he would.

"I've figured out where I can access those records you were asking about," I say as coolly as I can manage.

"Lander's phone records?" he asks, his voice registering surprise.

"Those are the ones," I reply. "I can give you that . . . But unfortunately your other request isn't feasible."

There's a long pause on the phone and then a low laugh. "Very well, I'll drop the request, for now. However, I will be stopping by there in about forty minutes."

"Why?"

"Because it's my home and I can come in and out of it as I please," Travis replies. "Let Jessica know, will you?"

Before I can respond the phone goes dead. I raise my head to meet Jessica's eyes with a smile. But I can immediately tell it's too late to reassure her. Even through the haze of drugs she saw . . . something. She knows the conversation wasn't about business.

"Mr. Gable will be stopping home in about forty minutes."

"Why?" Jessica asks, unwittingly repeating my own

reaction to the news. She studies the magazine, although I'm not sure she's actually reading the words.

"That's a very good question," I admit.

And it's a question I'm a little worried about.

She smiles weakly and runs her palm over an image of a girl selling perfume and sex. "Perhaps," she says, "I'll show you the shoes some other time."

chapter twenty-nine

A full hour later Travis arrives and heads straight into Jessica's office, where we're working out the seating arrangements for the upcoming fund-raiser dinner. His walk is less a strut than it is the stalking gait of a predator.

Jessica opens her mouth to say hello, but my charming employer doesn't acknowledge his wife at all. Instead he smiles down at me, more warmly than he ever has before.

It's enough to scare the shit out of me.

"Bell," he says, "you look beautiful as always."

I glance toward Jessica. She has her head down, but even from this angle I can see that she's fighting for composure.

"Thank you, Mr. Gable," I begin. "Mrs. Gable and I—"

"I thought we could have a family dinner tonight, Travis," Jessica interjects. "The children will be home early and—"

"And how would you know what time my children are going to be brought home?" Travis asks without bothering to turn and look at her.

"They're our children, Travis," she says with a nervous laugh. "It's important that I keep up with the structure of their day. Is it so odd that I would memorize their schedule?"

I look away, hoping Travis didn't have time to read my knee-jerk reaction to that. Jessica didn't memorize a thing. I checked the calendar just twenty minutes ago and told her what the kids had scheduled today. But I don't want the credit. I want Travis to believe that Jessica is being a halfway decent parent. I want him to soften toward her, if only for a few minutes.

If only long enough to get his attention off me.

And for a moment I think I'm getting my wish. Travis finally turns to face her. "I'll call the nanny," he says. "I'll ask her to take Braden and Mercedes out to dinner. You shouldn't be around them tonight."

"But . . . I promised Mercedes we would play Chutes and Ladders tonight after dinner—"

"Then you're going to have to break your promise to your daughter."

Jessica shakes her head as she mouths the word *why*.

"You're stoned, Jessica. You're a complete mess. You're not fit to be around any child."

"But I . . . I only took the pills you gave me," she protests.

"Are you blaming me for your addiction?"

"No," Jessica responds quickly, immediately getting to her feet. "I didn't mean—"

"If you like I can just stop giving you the pills. See how that goes."

"No! I mean . . . I . . . I need them . . . You remember the last time I tried to do without them . . . It's my medicine . . . my *prescribed* medicine . . . I . . . I'm—"

"A joke," he finishes for her. "You're a complete joke."

Jessica, seemingly unable to form any more words, is reduced to just shaking her head and holding back tears.

"Don't worry, I'll keep getting you your *medication*," he says, adding extra sarcasm to the last word. "Maybe I'll let you play a game or two with my daughter tomorrow if you're sober enough to speak clearly. And you are right about one thing: it might be nice if I took them out to dinner tonight." He turns back to me, his smile animated with cruelty. "Would you like to join us, Bell? I'm sure my children will love you."

"I . . . I don't . . ." I fumble, finding myself just as discombobulated as his wife.

"They're very well behaved at restaurants," he assures me. "Despite their mother's weak-willed sloppiness they're surprisingly disciplined in their behavior."

"I . . . I have plans tonight," I stammer.

"Why don't you see if you can cancel them," he suggests. "I want to show you that not everyone in my family is weak. I'm sure your days with Jessica have lowered your opinion of us. I bet you have to take a shower when you leave just to get the stench of her neediness and addiction off you."

Jessica has her hands clasped and pressed against her chest, and her knees are bent as she twists her body away from us as if she's actually being deformed by the humiliation Travis is heaping on top of her.

The whole scene feels surreal to me. Like someone just turned the home office into a stage and now Travis, Jessica, and I are performing a modern version of *No Exit*. All we're missing is the valet.

But then, this shouldn't be a surprise. It's not like I walked into this situation blind. About a year ago I briefly dated a boy who was cute, stupid, and incredibly low maintenance. He would have been content hanging out all day shooting hoops, playing pool, and making idle small talk about pop culture. But that's not why I went out with him. I went out with him because I wanted to get to know his sister, a nice, middle-aged woman named

Sara who had just gotten a job as a day-care provider in Brooklyn. Before that she worked as a nanny for a wealthy couple who lived on the Upper West Side: Jessica and Travis Gable.

"That's one fucked-up *family,*" *Sara had slurred more than once over the beers I bought her at the pool hall where we watched her brother play every Friday night. "I had to drag the kids from one activity to another just to keep them out of their parents' way. And the girl's just a baby, so I mean how many activities can I come up with for her, right? Oh, and the wife, Jessica? She's suicidal, and I think her husband wants her to do it too."*

"God, what makes you say that?" I had pressed.

"Lots of reasons . . . But I guess the biggest one is that I once walked in on her holding a knife to her wrist."

"What?" I swiveled back and forth on my bar stool, trying to figure out how I felt about the woman who helped set up my mother for murder committing suicide.

"Yep, I accidentally walked in on her in the bathroom and she was just standing in front of the mirror with this glassy stare. In her hand was a kitchen knife, and she just had it, you know, resting against the underside of her wrist as if she was still making up her mind about whether or not to go through with it."

"Wow," I whispered.

"Yeah, It was freaky. And when she saw me she just put the knife down on the counter and walked out of the bathroom, like I wasn't even there. Later when I asked her about it she said that it never happened. She called me a liar, and when I tried to push it she slapped me across the face so hard it actually left a mark. Then she accused me of sleeping with her husband. Said I was nothing more than a common whore." Sara shook her head, seemingly still amazed by the memory. "The woman is just totally out of her mind. So then I tell her husband about the knife incident . . ."

"And?"

"And he thanked me for telling him and said he'd take care of everything. But here's the thing. He actually seemed happy about it."

"Happy about . . . Wait, what was he happy about?" I had asked, genuinely confused.

"Happy to hear that his wife was suicidal. You could just tell that he was trying to hold back a smile."

"Huh." I waved over the bartender and ordered Sara another beer. Once it was served I propped up my elbows and started tearing at the edges of my napkin. "Do you think she'd ever actually go through with it?"

"Maybe," Sara had mused. "I don't really get what keeps her in the marriage, but it isn't love for him, and I don't *think she loves her kids either. I think maybe her husband has something on her . . . or maybe they have something on each other. You know, keep your friends close and your enemies closer? Still, it's clear she's afraid of him. And part of me thinks that given the chance, she'd run."*

"You mean leave?"

Sara had shaken her head and stared long and hard into her beer. "No," she had said carefully. "I mean run."

And now here I am, witnessing all the abuse Sara witnessed. Although I have to think Travis is turning it up a notch. If I had to guess, he gets a little more sadistic every month, hoping to find her breaking point. Trying to formulate the right words, words that will drive her to pick up that knife.

It's not pleasant to watch. But it is useful.

The house phone spits out a short, high-pitched ring. It's the noise it makes when there's a call coming in from the front desk of the lobby. Travis, clearly irritated by this interruption of his little torture session, snatches up the phone. "What."

There's a pause and his forehead creases. He gives me a sharp look. "Why, yes," he says slowly. "Send him up."

He hangs up the phone, his eyes still on me. "My brother's here."

I freeze, momentarily stunned. This can't be happening.

"It seems like you and Mrs. Gable need a little time to talk," I say quickly. "Would you like me to meet your brother at the elevator and ask him to come back later?"

"No," Travis says slowly, his expression moving from cruel to cold. "But I would like to know why he's here. Surely no one in this penthouse was expecting him, right?"

"No, of course not," Jessica says, wrongly assuming the question is directed at her. She clears her throat before adding, "I never invite Lander over—"

"Dear God, when will you shut up?" Travis hisses, looking down at his browbeaten wife before quickly shifting his eyes back to me. I see the unspoken question.

And I don't have an answer.

I don't *know* why he's here! Has he decided not to go along with keeping our relationship a secret after all? Why would he do that? I've set up a rather elaborate mousetrap, one in which Travis knows about the affair that he thinks Lander is keeping from him, which Lander is keeping quiet about because I've asked him to. Getting each one to think he's using me to spy on the other has been working great so far. But if Lander has decided to come clean, I'll be the only mouse in danger.

There's a knock on the door and for a second no one moves, as if we all expect that the guy knocking is the boogeyman rather than a family member, although I suppose all too frequently the two are the same.

Jessica snaps out of it first.

"I'll get it," she whispers. On unsteady feet she makes her way out of the room to the front door.

"You asked him to meet you here?" Travis growls under his breath.

"No!" I insist in a harsh whisper. "I have no idea why . . ."

Lander walks in with Jessica by his side. "Ah, Travis. I heard you came home for lunch. Glad the rumor mill bases at least some of its gossip on fact. I . . . Oh, hello." His eyes turn to me. "I didn't know you had company."

Neither Travis nor I move. Again, it's Jessica who comes to the rescue. "Lander, this is my . . . *our* . . . new personal assistant, Bell Dantès."

"What a beautiful name," Lander says as he steps forward, offering his hand. "I'm Lander Gable."

Tentatively I shake his hand. "It's a pleasure to meet you."

"Did I forget to tell you I have a new assistant?" Travis asks, enunciating each word carefully as if testing the waters. "I've been rather distracted of late."

"Life's been busy for all of us," Lander says, making himself comfortable on the couch and smiling up at Travis. "I actually have a dentist appointment around the corner and I thought I'd stop by and let Jessica know that I'd like to go to the fund-raiser for Highkin after all . . . assuming there's still space."

Travis leans back on his heels and studies his younger brother, curiosity blunting some of his anger. "I didn't think you liked Highkin."

Lander shrugs nonchalantly. "You like him, Dad likes him . . . Maybe I should at least give the man a chance."

"It's a thousand dollars a plate."

Lander's lips curl up into a little ironic smile. "I'm good for it."

"Will it be just you?" Travis asks provocatively.

Lander hesitates for a moment before turning to Jessica, who is sitting in the corner trying to make herself as small as possible. "Jessica, will most of the attendees be bringing a plus one?"

"Most of them," Jessica says in something just above a whisper. "Of course, it's not a requirement . . ."

"But I don't want to be the odd man out. Maybe there's someone you could set me up with?"

At this Travis's eyes narrow, but Jessica, oblivious to the true dynamics of what's going on, nods her head. "I'm sure I could come up with a name or two," she says vaguely. "You're not a difficult man to fix up . . . Although you are so picky, Lander. I can't remember the last time you dated a woman for more than a week."

I can. But I keep my eyes on the floor, not saying a word.

"I know, I'm a challenge." Lander laughs. "Perhaps you shouldn't set me up after all. I'll undoubtedly do something unforgivable during the evening and your friend will hate you forever for putting her through the hardship."

"'Unforgivable'?" Travis repeats coolly.

"Oh, you know." Lander sighs. "I won't give my date enough attention, or I won't be able to feign interest in her career. Or when she asks me if I'll respect her in the morning, I'll tell her the truth. I've never been good at pulling my punches, and that doesn't really work out well for me in our circles." He taps his fingers against his knees as he pretends to think.

And then he turns to me.

"How about you, Bell?"

"Me?" I ask weakly. I cast a glance at Travis, but I can't read him. Lander seems to have us all a bit off guard.

"It'll be good food and good drinks, isn't that right, Jess?" Again Lander smiles at his sister-in-law.

"Well, yes, Bell actually helped a bit with sorting through the RSVPs and pledges, although most of it was planned before we hired her . . ."

"Oh, you helped?" Lander gets to his feet and faces me. "Well, now you *have* to come."

For a second I feel a little dizzy. I can feel both Travis's and Lander's eyes on me as I try to come up with a response. Finally I venture a small smile and lock my eyes on Lander. "Forgive me, Mr. Gable—"

"Lander," he corrects.

"Forgive me, *Lander*, but you didn't exactly make yourself seem like a great date just now."

He smiles, a slow, knowing, and incredibly sexy smile.

"So use me," he says sweetly.

"Excuse me?" I ask, my voice catching in my throat.

"For the dinner, of course," he clarifies, his smile widening. "I'm offering you a way into an event that might otherwise be financially out of reach. It'll be fun."

I look over at Jessica. There's a flash of something in her eyes that I haven't seen from her before. It could be amusement, but it almost looks like . . . like triumph.

Of course. She wants Lander to hit on me. She wants him to make me absolutely unavailable to her husband.

My eyes travel to Travis. His look is easier to read. He just wants to throttle someone.

And yet, what can he really say? He knows I'm dating Lander. And I told him that Lander wanted to keep our brief history as a couple a secret, and Lander has just reinforced that narrative by this interaction. Why he wants Travis to know he's interested in dating me now is a mystery, but he's still lying about when we met. And it *was* Travis who asked me to continue my relationship with Lander. So he can hardly fault me for any of this. And if Micah is watching, seeing me dating Lander out in the open, in full view of his family, it'll make me look less subversive. It might even make Micah think that I've taken his advice.

I smile flirtatiously at Lander. "I can't imagine why you would want to spend a thousand dollars on a girl you don't know, but I'm certainly not going to refuse the invitation."

"I'm not spending a thousand dollars on you," Lander says dismissively. "I'm spending two thousand dollars on a politician who is important to my family." He pauses and lets his eyes roam over me . . . although the look is a little less crude and a lot less insulting than the ones his brother gives me. "Since it's only our first date, I think . . . I think I'll spend only fifteen hundred dollars on you."

I shake my head. "Excuse me?"

"For your evening wear," Lander says. He turns to Jessica. "Do you have time to take her shopping for a dress? You do have a beautiful sense of style."

"Oh, Lander," Jessica says, her voice almost sultry as she rises and crosses the room to take the seat next to him. "You're such a flatterer and so very impulsive, but"—and here she stops to give him a playful kiss on the cheek—"that's why we love you. Isn't it, Travis?" She flashes a pretty but undeniably taunting smile at her husband.

It's a subtle provocation, but for Jessica it's huge. My mind flashes back to the day Travis hired me. I remember the outburst and mild defiance that Jessica demonstrated and maintained for the space of two minutes.

For two minutes she was defiant. For two minutes she stood her ground and she lashed out. And now there's this little glimpse of her desire to strike back.

Jessica turns her smile toward me. "Tomorrow, instead of going through emails and organizing fundraisers, we'll take a girls' day out. We'll start at De la Renta and work our way down to Lanvin. Or maybe we'll just head straight for Bergdorf's. You've been such a help to me in the few days you've been in my employ. You've certainly earned a little fun."

"She works for *me*!" The blood has rushed to Travis's face, giving his normally cool complexion the heat of aggression. His eyes lock on mine. "You work for *me*. If you want to go shopping during the workday, you ask *me*!"

"I suppose it doesn't need to be during the workday," Jessica says, her voice now slipping back into uncertainty. "We could go after you're done or during the weekend—"

"She needs to ask *me*!"

"I don't think the labor laws would support you on that," Lander says, his arm casually draped across the back of the couch. "She gets to decide what she wants to do in her free time."

"Really," Travis says flatly, turning his glare on Lander. "And what do *you* think she likes to do in her free time?"

"I wouldn't know," Lander replies easily. "We just met. All I know is that it's her decision." He cocks his head to the side. "Are you all right, Trav? It's unlike you to get worked up over something so trivial as a shopping trip."

"I'm hardly worked up," Travis says, his voice immediately dropping back to the casually rapacious tone I've become accustomed to. "But I do find this whole thing a bit impulsive, even for you. Bell had a point when she asked why you would want to spend so much on a stranger."

"Really?" Lander asks, his brow crinkling in puzzlement. "It's certainly no more impulsive than when I took that waitress from the Millennium Club to Belize for the weekend."

A nervous smile pulls on Jessica's lips. She clearly finds that amusing.

I don't. I didn't know about the weekend in Belize.

But the reference does seem to have the desired effect on Travis. He hesitates before giving a curt nod of acknowledgment. "You're right, your behavior isn't surprising, just typically irresponsible. That incident with the waitress ended up costing you your membership."

Lander shrugs nonchalantly. "If I had liked the Millennium Club, I wouldn't have allowed them to take my membership. But as you know, it wasn't my scene. So my behavior wasn't irresponsible; I simply decided to take what I wanted and discard what I didn't. And now I want to buy your assistant a dress and take her to a fund-raiser. Is that really an issue?"

"No," Travis says slowly. He throws Jessica a look and she immediately gets up and moves back to her seat in the corner as if she's getting out of the way of an anticipated explosion. "If this is what you want to do I have no interest in stopping you," he continues. "I'm glad you came around about Highkin. He will be useful."

"I'm sure of it," Lander replies. "I only wonder that you have room in your pockets for another politician."

"Well," Travis says with a small smile, "it's a good thing my pockets are so extraordinarily large."

"Yes," Lander says distractedly as he reaches inside his jacket for his checkbook. "Jessica, I'll write you one check for the dress and another for the fund-raiser. Will that work?"

"Perfectly," she whispers. Her two minutes have clearly been spent and she's now turned back into a pumpkin.

Lander whips out a pen and walks over to the desk as Jessica, following him at a safe distance, tells him who to make the fund-raising check out to.

Travis doesn't object and instead busies himself with the emails on his phone. And yet, even though his eyes are on his screen, I can't shake the feeling that he's watching me. It's like he's sending me a silent warning . . . or perhaps a threat.

When Lander's done he puts his checkbook back into his pocket, only to pull out his cell. "So that's all settled. Bell, can I have your number so we can make arrangements?"

I rattle off the number he already has and he makes a show of typing it in. Travis looks up from his own phone, his expression hard and impatient. "It was good of you to stop by, Lander."

"As I said, it was on my way. I'll see myself out," Lander replies, easily taking the hint. "Always a pleasure, Jessica." And then he turns to me, his smile filled with mischief. "I look forward to seeing your choice of attire."

None of us move as he walks out of the room, and we stay silent until we hear the sound of the front door clicking closed.

The slow way Travis's head turns in my direction reminds me a little of the Komodo dragon I saw at the Bronx Zoo. It's a leisurely movement, almost nonchalant, and yet you just know that whatever has attracted the beast's attention is not long for this world.

"I need to talk to Bell alone," he says coolly.

"Travis, I really—" Jessica begins, but he stops her with a small gesture of his hand.

"I can talk to her alone in here or she and I can speak privately in the bedroom while you wait for us. Your choice."

Jessica's shoulders rise up to her diamond drop earrings but she doesn't say anything. Instead she just turns around and leaves her office, closing the door quietly behind her.

"She's very . . . tolerant," I venture, because at this point *not* saying something feels conspicuous.

"I usually don't talk to her like that in front of company. I only make an exception to that rule when we're in the presence of people I trust or people who don't have the credibility or influence to sway the opinion of anyone who matters. You fit into both categories," he says irritably. "Go after him."

"Excuse me?"

"Go after Lander now and find out what the hell he's up to."

"But he said he has a dentist appointment."

"Are you stupid?"

I look at him blankly, pretending not to understand.

"He doesn't have a goddamned dentist appointment! What he has is an agenda. Go find out what it is. Now, Bell, or that sex tape will be the least of your concerns."

I really wish he'd stop bringing up that tape. If he does end up posting it on the internet it won't be the worst thing in the world, but oddly enough, knowing that millions of strangers could see it is less disquieting than knowing that Travis already has.

I also think that confronting Lander can wait. I want to find a way to get Travis to talk about Javier and maybe even about Micah. But if Travis doesn't think I'm completely under his thumb he won't share anything with me. So reluctantly I grab my purse and nod my consent. "I'll let you know what I'm able to get out of him," I say.

As I pass a sulking Jessica in the hall, I realize that I can at least be grateful that my private exchange with Travis was far too brief for Jessica to assume that we did anything other than talk . . . unless of course Travis has issues that I don't know about.

chapter thirty

When I get to the street I'm not exactly sure where to turn. This latest series of events has me rattled and dazed. Lander has sort of kept and broken his promise to me at the same time. And Travis has apparently fed his inner asshole Miracle-Gro to the point that his dickishness can barely be contained. While Jessica . . . Well, Jessica's the same pathetic mess she always is, so at least there's that.

I wander down the sidewalk, halfheartedly fishing for my phone inside my purse so I can call Lander and find out where he really is.

But when I turn the corner he's there, waiting for me with a smirk.

"What was that about?" I ask as I approach, more curious than cross.

"It's simpler this way," he says.

"Simpler for who?"

"Both of us I should think." He's leaning nonchalantly against a building, looking like a cross between a young Gordon Gekko and James Dean. Only Lander can make a suit look rebellious. "You don't have to pretend not to know me anymore, so that should make things easier for you. As for me? Well, now you can tell Travis that you're in the position to get the inside scoop on me. My brother doesn't trust me? Let's give him some cooked-up dirt and see where it takes us."

I am no longer in the middle of one of Sartre's plays. I'm in the middle of The Twilight Zone.

"I . . . I haven't agreed to that," I stammer.

"And what have you agreed to, Bell?" he asks. "What bargains have you made with your demons? Because I suspect you've made a few."

"I think," I say slowly, "that I could ask you the same question."

Again he smiles. An elderly couple walks past us, hand in hand, while a thirtysomething woman wearing a tightly fitted dress passes them with a longing glance. The world is moving at the pace it's supposed to move . . . except for Lander and me. We're in this holding pattern as we try to parse each other's moods and secrets.

Lander has his own plans, plans that I know nothing about despite all my research. I should never have made him a target. Targets should be simple, like Jessica, who is the equivalent of a red bull's-eye; to take her down all I need to do is keep a steady hand and a focused eye. Or like Travis, who is a hawk: difficult to shoot, but easy to spot and identify.

Trying to make a target out of Lander is like trying to shoot an entire colony of killer bees. Destroying him, even *containing* him, may be nearly impossible, and yet I suspect that he has a unique ability to destroy.

Travis is in trouble.

"Will you help me feed Travis some false information, Bell?" Lander asks. "Will you help me put some wheels in motion?"

He's asking me to do what I'm already doing. I wish I could tell him that. I wish we could laugh about it and work like a true team, the way bees are meant to work.

But I can't do that. I lift my face up to the sun and close my eyes. "I will, on one condition."

"What's that?"

"I want to know what the deal is with this waitress. We've been together almost every night this week and you still haven't offered to take me anywhere."

Lander laughs and shakes his head. "That was a long time ago. I was about your age when it happened, I think. It didn't mean anything. I just wanted to take a vacation and I wanted someone to sleep with while I was there. She said she was game, so I took her. I was kicked out of the club because their staff isn't allowed to fraternize with the guests . . . and when the manager tried to fire her I lost my temper." Lander shrugs and sighs. "I'm not pleasant when I lose my temper."

"Sooo, you're like the Hulk."

Lander chuckles softly. "Something like that. But really, Travis is right; I didn't handle the whole thing well. Like I said, I was young."

"Like me."

"Like you." He crosses his arms. "So will you feed some false information to Travis or not?"

"Oh, I'll do it. But if we last six months and you still haven't taken me on a trip, we're going to have problems."

"Fair enough," he says as his eyes follow a passing pedestrian as tall as an NBA player with a dog the size of a toaster. "Why did he send you after me? He is the reason you're down here, right?"

"He wants me to get a sense of why you're coming to this dinner. He doesn't believe that you actually want to support this politician."

That's not entirely accurate, but I don't feel guilty about misrepresenting Travis's request. At this moment the lies are so much more logical than the truth.

"Right," he says slowly. "But what could you realistically get out of a man you've supposedly just met?"

"Maybe he's testing my skills as an interrogator."

"Tell him I said I think I'll be able to make some good business contacts at the dinner. And tell him that you made plans with me tonight."

"*Are* you making plans with me tonight?"

He reaches forward and brushes my cheek with his hand. "Meet me at my place at eight. I'll have champagne chilled and dinner delivered."

"I might tell Travis that we're just meeting at a restaurant," I say with a smile, "since we just met and all."

"Very well, tell him that," Lander says. "That is, if you think you're capable of carrying off the lie."

It's a funny line. Probably funnier than he realizes.

I leave him without another word. I'm almost back inside Travis's building when I get the text.

Are you being good, Sweet?

My steps slow to a stop and I take a moment to look around. Am I being watched? Shivering slightly I text back: Yes.

I wait to see if another text is coming, but there's nothing, and eventually my screen goes dark.

As I walk back into Travis's building I have to remind myself that I'm the predator . . . not the prey.

chapter thirty-one

When I get back up to the penthouse it's Jessica who opens the door for me, a half-emptied martini glass in her hand.

"He's waiting for you in my office." I can tell by both the phrasing and her tone that she's still forbidden entry into that particular room. I offer her my best what-can-I-do smile, but she just glares at me through tear-filled eyes and watches as I too disappear into what is supposed to be her space.

"What did he say?" Travis snaps the minute the door is closed.

"He says that he wants you to know that we're dating. He thinks you're going to ask me to spy on him. It's a test."

"A test?"

"Your brother doesn't trust you," I say simply.

Travis turns his back on me and stares out the window. "Throw him off the scent."

"You want me to tell him you don't want me to spy on him?"

"Don't be an idiot. That would be like Russia saying they don't want to spy on China. It's a blatant and easily spotted lie. No, when I tell you to throw him off the scent what I mean is I want you to pretend that I'm trying to get *different* information from the information I'm actually trying to get. Tell him I suspect him of betraying the family. Tell him I think he's feeding information to HGVB's competition. Tell him I think he's about to jump ship and I want to know what kind of lifeboat he's built himself."

"You really want me to tell him all that?"

"Well, don't be *obvious* about it!" Travis whirls around. "Lead him to believe those things, that's all. You're a smart girl, you work it out."

"But . . . how can I throw him off the scent when I don't know what the scent *is*?"

"Excuse me?"

"I don't know what information you actually want me to get, other than his phone records. What do you *really* want me to find out, Mr. Gable?"

Travis hesitates, and then I see a slow calm descend

on him as he slips his hands into his pockets. "Find out what his interest is in Talebi."

The request startles me. I had almost forgotten that I had planted that particular seed.

And yet the reminder makes me unspeakably happy. When I mentioned that name to Travis it had been a shot in the dark. The fact that I actually managed to hit something is a little stunning.

"Can you give me any information that might help me draw him out on that score?" I ask. "For instance, does Talebi work for the bank? If so, perhaps I should start by asking him about his coworkers in a more general sense before zeroing in. Or maybe he's a client? Should I start by asking him about his accounts? Or—"

"Just ask him why he wants to know whether or not I mentioned the name Talebi," Travis says impatiently. "He's the one who brought it up, right? You don't need any better excuse to ask him about it than that."

I nod, quietly tucking away my disappointment.

Travis looks at his watch. "I have to get back to the office."

"Wait," I say, taking a step forward. "I wanted to ask you . . . I, um . . . Do you think I did a good job last night?"

"What are you talking about?"

"As a translator for Javier. Despite being bilingual,

I've never actually acted as a translator before. Did I perform satisfactorily? What about Javier? Is he happy with how the information was relayed?"

I watch Travis's face carefully, looking for any sign that he might know something that he's not letting on.

But instead he just shakes his head again and pushes past me. "Trust me, Bell, if I have a problem with your performance you won't have to ask."

I sit down on the sofa as Travis exits and try to stave off dizziness.

Moments after I hear the front door open and close Jessica comes in. "I'd like you to leave early today."

"Jessica, the way Mr. Gable behaved . . . It wasn't based on any encouragement I've given him. I would never—"

Jessica holds up her hand to stop me. I notice that the cocktail glass that was half empty before is now completely drained. "Just go," she says softly.

Without another word I get up and gather my things. "I'll be back tomorrow morning at ten," I say, and when Jessica doesn't answer I make a quiet exit, secretly thankful for the respite.

A few blocks from my home I find Mary sitting on the sidewalk. She has a whole stack of coloring books now, two boxes of colored pencils, and a small sharpener, all stacked and lined up with the precision you would expect from a preschool teacher preparing for class.

As I step up to her she flashes me a big smile. "Hi, I'm Mary."

"I know," I say quietly.

"Your family's real nice," she continues, looking down at her new supplies. "They gave me the money for all of this and a good meal too. I ate at Red Lobster last night. I just walked right in and ordered up a four-course feast! And all they wanted in return was my help in getting you to talk to them. Did you talk to them?" she asks as she opens up a coloring book filled with images of Dora the Explorer. "You should always talk to family, you know. I would have helped them even without the money. But the money, that was real nice. Been a long time since I've had lobster."

I think about the Clif Bars in my purse and suddenly feel ashamed. I've been treating Mary like she's a dog, not a person. Giving her the occasional treat or toy. Micah and Javier were able to buy Mary's trust simply by offering her the means to feel human for a night.

"Maybe someday we should go to a better lobster restaurant," I say, thinking about the duffel bag full of money still in my apartment. "Maybe Ed's Lobster Bar in Soho."

Mary shakes her head. "I don't like that part of town. I like it right here in Harlem where my people are." She looks at me suspiciously, seeming to notice my tailored attire for the first time. "Are you sure you're from around here?"

"Yes," I say with a sigh and take a seat next to her on the curb. "I'm your people."

"And did you talk to your family?"

"I spoke to the men who gave you all this, but they're not family."

"You can't disown family," Mary says, shaking her head so hard a green pencil she had in her hair comes flying out. She picks it up primly and uses it to color the clouds of Dora's world. "You can't pretend you don't belong to them and they don't belong to you. You share the blood, that's what matters. Can't pretend you don't."

"I don't share their blood," I say softly, not sure if I can convince her of that or even sure if it's worth my while to try. "The only family I ever had was my mom."

"Huh." Mary's pencil is working furiously now as she makes green drip from Dora's mouth so it looks like she's been eating this artificial sky Mary's creating for her. "So where's your mama now?"

"She's dead."

Mary looks up, startled. I'm a little startled myself. I've never said those words aloud in quite that way, without poetry or venom. Just stating it as a fact the way you might tell someone that you didn't win the lottery, the disappointment so expected it's barely worth noting.

"You alone in the world?"

"Yes."

"Me too," she says as she pulls out another pencil, this time from the box, and gives Dora a pink sun. "Whatcha gonna do about it?"

"What do you suggest?" I ask. "Coloring books?" I hear the sarcasm in my voice and instantly feel ashamed, but Mary seems unfazed.

"Nah," she says. "Colorin's my way. Everybody's gotta find their own way to be alone in this world."

"I had a plan," I say as a large truck goes rumbling by and a passing teenager throws his empty Coke can into the gutter.

"What kinda plan?"

"The kinda plan that I thought would help me handle being alone, I guess," I say with a sigh. "It's been sort of a big focus for me. It's a very, very detailed plan. But it's gotten complicated. So complicated I can barely tell what's going on anymore or who's doing what. It literally makes my head spin."

"That's good," Mary says mildly as she pulls out a lavender pencil.

"That's *good*?"

"Sure. When your head's spinnin' you forget about being lonely . . . Too busy being dizzy, I imagine. If you just focus on the emptiness it'll swallow you up just like it was a big black hole."

A big black hole . . . Yes, that's what loneliness is. I'm a little surprised by the wisdom of Mary's insights, but then, unhappy, lonely people usually make the best philosophers. Happy people usually try not to see people like Mary. They pass them on the street without so much as a cursory glance as they rush home to their loved ones. But Mary sees *everyone*. She doesn't have the luxury of blinders, so it makes sense that she might have a better grasp of what life really is and what it isn't.

"Ever think about being a therapist, Mary?" I ask absently.

Mary smiles as she colors in the earth beneath Dora's feet. "I'd rather be a lobster catcher. That lobster last night was *good.*"

I laugh, pull my wallet out, and hand her a twenty and a ten.

"What's this for?" she asks politely, but she does snatch the money from my hand.

"For the therapy session," I say as I get to my feet. "And for Red Lobster."

I walk the last block home mulling it all over. Although I know Mary's right about every distraction being a blessing, I can't help but think that these are blessings I could do without. I actually feel cheated. It's as if I had spent all of 2007 coming up with a plan to destroy Lehman Brothers only to find out that they had decided to implode themselves. Clearly Travis and Lander are going to tear each other to shreds with or without me, which gives the desired result, but without any of the satisfaction.

And Micah and Javier went to all that trouble to scare the shit out of me last night, and to what end? So they could keep me from undoing men who are intent on being undone? Lander and Travis are making all of our subversive tactics and threats completely irrelevant. It's just not right.

When I get to my apartment I throw my purse onto my bed next to the duffel bag. It feels odd leaving thousands of dollars in cash in my apartment, but then again no one in their right mind would think to look for that kind of cash in this particular rat hole.

"It's all right," I whisper to myself. "It's only stage one." And it's true. Travis is using me as a double agent against Lander, and Lander is using me as a double agent against Travis. Neither one of them seems to be able to grasp the fact that I'm my own agent working exclusively for myself. I'm the only one with a bird's-eye view of the game.

That's stage one.

And while Travis has his fur up over Lander, he's completely oblivious to the quiet setup I'm orchestrating from Jessica's computer.

Although Travis seems hell-bent on making that job easier for me too. I don't know what keeps Travis and Jessica together, but if he wants her to disappear he's going to get his wish.

And Travis will never see it coming.

Of course, it'll look more believable once I know what shady dealings he's involved in. Then I can make it look like Jessica knows too, and of course she might. But what's important is that I'll make it look like she might be on the verge of spilling the secrets. Jessica's posts about spousal abuse will be damning, but to ensure that someone of Travis's means actually goes to prison I'll need to show that he has something to gain from the murder and a lot to lose if he doesn't go through with it. And once they convict him of the white-collar stuff it'll be so much easier to believe that he lost control in other areas as well.

A little truth, a little fiction. It's a potent and delicious dish that I've stolen directly from the Gables' recipe book.

I sit on the bed and carefully open the duffel bag. Fifteen thousand dollars . . . Considering what Micah thinks he's buying the price seems a little low. Then again, he doesn't really need to pay me anything. If I were capable of complying, his threats would have been enough. But I can't comply. It would go against my very nature. So no amount of money would do the trick.

Still, if Micah catches even the faintest whiff of what's going on, not only will he subject me to unthinkable torture, he'll make sure that Travis gets off.

That can't happen. And yet I'm not sure of how to prevent it from happening. And the horrible truth is that the white-collar stuff that I'm hoping to expose might very well directly involve Micah. Bringing down the Gables will be a dangerous task, but to take down a mob boss with them? That's a death-defying feat.

So question number one is, do I have the ability to defy death?

And question number two is, what about Lander?

I pick up a handful of bills and flip through them, trying to make them create that sound, the sound money makes in the movies when the bad guy holds a rubber-banded stack of bills to his ear and makes them rustle like a deck of cards. In the movies he can tell how many bills are there just by listening to that noise.

It's total bullshit, of course. Bills can never sound like plastic cards. You can't count money by listening to it any more than you can get to know Lander by watching him from afar.

I wish I had worked that out earlier, the part about

Lander. I had pegged him as a movie-style villain. If that had been the case, I would have made sure he was also implicated in whatever crimes Travis was up to. I would have made Jessica's disappearance look like a conspiracy hatched by the two brothers. Travis and Lander would have spent most of their time trying to prove each other's guilt and very little time working together in a productive manner.

But Lander isn't a movie villain. He's Lander. And I don't want to treat him like he's his brother's clone, because he's not. They deserve different fates.

I know what fate Travis deserves. I'm not sure about Lander.

I know what I want him to be deserving of. I want him to be deserving of me. I'm fully aware that's a punishment of sorts, perhaps for both of us. But I'd like to think it's a fitting punishment. It'd be nice to think that we're Catherine and Heathcliff, or Valmont and Merteuil from *Dangerous Liaisons*. All completely screwed-up individuals who were cursed to love and torture each other. A lifetime of love and torture at the hands of one special individual. It's all any of us can reasonably ask for. The perfectly happy, all-American families with their white-picket-fence homes and ice-cream-soda weekends? Norman Rockwell dreamed those people up between his wife's depressive-alcoholic episodes.

And that Disney princess dream, complete with the prince and the horse and the pretty white castle? I gave *that* up on the day they took my mother from me.

But now, for the first time in my life, I find myself craving something else. I have a new dream, one that doesn't directly involve revenge.

For the first time I find myself longing for the torture of love.

chapter thirty-two

I have no idea from where Lander ordered this chilled peach soup or the grilled chicken breast with the grapefruit glaze sitting on the plates in front of us—I didn't even know you *could* order such things to be delivered. But as we sit in his formal dining room, a bottle of Reserve Brut chilling in a silver bucket, I remind myself that when you're rich anything is possible.

I wait for him to mention Travis or Jessica or the impending fund-raising dinner, but he avoids all of those subjects. Instead he works on my edges, trying to find quiet ways to push past my defenses.

"What's your favorite book, Bell?" he asks. He dips his spoon into his soup and takes a small sip, as if the question was casual and not an attempt to learn who he's been sleeping with all this time.

I think about making up an answer that will sound right, but when I open my mouth I surprise myself by telling the truth. "I think . . . I think *The Princess Bride* is my favorite."

Lander stops, clearly surprised. "*The Princess Bride* . . . the movie with Billy Crystal?"

"No," I say impatiently. "The book that came before the movie. I hate movies based on book adaptations."

"It was a fun film—"

"I didn't say I hate *that* movie. I said I hate movies based on books in general. I don't want to see someone else's version of a story that I've already played out in my head. They never get it right. They can't. They're playing for the masses. A movie will always belong to a crowded theater, but a book is personal. It's an individual and intimate experience shared exclusively between the author and each individual reader, and when they turn books into movies they take that element away."

"I never thought of it that way," Lander admits, "but you're absolutely right."

"It's just not my thing. The truth is, I'm a selfish person," I say with a light laugh as I lift my champagne flute. "I know it's bad, but I don't like sharing. I don't like sharing my experiences, I don't want to share what's in my head or—"

"Or what's in your heart."

I sip my drink and let the bubbles play on my tongue. "You've got to stop finishing my sentences, Lander. You don't always know what it is I'm going to say."

"Did I get it wrong that time?"

I smile and put the glass back on the table, unwilling to answer.

"I can finish your sentences because we think alike," he says mildly.

"What do *you* like to read?" I ask, ignoring his last comment.

"I've always enjoyed Shakespeare."

"What's your favorite play?" I ask, even though I know it's *Macbeth*.

"*Macbeth*. *Hamlet* and *Titus Andronicus* are also favorites."

"You like 'em dark," I note.

"I like things I can relate to," he replies. "It's easier for me to connect with a tragedy than a farce."

I nod, fully understanding.

"And what kind of music do you like? What's your favorite band?" he continues. "I can't believe we've never talked about this. Wait, let me guess, you're a Linkin Park girl . . . or maybe Nine Inch Nails. I can see you as a Nirvana enthusiast too."

"Christina Aguilera!" The name bursts from my lips before I can stop it.

Lander looks at me, clearly startled. "Christina Aguilera?"

I feel my cheeks redden and I duck my head down to try to hide it. "I listened to her when I was young," I say softly. "My mother would play her all the time when we were home. We would dance around our little living room to 'Come on Over Baby' and 'Genie in a Bottle,' and when 'Beautiful' came out, my mom said it was her song. I thought it was a little sappy at first but eventually I came around."

Lander reaches forward and tucks my hair behind my ear so he can better see my face. Still, I won't meet his eyes. "Did your father like her too?"

"I've never met my father."

"Ah." He sighs and shakes his head. "So where's your mother now?"

"She's gone."

"Gone where?"

Finally I lift my head and meet his eyes. "She was killed when I was still a kid."

He takes a moment to absorb this, his gaze sliding away from me to an abstract painting on the wall. "Do you want to talk about how it happened?"

"No."

He nods his acceptance of this. "If she was killed when you were still a kid and your father wasn't in the picture . . . what did you do?"

"I grew up."

A sardonic smile plays on the edges of Lander's lips. "Tragedy tends to do that to people. It ages them."

"Yeah," I agree with a sigh. "That's probably why so many of the high schoolers on *Glee* look like they're about thirty. If they sing 'Total Eclipse of the Heart' one more time they'll be ready for social security."

Again Lander looks startled and then he breaks out laughing. I find myself giggling too and then something in me just sort of breaks and succumbs to a full-on belly laugh. Tears start trickling down my cheeks and I have to hold on to the table to steady myself. It's not that what I said was so funny; it wasn't. But talking about my mother here, like this, to Lander . . . It feels like a relief. And maybe for him it's a relief to hear me reveal anything about my life at all.

So we laugh and we laugh until our breath fails us and we wash down our merriment and tears with champagne and good food. We bring the conversation back to the trivial, and I ask about his favorite artists and vacation spots (Degas and Jackson Pollock for the former; Paris and the small villages of Vietnam for the latter). He asks about my favorite places to shop in New York and where I get my news (Friends Vintage and Angel Street Thrift Shop for the former; public radio and the *Village Voice* for the latter). We talk about television and the few movies I do like and the many movies he loves. We talk about his love of puzzles and how it was his mother who introduced him to the world of anagrams and how they used to send each other coded notes all the time when he was in elementary school. He admits to having pretended he was Galileo sending secret notes to Kepler, and I'm embarrassed to admit that I used to pretend that I was Cinderella getting princess lessons from my Fairy Godmother (aka my mother).

I tell him just how much I love to read.

Naming my favorite book was one thing, but spelling out my obsession with reading in general? Well, that may not seem like such a big admission for most people, but for me it is. My rebellious streak started at ten, and since then I've kept my love of books a secret. I admit to Lander that I've read everything from Faulkner to Charlaine Harris. I've read Brian Greene's science books and the political books of Bob Woodward. *The Odyssey, The Canterbury Tales, I Know Why the Caged Bird Sings,* the Shopaholic books—I've read *everything.* I expect him to be surprised by this, but Lander just nods his head and gently fishes for more, asking about my thoughts on specific novels and authors, asking if I ever thought of writing myself (no, not for publication) and if I prefer ebooks to paperbacks (I'm good with either).

"Are you self-educated or did you go to college?" he asks.

"So many questions," I say with a sigh as I scoop up the last bite on my plate. "Shouldn't we leave a little to be discovered over time?"

"Oh, I suspect that even if I had a lifetime to make inquiries I'd still be discovering new things about you." He picks up my hand and runs his thumb back and forth over the inside of my wrist.

I remain quiet as his touch moves from my wrist to my arm, tracing the vein where the life source is held. "If you took that much time to learn about me," I finally say, "you'd discover that I'm not a good person."

Lander's hand stops and he looks up from my arm and into my eyes. "And if you took that much time to examine *me*," he says, "you'd discover that I'm worse."

I giggle. I'm a little thrilled by the darkness of it all, and the mere mention of taking so much time together fills me with a disturbing sense of hope.

"We haven't talked about Travis yet," I point out. "If we're going to feed him false information we'd better figure out exactly what kind of false information will be most beneficial."

"We'll get to the subject of Travis."

"When?"

He flashes me an impish grin. "I thought we'd talk about it over dessert." He leans forward and touches his lips to my neck, sucks gently at the skin as I feel goose bumps rise all over my body. No one can excite me the way Lander can. No one can challenge or worry me in quite the same way. We're two creatures shaped by heartbreak and rage.

We're two people who belong together.

His hands are in my hair as my hands move down to his pants. I can feel his erection reaching for me as his mouth moves to my ear. With one arm he pushes the dishes out of the way. One of them falls, landing on the hardwood floor with a crash just as Lander lifts me onto the table. I wrap my legs around his waist and my hands are in his shirt. He has just the lightest scattering of chest hair, which is coarse against my fingers.

"I want to see you," he breathes, his lips by my ear, his hands now up my skirt, stroking my thighs.

I smile and lean back just enough to pull off my shirt. He can see my hardened nipples peeking out from the black lace flowers of my bra. I wrap my arms around his neck and nod, inviting him to expose me.

His fingers work quickly and the bra is soon dangling from my shoulders. Seconds later it lies among the shards of ceramic on the floor.

His hands are so warm as they touch me, caressing the skin of my breasts as I arch my back, offering myself on his table as if I'm a delicacy.

One of his hands slips between my legs, and just the

smallest movement of his fingers causes the thin fabric of my thong to delicately scrape against my clit.

"Are you wet for me, Bell?" he asks, his whispered voice gliding over my skin.

"Yes," I whisper back. He shakes his head, unsatisfied with my answer.

"Yes, *what*?"

I close my eyes as he lowers his head, gasp as his teeth graze my nipple. "Yes," I say again, "I'm wet for you, Lander."

I feel his smile against my skin. With little effort he lifts me enough to pull off my panties and then my skirt.

And now I'm wearing nothing.

He pushes me onto my back, my legs dangling off the edge of the table.

"You're going to spy on Travis for me," he says, his hands moving from my calves, to my hips, to my stomach, to my breasts.

"Yes."

"Will you enjoy it, Bell?"

Again his fingers slide between my legs and he's touching me as I writhe before him.

"Yes."

"Yes, what, Bell?"

"Yes, I'll enjoy it."

His finger pushes inside.

"You won't disappoint me, will you, Bell?"

"No," I breathe. His thumb moves to my clit. "I'm not going to disappoint you in any way."

"That's good," he says. "It would be a shame if you did, particularly when you're so capable of bringing me so much pleasure."

I bite down on my lip before replying, "I always give as good as I get."

His smile spreads into a grin and his fingers continue to play. I can feel myself being brought closer and closer to the edge.

"I want you to tell him that you overheard me on the phone. Tell him I addressed the person on the line as Mr. Talebi."

That name again. I want to ask what it means, but then Lander's thumb starts making little circular movements, adding a new and exciting sensation. I cannot question him now. All I can do is agree.

"What are you going to do, Bell?" he asks as he brings me closer and closer to orgasm. "What will you say to my brother?"

"I'll . . . I'll tell him . . . tell him that you were speaking to Talebi," I gasp.

"Say it again," Lander says. "I want to make sure you memorize your lines."

"You were speaking with . . . Oh, God!"

"No," Lander says. A second finger pushes inside, making me whimper in pleasure. "I don't speak to God. Who will I be speaking to?"

"Talebi," I moan.

"That's right. You'll tell him that for me. Won't you?"

"Yes." I'm so very close I can barely stand it.

"Do you like spying for me, Bell?" he says, his voice low, teasing. He knows the answer.

"Yes," I say again.

He leans over me, whispering into my ear, "You will be my little spy, stealing secrets and exploiting them for my entertainment."

I moan. My whole body is trembling.

"And do you know why you'll do these things for me, Bell?"

"Why?" I breathe. "Tell me."

He raises himself slowly, looking down at me as I writhe. "You'll do it because you'll like it. You like the game."

"Yes!" I reach for him, but as my hand extends, the ring of the doorbell echoes through the penthouse.

Someone is here. And not just in the building. Someone was granted access to this floor and is right outside.

I try to get up but Lander gently pushes me back down. "I told you I ordered dessert, didn't I?"

My heart is pounding so hard it seems to make the entire table vibrate beneath me.

"Will you come get the door with me, Bell? Will you give me that pleasure?"

I don't know what to say. I don't know who's out there. I don't know what this is about.

And then I'm struck with the strangest realization:

I *trust* Lander.

I trust that whatever happens, whatever he has planned . . . I'll like it.

My heart is still pounding, his hand is still moving on me, and through barely parted lips I once again say, "Yes."

And suddenly, just as I think I'm about to orgasm right here, on this table with God-knows-who waiting outside the door, he takes his hand away and then pulls me to my feet. I can barely keep my balance as he leads me out of the room, naked, and into the hall to the front door. I stand only a few steps behind. I'm tempted to cover myself, but instead I reach forward and take Lander's arm, holding on to him tightly as he opens the door.

"Hi, I—" begins the man standing in the threshold, an insulated bag in his hands. But of course he doesn't finish his sentence as his eyes land on me. He's young, maybe my age, maybe a college student working part-time delivering desserts to wealthy patrons.

But whoever he is, he's never seen anything like this. I can tell by the way his eyes wander over me, his mouth hanging open in shock, his eyes alight with desire.

"Ah, you brought the ice cream," Lander says smoothly, turning to me, keeping the door open wide. "This place has the best ice cream in New York, all made on the premises, of course. They don't usually deliver, but they made an exception for me." He wraps his arm around my waist, his hand moving to my hip. "Please put it in the kitchen," he says to the man.

The deliveryman nods and steps inside, never taking his eyes off me. Slowly, ever so slowly, he walks past, pivoting to watch me as he does.

"The kitchen," Lander says, a little more sternly this time, and as the man turns to obey orders, Lander pushes me against the wall and kisses me fiercely. His hands are everywhere—my butt, my inner thighs—and then up, once again slipping inside my core just as our audience reemerges from the kitchen. He pauses to watch as I claw at Lander's back.

I look over at the man. He's got shaggy black hair that falls into his eyes, and the stubble on his face is so faint it can barely be seen.

Lander's toying with me, making me shiver, but still I manage a smile for our visitor. "You can leave now," I say coyly as Lander continues his ministrations.

"But I need to give him his tip," Lander says, pulling a fifty out of his back pocket and placing it in my palm. His right hand never leaves me, never stops moving. Once again I'm coming close to losing control.

The stranger moves closer. He's studying me now, watching the way Lander is making my body quiver and sing. His eyes linger on my breasts before falling to where Lander is touching me. I can see that he's hard for me. I can see that he wants to touch me.

I reach out my hand . . .

. . . and give him the fifty.

"She's beautiful, isn't she?" Lander asks as he presses his finger in deeper, and I find that I can't suppress my moan.

"Yes," the man whispers. "May I . . . may I touch her?"

"No," Lander says, leaning down to kiss my shoulder. "Only she chooses who can touch her. And she's chosen me."

I close my eyes at that. He has no idea why he was chosen. He doesn't know that the woman whose body he can manipulate so easily has made it her life's work to manipulate his world.

"May I touch you?" the man asks me, bypassing Lander in his desperation for satisfaction.

I open my eyes and stare into the brown eyes of Lander,

my lover,

my choice.

"No," I whisper.

Lander smiles and with one hand he opens the door wide again. If anyone were in the hall they'd be able to see us. But no one is there and, very reluctantly, the deliveryman walks out the door. He turns to say one more thing, or perhaps he just wants to burn the image into his memory, but Lander lets the door close and then suddenly we're alone again.

And I'm on fire.

In an instant I have his pants down. I'm pressed between him and the wall and I lift my legs and wrap them around his hips, allowing him to lower me onto him. I feel him thrusting with unhindered force inside my walls, making me cry out his name again and again as the orgasm finally overtakes me. I claw at his skin, bite down on his shoulder. And when he pulls me away from the wall and lowers me to the floor I don't protest. Instead I run my fingers against his polished floor as he continues to ride me.

Then, with one swift motion he turns and I'm on top. I sit up, never breaking our connection. His hands go to my hips and he slides me forward and back, making sure that he hits the spot that he knows drives me wild. I throw my head back and pull at my own hair. It seems impossible that my body can handle such an intense ecstasy. Surely I'll shatter or break.

He moves his hands up just a little higher so now I can feel his palms on the small of my back as he gently pulls me down to him. I put my hands on either side of his head and curl my feet around the insides of his knees as I take control, moving my hips, rubbing my clit against him as I press my breasts into his chest.

We're so thoroughly connected you would think we were one.

Grinding slowly I push him farther and farther inside me until control becomes difficult for both of us.

His grip moves to my thighs, encouraging me, increasing my pace. He's the only thing I can focus on. The room itself is a blur, controlled chaos.

Tonight I let a stranger see me. It felt wild and crazy and dangerous . . .

. . . and I never lost control.

I look down at Lander and see the intensity of his gaze, which I can feel as surely as I can feel him inside me. The penthouse is silent except for our rough and uneven breathing.

I start moving even faster and his hips move with mine before he abruptly flips me over again. Now he's on top, and each thrust is so powerful that the explosion can no longer be contained.

But it's a sweet explosion. I shake with pleasure as Lander releases himself inside me, filling me, throbbing inside me, making the moment complete.

It's decadent.

It's devious.

It's fantastic.

It's us.

chapter thirty-three

Hours have passed and now we lie in his bed, him sleeping by my side. But me? I couldn't be more awake. I *should* be looking through his things right now, but I don't want to.

I want to talk.

I nudge him gently with my elbow, and when he doesn't respond I jab him with more force. "Are you awake?" I ask as he moans and turns in my direction.

"Well, you just jabbed me with your elbow."

"So I guess that's a yes?"

"Bell."

"Who is Talebi?"

There's a silence in the room. I can't see him but I can feel him thinking.

I turn onto my side so now I'm looking at his silhouette, his features completely lost to the darkness. "If you want me to help you, you have to," I say.

"Have to what?" he asks.

"You have to trust me," I reply. "That's what you're thinking, isn't it? You're trying to work out if you can trust me or not."

Silence.

I release a loud, exasperated sigh. "If you don't tell me, I'll research it. I'll find out one way or another."

"I trust you, Bell," Lander finally says. "I just don't know if this is information that will help or hurt you. It's easier to stay clean if you're ignorant."

"I don't want to be ignorant, and a little dirt isn't going to kill me. If it gets to be too much I'll wash myself off and walk away."

"It's not always that easy." His voice is softer now, tempered with both concern and affection.

"You need to tell me, Lander."

Another long silence and I'm about to continue my argument when he finally speaks up. "I think Talebi is feeding Travis information."

"What kind of information?"

"Information about other companies. Companies that HGVB's top clients are investing in."

"Oh," I say, trying to keep the disappointment out of my voice. "You mean like insider trading?" I can't think of a crime less shocking or scandalous than insider trading.

"A lot of insider trading and a lot of corporate espionage."

That perks me up. I'm not entirely clear on what qualifies as corporate espionage, but it certainly sounds more interesting than insider trading.

"Talebi and some of his associates get information on companies that they aren't sharing with the shareholders. Sometimes it's drops in profit that haven't been reported yet but will be. Other times it's product development information that if leaked to competitors will weaken the company. I think Talebi is giving this information to Travis for a fee and then he's advising a few key investors to short the stock. They do, the information comes out or is mysteriously leaked, and our investors get rich."

"And the companies?"

"It's bad for them," Lander admits. "The smaller ones fold. The bigger ones certainly survive, but they all suffer and frequently someone inside their ranks gets the blame for the leak. If I'm right, innocent people are being fired and blacklisted from the industries they've spent their lives working in."

This time it's me who lets the room fall into silence. Up here on the fifteenth floor the sounds of the city are muted to the point of being practically nonexistent. But the thoughts reverberating through my brain are very, very loud. I'm almost surprised Lander can't hear them. Travis isn't looking for companies to invest in. He's looking for companies he can bet against. And once he places the bet, he makes sure that the company goes down. And if innocent people are hurt by this? Well, Travis has never been concerned with the welfare of innocents. Just ask my mother.

"How illegal is this?" I ask.

"Very illegal."

"Illegal enough to bring down a bank?"

Lander barks out a dry laugh. "Nothing brings down a bank. Haven't you been paying attention over the last several years?"

"Is it enough to send someone to jail, then?" I ask, not bothering to acknowledge his rhetorical question.

Lander hesitates, and the bed shifts beneath me as he turns onto his back.

"Two years ago I would have told you no. But the Justice Department is getting tougher. People have had it with bankers and their disregard for the law. If I'm right about this—and I might not be, Bell—but if I am, the Justice Department might demand their pound of flesh just to show people they're doing something. A figurehead to take down."

"And you think Travis is behind this?"

No answer.

"Lander, are we talking about Travis or not?"

"I don't know," Lander says quietly. "Like I said, I don't even know for sure that HGVB is involved in this whole thing or if anything's actually happening. I've just noticed some coincidences that look very suspicious to me. That's all. If something is going on, I have not been brought into that loop. But I have my reasons for being concerned."

"But what if it is Travis? What will you do?"

"I'll handle it," he says firmly. "I promise you that much, but you have to let *me* handle it. I appreciate your spying on him for me, but no matter what you find out, you can't go reporting it to the authorities and you certainly can't confront or question Travis. Just give the information to me."

"You don't want my help?"

"I want your help getting some wheels moving, that's all. You're a brilliant woman, but you don't have the specific expertise to know exactly what to look for or how to approach all this. If you went to the Treasury Department with this now, with no evidence, they'd dismiss it out of hand . . . and you would also tip off the wrong people."

"But if you get the evidence that proves that Travis is

involved in this kind of illegal activity, what are you going to do?" I press.

He pauses long enough to take a deep, cleansing breath, and then in a slow, steady voice he simply says, "I'll stop him."

Relief floods through me with the force of a raging river. The man I thought Lander was, the one I set out to destroy, would have protected Travis out of family loyalty, or maybe just for the sake of convenience and profit. But Lander is not the man I thought he was.

Which means I can be with him . . . even work with him.

It's perfect.

I reach out and touch his arm, connecting myself to him, feeling what it's like to be with someone I can both trust and respect.

"Lander—" I begin.

"I'll stop him without anyone having to go to jail."

I freeze. "How?" I whisper.

"I'll be able to sideline him or, if I need to, push him out of HGVB entirely. We'll quietly correct things at HGVB and make sure nothing like this happens again."

"That's it?" I can barely get the words out. He's telling me that he'll simply cover up the crime and move on. All those people and smaller companies that Travis has hurt in his quest for profits, nothing will change for them. Lander will deny them their justice.

"Trust me, it's enough," Lander says. "Without HGVB, Travis is nothing. And there's no point in his doing time. It won't fix anything and it will hurt his wife and kids as well as the family name. Plus it will damage the reputation of HGVB, and there will be fines, of course. Best to handle the whole thing in-house."

There will be fines. Companies have folded. People have lost their jobs, been blacklisted from careers they've spent their whole lives building. But Lander will sweep the whole thing under the rug so that HGVB doesn't have to pay a fine.

And so that the Gable name stays clean.

I pull back my hand and subtly shift away from him.

"So you'll help me plant a few seeds in Travis's head and then let me handle the rest?" he asks, oblivious to my change in mood.

"Of course, Lander," I say, working hard to keep the cold out of my voice. "I'll leave it all up to you."

Of all the lies I've told him since we met, that one is probably the biggest.

chapter thirty-four

The morning is difficult for me. Not in a pragmatic way; for once I actually had the foresight to bring my clothes to Lander's so I can leave for work directly from there rather than have to stop at my apartment. But I'm suffering from a hard-core emotional hangover.

I think he senses that something's wrong, but I don't volunteer my thoughts and he doesn't have much time to question me. He has to get to work himself and he has to be there by nine. I don't have to be at Jessica's until ten.

He agrees to leave me in the penthouse by myself.

Actually, it's not like he agrees to it exactly; he just does it. He seems to trust me.

Yesterday that trust was justified. Reciprocated. But now?

Sitting alone in his office, my hands pressed flat

against the smooth surface of his mahogany desk, I close my eyes, take a deep breath, and try to organize my thoughts.

"What do I do?" I whisper aloud.

And then as the obvious answer comes to me I open my eyes and walk over to Lander's file cabinet and start looking through his papers, trying to find something incriminating.

Because the obvious answer is simply this: *stick to the plan.*

I should be relieved. Everything is exactly as I originally thought it was. Travis is a criminal, Lander is a profit-hungry enabler—who cares less about innocents being hurt than about the status of his corporation—and their father is the asshole who unleashed them on the world.

It shouldn't surprise me that Lander wants to use his girlfriend to help his brother and HGVB get away with breaking the law. Sure, he's trying to stop them, but there's no justice in his plan, and they'll keep all their profits from Travis's dirty acts. Just last night Lander *told* me he was a bad person. He said he was worse than me, and God knows that's saying something.

So everything that's happening . . . it's *good.* Lander has literally spelled out what I need to be looking for. I just need to make it look like Jessica knows all about the espionage and that she's threatening to go public, and I'd better do it quickly because that woman could accidentally overdose at any time. Despite harboring some pity, I have absolutely no love for Jessica. And if she does commit suicide or overdose, I won't hesitate to find a way to make it look like a murder and pin it on Travis. But if she lives, that works for me too.

Travis is the kind of guy who would put a hit out on his wife if he thought she was going to betray him. Jessica knows that; after all, she was party to what happened to Nick Foley. So it shouldn't be too hard to convince her that she's going to be the next to go. I have to tell her that if she doesn't stage her own death she will actually die.

It amuses me to think about Jessica on the run, always looking over her shoulder, moving from one cheap motel to another, forced to use cash and take under-the-table odd jobs. *That's* the fate she deserves for her testimony against my mom. And who knows, maybe she'll actually sober up; maybe it'll help her in the long run. She certainly won't have the means for the drugs she's taking now.

As for her kids, well, as much as it pains me to admit it, I'm actually with Travis on this one. Jessica's not fit to raise a ferret, let alone a child. And if Travis raises them they'll turn into horrible little fascist monsters, and that's bad for everybody. No, Mercedes and Braden will be better off once their parents are out of the picture.

If I choose not to bring Lander down perhaps he'll be the one to raise them.

But I *have* to bring him down. He's one of the bad guys. He just told me as much.

It's simpler this way. I really need to be happy about this.

I pull out a copy of Lander's phone bill and study the numbers. I'm happy about this. Of course I am. This is great.

I take the bill and put it down on the desk. I should make a copy with Lander's printer and give it to Travis. I don't know if there's anything incriminating in here, but if I show it to Travis and he tells me to follow up on something, then I *will* know. And I can just keep fueling the flame between the brothers. It will be a betrayal of Lander's trust, but that's what I'm here for, right? He's the bad guy and I'm the necessary evil. That's how it's supposed to be.

But I don't *want* to give this to Travis.

I lean back on the desk and put my head in my hands. There have been times in my life when I've felt stupid and self-destructive and all sorts of other things, but this is the first time I've ever felt weak.

How have I come to this? I made assumptions about

who these people are, and across the board I've been completely accurate in my predictions. I got it all right. I'm *right*. How can I be having a hard time accepting *that*?

Again I take a deep breath and force myself to remember. I remember my mother crying. I remember her protestations of innocence that no one listened to. I remember what she looked like when I called her a killer and a whore.

I don't deserve a happy life. I can't forget that.

But I also have to remember that the Gables don't deserve happy lives either. They're the ones who started this. They literally got away with murder. I owe my mother justice. I can't have a real relationship with Lander. I probably can't have a real relationship with anyone. That's just the way it is. But if I let my mother down again, if I fail, my life is completely worthless.

There has to be justice.

I pick up the phone record and walk over to the printer, slip it under the lid, and press copy.

There has to be justice.

chapter thirty-five

When I get to Jessica and Travis's penthouse, Jessica answers the door before I even have a chance to finish knocking. Her eyes are red and I wonder what unique horror Travis has put her through this time.

"Shall we go shopping?" she asks, stepping out before I can step in.

"But I thought we were going to do that when I wasn't scheduled to work."

"You work," Jessica says between tightly clenched teeth, "for *me*. You're my personal assistant. Do you remember that? Or have you forgotten?"

"No, I . . ."

"For me, for me, for me!"

I take a small step back. It would seem that today's meds aren't sitting well.

"I want to go to brunch," Jessica says as she carefully locks the door behind her. "That's where we're going, to brunch. And then we're going shopping because you work for me."

"You're right," I say slowly. "I work for you."

A small but victorious smile plays on Jessica's lips. "Good girl."

She actually pats me on the head . . . like a *dog*.

I take a deep breath. It's fine. All of this is fine. In the end Jessica will be the one with her tail between her legs.

For the first half of brunch, Jessica and I sit in silence, mostly because she can't stop drinking long enough to get more than a few words out. On the plus side, she sips her Bloody Mary very slowly. It would really be fine if she would only give herself more than a few seconds off between each leisurely sip. And in combination with the drugs . . . well, it's not good.

My phone vibrates in my purse and I glance down at it to see a text from Lander.

How is my beautiful spy?

I look up quickly at Jessica as if she might have been able to read from my expression the context of the message. But of course her eyes remain on her glass. It was so careless of Lander to text me something like that while I'm working.

My mind flashes back to what it felt like to be on his table, his fingers inside me as he fed me my mission. *You will be my little spy, stealing secrets and exploiting them for my entertainment.* I had relished that moment. The very idea that we could work together to undermine Travis had been seductive.

But that was just a game. We were role-playing, as couples are wont to do in those circumstances. Lander doesn't want to work with me. He wants to use me. And I can never be his spy . . . only his traitor.

And that is the tragedy of us.

As Jessica continues to ignore me, I reach into my purse and answer back, Shh! Quiet, lover, I have work to do.

"Who are you texting?" Jessica snaps, as if she just noticed that I was still on the other side of the table.

"Just my neighbor. She wants me to watch her dog when she—"

"Fine," Jessica says, already bored with my lie. I sigh and zip up my purse, futilely trying to push Lander from my head.

It's only about forty minutes into brunch before Jessica's starting her third Bloody Mary. And she's getting sloppy.

"You lied to me," she slurs with a smile.

"What? Jessica, I've never—"

"Oh yes you did!" She laughs and wags a finger at me. "*You* said you weren't sleeping with my husband."

"I'm not," I say coolly. "Would you like to go to his office right now and ask him? We can do that. I don't think he'll lie to you."

"Yes, why hurt me with lies when the truth will do?"

I sigh and glance around the restaurant. I'm pretty sure this isn't Jessica's normal lunch spot. It's about as close to a dive as you can get in this part of town. The exposed brick walls are nice, but the place is dark despite it being late in the morning.

"You choose to stay with him and he chooses to stay with you," I say impatiently. "Obviously there's something still there between the two of you. Why don't we go back to his office and you can talk—"

"I stay because if I don't he'll take my children," she snaps, before adding, "my children and . . . and other things."

By other things I assume she means her Bergdorf card and her happy pills. She barely knows her children so I can't imagine she's too broken up over the possibility of losing them.

My eyes wander to the door. I should be back at Jessica and Travis's penthouse writing more incriminating posts. Plus I need to find evidence that Travis is working with this Talebi guy—and I *really* need to figure out what his connection is to Micah and Javier. There's no legal reason that I can think of that would prevent HGVB from doing business with Mexican or Russian banks, so there's got to be something else that I'm missing.

When I started this thing I assumed that I was going to have lots and lots of time. Time to build Jessica's paranoia, time to plant the right information in the right places, time to set Travis up for murder, time to orchestrate Jessica's disappearance . . . But if Lander is already onto the crimes Travis is committing and if he finds a way to sufficiently cover them up, all *my* plans will fall apart.

Time is now of the essence.

What I don't need to be doing is sitting here, twiddling my thumbs while Jessica gets wasted.

"And," Jessica continues as if she hadn't taken a full two-minute break from our conversation, "Travis stays because I know too much."

My eyes snap back to her. "What did you say?"

Jessica shakes her head, staring into her drink. "I'm so good with secrets. And I'm not a bad actress. Without me, where would they be?"

I lean forward, my focus now completely on her, my smile sympathetic. "Where *would* they be, Jessica?"

"I've stood up for this family," Jessica says, shaking her head a little too hard. "The *Gables*." She says the name as if it's the most ridiculous word in the world. "To listen to Travis's father you'd think he was the pope! Completely infallible! Walking on water and turning water into wine."

"Okay, I don't think it was the pope who did those things, but let's get back to *you*. You were telling me how you stood up for the family."

"Liars," she says, taking another sip of her drink. "They're liars. When Travis and I met he told me it was love at first sight, but he didn't love me. He loved that other bitch, the one who dumped him. But never me!"

"Wait, who did Travis love?"

"Not me!" Jessica practically screams. "That's the only important part. He's never loved me! The Gables lie! Liars, every one of them."

"But at some point, *you* loved Travis," I say gently.

"I did." She puts her glass down a little too hard, causing the waiter, who is across the room, to give us a worried look. But he doesn't come over. He's probably worried she'll try to order a fourth Bloody Mary and he'll have to refuse her service.

"I loved him," Jessica continues. "I didn't used to be a liar . . . he turned me into one. They all did."

"How'd they do that, Jessica?"

"By getting me to help them stay above the law, that's how! Do you know how many shattered lives paved the way to the Gables' success? You have no idea what these people have gotten away with! Travis, Lander, Edmund, not one of them is innocent! Their money is dirty, all of it! The only laws they care about are Darwinian! They——" She freezes, her mouth still open as if waiting for the next sound to come out. Her eyes clear and I can see she's having a brief moment of lucidity within the ocean of intoxication. "I don't know what I'm saying," she says, her tone suddenly fearful. Then she gets ahold of herself, pushes her drink a little farther away. "You shouldn't listen to me. I'm drunk. I shouldn't be drinking this early."

"It's okay, Jessica, you can talk to me."

Her bloodshot eyes narrow. "You will call me Mrs. Gable, and no, I can't talk to you," she slurs. "You fucked my husband."

I take a deep breath. Why would anyone sleep with her husband when her brother-in-law is single and so intensely enticing? Any woman who dared to be with Travis must know that she would be expected to please him, not the other way around. But Lander? When he kisses my shoulder, when he slides his hand along the inside of my thigh, that's for my pleasure. When he sucks gently on my neck, even when he whispers requests into my ear, it's all designed to enhance the delectation of the moment, not for *him*, but for *us*.

He opened the door for that deliveryman, he touched me and played with me, all the while knowing it was a game I relished.

No, I have never had any desire for the Gable man who belongs to Jessica. Hurting Travis will be fun. But hurting Lander? That might end up killing me.

"Mrs. Gable," I say soothingly, "I didn't sleep with—"

"Then you *will*!" she snaps. "Travis always gets what he wants. He and his brother, they're not so different as they seem. Everybody thinks Lander is the charming ladies' man. They think that women fall for him because of his smile and his . . . his *presence*, while Travis's mistresses are just with him for his money. But with Travis, it's never about money. Not in his business, not in his personal relationships, not even in his parenting. It's about power. And power gets you what you want." She sits back in her chair and shakes her head. "If he wants you, he'll have you. Power gets you everything."

"Right, well, power can come in different forms," I say dismissively. "And you have power too. The secrets you keep for him, that's power, Jessica."

She glares at me from across the table, her hands clenched into fists. "You're right, Bell. I have power. And I will never share that power with you."

The declaration hits me with the force of a slap.

Lander and Travis have both been suspicious of me at times, but they have never been suspicious of me for the right reasons. I've long since determined that Jessica is the least intelligent of the three . . .

. . . and yet she's the only one who seems to have pegged me perfectly.

I underestimated her. I didn't bother with any real finesse while trying to draw her out. And now she knows what I want. Which means she will not give it to me.

For a full minute we sit in silence as I desperately try to come up with a way to undo the damage, to backtrack, to make her see me as less of a threat. But there's no wavering in Jessica's glare. Finally her eyes move away from mine. She opens her purse and pulls out a tube of forty-eight-dollar lipstick and a heart-shaped Tiffany pocket mirror.

"So," she says as she carefully drags the color across her lips. "Shall we go dress shopping now?"

A few hours later we're in Saks and I'm carrying three different shopping bags, all of them filled with things that Jessica has bought for herself. I have tried everything to endear myself to her again. I've complimented her style and her figure. I apologized for getting in her way when she "accidentally" bumped into me and spilled some of her Fiji water down my shirt. I've zipped her in and out of countless garments. But she's barely talking to me. And when she does it's only to issue an order or an insult. She's moderately more polite to the commissioned saleswomen, who are falling all over themselves in an attempt to please her.

"I do love retail therapy," Jessica says with a sigh as she hands the saleswoman another thirteen-hundred-dollar scarf. The young, raven-haired, conservatively dressed saleswoman smiles enthusiastically, politely ignoring the fact that Jessica is having a hard time standing or enunciating. I had hoped that she would be sobering up by now, but she popped a pill less than a half hour ago and appears as plastered as ever. She turns to me with a lopsided smile. "I guess we'll have to get you that dress now. Fifteen hundred dollars isn't much to work with, but I suppose we can find something.

"Can you find her something?" she asks the saleswoman. "She needs a dress for a black-tie dinner. My brother-in-law would like to fuck her, so he's paying." She laughs at her own joke as the other woman and I exchange uncomfortable looks. The statement isn't just insulting, it's ridiculous. She's known Lander for years now, so she should know that when Lander wants to sleep with a woman, all he has to give her is an invitation.

"No more than fifteen hundred, and that includes the shoes and any other accessories," Jessica continues, now leaning on the counter for support.

"Of course." The saleswoman turns to me. "Do you have a favorite designer?"

Jessica laughs again. "How odd that you would think she knows a thing about designers. Well, maybe she knows Carolina Herrera. She's a Mexican too, isn't she? Anyway, just find her something decent." She looks around the room. "Is there somewhere I can sit? I'm feeling a bit dizzy."

I raise my eyebrows in mild surprise as Jessica is led to a small love seat placed strategically by the restrooms. Jessica's so rarely sober I had sort of assumed that dizzy was her new normal. Then again, I probably shouldn't complain. My best hope is that she gets so wasted that she doesn't remember our conversation at brunch. Hell, maybe she won't even remember that she was with me today. Still, I'd prefer not to leave her now. If she does end up remembering, I'm going to have a lot of making up to do.

"Shall I stay with you?" I ask, but Jessica shoots me a look so venomous I actually take a step back.

"I think we should look at Nicole Miller and Badgley Mischka first," the saleswoman says, tacitly leading me toward the escalator. "They have many lovely dresses within your price range."

I smile and nod, trying to quell my nerves. I'll just buy any ole dress and get back to Jessica. Surely it won't take too long. It's not like it needs to be perfect.

But it'll be nice, having Lander see me in a formal dress. I'm always dressed so casually with him. Will my wearing a floor-length gown cause him to see me differently? Will he tell me I'm lovely as he escorts me through the crowd?

I give my head a little shake. These are useless thoughts. I can't indulge in them.

"I'm Tanya, by the way," the saleswoman says, her posture regally straight as she demurely clasps her hands in front of her.

"I'm Bell," I say as we begin our ascent.

"Oh, I love that name!" she replies. "I . . . um . . ." She turns her head to make sure no one else is in hearing distance. "Will your friend be okay?"

"She's my employer, and she'll be fine," I say tersely. Tanya immediately seems to regret asking and I feel a little guilty for my attitude. It's not her fault that Jessica is . . . well, Jessica. "She's just had a bad day," I explain as we step onto the next floor. "So she started happy hour a little early."

Tanya doesn't say anything, but I see her eyes dart quickly to the wall clock. It's not even two.

"I'm her personal assistant," I explain. Obviously I'm

not required to start up a conversation with this woman, but I'm feeling anxious and chatty.

"Oh," she says, pleasantly enough. "That sounds like . . . challenging work."

I giggle and Tanya tries to suppress a smile before giggling too. "We all have to start somewhere," she reasons as she walks me past the featureless white-faced mannequins to a collection of dresses. She stands back, waiting for me to make a selection.

But I can't. I thought I could just grab a dress and be done with this, but now, staring at rows and rows of all these elegant, expensive gowns . . . I can't even get myself to touch them. It's one thing to help Jessica shop, but now that I'm confronted with the idea of getting something for myself—something from *Saks*—it's just sort of intimidating.

It's funny if you think about it. I brazenly went after one of the most powerful families in New York, but now I'm standing here, overawed by a bunch of dresses on a rack.

Tanya's watching me and I can see the flash of understanding when I meet her eyes. "Why don't I pick a few things out for you and we'll go from there."

I nod, grateful for the rescue. As Tanya steps forward, I feel my phone buzzing in my purse. I reach in and see that I have a text from Travis: Where are you?

I step away from Tanya as she goes through the gowns and text back: Jessica wanted to go shopping. She insisted.

I could lie, but what's the point? My phone buzzes again.

I did not give you permission.

I suppose the point would have been to avoid this conversation.

She wouldn't take no for an answer. Most of the shopping is for Mrs. Gable. I'm just here to carry her bags.

Ten seconds after sending that text I get a call.

"I told you—" he begins, but I interrupt.

"I have the phone records." I walk a little farther from the dress section to an area where there's no one around to overhear me.

"Then why don't *I* have them?" he snaps.

"I'll stop by your office after dropping off Jessica," I assure him. "I'm doing everything you've asked me to do, Mr. Gable. I just have to do what your wife asks too . . . at least to a degree."

"Did you find out about Talebi?"

I hesitate. "I don't know how Lander first heard the name, but he thinks Talebi might be a big investor that you're bringing to the bank. I think he wants to surpass you at HGVB, maybe even push you out. Are you maybe about to make some kind of big deal he might want to subvert, or beat you to the punch on?"

Another long pause on the other end of the phone.

"Mr. Gable, are you there?"

"Are you serious?" Travis asks. "He thinks he can outdo me in *business*?"

"Well, yes. That's essentially what he said. He thinks it's time for a new Gable to take his place on the top floor."

"Just bring me those records," Travis says, his tone dripping with disgust and disbelief. And then he hangs up.

It's the disbelief that worries me.

"Bell, are you ready?"

I look up to see that Tanya is standing several feet outside the dressing rooms. "I've selected some dresses for you."

I smile sheepishly and follow her to the room.

When she opens the door I literally gasp. I haven't made a noise like this outside of a sexual encounter in years. But these dresses are stunningly beautiful. White, purple, pink, red, and green. There are edgy gowns made of leather and chiffon, while others are made of silk and lace.

"I'll come check on you in a moment." She exits quietly, closing the door behind her.

I reach for a silk chiffon dress in the palest of pinks

with delicate little beaded shoulder straps. It's so insanely romantic . . . probably too romantic. I'm a seductress, not an ingenue.

I hold the dress up to me. I absolutely do not have time for this right now. I came *so* close to getting Jessica to spill her secrets. Would another cocktail make her more talkative or more hostile? Or would it just kill her?

I'm not ready for that yet.

The dress probably weighs half an ounce. It's so light and airy, almost whimsical. When I was a little girl I dreamed about gowns like this.

I hang it on the peg and pull off my shoes before taking off my shirt and skirt. I should have found a way to mention Micah's and Javier's names to Lander. Micah made it sound like he might know both brothers. And I still have to find a way to get Micah to trust me a little more. The last thing I need is for him to blame me when Jessica disappears.

I take the first item off the hanger and carefully step into it. I've never tried on a new designer dress before. It's incredibly soft against my skin, almost like a caress.

Is Jessica really onto me? Is it possible that she knows more than she pretends?

I slip my arm under each strap and pull it up just as I hear a knock on the door.

"May I assist you with the zipper?"

I step back and open the door. Tanya is standing there with a shoebox in her hand and a big smile on her face.

"Oh, you did try the Mischka on first! Good!" She immediately puts the box down and zips me up as I stare at my image in the mirror. Artfully draped ruffles enhance the gentle V neckline of the finely tailored gown. It gathers softly on the right side of my waist, which marks the beginning of another delicate cascade of silk-chiffon ruffles that fall along the side of the slender skirt.

"Here," Tanya says as she bends down by my feet. "Try on the shoes." She pulls out a pair of high-heeled platforms that are only a slightly darker pink than the dress. "They're Italian patent leather," she explains as I sit down in the chair and allow her to fasten the double straps around my ankles. When I stand up again I'm about six inches taller, but I look so completely feminine . . . and innocent . . . and pure.

Tanya stands behind me, admiring my reflection in the mirror. "You look like a princess," she breathes.

The comment takes me back a little farther than I'd like to go . . .

"You were wonderful," my mom had gushed as she walked me home after the third-grade performance of

Sleeping Beauty. *"You know what? I think you really are a princess."*

"Mama!" I had laughed, skipping along the cracked sidewalk, still dressed in the Aurora costume she had made for me. *"For me to be a princess you'd have to be a queen!"*

My mother looked at me sharply. *"Are you kind to people when they talk to you?"*

I nodded and played with the ruffles on my dress.

"Are you graceful?"

I had hesitated at that before answering shyly, *"I think I dance okay. Does that count as graceful?"*

My mother had to wait to answer as a police car drove by, its siren wailing. *"Yes,"* she said finally. *"It counts. Do you try to help those who need it?"*

Again I had to think before answering. *"Sometimes at recess I help tie Eva's shoes when nobody's looking. She's not so good at it, but she's too embarrassed to admit it, so I help."*

"That is helpful," my mother confirmed. *"You have grace, kindness, and compassion, and in my book that makes you a princess."* And then she leaned down and whispered in my ear, *"And with that you've made me into a queen."*

I had giggled in delight and continued to skip as cabs honked their horns and drunk men on the corner shouted obscenities. None of it mattered. I was a princess. And when

I grew up I would keep wearing princess dresses just like the Aurora dress my mother made me.

The images of my youth dissipate as I continue to look at my reflection. In the mirror is the image of the woman I wanted to be when I was eight. But I'm only playing dress-up. Inside I'm not a princess. If anything I'm the witch.

In all those fairy tales I once loved, the witch always used spells to make herself beautiful. But before the happily-ever-after ending, the witch's spell would go wrong and the whole world would see how ugly she really was. That's how fairy tales work.

And in a fairy tale, Lander would see me cloaked in layers of magical silk chiffon, and he would fall for me because he would mistake me for someone else: an innocent, beautiful princess . . . and then the real princess would step forward and he'd realize that it was all a trick.

And then he would have his minions tear me apart.

It's so easy to be seduced by royalty. Lander with his perfect smile and gentle hands . . . hands that he keeps clean, just like a real Prince Charming. But when he realizes I'm the witch, he will find a woman who is more pure and less challenging to be his companion. And he will oversee my ruin with that same winning smile.

Because in the real fairy tales, Prince Charming never forgives. When it serves him, he's ruthless.

I just wish I didn't find that quality so alluring. But more than that, I wish I could be a princess. I wish there was a way we could be ruthless together, condemning his family to our dungeons while we throw lavish balls in our castle.

But we can't. Because he doesn't want to jail Travis.

And even if he did, it wouldn't work. Because I'm the witch.

I lower my eyes. "It's a beautiful dress," I whisper.

"Would you like to try on the Nicole Miller?"

"No, I'll take this one." I gesture for her to help me with the zipper again. "Just make sure Mrs. Gable doesn't slip into a coma before she up-fronts the money."

Tanya laughs and exits the dressing room.

Slowly and with regret I slip the dress from my shoulders, shedding myself of the pretty spell.

chapter thirty-six

Upon reuniting with Jessica, I had been initially confused by how she had become more, not less, intoxicated while waiting for me. But that was before I found the half-empty flask in her handbag. By the time I get her home she's barely conscious. The nanny is there with Braden and Mercedes when we walk through the door.

"Mama!" Mercedes giggles, but then she stops when she sees her mother's uneven steps and glassy eyes. Braden turns his back in disgust and marches off into his room as I pull Jessica into hers.

"They hate me," she says as she drops down onto her bed. I quietly put down her many shopping bags and place my own by the door. I turn on the lights but use the dimmer switch to keep them low.

I refuse to reassure her about her children. Mercedes

may not hate her yet, but if Jessica keeps this up, her daughter will get there.

Jessica is staring up at the ceiling. Her skin, which she pampers with expensive products and body scrubs, appears to have a slightly bluish tint.

"Jessica, you might want to throw up," I advise.

"Why on earth would I want to do that?"

Reluctantly I sit down on the side of the bed and reach to take her arm. She tries to pull away, but she's so out of it she can't manage to do it. I press my finger against the inside of her wrist. "Your pulse seems a little weak. I think you might have alcohol poisoning. Really, you should throw up."

"You'd like that, wouldn't you," she slurs. "You want to see me on my knees, completely helpless and incapacitated while you take him from me."

"Mrs. Gable," I say, unable to hide my exasperation, "why on earth would anyone want to take your husband? And why are you so worried about losing him?"

"You think he'll just let me walk away?" she mumbles, her eyes falling closed. "My God you're an idiot. A stupid little whore."

I bite down on my lip. I'm not sure how to handle this. Part of me thinks I should be careful, even subtle, but Jessica is too drunk for subtle, and although I don't know if she'll remember brunch or not, I'll be shocked if she remembers this.

"Mrs. Gable," I say softly, "do you think he'd hurt you if you tried to leave?"

"You're a whore," she whispers back and breaks into a fit of drunken giggles.

I sigh; at least when Lander accused me of something similar he called me a courtesan. You have to respect a man who can phrase his insults so elegantly.

"What if there was a way for you to leave safely?" I ask. "What if you could start a brand-new life without him?"

Slowly, and with effort, she turns her head and looks up at me. Her eyes are unfocused but the desperation there is crystal clear. "Help me," she whispers.

I open my mouth to respond when I hear the front door open and some quiet, urgent words exchanged in the hallway before the door to the bedroom is swung open and Travis stands before us.

"Bell, I need to talk to you," he says coolly.

I stand up as Jessica mumbles something unintelligible. "I think she might need to go to the hospital," I say urgently.

"She'll be fine. Just get her another drink."

"What?"

"It's what she wants, isn't it?"

"She's *blue*!"

Travis turns the lights to full illuminative power as Jessica moans in protest. He strides over and picks up her arm, stares at it for a second, and then drops it back down on the bed. "Her coloring is fine, or at least it's good enough. Do you want a drink, Jessica?"

"Yesss," she whispers.

"Get her a drink."

I stare at Travis, unable to move. "I . . . I can't."

"You were a bartender, Bell, you know how to do this."

"No, I mean . . ." I stare down at Jessica. I hate this woman. I *really* hate her, and I knew she might commit suicide when I took the job. I practically counted on it, but now that we're here I . . . I just can't be an extension of his cruelty. I can't be the one who kills her!

"Your kids are here," I remind him, a little desperately.

"I told the nanny to take them out for pizza. Really, Bell, she's just going to pass out. I don't see what the problem is. But if you'd rather she suffer through this, fine. She can get her own drink. Regardless, I need to talk to you, now."

I look from him to her and then to him again.

Sara was right. He wants her to die. It's why he's so intent on regularly humiliating her. Like me, he wants her to disappear.

But now that we're here, in the moment of truth, I realize that he has the advantage. Travis is simply more merciless than I have ever been or ever could be.

And now I don't know what to do.

Travis walks back to the bedroom door. "Shall we speak in the office?"

"Yes—I mean . . . I'll get her a drink and meet you there."

He registers pleasant surprise. "Fine, be quick."

When he walks out I count to fifteen and then rush to the kitchen, where I pull out a double-old-fashioned glass, throw in some ice cubes and a small slice of lemon, and fill it with water. In less than a minute I'm back by Jessica's side. "Here," I say, pressing the glass into her hand.

"What is it?" she whispers.

"Vodka."

A small smile plays on her lips and she manages to prop herself up and sip from the glass.

"I can't taste the alcohol."

"It's there, you're just too drunk to notice it. Drink more."

She nods and sips.

"I have to go talk to your husband now, but I'll get you another before I leave, okay?"

"That's so kind of you."

"Oh my God, you have no idea." I stand up and leave the room, pulling out my phone as I do.

When I step into the hall I almost bump into the

nanny, who is ushering the children out. "Button your coats, it's cold outside," she says cheerily before turning to me and whispering under her breath, "Can you believe this shit?"

I shake my head and make a face that makes her smile as she walks out.

I glance toward the office, where there's a soft glow. I look down at my phone, take a deep breath, and text Lander.

Your sister-in-law may be on the verge of drinking herself to death and your brother's all for it. If that bothers you, you might want to get over here.

I throw the phone back into my handbag. I'm not even interested in seeing his response. I'm so insanely pissed at myself right now. How could I be so . . . so empathetic? And now I'm turning to Lander for help? I shouldn't be turning to Lander for *anything*! What is wrong with me?

I stride into Travis's office and throw myself down onto the chair across from the love seat where he sits.

"What's wrong with *you*?" he asks.

"Nothing, everything's just great. Here." I pull Lander's phone records out of my bag and hand them over to him. "I don't know if they're worth anything, but now you have them."

"So I do," he says as he scans the documents. "Now,

why don't you tell me why Lander wanted to know if I was acquainted with someone named Talebi."

"I *did* tell you, he wants—"

"To be a managing director?" Travis says with a raise of his eyebrow. "My brother isn't stupid. If he wants to get ahead at HGVB he doesn't need to knock me out of the way to do it. He's good at his job and he's a Gable. Our family is literally the *G* in HGVB. There is more family nepotism in this particular financial institution than any other I know of. If he continues to do his job well he'll be promoted soon enough, as will I, and eventually we'll reign together. He may not stay in the investment banking division but he'll have power, money, and prestige, which is what everyone wants in this business. So let's try this again, shall we? Why does Lander want to know about Talebi and what does he want to know about him? Or better yet, why are you lying to me?"

"I'm not—I'm not—"

Travis holds up his hand to stop me. "There are men who find stammering, weak women to be cute. I don't. So take a moment and get yourself together and answer my question with more efficiency."

"I'm not lying to you, Mr. Gable. I'm just relaying what Lander told me."

"Ah." Travis drums his fingers against his knee as he studies me. "It's hard for women, isn't it?"

"What's hard?"

"Having sex with a man without getting emotionally involved. How many times have you fucked my brother now? Five times? Ten? Twenty? Has he made you come every time?"

"Mr. Gable, I'm not getting emotionally—"

"We've moved on from that question; now I've asked you another. How many times have you fucked him and how many times has he made you come?"

I press my lips together and glance toward the door.

"In the video," Travis says as he gets to his feet and walks behind me, "you came while you were on a table."

I can feel his hands touching my hair. Again I glance toward the door.

"He had just turned you on your back," he continues. "And then he rode you like a man would ride any good mare. And you just couldn't get enough. And then the two of you came together. Very romantic. And as far as I could tell, he wasn't wearing a condom. Wonderfully thoughtful of you to let him come inside you. He certainly seemed to appreciate it."

"Mr. Gable, I think we're getting off topic."

"No." Travis's hands move to my shoulders, which he massages with firm, steady movements. "We're definitely on point. You have fucked my brother and he has made you come over and over again, and now you're attached, and you're lying to me in order to protect him."

"No, that's not what's going on," I insist. "He's just a good time, that's all. And I've been enjoying this little spy game you've gotten me into. It's fun, a bit like a Bond movie."

"And that would make you a Bond girl, wouldn't it?" His hands are moving a little farther down, toward my breasts.

I abruptly stand up, putting distance between us by walking over to the window before turning to face him. I despise being alone with Travis, and I hate it when he goads me. But most of all, I hate that he's right. Not about my supposed attempts to protect Lander, but about my emotional attachment.

My feelings for Lander are not what they should be. Not at all. I've fallen for my mark. And the worst part is that I may not be protecting him, but I desperately want to. I don't want to play by the rules of my own game.

"It's not just that he wants to get ahead," I say, trying to keep my voice cool. "He wants to hurt you when he does it. Your brother doesn't like you, Mr. Gable. He wants to see you suffer. He knows that the best way to do that is to undermine your career while promoting his own. I'm not lying to you."

"No? That's good." Slowly he advances on me and

then carefully he puts a hand on either side of my head, the pressure he applies a little too strong to be comfortable. "I really don't like it when people lie to me, Bell. It makes me a little crazy. But"—and with this he removes his hands from the sides of my head and gently strokes my cheek—"your story about Lander wanting to hurt me? That rings true."

I almost collapse in relief. But I hold it together, keeping both his gaze and my composure.

"You know what would be even more convincing?"

"What?"

"Take off your clothes."

"*What?*"

"You say Lander means nothing to you. Prove it. Have sex with me. Or if not me maybe I should call in L.J.? He says you weren't very respectful last time he saw you. Perhaps I should call him over and you could make it up to him. He seems to think a spanking's in order."

"Mr. Gable—"

"Or perhaps Javier?"

"Javier?" I breathe. "Why would you suggest him?"

"I ran into him while having lunch at Del Posto," he says. "I couldn't understand much of what he said, but your name did come up. He'd like to see you. I believe he would like to see much more of you than he can see at dinner. Shall we call him, Bell?"

"No," I say a little too quickly. There's no way that was an accidental meeting. Perhaps it was Javier just trying to get his "turn" with me, as Micah so delicately put it. Or perhaps it was the gangsters' way of reminding me that they are keeping tabs on me.

But at the moment it's just a reminder of the precariousness of my situation.

"Very well then, not Javier," Travis says with a smile. "It can be any man you want, or woman for that matter. I certainly wouldn't want to impose my tastes on you. But do choose someone. I do want to see where your loyalty lies. You say it's not with my brother? Show me the evidence."

There's a way out of this. There's always a way out. I can keep his trust, or if necessary, regain it, without turning into a whore.

But I don't know the way out. I don't have a map for this detour. "You say I can sleep with anyone," I say slowly.

"Anyone except my brother, who you're already taking care of."

"But"—I pause, sucking in yet another deep breath—"you want me to sleep with you."

"It's simpler that way," he says smoothly.

"How so?"

"Neither one of us is at risk of becoming attached."

I force a laugh. "So just sex."

"This is my test, Bell. It's not difficult to pass."

"Okay."

Travis's eyes light up with lust and triumph as he reaches for me, but I sidestep him, putting distance between us. "Okay," I say again, "but not now."

"Why not?" he asks, a little bemused, a little irritated. "You have to work up your nerve? Or perhaps you really do have to decide where your loyalties lie."

"Or perhaps," I say, mimicking his tone, "I don't want to have sex with you while your wife is dying of alcohol poisoning in the next room. I like things dark, but even I have my limits."

"She's not dying—"

"It's close enough. I'm not doing this now and I'm not doing this here. Not with her nearby like that."

Travis's jaw moves from side to side. If it completely unhinged right now and he turned out to be some kind of predatory alien being, I don't think I'd be surprised. "Do you have a date in mind?"

I shrug. At this point I'm just stalling for time, giving myself room to think. I try to come up with an answer that will appease him while still procrastinating for as long as possible when someone knocks on the front door.

Travis looks surprised for a moment and then shakes his head. "If they didn't have to ring from the lobby it means it's the nanny. She must have forgotten something." I follow him out of the room as he goes to the door, flings it open, and is confronted by Lander.

"Hi, bro," Lander says, his smile easy and his posture relaxed. "Jessica called me, said she needed some last-minute help with this political fund-raiser."

The sound of his voice immediately calms me. I can't help it. I can't make him affect me in a different way than he does. Things were getting out of hand and now, just hearing him speak, knowing that he's occupying the same space as me . . . I can breathe again.

He once told me that we're all just puzzle pieces needing to make our connections, linking our lives to others to find out where we fit best. Lander and I fit. I don't want that to be true, but all other connections feel unnatural and awkward. Together, we form a picture that makes sense.

"Since when have you been interested in helping Jessica with her fund-raisers?" Travis asks, jarring me out of my thoughts. I'm standing behind him so I can't see Travis's face, but I can see the tense position of his shoulders.

"I'm not," Lander admits. "But she's family and it's not like she asks often. So where is she?" he asks, pushing past his brother. He spots me for the first time and flashes me a smile and a quick wink before calling out, "Jessica?"

"She's in there," I say quietly, gesturing to the door with my thumb.

Lander knocks as Travis tries to intervene. "I don't know why she called you, but she's resting now."

"I just *told* you why she called, but if you like we can ask her now," Lander says and knocks again before just opening the door.

"That's her bedroom," Travis snaps.

"Really?" Lander asks as he peeks into the dimly lit room. "I thought the bedroom belonged to both husband and wife." He pushes the door all the way open and steps inside.

And there's Jessica, moaning softly as she lies across the bed, her head partially lolling over the edge and a pool of vomit on the floor.

Travis recoils in disgust, but Lander just moves her hair back from her sweaty forehead. "Jessica, do you remember calling me? You said you needed help?"

Jessica opens her eyes and looks up at her guest. "Oh," she says softly, "I don't feel very well."

"It looks like you might have had a little too much to drink."

"Lander?" she asks, as if she's just now figuring out who he is.

"Yes, it's me, you *called* me. "

"Oh yes." Her eyes fall to half-mast. "Your girlfriend's a whore."

"I don't have a girlfriend," Lander corrects. "If I did I wouldn't have asked your assistant to accompany me to the fund-raiser dinner."

"Oh yes," she whispers. She's almost out again.

Lander presses two fingers against the vein in her wrist. "It would appear that I've been drunk dialed," he says, looking up at Travis. "Funny, because she sounded coherent on the phone . . . Well, coherent by Jessica standards. Still, she's not looking good. Her pulse is weak and her coloring?" He turns on the nightstand lamp and Jessica moans again. "Even worse. You're going to need to take her to the hospital."

"You expect me to drag the Gable name through the dirt by allowing people to see her like this?" Travis asks incredulously. "She'll be fine."

"Maybe," Lander says, standing up and facing his brother. "Or maybe not. With your permission I'd like to drop the normal civilities and be honest with you."

Travis smirks. "You have my permission."

"Good. Because the truth is, I don't like your wife. I never have. But she's the mother of my niece and nephew, so I think it best that we don't let her die. If you prefer, I'll take her in, bribe a couple of nurses to keep this as quiet as possible, which shouldn't be hard. We're bankers, not celebrities. No one's going to be calling the tabloids over this, and if Page Six had room for every socialite overdose, that column would read like a James

Frey book. Nobody wants that. So let's just take care of this."

Travis's eyes slide from Lander to me and then back to Lander. "Fine. It's unnecessary, but if it will make you feel better be my guest."

"Great." Lander looks down at Jessica. "I take it you won't be coming with me?"

"I don't have time for field trips," Travis says between gritted teeth.

"Very well." He leans down and scoops up Jessica in his arms, wrinkling his nose slightly, put off by the smell of her. "Bell, I'm going to need your help."

"And why is that?" Travis asks in a voice that implies that he knows the answer.

"I only have so many hands," Lander says irritably. "I could use help, and it seems appropriate that your wife's assistant help me deal with this." He looks over at me. "Your employer is in a stupor; I assume you're free?"

I nod, feeling more grateful than I can let on here.

My enemy has saved me.

chapter thirty-seven

The ride to the hospital is not pleasant. Twice Lander has to ask his driver to pull over so Jessica can throw up, which really takes the elegance out of riding in a limo. I seriously doubt I'm going to want to have sex in here again.

Of course I'm happy to be away from Travis, but the very fact that I'm taking Jessica to the hospital begins to infuriate me. I'm now fairly sure that Jessica's not going to die and that Travis was right, she probably would have lived through the night if left to herself. But still, I've never seen her this bad before, and if he's wrong and she *is* in mortal danger, I may have just blown the best setup I could have asked for. If she had died because her husband wouldn't help her, all I would have had to do was make it look like Travis had tricked her into taking the meds (snuck them in her Advil bottle, or just emptied a few capsules into her flask). That combined with his refusing to take her to the emergency room when she started turning blue and presto!—instant murder charge.

But no. I got soppy and weak! And now Jessica gets to torment the world for another day and once again I have to reformulate my plan. The absurdity of it affects me like a cheap amphetamine. I'm antsy and irritable and intensely disappointed in myself. I always thought my anger made me tough, mature, efficient . . . but being faced with so many of my own shortcomings brings out another side of me. I don't feel like a woman who can plan a battle. I feel like a girl who wants to pound her fists against the wall and scream.

And to make matters worse, Travis is onto me and if I don't figure out an alternative soon, I'll have to sleep with him or give up on the whole thing.

Of course, he didn't say I actually had to sleep with *him*. He just said I had to sleep with someone who isn't Lander. Theoretically, if we could procure him, I could pass this loyalty check by going down on Ryan Gosling. But here's another horrible truth: I don't *want* to go down on Ryan Gosling. I don't even want Ryan Gosling to go down on me!

And there are only two kinds of women who don't want Ryan Gosling to go down on them: lesbians and women who are in love with somebody else.

As Jessica dry-heaves in the corner I squeeze my eyes closed, silently cursing her while simultaneously berating myself. How awful is it that deceiving and manipulating Lander makes me feel weak and uncertain, while holding him makes me feel confident and strong? How did this happen?

When we get to the hospital, Lander takes care of everything. He really didn't need me at all, not even to fill out the paperwork, which he does swiftly and with little emotion.

"All right," he says, turning to me when they have wheeled Jessica away and hooked her up with the appropriate IVs and whatnot. "Let's go."

"We're not going to wait with her?" I ask with a sigh of relief.

"Good God, no." He takes my arm and leads me toward the exit. "The woman is a walking, talking public service warning."

I can't help but laugh at that.

This man can always make me laugh.

We get in the limo and go back to his place, neither of us speaking. When we eventually get back to his penthouse we both walk, somewhat numbly, to the living room. I have my purse, my shopping bag, and the toiletries I used last night, but I don't have clothes for work tomorrow, which means that if I stay here I'll have to get up early and go back to my apartment . . . which is probably good. I have thousands of dollars sitting in there un-attended.

"Would it be inappropriate to offer you a drink?" he asks doubtfully.

"I think I'll stick to Perrier tonight. Public service warning, remember?"

He smiles and excuses himself, returning shortly with two glasses of sparkling water garnished with slices of lime.

I stare down into my drink. "Will they send her to rehab?"

"Well, they'll suggest it, but they can't force her. It's not like she was brought in for disorderly conduct or a DUI. The police have no jurisdiction to get involved in this and Travis will certainly talk her out of it if she's tempted to get help."

"He'll talk her out of it? That's a pretty damning accusation," I mutter.

"No." He sits down on the couch and crosses his ankle over his knee. "It's just an obvious observation."

"Why doesn't he just divorce her?"

Lander doesn't answer right away and then sips his water before saying, "He has his reasons."

I stare at Lander and then turn toward the window. He knows his brother is encouraging his wife to kill herself, accidentally or otherwise, and he's not going to do a thing about it other than take her to the hospital *if* he happens to get a call. When he told me he was a worse person than I am he might have actually been onto something.

I simply can't be in love with him.

"What's in the bag?" he asks, gesturing to it with his glass.

"I got the dress today. The dress you paid for."

"Can I see it?"

"You'll see it at the dinner."

Lander smiles, amused by my refusal. "Did you happen to have the chance to mention Talebi to Travis?"

"Yes . . . it made him very nervous."

Lander chuckles and takes another sip. "Come here."

I walk over and sit by his side, staring out at the grayish black sky of the city. So I don't have the stomach to let Jessica die. I can still go with plan B and help her disappear. I won't even have to lie. Clearly her husband really does want to kill her, so maybe I just have to point that out and then suggest that it would be a good idea to get the hell out of Dodge. I'm sure I can pin her disappearance on Travis. Trying to make Travis look evil is like trying to make Putin look homophobic. It's just not hard to do.

And Lander's complicit in all of it. He's an accessory, an *enabler*.

And I don't care. I don't want to hurt him. I know he's not innocent, but he's not guilty either. Not the way Travis and Jessica are. Not the way his father is. I may not have all the details, but I now know this man. He's like me. He'll bend the rules a little to help his family, even when they screw up. He harbors anger and brutality and unwavering ambition; he finds satisfaction in the destruction of his enemies. But when he's asked to take a woman he dislikes to the hospital, he *does it*.

We have the same strengths; we have the same weaknesses. We fit.

When he slips his arm over my shoulders, my heart rate immediately increases. I want this man.

"I know you've had a hard day," he murmurs as he kisses my ear, just the way I like it, making me flush.

"Lander," I whisper, although I don't actually have anything more to say. He kisses my hair, my shoulder. I close my eyes, allowing myself to get lost in the tenderness of it. It's going to be okay. I've got to believe that. I have to believe that I can have my justice and still find a way to be with him. I *have* to have this.

Prince Charming may not be forgiving . . . but he doesn't necessarily have to know that there's anything to forgive either. I must make this work.

I turn toward him and our eyes lock, and he leans in just as his phone rings. He smiles and rests his forehead against mine. "Just one moment," he says and gets up to grab the phone, which he left on the bar on the other side of the room. When he stares down at the screen his expression changes.

"Lander?" I ask, but he holds up his hand for silence as he puts the phone to his ear.

"Hello, Father. I didn't expect to hear from you to-night."

I'm immediately alert. This is a conversation I want to hear. But Lander walks down the hall, into his office, and closes himself in.

Frustrated, I follow him and press my ear against the door, but all I can hear is murmuring and the sound of rustling papers.

Grudgingly I walk back to the living room and take a seat. It could be that they're talking about Jessica, or maybe Edmund's just calling to say hi.

But I doubt it. I've seen no evidence that Lander and his father have that kind of relationship.

To occupy myself and stop my wondering, I pull out my own phone from my purse and start idly flipping through my photos. I slow down when I get to Lander's pictures and anagrams. There are still a few I haven't worked out, like *E's Wolflike Indecency.*

I stare at the photo. It's by far the most disturbing of all of Lander's drawings. The man with the wolflike teeth and eyes is staring down at the other man, who is sleeping at his feet . . . or maybe he's not sleeping.

Maybe he's a victim.

I pull out a pen and a discarded receipt from my bag and start to work on it again.

YELLOW FINK DECENCIES.

Probably not.

OWL KNEELS DEFICIENCY.

Unlikely.

It goes on like this for a while. Lander's conversation stretches on and I try combination after combination. The sense of urgency I had while trying to solve the other anagrams isn't here now. I don't want to trap Lander. I don't even want to believe there's a reason to. I just want to know him.

When there's no more room on the receipt paper, I crumple it up, dump it into my purse, and pull out one of Travis's business cards. I stare at the picture again and then try the word *we*.

I sigh and glance back toward the hall. What the hell could they be talking about for this long? Lander's manners normally wouldn't let him go on like this with a guest waiting.

SILENCED

That sounds promising. I bite my lip and examine the letters that are left. There's still an *O*. And an *L*. And an *F* and an *E* . . .

My heart stops and the entire room suddenly gets very, very cold.

I stare down at my hand. I'm shaking . . . more than I was after that confrontation with Micah and Javier. I can barely keep hold of the pen. Still I manage to write the letters down, each one shakier than the next. It's unlikely that anyone else would be able to even read my handwriting.

But I can read it. I can read each word perfectly. I know the solution to the anagram.

E.'S. W.O.L.F.L.I.K.E. I.N.D.E.C.E.N.C.Y.

WE SILENCED NICK FOLEY.

I feel my stomach lurch in a sudden and violent cramp.

It lurches again and I have to run to the bathroom. Dry-heaving as I kneel over the toilet, I'm unable to purge myself of this new evil. There's a buzzing in my ears that's so loud it's impossible to believe that it exists only in my head.

I was fooling myself. There can be no question about it now. Lander was involved in Nick Foley's death. He was responsible for setting my mother up. He knew what was happening. He knew the truth.

And he never spoke it.

Sitting on the bathroom floor I find that I can't get up. My legs have no strength in them. This shouldn't be affecting me this way. I knew what I was doing when

I seduced Lander. I knew who he was. I knew what he did.

But on a very deep level I had stopped believing it. I stopped believing in his guilt.

I was only supposed to have sex with him, but somewhere along the line my heart got involved.

Of all the ways I've failed my mother, this is by far my biggest betrayal. It was bad enough when I turned away from her when I thought she was guilty. But now I know that she was innocent and I've been fantasizing about riding off into the sunset with a man who is basically her murderer.

"Bell?" I hear Lander's voice moving down the hallway. I stay curled up in a ball. I know I need to get myself together, but how can I do that? How can I be here? How can I walk out of this room and let that man touch me?

"Bell?" Now his voice is farther away, probably in the living room. I force myself to my feet and lean over the sink before splashing cold water on my face.

Pull it together, pull it together, pull it together.

I look up, stare at my reflection; water is dripping from my chin.

I can't be here.

I hear footsteps coming back down the hall. Coming toward me.

Quickly I pat my face dry and try to compose myself,

only to find that composure is completely beyond my grasp.

I can't be here.

"Bell?" His voice is soft this time, and it's right outside the door.

I open my mouth to tell him to wait, but no sound comes out. I watch the doorknob turn, stupefied and almost not understanding what I'm seeing. I take a step back as Lander pushes the door open. His expression is calm, knowing, and almost sympathetic.

"Bell," he says. And then he holds up my phone, the picture of his anagram still on the screen, and in his other hand is the business card with the solution.

Nick Foley's name is illegible. But *We Silenced* isn't. And that's all he really needs to see to know that I got the answer.

In a moment of panic I have been inexcusably careless.

And it's going to cost me everything.

He puts the items down on the bathroom counter and reaches for me, but I step back again. I can't focus my eyes. Lander is nothing more than a blur of color. He's a stranger, a dazzling monster. *I've never known him at all.*

"It's all right, Bell," he says calmly.

I shake my head, take another step back. I wanted to be with this man.

I thought I loved him . . . I fell in love with a monster.

"Bell?" he says again and then takes a deep breath. "No, that's wrong. I should call you Adoncia."

I blanch.

Adoncia. A Spanish name that means *sweet. My* name.

He's been playing with me. Toying with the girl whose mother he essentially killed.

He made me fall in love with him when all I wanted was to destroy him.

I look down at his hand, still extended, waiting for me to take it.

And something in me just snaps.

Taking a large step forward, feeling all my rage, gathering up all of my warrior's heart, I punch him in the face.

Lander reels back in surprise, but I'm not done. I lunge at him, claws out, but he grabs my wrist and we go whirling into the hall. Lander knows how to fight, but I've taken him by surprise. And here's the thing: I know how to fight too.

He presses me against the wall, restraining my arms. "Listen! Not everything is as it seems," he begins, but before he can finish, I slam my foot down on top of his, aiming for the instep. I can immediately tell that I haven't quite hit the right spot—nothing breaks—but still he's clearly in pain and his grip loosens just enough for me to free myself and punch him again, this time in the gut.

Again he grabs me, and as I struggle against him we fall to the floor. In some corner of my mind I'm beginning to understand that my real advantage is that he's trying not to hurt me. Weakness; his gallantry doesn't mean a damn thing to me now. We roll around in the narrow hallway as he tries to restrain me and I try to kill him. I scratch at his face, drawing blood. I aim a knee at his groin, but he twists to evade me. I think about the knives in the kitchen. I think about my early fantasies of stabbing him with a corkscrew.

I want his blood on my hands.

I manage to turn on my side and try slipping away to where I can grab a weapon, but Lander's shock has worn off and he immediately slams me onto my stomach, my cheek pressed hard against the floor. He holds me there as I struggle and growl.

"Adoncia," he says, breathing heavily. "We need to talk. You will let me talk to you."

chapter thirty-eight

In the dining room Lander stands across from me, leaning against the closed door that would give me my freedom, holding an ice pack against the side of his face. He's brought in his sketchbook, which now sits on the empty table.

Everything in me still screams *attack*. But I no longer have the element of surprise. I know I can't beat him head-on. It's why I've been trying for a strike from the shadows.

I've truly failed.

"I'd like to leave now," I say, my voice dripping with anger and frustration.

"No."

I hate the way he says the word. So calm and matter-of-fact. As if he isn't holding me against my will.

I look around me. It's not a big mystery why he brought me into this room instead of the others. There's nothing in here that can be used as a weapon.

"It was about ten years ago," Lander begins. "That's when I first met your mother."

I look down at my nails and think about how lovely it would be to dig them into his skin once more. How lovely it would be to gouge out his eyes.

"My father asked me to come to see him at his town house," he continues. "He told me ahead of time that if he wasn't there I should let myself in and wait for him, which I did. A few minutes after I arrived, Nick Foley's wife, Jenna, showed up. I don't know why. I hadn't been expecting her to join us. But she told me that my father had invited her, which was odd because I didn't realize that she and my father were close."

I bite down on my lip until I taste the blood. This man *needs* to pay.

Lander leans his back against the door, reminding me that I'm trapped in here. "I was too distracted by my own problems to give it much thought," he says. "My father had left my mother a month before, and three weeks after that I learned she had cancer. I had to tell him. I assumed he would help her through it."

I don't answer. I don't really care. I just want to kill him and leave.

"So there I was, making awkward small talk with Jenna while we waited for my father, and then, much to our surprise, in comes my father's new housekeeper. And as it turns out, she and Jenna knew each other. And that wasn't a good thing."

For the first time I look up from my nails.

"I didn't know their history at the time, but it quickly became clear that Jenna had recently discovered your mother's affair with Nick . . . Adoncia, I'm sorry, but your mother didn't handle herself well."

"Do *not* call me Adoncia," I say tersely, hating the way the name sounds on his lips.

"Your mother said things that, well, later would sound incriminating. I had to ask her to leave. A few weeks later Nick was killed and I testified. My testimony only dealt with that one argument. The prosecutors, as they do, helped the jury draw conclusions from that."

"Tell me," I hiss, "did Jenna say nothing to provoke my mother?"

"Jenna was definitely provocative."

"And yet somehow that didn't make it into your testimony."

"True," Lander admits with a sigh. "My father, who was following the case much more closely than I was, was convinced that your mother was guilty. He's the one who urged me to tell the police about the argument after the murder took place. And he also insisted that I be careful not to disparage Jenna while relaying the tale. He felt that Jenna had been through enough. That she had just lost her husband. That she was only saying what any scorned woman would say. And, although you may not want to hear this, your mother hurt her. She slept with her husband—Jenna was a victim. She was innocent of everything. I now believe that your mother was also innocent of some things. But not of everything."

I *hate* that he's right. Even now I know there was no excuse for my mother's behavior. And to make matters worse, she took Edmund Gable's advice; she waged an open war against Nick's wife. She made herself look crazy and, in retrospect, dangerous. It made setting her up so easy.

"'We silenced Nick Foley,'" I say, my voice low and angry. "That's what you wrote. You didn't write that my mother silenced him. You didn't write that your father silenced him. You used the word 'we' and then you put it in your little notebook and tucked it away in a drawer, hiding it from anyone who might find that statement troubling. And you've known who I am for God only knows how long—and rather than confront me, you played me. And now, *now*, you want me to believe that you had nothing to do with setting my mother up? That all you did was tell the truth as you knew it and that you just sort of stumbled into this thing blindly. That none of this is your fault. That—"

"We did silence Nick Foley," Lander interrupts, his eyes cold. "And yes, I did stumble into it blindly, though that doesn't mean that I didn't have the opportunity to see things clearly. I just wasn't paying attention. I was focused on my own mother, trying to please my father so that he would get her the care she needed."

"Oh right, *your mother*," I say, pretending to think about that. "That would be the woman who died alone because you went off to Oxford and couldn't be bothered with her, right? Is that the mother we're talking about?"

Lander grimaces and tosses the ice pack onto the table. "My father took my mother back. She told me she was in remission. They both told me to go to Oxford, and *Travis* told me that if I didn't, our father would blame my mother for holding me back. He told me that dear old Dad would stop taking care of her, that she would lose her health insurance and that would be the end of it."

"And you always trust Travis."

"I didn't think he would mislead me about *that*," Lander says, his eyes narrowing as he looks deep into the past. "I did everything they asked me to do. I went to Oxford for my graduate degree. I wrote my mother, occasionally we spoke on the phone. I wanted to come home to be with her, but there was always something she thought I should do in Europe, something my *father* wanted me to do and she would beg me to comply. And Travis was always calling, counseling me, telling me how tenuous my mother's relationship was with our father. He explained that while it was true that she was in remission she wouldn't be out of the woods until she was cancer free and stayed cancer free for a few years. We had to be vigilant. We had to keep Father happy. We had to keep the peace."

He says the last few words with so much sarcasm and venom that I actually shudder. I don't understand the point of this story. I'm not sure I want to . . . but I'm not really convinced that he's lying either. Still . . .

"I've done my research, Lander," I say, trying to keep the uncertainty out of my tone. "Your mother died alone in a small apartment. As far as I can tell, the prenup your father had her sign ensured that she got a little less than nothing. And although I wasn't able to get my hands on her health records, I'm pretty sure she *did* lose her health insurance. So your story—"

"Is a lie," Lander says in a low voice. "A total lie told to a naïve son. I didn't know it then. I didn't know it until she died, one day before my graduation ceremonies. It was Travis who told me. He looked me in the eye and told me that she was dead and that my father had finalized the divorce well over a year ago. He told me that they lied to me so I could focus on my studies and uphold the Gable name. And then he smiled."

"He . . . *smiled*?" He's trying to make me feel sorry for him. *Me*. But that won't happen. Never, ever again.

"He was amused by how easy it had been to fool me," Lander says quietly. "My father was slightly more gracious. He explained that while he couldn't make it work with my mother, they both wanted me to be successful. By graduating from Oxford I had granted her dying wish. Of course, he left out the part about her being left to die alone without proper care. About the pain her disease must have caused her, or the loneliness she must have felt. How they *really* got her to lie to me, I'll never really know. But as far as my father is concerned, he did a good thing. The point was that he looked out for his son. That's what was important to him. You see, my father is a cruel bastard. But my brother is simply evil."

I don't say anything. I'm staring at the scratches on his face, the slight bruise that's forming by his left eye despite the ice pack. I did that to him for a reason and now I'm doing everything I can to remind myself that this man is one of the bad guys.

He steps forward and I immediately step back, but it's the sketchbook he reaches for. He opens it up to a picture of three men. I've seen this picture before. It's titled *Bite, Torture, Ruin.* But the picture I took of it on my phone isn't so good. I took it too quickly and it's a little blurry. And I haven't figured out this anagram yet. Sloppy work on my part, but there had been so many anagrams to work out I had assumed that this one could wait. After all, what were the odds that the one anagram I didn't get a good picture of would be the important one?

But now, seeing it in person again, I study it a little more closely. One of the men in the drawing wears a suit with a nail where his heart should be. He's arm in arm with an older man who has his pockets turned inside out. He appears to be handing over the last of his money to a boy who has extraordinarily sharp teeth. The boy looks like he's going to take off the old man's hand with those teeth of his.

The boy looks a little like Lander.

"I'm getting kind of tired of games and puzzles," I snap. "Give me answers."

And please, God, I think, *give me solutions.*

Lander shakes his head. "Just look at the picture. I know you've seen this before. If you haven't gotten the answer it's because it's unexpected."

"Unlike *We Silenced Nick Foley?*" I ask sarcastically.

"Unlike *We Silenced Nick Foley.* You were definitely looking for that . . . You may not have wanted to see it, but you were looking for it. But I'm not asking you to look. I'm asking you to *see*."

Reluctantly I turn to the picture again. The features of the man in the suit and the old man are indistinct, giving them a rather anonymous quality that adds to the sinister nature of the drawing.

It's not until I note the briefcase being held by the man in the suit that things start to click. I hadn't noted that detail before. I mean, I saw the briefcase, I just didn't pay any attention to it. I didn't note that it was textured, as if it was made out of crocodile skin or something.

There aren't many people who have briefcases made of crocodile skin.

But Travis does.

I reach forward and put my finger on the old man. "Is that meant to be Edmund?"

Lander nods and smiles.

Again I look at the title of the drawing. *Bite, Torture, Ruin.*

Lander leans forward and writes out the letters individually. B. I. T. E. T. O. and so on until they stop looking like words and start looking like the puzzle fragments they are. And then, just like that, I see it. Without really thinking about it I pull the pencil from him and write the solution to the puzzle.

TRUE RETRIBUTION.

Lander delicately takes the pencil from me as I continue to stare at the picture.

"I've had a sense about you from the moment we met," he says quietly. "I knew that there was more to you than meets the eye. You're always so mysterious and there's something seductively devious about you. But it wasn't until you mentioned the name Talebi that I knew for sure that you had an agenda."

"That name again," I say quietly, my eyes still on the picture.

"A name that Travis could never have known. Talebi was one of the people I was thinking about hiring to help me expose my brother for what he is. He's not involved in insider trading and corporate espionage, Bell. Or if he is, it's not my primary concern." Lander takes a moment to pause, and I know he's doing it for effect, to try to draw me onto his side. "He's using HGVB to launder money for Mexican drug cartels and Iranian officials. I'm pretty sure about this, and I think Nick knew too. I think he was going to say something and that's why my family decided he had to go. I even have reason to believe that my brother enlisted members of the Russian mafia to pull off the hit, although I can't prove it."

"Oh, God," I whisper, grabbing for the back of a chair to help support me. The information is coming so fast, I'm struggling to wrap my head around it. But the words that keep singing to me are the words that are written on paper before me.

"When you mentioned Talebi," Lander says, clearly emboldened by my reaction, "it became clear that you were up to something, and at first I suspected that you were working with Travis. So I did two things. First I made sure that Travis overheard my end of a phone conversation between me and Talebi." From my peripheral vision I can see him make air-quotes around the word *overheard*. "I faked the call, of course, but Travis didn't know that. I made sure Travis thought that Talebi was someone who could be a threat to him, but I was extraordinarily vague about the particulars. Like he was someone who could make my brother look bad in the press or dig up some actual insider trading stuff. I had to make sure that you and Travis were looking in the wrong direction."

My eyes keep reading and rereading the solution to the anagram, my mind furiously going over all the things it could mean. The picture would suggest that he wants retribution against his family. Of course he could have planted this for me. He could be using this as a way to trick me again, to convince me that he's on my side.

But then, I found this sketch on the first night he

took me home. Before he could possibly have known what I was up to. And I found it with the anagram about Nick Foley. If it was a plant, why allow me to find that too?

"You said you did two things," I say hoarsely.

"Yes, the second thing I did was hire private investigators. I hired a slew of them, actually, and I promised an impressive bonus to whoever could figure out your identity first. The first one I hired found virtually nothing. The second one found even less. You've covered your tracks well. But the third detective, a man who used to work for the intelligence community as a sort of government-sanctioned hacker, he found enough for me to put the rest of the pieces together myself."

"And when was that?" I ask. *True retribution, true retribution, true retribution*—the words are marching around in my head like a chant. Like the revelation it is.

"That was this morning, Adoncia."

I inhale sharply. *True retribution.*

"My family set your mother up for murder. I didn't know it at the time, but I'd bet my life on it now. And they orchestrated the abandonment of my mother when she was sick and in pain. The murder, the money laundering, the cartels—it took me years of digging and scheming to get the information I needed to put all the pieces together. But now that I have, I'm ready for war."

Lander reaches forward and taps his index finger against the words I've written down. "Let's stop fighting with each other, Adoncia," he says softly, and gently he puts one hand under my chin and turns my face toward him so now I'm looking into his eyes. "Let's focus our energy. And let's bring Travis and my father To. Their. Knees."

I search his face for some sign of deceit or jest.

But all I see is honesty and vicious determination.

This man is not my enemy.

This man is my partner in crime.

Again, something inside me just snaps.

And immediately I'm on him. My lips crush against his as he draws me to him. I tear at his shirt as he yanks my skirt to my waist. I want him inside me and I want it now.

I pull at his belt as his hands move to my ass. I'm kissing his neck, his shoulder. I kiss the wounds that I inflicted on him less than an hour ago.

This man will be my partner, in crime *and* in love.

I don't think I've ever felt this kind of need or this level of urgency.

When Lander pulls my panties to the floor I reach for his belt, but before I can pull it off him he pushes me down onto a chair and kneels before me, tasting me, teasing me, making me insane. I reach my hands into his hair as his tongue circles my clit. This is delicious torment. I can feel myself literally throbbing for him as I throw my head back and call out his name.

Lander, *my* Lander.

My warrior.

The man who will fight by my side.

My orgasm is sudden and intense and Lander holds on to my hips, keeping me in place, making sure that I can't get away.

But I don't want to get away. Not now, not ever.

He rises up and lifts me into an embrace and finally I get hold of his belt and pull it off with speed and force. There can be no more waiting. As Lander pointed out, we've wasted enough time. I pull his pants and boxer briefs down and he steps out of them. This time I'm the one to fall to my knees, and I taste him, licking the head of his cock, running my hands up and down its length before tracing that small ridge that leads from the head to the base with my tongue, teasing him, making him so hard he moans, desperate for relief.

He yanks me to my feet and turns me around, bending me over so I have to support myself with my hands on the floor, my body a perfect upside-down V as he enters me. His thrust is powerful and deep, stimulating my clit from the inside as the unique angle allows me to experience him in a brand-new way.

Everything about this is new. He's not the man I thought he was.

He's *so* much better.

As he continues to thrust, his hand moves around me and finds my clit, making the sensation overpowering and complete. I know another orgasm is coming and I give in to it immediately, letting it overwhelm me, letting *him* overwhelm me.

He grabs me by the hair and pulls me up, turning my neck to the side with one strong hand so he can kiss me again. His other hand roams hungrily over my breasts, And the moment he releases me, I turn and push him down into the chair, straddling him. I lean back and place one hand on each of his knees before raising up to rest my ankles on his shoulders. I rock myself back and forth. He can see every part of me and I can see him. I can see what I'm doing to him. I can see him watching me. And now I can see who he is.

Hands on the small of my back, he encourages my motion. I know that he's close and I increase my pace, trembling as I do.

"Lander," I call out again.

"Adoncia," he whispers, and within moments I feel him come inside me with a volcanic strength. For a moment I don't move, I just want to feel him pulsing inside me.

And then finally, after I lower my legs and rest my chest against his, after I lay my head down on his powerful shoulders, I say, "Please," between panting breaths, "my friends call me Doncia."

I don't have to see Lander's face to know that he's smiling. It's a new beginning.

And it's *our* game now.

acknowledgments

I want to thank Rod Lurie for all his support and feedback and for putting up with me when I was completely freaking out about deadlines. And I want to thank my friends and family for being so patient and understanding when they didn't hear from me for weeks on end because I was completely caught up in writing. I don't know what I would do without any of you!

about the author

Kyra Davis is the *New York Times* bestselling author of *Just One Night,* the critically acclaimed Sophie Katz mystery series, and the novel *So Much for My Happy Ending.* Now a full-time author and television writer, Kyra lives in the Los Angeles area with her son, their leopard gecko, and their lovably quirky Labrador, Sophie Dogz.

Visit her online at KyraDavis.com and on Twitter @_KyraDavis.